K Cooper Griffin

chasing mercury

KIMBERLY COOPER GRIFFIN

NIGHT
RIVER
PRESS

The characters, names, and events as well as all places, incidents, organizations, and dialog in this novel are either the products of the writer's imagination or are used fictitiously.

Copyright © 2017 by Kimberly Cooper Griffin

Printed in the United States of America
First Edition 2017

Edited by Jamie May

Cover design by Erin Dameron-Hill at EDHGraphics
Interior design/layout by Matthew LaFleur

Night River Press
Denver, CO 80209
NightRiverPress.com

Chasing Mercury
ISBN-10: 0-9972190-6-8
ISBN-13: 978-0-9972190-6-7

Visit the author's website at http://kimberlycoopergriffin.com
to order additional copies.

Chasing Mercury *is dedicated to sweet Annilee,*
a gentle light that went out way too soon.

Also by Kimberly Cooper Griffin

Life in High Def

ACKNOWLEDGEMENTS

Chasing Mercury owes its life to my writing group; Lake McCleary, Carrie Repking, and Beth Escott Newcomer. You endured many a rewrite and tedious reading of this tome but it is far richer for your suffering.

Thank you, my Michelle Dunkley, faithful beta reader, precious friend. I get so much more from your reviews than you think I do. I live for the shoulder-dance, eyes-searching-the-heavens combo you do when you really like something. Seriously. I live for that! How are you still single?

Jamie May, you did it again, making me sound coherent, where once there was a string of words loosely resembling a story.

Summer Cooper Griffin, there is nothing I don't acknowledge you for. You are the center of my universe and always will be. Thank you for loving me.

Part 1

Nora

🌲🌲🌲🌲🌲

THE BOEING 737 ROSE TO SKIM the fluffy white clouds that had been slate-gray and impenetrable from the storm-splattered windows of the airport terminal below. After a two-hour flight delay out of Anchorage, where rain had been falling in a steady deluge all morning, the ride had pitched and thumped for several minutes during the steep ascent before smoothing out. The chimes sounded to signal they were at cruising altitude and Nora Kavendash opened and shut her jaw, trying to pop her ears. Tired and uncomfortable, she pushed her shoulder-length brown hair away from her face, loosened her seatbelt, and leaned her seat back. The two additional degrees of incline hardly gave relief to her travel weary body, but she closed her eyes, counting the minutes before the jet would touch down in Juneau. Her estimation, considering they were fifteen minutes into the flight and all the deplaning rigmarole once they landed, placed her back home in just over two hours. Back to her bed. Back to blessed, uninterrupted sleep. She tried to relax her shoulders, rolled her head from side to side, and settled in.

Red darkness painted the insides of her eyelids and a twitch began to flutter under her left eye. She pinched the tender skin hoping to relieve the spasm, but it didn't help. She was exhausted. The tired she felt was beyond the kind of tired that a nap in an airplane could touch—even if she could manage to nod off. She'd never been able to sleep on a plane. She opened her eyes and it felt like sand scoured her eyeballs. Unfiltered sunshine spilled into the aircraft through the open windows at the end of her row. The headache she'd been fighting for the last two days flared. From her aisle seat, Nora glanced over the two passengers separating her from the window. The young woman in the window seat had earphones on, concentrating intently on the video game she was playing. Nora contemplated reaching across the woman who was sleeping between them to ask her to slide the shade closed, but realized it was one window among several and it wasn't really worth the trouble. She sighed and leaned forward. Holding her nose, she closed her lips and pushed air into her sinuses. With a merciful pop, the pressure eased, and with it, some of the headache and a little of the crankiness she'd stored up over the last few days.

Nora sighed and relaxed but was impeded when she tried to sit back in her seat. A glance over her shoulder found that the middle-aged woman beside her was leaning halfway into her space. Gentle snores shook the loose skin of the woman's neck. Nora let out an exasperated breath. She'd once traveled regularly like this. How had she once dealt with the lack of personal space in the slowly shrinking seats and overcrowded flights? Humans weren't equipped for such close quarters. She gazed longingly up at first class, just two rows ahead of her. But there had been no first class seats available when the flight from Mexico into Seattle had been late and she'd needed to rebook the last two legs of her trip back to Juneau.

God, she needed this trip to be over. Nora summoned a little patience from her rapidly dwindling supply, and with a gentle nudge, she repositioned the woman back into her own seat, gently draping the airline blanket over the woman's lap. A cloud of faintly familiar perfume remained in the woman's wake. Agitated and unable to sleep, Nora moved her five-foot-ten frame like a contortionist to pull her backpack slightly toward her from under the seat in front of her. She slipped an e-reader out of the front pocket.

Reading device in hand and pocket zipped closed, she slid the bag back under the seat in front of her. The pack barely fit and she had to use her foot to push it. There was no room in the overheads on the sold out flight. The attendant had offered to check the bag when she boarded, but Nora hadn't dared let it out of her sight. Not with Aunt Mace's last chance tucked inside.

Nora's thoughts drifted to the last four miserable days of travelling and interminable waits between flights. The trip from Juneau, Alaska, to Mexico City and back had been a success as far as getting her hands on the drugs her aunt so desperately needed, but the delays that had occurred on almost every leg of her round trip journey had drawn it out to almost twice as long as she had originally scheduled. No opportunity for real sleep had left her on the brink of delirium. Weather delays, a schedule change, and a bizarre gang shooting at the Benito Juarez International Airport had extended her trip. The resulting fatigue she felt in the deepest core of her bones as she sat in the cramped airplane was beyond anything she had ever experienced. It weighed her limbs down, affected her mood, altered her sense of reality. She had tried to nod off on the hard plastic seats of a darkened terminal gate in Mexico when the airport had been locked down for several hours, but the shooting, along with the constant worry that she'd miss her next flight, kept her from drifting off. The huge cockroach that had ambled over her sock-clad foot at the security checkpoint hadn't helped, either. Sitting in her business class seat now, just a couple of hours away from home, she recalled the past four days, and wondered if she had somehow hallucinated the whole experience.

Flight attendants in first class now moved through the front of the cabin, attending to those lucky passengers who basked in an additional six inches of soft leather seat and eight inches of coveted legroom. Glasses were re-filled and pillows offered.

Nora watched a woman a few rows up from her offer to hold a baby for a harried young mother who was struggling with a bag of baby toys. The little girl bounced on the woman's knee with giggles that were almost contagious. Although Nora could only see the woman from behind, she remembered an easy smile and brilliant green eyes from when Nora had passed her seat during the boarding process. From her seat in business class, Nora observed the woman playing with the baby until an attendant pulled closed the light green fabric with the subtle design of leaves, separating first class from the rest of the passengers. Nora realized she had relaxed a little when the woman in the seat next to her settled against her shoulder and snored into the softness of Nora's favorite flannel shirt. She gently repositioned the woman back into her own seat without waking her, tucking the scratchy wool blanket between them.

Several minutes later, Nora's eyelids were sliding closed above the blurry screen in her hands when a hard jolt accompanied by a high pitched mechanical whine made her eyes snap open. She dropped her reader into her lap to grab the hand rest. Just as quickly, the disconcerting noise stopped and there was a moment of eerie quiet. Nora wondered if they had lost the engines, since the loud rumble that had nearly lulled her to sleep during their ascent was gone. But before she had a chance to get too worked up, the pilot's velvet voice came over the airplane's announcement system.

"Ladies and gentlemen, we've run into a little mechanical difficulty with one of our engines." A low mumble filled the cabin before the captain continued: "But don't be concerned, this aircraft is equipped with two engines, and the other is working normally. While one engine is more than capable of getting us to where we want to go, we're going to return to Anchorage just to be safe. Sorry for the inconvenience. We should be back on the ground in approximately thirty-five minutes, where the airline will assist you with adjusting your travel plans. Please remain in your seats with seatbelts fastened for the remainder of the trip. Flight attendants, please cease beverage service and stow the carts. Ladies and gentlemen, once again, on behalf of North Star Airlines, we sincerely apologize for the inconvenience."

The pilot's voice was calm and reassuring, and Nora pictured the beautiful woman with mocha skin and sparkling brown eyes who had stood in the cockpit doorway, just behind the flight attendant. They had greeted each of the passengers boarding the airplane. At the time, Nora had added the presence of a female commercial airline pilot to the very short mental list of good things she had encountered on her trip. Now, listening to the pilot, she was comforted to hear the calm voice. She wondered if learning to speak that way was part of their training. The rest of the cabin must have felt the reassurance too, because the mumbling din quieted, and she could finally make out the gentle hum of the other engine droning away in the background, doing its important job.

The plane began to bank in a wide turn and Nora sighed. Four days of constant travel seemed like a nightmare now. The thought of spending more time in an airport—even one devoid of gang wars and cockroaches—made her shoulders droop. The siren's song of her feather bed became a discordant wail.

"Holy Christopher, patron saint of all travelers, pray for us all," muttered the woman next to Nora. Now wide awake, though her eyes were tightly squeezed closed, the woman's lips moved against a small gold medallion she held in her hand. She kissed it and tucked it and its chain back into her blouse. Nora watched as the woman crossed herself several times before she proceeded to rock in her seat, wringing her hands and whispering quietly.

Nora picked up her reader and hoped the woman wouldn't start talking to her or ask her to pray with her.

Consistent with her luck throughout the trip, the woman plucked at her sleeve. "That was scary. My heart is still racing. The pilot seems to know what's she's talking about, though, doesn't she?"

Nora was tired and uncomfortable, but too polite to ignore her, so she smiled and nodded. She guessed the woman was in her late fifties, and from the way she intently searched Nora's face, she was trying to figure out how anxious she should be. Nora felt an inordinate amount of pressure over the scrutiny and resented the imposed responsibility to reassure the woman that everything would be okay.

The jolt had startled her, but she'd been in far dicier situations and she felt safer in the air than she did in her car. Many of the missions she had flown in Search and Rescue while serving in the Air National Guard had been done in inclement weather. One time, just flying for business, she had exited an airplane via an inflatable slide when something inside of the cabin began to smoke during an otherwise smooth landing. Flying was little more than a complicated car ride for her. They had one good engine. She was aware of the regulated maintenance schedules for commercial airlines. The pilot and flight attendants were calm. Her heart rate had already returned to normal.

"Yes. I'm sure everything is fine. We'll just go back and get booked on another fl—"

Another hard jolt shook the plane and Nora experienced a flash of guilt for trying to provide false assurances, but the feeling of the seatbelt going taut across her lap eclipsed it. An uncomfortable and disorienting sense of floating filled her belly and head. An incessant bell sounded throughout the cabin, signaling the flight attendants to immediately take their seats. She felt blindly for the woman's hand beside her and wrapped it around the armrest and then placed hers over it, linking their fingers. Nora refused to look at her. She couldn't bear to see her own fear reflected in the woman's eyes. She heard what she thought was the beverage cart rattle loudly behind her and several cans of unopened soft drinks rolled down the center aisle a second later. A few overhead storage compartments opened, and startled voices murmured all around her, but otherwise, the cabin was strangely quiet.

"Flight attendants, secure all items and return all passengers and your-selves to seats immediately." The smooth voice of the pilot issued from the cabin speakers. There was no sound of panic in it, but the tone left nothing to question. They were in serious trouble. "Ladies and gentlemen, if you haven't already done so, fasten your seatbelts and make sure they are tight across your lap. Stow all trays and loose items as best you can. Make sure seats are in the full upright position. If you cannot secure an item, please hold it secure in preparation for a forced landing. Place your feet flat on the floor beneath you, knees together. Lean forward, place the top of your head against the seat in front of you, and put your hands behind your head, lacing your fingers together. If the oxygen masks deploy, make sure you affix yours before helping others. Your seat cushion can be used as a floatation…"

Obediently, Nora let go of the woman's hand and assumed the position, but in defiance of other instructions, she quickly pulled the straps of her bag around her ankles. There was no way she was going to leave it behind if they had to evacuate when they landed. She didn't have time to stow her e-reader, so she stuffed it down the front of her shirt and then laced her fingers behind her head as told. The woman beside her began to sing a song in a breathless and frightened voice, but in all of the commotion Nora couldn't hear the words and she didn't recognize the tune. A baby's cries filled her ears. Her heart lodged in her throat. Nora thought of the baby in first class. She chanced a glance up the aisle. The curtain that had been pulled closed between first class and coach was swaying open and closed with the jerking movements of the aircraft. She couldn't see the baby but a few inches of the blond woman's body were visible. She appeared to be sitting up. Her arm was across the armrest, hand relaxed, dangling limply from the wrist. In the turbulent jostling movements of the plane, the woman's hand fell from its perch and her head lolled slightly to the side so the woman was leaning into the aisle. Nora noticed the woman's seatbelt was dangling, unfastened from her seat. She had time for disbelief when she realized the woman was asleep or unconscious.

Nora had no time to react.

The world became a blur of noise and disorienting motion. Everything happened at once, and it happened so fast, Nora didn't have time to determine if she was up or down, moving forward or backward, alive or dead. She kept her hands intertwined behind her neck and squeezed her eyes shut. The top of her head banged against the back of the seat in front of her as she tried to remain tucked in the crash position. Objects fell from the overhead compartments and whisked past her. She didn't dare look up. The woman beside her bounced against her and Nora felt the woman's arms reach out for her and slide away. Again, Nora didn't dare look up. She felt everything at once and nothing at all. The circumstances were so foreign to anything Nora had ever experienced, she felt disconnected from what was happening around her. Her heart bashed inside of her chest, but she kept her eyes closed tightly and her head down as best she could. It seemed as if her world had constricted into the small tight ball she had coiled into, and there was nothing else.

With a bone-crunching lurch, Nora was tossed back against her seat and she sensed she was hurtling through space. She tried to bend forward to resume the crash position, but the forward momentum of their trajectory plastered her to her chair. Time seemed to slow down even as everything else sped up, and a loud roar filled her head. She had no concept of how long the hellish descent took, and she lost track of how many times her sense of equilibrium flipped and spun. The fear encapsulating her seemed to be a black gel surrounding her, muting the sensations, silencing the noise, pressing her deep into the firm cushion of her seat.

When the unreal commotion suddenly stopped, a deafening silence fell upon her, thick and heavy. Nora wondered if she were still alive.

It was the slow realization of the thundering of her heartbeat in her ears and the shuddering sound of her breath that made her think she might not be dead. Her eyes, which were wide open, saw nothing. Her left hand clutched the armrest; the other had a claw-like grasp on the fabric of the seat cushion, even though she remembered having both hands behind her neck just moments before. Terror manifested itself in an inability to move and Nora struggled against it, yet she couldn't seem to force herself into motion. A new fear that she might be paralyzed triggered a cold flash that moved through her. Maybe she was dead. Was this what death felt like?

She had no idea how long she remained there, motionless, sightless, in the horror movie company of her own breathing, trying to decide if she were alive or dead. Or somewhere in between. It seemed like an eternity.

The prickle of something on the back of her neck convinced Nora she could feel, and therefore possibly move. With a concerted effort, she let go of the armrest and lifted her hand and the whisk of fabric over her skin validated that she was alive. She went to rub her eyes and discovered the blindness was a blanket draped over her face and torso. With a terrified grunt, she flung the covering off and squinted into the sudden brightness. The overpowering scent of the perfume of the woman beside her disappeared. When her eyes adjusted, she looked around. She was lying on her back, still strapped into her seat. Above her was a thin swath of blue sky, framed by tall pine trees. To either side of her were smooth gray rocks, standing like sentinels above her. After long moments of struggle, her shaking hands were able to unbuckle her seatbelt, and she tried to roll away from the seat, but her legs would not follow. Panic seized her before she realized it was the straps to her backpack that were still wrapped around her lower legs. She laughed with relief and the sound came out in an unfamiliar bray, the cackle of an insane woman. She untangled her legs and kicked the bag away, rolling from the seat and onto her knees on the pine needle covered earth where anxiety grabbed her. Next to her now was just her seat lying on its back. There were no others. One moment, she was crowded into a small space with too many other people, the next she was all alone. It was impossible to contemplate. All she could think was that Aunt Mace was expecting her home. Nora pulled her pack to her and checked her precious cargo. The plastic bag filled with rapidly dissipating dry ice used to chill the medication that needed to be kept refrigerated was undamaged. She zipped her pack and looked for her phone. Finding it in the front pocket, she switched it out of airplane mode but found she had no signal.

Nora slid her phone into her back pocket and stood up. With tentative movements, she ran her shaking hands over her body, taking inventory. She didn't feel any pain. Everything seemed to be intact. The hard square shape of her e-reader slid out from the bottom edge of her shirt and landed at her feet. She stared at it in disbelief, an artifact of normalcy, when she wasn't sure what normal was anymore.

Nora picked up the device and stepped around the seat, noticing the torn metal where the adjoining seat had been. A thick layer of dirt and pine needles had collected around the headrest and in the chair, indicating that the seat had slid headfirst before it had come to a stop. She dropped the e-reader into the seat. Her eyes traced the disturbed path of forest debris, and she realized that her seat had skidded at least a hundred feet before it came to rest between two huge rocks. She pulled a handful of pine needles from the collar of her flannel shirt. How had she not been bashed against one of the trees or the large rocks strewn around the immediate vicinity? It was against all logical probability that she wasn't dead.

Evidence of the crash surrounded her, a wide swath of plowed up dirt and broken trees. Nora began to walk, and then run, toward where she thought the airplane would be. She couldn't see the aircraft, but its slide path led her over a slight rise. She looked frantically around her as she raced through the forest, hoping to see other survivors. There was no smoke and little debris aside from the torn up vegetation and disturbed earth. She caught a whiff of airplane fuel, but it was faint, and then it was gone. It was silent save for the sound of her own pulse pounding in her head and her feet hitting the uneven ground. There was no birdsong, no insect noise, not even the sound of the wind in the trees. Nature seemed to hold its breath while she processed the scene. Skirting around a large rock in what had become a full sprint, Nora saw one of the aircraft's wings propped against some trees. The sight distracted her long enough that she almost didn't notice the path disappearing into empty air. With open space careening toward her, she sat back hard, grasping at the ground with her hands. She skidded to a stop on her butt, the heel of her foot caught on a root barely a half-inch in diameter dangling in a loop from the edge of the cliff. It was all that stopped her from the forward momentum that would have launched her into the deep abyss below.

Heart in her throat, she immediately switched course, performing a frantic crab-crawl backward until she was several feet from the edge. On solid footing, she leaned back on her hands while sweat streamed down her face, instantly chilling her in the cool autumn air. She tried to catch her breath, her respiration and heart rate careening, the sound of her raspy inhalations stark in the otherwise eerie quiet. Light-headed, the sense of surrealism she had felt in her exhaustion on the plane was a total contrast to the complete sense of hyper-awareness she felt now. The ravine in front of her was the width of a football field, with the thick forest picking up on the other side, stretching into the visible horizon. From where she sat, she couldn't see to the bottom of the ravine and she wasn't very keen on getting too close to the edge to check it out. But she was pretty sure the plane was down there, and she needed to see. Although it terrified her, she crawled over to a nearby tree that jutted out over the crevice. Summoning her courage, she stood on shaky legs, hooked her arm around the trunk, and leaned over. Instant vertigo made her head swim, but Nora shut her eyes and took a deep breath to control herself. When she felt a little better, she slowly opened her eyes. Five hundred feet below, the hull of the airplane littered the ravine floor in one large piece and a thousand smaller ones. The other wing rested several feet away. Little else was recognizable.

She needed to get down there to look for survivors. She searched for a way to descend. The bottom of the ravine narrowed to what looked to be no more than two hundred feet across, with nearly vertical walls going straight down. Looking to her right, the icy façade of a glacier filled the narrower end of the ravine. To the left, it bent out of sight. Aside from a small stream of water worming away from the glacier, there was no movement, except for a thin black stream of smoke snaking up from one of the larger sections of the plane, threading its way upward before hitting open space and blowing in the opposite direction. Nora searched up and down the narrow canyon for a path that would take her down. As she was looking away from the crash, she heard the first explosion, and she turned toward the sound just in time to see a second, much larger, explosion. A ball of heat raced past her, forcing her backward, and she instinctively rolled into a ball behind the trunk of the tree she'd been holding on to and covered her head with her arms. Several smaller bangs and thuds continued to sound, and Nora imagined the fuselage blown to bits, with the metal raining down.

When the explosions ceased, Nora tentatively peered around the tree and leaned over to look into the now thicker smoke billowing from the space below. It was difficult to see, but between clouds of smoke, she was able to discern the largest section of plane, which had flames coming from each end. The smell of jet fuel and burning electrical components filled the air.

She sank to her knees, hugging the tree, and stared at the burning wreckage with a leaden weight filling her chest. How many people were still in the airplane? She felt helpless as she watched the conflagration burn uncontested. Her limbs were useless, hanging heavily from her body, and even if there had been a convenient way down into the ravine, she knew her body wouldn't take her. The heat that reached her from the distance told her it wasn't safe anyway. She'd have to wait until the fire burned down before she could get close enough to look for survivors.

Nora tore her eyes from the flames and shook her head to clear the fogginess trying to block her thoughts—thoughts too painful to contemplate but too important to ignore. Images of the people she had seen on the flight flashed through her mind: the smiling pilot, the woman sitting next to her, another woman with green eyes and a dazzling smile, a laughing baby girl. A hand seemed to reach into her chest and squeeze her heart the tightest at the thought of the baby. Abruptly, she was back at the airport in Anchorage.

A frazzled mother was sitting in a seat across from her at the gate, surrounded by a diaper bag, a carry on, her purse, and a sippy cup, while watching a baby pull herself up on the seat next to her. The woman glanced at Nora and smiled, a look on her face seeming to apologize for contributing to the already frenetic energy bustling through the boarding area. Nora loved kids but was exhausted on the last leg of a frustrating and extended trip. Normally, she'd play peek a boo with the baby to distract it to give the young mother a little break. But just watching them made her more tired.

So she'd returned the smile, but leaned back in her seat and closed her eyes, blocking out the noise and activity all around her.

Snapping back to her new reality, standing above a canyon with the heat of an inferno blowing toward her, she wondered if the mother and baby were down there. She pushed the thought away. It was an unfamiliar response for her. She was used to dealing with difficult situations with a determined and practiced calm. Her composure had helped her in countless situations. This time was different, though. This was too close, too much to deal with all at once. She let her mind shut down. She'd deal with the unthinkable later, when she didn't have to worry about survival. For now, she would do what she needed to do to help herself and any victims she found.

She turned to retrace her steps, searching carefully for survivors among the trees on either side of the churned earth left in the wake of the crashed airplane, expecting to see others like her who had been thrown out above the ravine. She couldn't be the only one left.

She saw no evidence of other people and there was less airplane debris than she would have thought in the path of destruction that led away from the edge of the cliff. There was the wing she'd seen leaning against a group of trees and an engine lying not too far from it. Not far from that was what looked like a section of plastic from the inside of the airplane cabin with a space where a window should have been. Further away was a piece of fabric attached to something partially buried in pine needles. A nearly intact and upright beverage cart with all of the drawers still in it sat against tree. She stopped and stared at it. The cart looked like it had been set there on purpose, as if beverage service was a natural event in the Alaskan wild. Away from the flames and most of the carnage, she was surrounded by an eerie quiet.

She was alone.

A surge of pent up anxiety clapped around her. Her head throbbed. She began to feel light-headed. She sat down and dangled her head between her knees.

When she felt better, she got back up and walked back to where she had left the airplane seat, nestled between the boulders. She stared at the seat for a long time, her mind unable to process what had happened. A jumble of emotions railed through her, but she couldn't form a coherent train of thought. She righted the airplane seat and leaned it against the rock. Ripped from the adjacent seat and its mooring, the chair only had one arm and part of one metal leg attached to its bottom. It leaned to one side when Nora tried to set it upright, so Nora propped it up on a low, flat rock, and then carefully dropped down into it. Energy coursed through her, and she tapped her foot on the pine needle strewn ground.

Where was she?

She looked at her wrist, which sported a mountaineer watch she had worn since her days in the Air National Guard. In addition to the time, which was just before noon, it told her she was at an elevation of 1,986 feet, and it was 57 degrees Fahrenheit. Her analytical brain kicked in. The longitude and latitude displayed were interesting but provided her with no real understanding of where she was, since she wasn't familiar with the area. Based on the time they had spent in flight, she guessed they had come down somewhere near Valdez, Alaska, in the Chugach Mountains. Unless the flight plan had taken a less than direct path from Anchorage to Juneau, it had flown along the coast of the Gulf of Alaska, and she pondered how lucky she was they hadn't had to make a water landing. Would it have been smoother than landing in the rough terrain of the Chugach range? Did the pilot make a choice, or was the choice made for her? She ignored the what-ifs and wondered how long it would take for help to arrive. It was a heavily wooded area, but they weren't too far from Anchorage, so hopefully it would be soon. Surely the airplane had some sort of homing beacon on it, and the pilot would have called in their location as they went down. She couldn't see the plane or the smoke from the fire through the dense forest from where she sat, but she could smell it, and she figured the smoke would also guide search and rescue toward their location.

Nora looked up at the cloudy sky, thankful it wasn't raining here as it had been in Anchorage.

She heard Aunt Mace's voice in her head. It was the last conversation she had with her before boarding the flight in Anchorage.

"The flight's delayed so I'll be a little later than I told you last time," Nora had explained.

"Another delay? I'll bet it's a set up between the airline and the airport. If they trap you there they force you to buy their overpriced food," huffed Aunt Mace.

Nora heard one of Aunt Mace's friends, Elphie, in the background: "She should have packed sandwiches. They'd have been better than that Styrofoam crap they try to pass off as food in those places!"

"I don't know about that," Nora said with a laugh. "It's just raining pretty hard and I heard one of the gate attendants tell someone they were finishing up some scheduled maintenance."

"I wouldn't get on one of those sardine cans if you paid me! Are you keeping dry?"

"I'm safe inside the building, Aunt Mace. I'm fine."

"Well, trust your gut, Eleanor. You hear? If it doesn't feel right, don't get on that plane."

"It's just a little rain."

Back in the forest, beneath the dense canopy, it was relatively dry. The clouds above were interspersed with patches of blue she could see through the small gaps between the treetops. The clouds had dark gray centers, though, and there was a heavy feeling in the air. The daylight held the silver-gray tinge that signaled pending rain to Nora. Living in Alaska for the last four years had taught her that a weather system was rolling in. Nora hoped she was wrong. She didn't need a storm to compound her already dire situation. Even so, she should probably find somewhere to stay dry if it rained.

Glad to have a problem to solve to keep her mind busy, Nora wondered what she could use for shelter. A panel from the plane, one of the few pieces of debris she'd seen that hadn't landed at the bottom of the ravine, seemed like the best immediate possibility. She could use branches from the broken foliage, too. A cave would be better. It didn't have to be huge, just big enough to keep her dry. Unless there were others. There had to be others.

She pushed herself up from the chair and decided to search in the opposite direction from the ravine. The woods were less damaged in that direction, and she tried to envision how the airplane had come down. Examining the path of broken vegetation and upturned earth before her, it looked like the plane had touched down just feet beyond the rock formation where she had come to rest. Her seat must have been thrown from the plane just before it landed, which didn't make sense because airplanes didn't just open up and disgorge passengers like that. But, then again, as brilliant as she was at software design, she had to admit she didn't know thing one about the physics of aerodynamics or crash analytics. That didn't keep Nora's mind from trying to piece together the puzzle of how she had survived, though. Maybe the plane had cracked in half somehow, or had fallen apart due to the mysterious forces of velocity as it tumbled from the sky. Maybe the jolts she had felt were an act of terrorism and a bomb had gone off, ripping a hole in the structure. Maybe the plane had first touched down somewhere above her and had bounced down the mountainside. Maybe it was a mix of those ideas. Maybe it was something entirely different. Maybe she would never know.

She walked the path of her seat's long slide, disturbed pine needles and tortured earth providing a visual guide. She guessed the thick layer of leaves that covered the forest floor probably cushioned her fall and slowed the speed of the slide. Observing the density of the tree growth and the scattering of large boulders all around, she shuddered. That her seat hadn't tumbled and banged her up in the process seemed improbable. That she hadn't suffered so much as a scratch in the ordeal seemed like an impossible feat. That she wasn't still in the plane, at the bottom of the gorge, burning alive in the fire, seemed like a miracle.

All of this went through her mind with an emotional register of zero. Observations and facts were all that computed.

She was grateful for the hiking boots she wore as she stepped around rocks and strode through countless years' worth of fallen leaves and trees. Picking her way around the rough barked columns of evergreens, she walked until she came to a wall of smooth rock about a hundred feet high. She had a moderate amount of rock climbing under her belt, but she wasn't a free-climber. The wall before her, with its almost completely smooth façade and gentle inward sway, was well beyond her skill level, even if she had all the equipment she was used to.

She looked along the wall's base in both directions and didn't see a way up or around it. Picking her way along the base of the cliff to the right, she found it soon came to a sharp drop-off into a deep crevice, an offshoot of the ravine behind her. It was narrow, just several feet across, but too wide to jump. She retraced her path the other way and found the wall swooped around in an arc until it hit the edge of the main ravine that the airplane had fallen into. This gave her a wider view of the area she had just traversed. The face of the glacier she had seen sloped up and back. It appeared she had landed on a pie slice-shaped ledge on the side of a steep mountain, and from what she saw, it would be difficult, if not impossible, for her to climb higher to see what was above her.

Below where she was standing, there was a steep game trail leading down into the ravine where the airplane rested. From where she stood, she couldn't see the aircraft around the curve of the ledge, but the smoke from the fire billowed toward her. Thick and acrid, the smoke stung her eyes and burned her lungs. She pulled the neck of the t-shirt she wore from under her flannel shirt over her nose and mouth to filter some of the dense smoke. She coughed, feeling impotent. Her earlier assessment still held, it was too dangerous to make the descent—at least for now.

Rather than dwell on whether there were other survivors below her who she couldn't get to, she churned through what she had experienced in the— she looked at her watch—ninety minutes since the airplane had fallen from the sky. She guessed that the plane had hit somewhere above her, then it had touched down on the small wooded shelf she was on, where it had slid for a short distance before finally plummeting into the ravine. A flash of hope filled her. Maybe there were other survivors stranded on the mountainside above her. An image of the woman who had been sitting next to her during the flight filled her mind. If Nora had been thrown clear, maybe her seatmate had been, too. A manic sort of hope rose in her at the thought that others might be safe on the mountain above, and maybe in the ravine below, if they had gotten free of the wreck before the explosions. When rescue came, they'd all be saved. She just had to stay close and wait.

Nora retraced her steps back toward the small copse of rocks where her seat had landed, her psychological home base. On her way, she found two plastic wrapped airline blankets lying on the thick layers of pine needles coating the forest floor. They were small and flimsy, but if help didn't come before nightfall, they would keep her warm along with the one she'd been covered with on the chair. Feeling grateful for her find, she came to the crash path and carefully stepped over broken tree trunks and clumps of churned up soil.

She walked around the newly exposed roots of a tree lying on the ground, trying to grasp the reality of her survival. Something caught her eye. She was so focused on everything that had happened that she almost missed it. A color, golden and unnatural in its surroundings, peeked through a mound of dead pine needles and soil next to the fallen tree. She bent to push the debris away. Shocked, she jerked her hand back when her fingertips swiped across a soft, wet expanse of skin, dark and caked with mud. Nora looked at her fingertips and realized they were covered in blood. She stood and fell backward over a branch in her hasty retreat, dropping the blankets she had been carrying. Her heart beat erratically in her chest.

A body. She had found a body. And she had touched it.

Fear and horror inundated her, but what was this reaction? Her first response was to run? She had been trained for this sort of thing. Disgusted with herself, Nora moved closer to the body. She studied the mound before she found the courage to brush aside more leaves and realized she was looking at a woman's face framed in disheveled blonde hair. Nora brushed away the soil and dead foliage that almost concealed her. One side of the woman's face was caked with mud, while the other side, once cleared of the loose pine needles, was relatively clean. Maybe she wasn't dead.

"Hey! Are you okay?" she shouted, knowing full well the woman was not okay. But what do you say in a situation like this? She brushed aside more of the needles and found an arm. She ran her hand up to grasp the wrist and felt for a pulse. Nothing. She tried the carotid artery in the woman's throat, and although the skin was warm and pliable, after a moment of trying not to concentrate on her own pulse hammering through her own body, Nora wasn't able to detect a pulse there, either.

Initially, she thought the dead woman's torso—or at least her legs—were pinned under the fallen tree, but as she cleared more of the dirt, Nora found the woman was merely pressed into the juncture between the tree and the ground beneath it. It was just earth and leaves covering her. The dead woman wore a blue button-up blouse, over a white v-neck t-shirt and jeans. Recognition washed over her. It was the woman with green eyes who had been seated in first class, fourth row from the front, next to the aisle. Seat 4B.

She cleared the pine needles from around the woman and scanned the area, both terrified and hopeful she wouldn't see other bodies, and, god, please not the baby. She got up. Concern over the woman, beyond her help, lost out over the sudden possibility a child might be out there somewhere, alone, hurt, and terrified. Nora listened for cries and canvassed the area, looking around branches and fallen trees, carefully kicking away mounds of pine needles. In an ever-expanding circle she moved, leaving no area unsearched, until she finally stood at the rim of the ravine, satisfied that the baby, or any other victims, were not there. She looked down at the fire continuing to burn far below her and felt the brutal knowledge of the lost lives sweep through her. Sweating from the effort of her search and the shock of what she had just confronted, Nora wiped away the tears streaming in a silent river down her hot face. She shivered in the cool afternoon air and went back to the woman's body. She knelt next to her wondering what to do next.

Aside from a deep gash on her forehead, the woman showed no other outward signs of the injury that had killed her. Leaves and dirt congealed with the wetness covering the side of the woman's face. Tentatively, trying not to touch any more of the blood, Nora reached out and brushed away some of the hair that fell across the woman's closed eyes. Her finger swept across a cheek, and Nora was surprised to feel it was still warm. She knew it didn't take long for a body to grow cold after death, especially outside. She looked at her watch—two hours and five minutes had passed since the crash. Any hope that the woman had died instantly left her.

Nora stared at the pretty face for a few minutes, taking in the solemn moment. She picked away a pine needle from the woman's high cheekbone and wiped a smudge from her defined jaw. She looked like she was merely asleep, her full lips slightly parted and her long dark lashes lying against the skin below her closed eyes—eyes that she knew were green and sparkled when she smiled. Nora felt the need to do something—anything—to mark the woman's passing. With shaking hands, she cleared the rest of the pine needles, sticks, and bits of bark from the body, settled the woman's limbs in a neat position, and sat down next to her. Taking one of the woman's hands in her own, she lowered her head, at a loss for thoughts, almost wishing she'd had just a little religious or spiritual experience in her background to help her through a moment like this.

The hand she held was cold and limp. She didn't know the woman, but she remembered her in the reflection of the little girl's smile. Grief swept through her then, and she allowed herself to cry again, this time with gut wrenching sobs and jagged breaths. Really scary things had just happened to her. People had died, but she was still alive, and that was something to be thankful for. A torrent of guilt rose in her. But she couldn't give up. Not yet. She had to survive. She had to keep living because this woman and so many others had died. Nora gently placed the hand she'd been holding upon the front of the blue blouse. She straightened out the collar and stroked the top of her hand. She noticed she didn't wear any rings, but the slight indentation and tan line on her left hand indicated a ring had been there recently and for a long time. She thought about the people the woman had left behind, the baby she'd made smile. Sadness swept through her and Nora pulled away.

The woman's chest rose as Nora sat back. It was so slight Nora thought she had imagined it, maybe even wished it. She stared to see if it would happen again. Then, a seemingly impossible amount of time later, it did, ever so shallow, barely a rise, but a breath, nonetheless.

The woman was alive! Maybe barely, but she was breathing, and that was all that mattered. A huge sense of obligation descended upon Nora. She had to take care of her. She was responsible for her survival.

"Hey! Wake up! Wake up!" She shouted, bending low and close to her face, listening for a breath, checking to make sure nothing blocked the woman's breathing—something she should have done initially, but she refused to berate herself for it now. She shook her—not enough to injure her more if there was something broken inside, but enough to wake a person if they were asleep.

Nothing.

She held the unconscious woman's hand and a gust of wind lifted the hair from Nora's brow, a reminder that rain was on the way. Through the narrow opening in the canopy along the path of downed trees, she saw the sky had turned a cold, hard gray. The clouds looked low and foreboding, the kind that clung to the earth not far from the sea, moving in, gathering heaviness as they moved across land. Nora hadn't seen the ocean, but she could feel it close by. For some reason, it gave her a sense of her bearings, which fueled her hope. The tops of the trees bent restlessly in a strong wind Nora could not yet feel, except for an occasional gust that chilled her skin.

Nora looked down at the unconscious woman and considered her next steps. With rain almost certain, she couldn't leave her where she was, but she didn't know what to do. Was it wise to move her? What about internal injuries? Candidates for shelter were sparse. She had been all over the immediate area and she hadn't seen any caves or even a hollowed out tree they could use. Then she thought of the wing near the edge of the ravine. She couldn't see it from where she was because of the slight rise, but she remembered it was propped up against some trees and rocks and there might be some shelter under it if it was stable. She had to go check, but that meant leaving the woman alone for a few minutes. She didn't want to, but she had no choice.

Before she left to assess the sheltering possibilities of the wing, she tore the plastic from the two blankets and spread the small wool covers over the woman's legs and torso.

"I'll be right back. Don't go anywhere," she said as she tucked the scratchy fabric around her. She might as well have been talking to herself, but it felt good not to be alone.

Near the wing, several feet away from the edge of the ravine, the wind was strong, carrying the smell of smoke with it. The hunk of metal was as she remembered it, battered and slightly bent, but still mostly in one piece. A faint smell of jet fuel lingered in the area, but the engine had come off and was lying partially embedded in the soft earth a short distance away. The wing was laying upside down, with the thickest, longest edge resting on the ground, and the high side leaning against a copse of trees. The opening underneath faced away from the nearby ravine, blocking much of the wind. The part of the wing that had been connected to the body of the airplane rested against a short crop of rocks, partially blocking off that side, forming a half sort of A-frame space beneath. She stooped to look under it and saw there was plenty of space beneath.

Up close, the wing was thicker than she had expected. Many of the flaps were extended and bent as a result of the crash. Nora estimated it was about forty or forty-five feet long, and at the widest, about ten feet across. The height of the space under it went from the ground to about four-and-a-half feet tall at the highest part. Blocked on the two sides, it looked like it would provide a good shelter from the rain and wind.

Nora pushed and pulled on the heavy metal structure to make sure it wouldn't shift and crush them, but it didn't budge. To be sure, she walked around to the other side and climbed on top of it, using one of the metal ridges that went up the bottom of the wing surface for support. She bounced on it first, and then jumped. The heavy thing still didn't move. Relieved she wouldn't have to build something from tree branches, Nora jumped down and made her way to the panel she had spotted earlier. She needed a litter to transport the injured woman.

Nora easily found the panel again. The curtain was barely attached to it, held on by a single rivet, and she pulled it free. She dropped it on top of the panel and dragged it back to where the woman was lying. It was heavier than she had expected, but there was a coat hook on one side that gave her something to grasp, making the task a little easier. She placed the makeshift stretcher next to the woman, who was resting exactly as Nora had left her. Nora waited to see the slight rise of chest that told her she was still breathing. When she saw it, she realized she had half-expected her to be dead when she returned. She shook the morbid thought away and busied herself with the careful transfer of the woman onto the panel. She didn't want to add to her injuries. The woman was like a limp doll. Nora felt along her limbs for broken bones and didn't find anything obvious as she positioned her on the flat surface. Aside from a few scrapes, and the gash on the woman's forehead, she didn't notice any other injuries. The woman herself gave no sign she felt any discomfort—or anything at all, for that matter.

A thought occurred to Nora as she centered the woman on the stretcher. "Sorry about this," she said as she pushed her hand into the woman's pockets. The first pocket revealed a tube of lip balm, along with a wrapper for a protein bar. The second pocket contained a blister pack of 25 mg tablets of decongestant with three empty spaces. If the woman had taken three at one time, it could explain why she had been asleep on the plane. She pushed the items back into the woman's pockets before she rolled her slightly to the side to reach into a back pocket. More than ever, Nora wanted to know who this woman was. She found a folded piece of paper that revealed itself to be a ticket sleeve. Inside were a boarding pass and a luggage check slip for one bag. Bingo. The woman's name was Grace Trackton. Seat 4B. Boarding passes from LAX to Juneau, Alaska, via Anchorage.

"Grace? Hey, lady from 4B? Can you hear me?" Nora studied the woman for a sign of recognition. She remained unresponsive. Nora refolded the papers and slid them back into the pocket she'd pulled them from. "Well, anyway, hello, Grace Trackton. I'm Nora Kavendash. Do you mind if I call you 4B? I think I like it better."

When her patient was placed squarely on the panel, Nora twisted the thin fabric of the curtain into a rope of sorts, slid it under 4B's upper back, and pulled the ends up and under her armpits to make a sort of harness. She then tied the ends around the coat hook that protruded from the flat panel just above 4B's head. After draping the blankets over the woman, Nora assessed her work and then took off the flannel shirt she was wearing and tied it around the woman's torso to secure the blankets and to keep the woman's arms at her sides so she wouldn't slide out. It looked awkward, and it didn't look terribly secure, but it would keep her patient from sliding off the stretcher when she lifted it by one end and started to drag it. The parts of the curtain that ran up to tie to the coat hook served additionally to stabilize her head. Nora was pretty proud of her work.

Nora hefted the panel under 4B's head and pulled. It was hard work and she had to take several breaks on the way to move debris from her path and to catch her breath. 4B's head moved a little from side to side, but other than the jostling from the ride, which Nora tried to minimize, she still hadn't moved on her own. Finally, they made it to the wing and Nora smoothed an area before she slid the contraption, woman and all, beneath the shelter. She crawled in after and studied 4B as she untied the harness. Checking to see if the woman was still breathing was becoming an obsession for Nora. The woman's chest rose about four times a minute. Fresh blood seeped out of the gash on 4B's forehead, probably a result of the bumpy ride. Nora took a closer look at it. It would probably stop again on its own, but it needed stiches—something she wasn't sure she was willing to try even if she did have the right supplies. The best she could do was clean the wound and put a bandage on it. The good thing was the new flow of blood had washed some of the dirt away, but small bits of soil and leaves still clung to the area around it. She hoped the tiny first aid kit she kept in her backpack would have what she needed to attend to the wound.

"You've got a nasty cut on your forehead, 4B. I'm going to see if I have a bandage big enough to cover it. My backpack is over by the rocks. I'll be right back."

Shaking her head at herself for talking to an unconscious woman, Nora crawled out from beneath the wing. As she stood, a gust of wind rounded the metal slab carrying some of the thick smoke that blew up from the drop-off. The rush of air was stronger than before and buffeted her. Nora shivered. The effort of dragging the woman to the wing had made her sweat, and the rapidly cooling air was starting to get chilly. A drop of rain hit her face. They had made it to the wing just in time. The sky had grown darker, indicating that the storm that was coming might be more than just a light rainfall.

Nora moved back under the wing and tucked the blankets more securely around 4B to keep her warm against the falling temperature. The individual raindrops became a smattering. She would have to hurry to get her backpack.

"Okay. Now I mean it. I'll be right back," she said to her unconscious companion. She crawled out from under the wing again and jogged back to the rocks, which were a few hundred feet away. She pulled her pack over her shoulders and was turning back, when she stopped. On a whim, she grabbed the airline seat and started to drag it back with her. It was heavy and awkward, but she didn't want to leave it behind. By the time she returned to the wing, the rain was sounding a regular patter against the metal surface.

"I'm back," said Nora, ducking into the space below the wing, pulling her cargo in after her. She was out of breath and a little damp from her hurried trip through the light rain. She dropped to her knees beside 4B, who hadn't moved. She was still breathing, though. Nora resituated herself so she was sitting cross-legged, facing the woman, she shrugged out of the backpack, pulling it into her lap. She found the small first aid kit in a side pocket, along with an unopened bottle of water she'd purchased at the last airport. She blew out a small laugh when she thought how Aunt Mace would have reacted when she told her how much she'd paid for it. She then selected a clean t-shirt and set all of it on the panel next to 4B's limp arm. She closed her pack, placed it aside, and then turned to study the unconscious woman's wound.

Aunt Mace would laugh to see her now, playing doctor like she knew what she was doing. The outdoorsy, physical aspect of search and rescue was why she had joined the service, not the medical part. She really didn't like the blood and guts part of it, but she had done it when needed. Trained to do emergency triage out in the field, she'd set bones, staunched bleeding, and once, even helped deliver a baby. Cleaning this wound was nothing to her. But Aunt Mace knew that, given the choice, she'd rather let someone else deal with the gory parts. There was no one else out here to do it, though.

Nora used some of the water to clean her hands. Then she squirted a generous amount of anti-bacterial hand gel she found in the first aid kit into her palm and rubbed her hands together. Once her hands were clean, she carefully picked most of the hair and larger pieces of debris from the area around the wound before she soaked the edge of her t-shirt in water and cleaned the area, starting from the edges in. Thankfully, the cut wasn't as large as it seemed and the bleeding had already slowed again. Most of the ugly mess washed away from smooth skin, revealing a deep cut about two inches long running vertically from the hairline to down above the woman's left eye. When Nora poured water over it to wash the last of the dirt away, a flap of skin folded up revealing a white line of bone. Nora, had to remind herself that she was normally fine with blood, as she continued to rinse away as much dirt as she could before she pushed the flap back into place. Finally, she applied a liberal coat of anti-bacterial ointment onto a gauze pad and placed it over the wound before she taped it down.

4B didn't react to anything during the entire procedure, and Nora wondered about the extent of her injuries. Nora had better than average medical knowledge, but anyone with any sense knew head injuries could be very serious, and she knew the longer 4B remained unconscious, the less of a chance she had of ever waking up, especially without the medical attention she so obviously needed.

Nora stashed the first aid supplies in her pack and then pulled the battered airline seat next to the panel the woman was lying on. She braced the unsteady base of the seat with a few loose rocks, sat back in the cushioned seat, and studied 4B's pretty face in the darkening shadows. The temperature was rapidly falling with the rain and the coming night. Nora pulled a hooded sweatshirt from her pack and put it on. She laid another over her lap and wished she had something to build a fire. She knew it was unlikely a search party would continue to look for them in the dark, but if help didn't come by morning, she would climb down to the smoldering airplane and see what she could see.

4B's chest rose and fell steadily. The fading light was already making it hard to see. Nora pulled a travel flashlight and her harmonica from the top compartment of her backpack, and sat back in her chair. As she blew into the instrument and the first few warbling notes filled the air, she willed the woman to wake up.

🌲🌲🌲🌲🌲

Nora awoke with a start, her hand squeezing the hand of her unconscious companion. It was very early the next morning and the other woman slept on. Heart racing, she took stock of where she was, and sat up a little straighter. Adrenaline raced through her body, but she was groggy. The final moments of the plane crash she had been reliving in her dreams faded quickly from her mind, the cries of a baby echoing in the fading darkness. She stretched, trying to ease away the stiffness caused by sitting still for so long in the cold night air. Several times during the long night, she'd thought about curling up next to 4B to share the blankets and body warmth, but the strangeness of getting so close to a person she didn't know, someone who might die at any moment, kept her in her chair. Surprised she'd actually nodded off, she picked up the harmonica that had fallen near her feet, rubbed it on her pants leg, and dropped it into her shirt pocket. The watch she wore with the self-illuminating dial indicated she had only been out for a few minutes. That meant she had been awake almost all night, listening to every sound of the dark and unfamiliar forest, conserving the battery of her small flashlight, and wishing she could make a fire. She watched with relief as the first weak morning light crept through the treetops. In the gloom beneath the wing, 4B was exactly as she had last seen her. Nora let go of the woman's hand, tucking it under the thin blankets against the woman's side. 4B may have been unconscious, but the limp hand wrapped in hers had been a comfort to Nora during the long, dark night.

Nora poked her head out from the wing. Through a small break in the treetops, she saw the clouds were grayer and lower than before. The smattering of rain had stopped some time during the night without ever really turning into a steady rainfall, but the damp scent of rich earth and pine tinged the air. She shivered and worried the cloud cover would hinder rescue efforts.

Nora ducked back into the shelter and pulled the blankets up over the unconscious woman's shoulders. Back out in the wind, her dark brown hair whipped against her face as she lifted her arms high and twisted the kinks out of her lower back. She pushed the strands behind her ears and walked around the wing to the edge of the ravine. As she had done the day before, she held onto a tree trunk and leaned over to look down. She half-expected to see flames, but the fire had almost burnt itself out overnight. Occasional lazy billows of black smoke rose from the wreckage, indicating the fire still smoldered. She studied the area surrounding it, looking for signs of anyone down there. Nothing moved in the early morning shadows. She hadn't expected to see anything, but still she was disappointed.

Blurry from exhaustion, she checked on her patient one more time, and then picked her way along the rim, over to where the cliff rose up. She found the game trail and started down. It wasn't a very friendly trail. She slid about as much as she hiked, but she managed to get all the way down. She just hoped she'd be able to make her way back up again.

By the time she arrived at the bottom, the morning sun had lightened the thick gray sky. The floor of the ravine was more rugged than it looked from above, the result of a millennium of glacial surge and retreat. A narrow stream of water ran from the glacier and through the middle of the ravine, but other than that, the floor was a barren, boulder-strewn ally. Nora walked through the rocks toward the wreckage, intending to keep a wide berth. As she drew closer, she could smell the effects of the fire. As she circled the wreckage, she found the entire other side of the fuselage had been torn away. The sections still retained some shape, and although the insides were now completely burned out, and black smoke continued to waft out of it, she couldn't see any flame. It was hard to tell how much of the plane was actually down there.

More debris littered the floor on the far side and Nora walked among it, not sure what she was looking for, but hoping for signs of survivors.

She wasn't expecting it when she came across the first body.

Stepping around a waist-high boulder, she saw him spread at an impossible angle, burned and unrecognizable. At first, she didn't know she was looking at a dead man. When recognition hit her, it still didn't seem real. She just stared, trying to make sense of the position he was in. And then it hit her. He was broken and twisted, and horror washed over her. Sick to her stomach and frightened, she turned and walked away, but a few feet in that direction, she found another body. Burns left the body almost unrecognizable.

Part of her had known she'd find bodies in the wreckage, but for some reason, she hadn't thought it through before she approached the scene. Her focus had been on finding survivors. She had no idea what to do about bodies.

Her tour in Search and Rescue hadn't prepared her for this. She'd never gone on any missions that required emergency response to major events. Her time in had mainly consisted of drills and exercises. And when she hadn't been practicing, she had been helping local agencies find lost or hurt hikers in the Colorado mountains and helping stranded rock climbers down from places they shouldn't have attempted. Aside from funerals, the one and only time she had come close to a dead person was a hiker who had been hit by lightning on Pikes Peak. Some of her unit had been deployed to the Middle East, where they had seen and talked about the death they'd witnessed there, but since she had been a full-time college student during her time in the Guard, she had been spared the nightmares her team members had been haunted by. Now, she felt wholly incapable of dealing with this situation.

Her search found no other survivors. Just bodies.

Unable to process the carnage, she shut down her emotions and concentrated on finding anything that would help her and the woman from 4B to survive until help arrived. With numb concentration she collected what she thought would be useful. Among her finds: a couple of backpacks; a length of rope; a professional-sized first aid kit that contained more airplane blankets; a tote bag containing several bags of gourmet beef jerky; half-dozen bottles of water; a jackpot computer bag that contained two apples, a hoagie sandwich, a sleeve of fig cookies, and an unopened bag of trail mix; a red ball cap; a pilot's suit jacket; a few handbags, in which she had found two lighters, three candy bars, a pack of gum, a package of sunflower seeds, and two travel bottles of hand sanitizer; and a box of airline peanuts.

Several suitcases were scattered along the floor of the ravine, but Nora couldn't find the courage to look through them. She'd save them for later if the situation came to that. She tried not to think about it, though.

🌲🌲🌲🌲🌲

Back at their makeshift camp, Nora crouched next to the fire she'd started in a ring of rocks she had assembled under the shelter of the wing. On the pallet, a safe distance from sparks, 4B lay motionless near the rock wall. The weather had cleared up some, but help had still not arrived. Nora shivered, more from the stress of their situation than the cold. The gray clouds that had threatened to douse them the day before were mostly gone. Blue sky tinged with sunset pink had emerged, but it was still cold in the shade. Visions of what she had seen in the ravine tried to fill her mind. She pushed them away. If she spent any energy on that, she might break down and she couldn't afford it. Not when she had 4B to keep safe. She watched the smoke from the fire roll out and away from the shelter.

"It's nice and toasty now, huh, 4B? Your old pal Nora reclaimed her badge in campfire building today."

She poked the long stick she was holding into the fire and smiled at herself. She felt a little weird talking to the unconscious woman, but it comforted her and helped to pass the time.

Not being a smoker, she hadn't expected to find a lighter or matches in any of the carry-on items she'd found, thinking they weren't allowed beyond the airport security checkpoints. She was glad she was wrong.

It was her father's advice, and not the search and rescue instructor's, that had echoed through her mind when she had built the fire.

"Put the dry leaves in a pile and make a teepee with the sticks we gathered, Hasenpfeffer. Space them apart so the air can flow. Fire needs oxygen. It needs to breathe."

"Like this, Potato Head?" she asked, when she was nine and intent on the job of setting up the fire they were making. It had been serious work, but she'd still gone along with their game of calling each other food items as endearments.

"That's perfect, my little brisket!" he'd said proudly. "Now you'll never go cold if you get lost in the woods."

She thought back to all of the times her father had taken her camping as a child. Hikes, whitewater rafting, horseback riding, teaching her how to play the harmonica—hundreds of cherished memories paraded through her mind. She was grateful it was the pleasant memories that came to her now, and not the darker ones from later on. As she watched the fire, she let her mind linger on the good times: her father's strength, his easy smile and the safety of his nearness. Those memories kept her calm.

She glanced over at the sleeping 4B. There had been no other survivors down there. It was just the two of them now, and she didn't have the luxury of dealing with her emotions. She carefully added another piece of wood to the flame. The fire was crackling and popping, casting an almost cheery light through the underside of the shelter. She opened one of the airplane-sized bottles of wine she'd discovered in the back of a drawer of the beverage cart she'd found. There were thirteen of the little bottles, and she was tempted to drink them all right then. But she wouldn't. She drank half of the bottle and then set it down before she took the harmonica from her shirt pocket and began to play. It helped to keep the loneliness and fear away.

★★★★★

"Careful. You have a nasty cut on your forehead," Nora said as she slid her harmonica into her shirt pocket. She caught one of 4B's hands just before it landed on the soiled bandage that covered her furrowed forehead. She held the woman's hands still and watched 4B regain consciousness.

It was mid-morning of their third day in the wild and Nora had been playing a tune on her harmonica when the woman had started to stir. The sudden quiet was broken by the new sound of her patient's moans. 4B hadn't moved a finger in over two days. The unexpected movement had startled Nora, who slid out of her seat to kneel next to the woman, holding her hands and willing her eyes to open.

The woman continued to move weakly, uttering incoherent snatches of words between moans. She shouted a word—"milagro!"—and then fell to mumbling. Nora couldn't understand any of what she said, but her heart pounded in her chest. Awake! She was awake! 4B's eyelids fluttered, and then opened, revealing a brilliant green that disappeared again when the lids slid shut. The woman turned her head away from the light spilling in through the open side of the wing they were under. Nora was taken by how stunning the woman was. She'd thought her beautiful before, but animation gave a new depth to her beauty. It was a fleeting assessment, though, as concern over the woman's well-being eclipsed other thoughts.

"Is the sunlight hurting your eyes?" asked Nora, grabbing the sweatshirt she taken off earlier and using it as a shade against some of the sunlight that now peeked between the late afternoon clouds. "That should be better. I've blocked the glare a little."

At the sound of Nora's voice, 4B opened her eyes again and turned her head toward Nora. In the next second, she closed her eyes again and was still. Nora hadn't realized her isolation until those eyes had seen her—and then didn't.

"4B? Are you still awake? Or did you fall back asleep?" Nora asked barely above a whisper, afraid to startle the woman. Afraid it was neither.

The woman's eyelids parted slightly, fluttering, the hand wrapped in Nora's tightened around her fingers. She moaned again and Nora exhaled. Green eyes—the color of new leaves, Nora decided—opened and then remained focused on Nora in a squint. Exaltation flared within Nora.

4B stared at her for several seconds and Nora wondered what to do. What was the woman thinking? Were there more injuries she couldn't see?

"Who are you?" whispered the woman. The words were so faint, Nora barely heard them.

Nora used the back of her hand to wipe away a sudden and unexpected surge of tears that blurred her vision. She cleared her throat and smiled.

"I'm Nora Kavendash," she said. "I can't believe you're awake." Nora continued to stare at the woman, who grimaced and rolled her head back to center. The movement appeared to take considerable effort, as if her head were heavy and painful. The woman tried to swallow.

"Thirsty." The word was barely audible.

Nora let go of 4B's hand and picked up the bottle of water that was sitting next to her chair. She unscrewed the top and was about to offer it to the woman, but just as she turned back, the green eyes lost focus and slid shut. She tried to wake her again, but short of slapping her, she couldn't rouse the woman. She replaced the cap on the bottle and relaxed into her seat.

Although the woman slept, she seemed more present now. The animation, although less active in sleep, was still there and Nora studied the woman's beautiful features. An unexplainable emotion linked Nora to her now. The woman's chest rose more often with deeper breaths, her eyelids fluttered with internal thoughts, and her fingers twitched as she slept. The hand Nora clutched was warmer, and her color was better. Nora dared to think the woman would be okay, and the anxious pressure that had made it hard for her to breathe eased.

She studied the woman, a habit she'd settled into as she'd passed the time since she'd found her. Now that her color had returned, the woman's face had gone from pretty to beautiful. Free from the dirt Nora had washed away when she'd cleaned the wound, the skin was smooth and clear, and with the subtle animation of consciousness, the woman's features came to life. Her lips, now a darker pink, were slightly parted to show perfect white teeth. Nora leaned forward to move a strand of hair away from the woman's cheek.

"I think you're going to make it, 4B," she said as she rubbed the woman's hand between both of hers. This time when she spoke, the woman squeezed her hand.

🌲🌲🌲🌲🌲

Twenty minutes later, Nora stared into the fire thinking about rescue. As the days passed, her hope waned and she tried to think of plans should help never arrive. How long should they wait? When would 4B be well enough to hike? What would they do for food when the meager rations she'd collected ran out? Questions spun through her mind in a haze of doubt and fear.

When Nora looked up to check on her sleeping patient, two green eyes stared back at her.

"Hi," she said, sitting up. She tried to push her dark thoughts away. "You're awake again."

The woman nodded and Nora realized she was still holding her hand. She let go and the woman slowly withdrew it, pulling it under the blanket.

"How do you feel?" asked Nora. The woman closed her eyes and swallowed. Nora could see she had trouble with it. "Are you thirsty? Do you need a drink of water?"

"Yes, please," the woman croaked. Nora dribbled a little water into the woman's open mouth and felt a pang of pity at the look of relief she saw reflected in the woman's face. Nora poured and paused, poured and paused, until 4B sighed and relaxed.

"Where am I?" the woman asked, using a shaking hand to wipe her mouth and then pull the blanket up to her neck.

Nora didn't know how to answer the simple question. The woman was barely coherent—she should let her adjust to being conscious before getting into the details of their situation.

"You're safe," she offered, hoping it was enough for now. She saw the woman's eyes slip down to the bottle in her hand and she handed it to the woman, who tipped it to her mouth, gulping greedily.

"Thanks," said 4B, swallowing and wiping away the drops that escaped down her chin.

"You're welcome," said Nora.

"Where am I?" the woman asked groggily, weakly turning her head to look around.

Nora tried to figure out how to answer the question. She was saved from having to answer when 4B blew out a breath and closed her eyes. She was motionless for so long that Nora thought she'd gone back to sleep until the woman opened her eyes and looked at her.

"You told me your name, but I can't remember it."

"It's Nora."

"Nora, I'm having a hard time thinking. Where are we? What are we…?" 4B squeezed her eyes shut with a grimace.

"Are you okay?" asked Nora, resting a hand on the woman's shoulder. "What hurts?"

"Everything. Mostly my head," said the woman, squeezing her eyes shut.

"You knocked your head pretty good in the crash. You probably have a concussion. Is there anything else hurting you?"

"Crash?" asked the woman opening her eyes with a slightly confused look on her face.

"Do you remember how we got here?" asked Nora.

The woman drew her eyebrows together in concentration.

"I don't think I do."

"What's the last thing you remember?"

The woman's lips moved, and when Nora leaned in to hear what she said, the woman mumbled she was tired and then drifted back to sleep. Nora eased the bottle from her limp hands and screwed the lid closed.

Later that afternoon, Nora stared into the fire. She absently shook the spit out of her harmonica and licked her lips. It had been a long time since she'd played so much and her lips were a little sore. She was thankful for the lip balm she'd found in 4B's pocket. She'd used it on both of them. The music was a way to pass the time, though, and she was glad she'd slipped the instrument into her bag before leaving on the trip. She rubbed the silver harp with pearl inlay on her jeans-clad leg and slipped it back into her shirt pocket.

"That was nice," said the woman. "What were you playing?"

"Hey, you're back again," said Nora with a smile, turning to see the brilliant green eyes watching her. It had only been ten minutes or so since they'd dropped shut. They were more aware this time. "It's a harmonica."

"I know it's a harmonica," replied the woman with a good-natured roll of her eyes. "I was asking about the song."

Nora laughed, feeling a little stupid. The woman was injured, not an idiot.

"Just an old song my father taught me. It's called 'Heart of Gold.'"

"I liked it. Nora, right?"

"Yep, that's me. How are you feeling?"

"Thirsty. Not as groggy, but kind of sick to my stomach." 4B closed her eyes, and with a great deal of effort, rolled to her side facing Nora. She put both of her hands beneath her head and swallowed with visible discomfort. Nora considered the change in position a good sign and unconsciously smoothed back the hair on the woman's forehead, careful of the white bandage, ready to help her if she got sick.

"You were out for a long time."

"Out? What… what happened?" 4B asked. "It feels like I swallowed a bag of glass."

Nora offered the water bottle and 4B rolled to her back. Nora propped her up with an arm around her shoulders so she could take a sip of water. "Easy. Take your time. We have plenty," she said as 4B gulped the water.

"Did I ask what happened?" asked 4B, out of breath from drinking so quickly. She held onto the bottle as if it were precious.

"There was a crash."

"You told me that before, right?" asked 4B "Was I driving?"

She thought she'd been in a car? "No. We were in an airplane. Do you remember any of it?"

Nora watched 4B's face. She looked like she was trying to remember.

"An airplane? No. I guess I don't. Should I be freaked out that I don't remember? I feel like I should be freaked out." 4B shut her eyes and was quiet for so long Nora wondered if she had fallen asleep again until 4B reached up to feel the bandage on her forehead.

"You have a cut on your head. You must have hit it pretty hard. Do you remember how?"

The woman's forehead wrinkled in deep concentration.

"No. But it hurts like hell."

"What's your name?" Nora asked, trying some of the questions she'd been trained to ask of trauma victims. "Do you know what year it is?"

4B opened her mouth as if to answer and then shut it. She opened her eyes again and stared hard at Nora, as if she'd find the answer in Nora's face.

"I… I don't know. It's right there, but I can't see it." Still clutching the water bottle, 4B struggled to sit up. She looked like a turtle that has been placed on its back. "The light is so bright. Makes my head hurt."

Nora could see a cascade of emotions slide across 4B's face as she tried to make sense of what was going on around her.

"Maybe you should lie back down."

"I'd rather sit up."

"Then let me help you. We'll go slow."

4B allowed Nora to take the water bottle from her and help her to sit up. She sat motionless, crossed-legged and slouched forward. Nora thought she looked so fragile with her hair dangling in front of her face and her hands limp on her knees. The wool blanket was now pooled in her lap, and she rested her head in her hands. Slowly, she moved her fingers back to the bandaged wound on her forehead and through her dirty hair. Nora watched helplessly.

"My head hurts," 4B said, pushing her hair back and exploring the dimensions of the bandage. "Sorry. I'm whining." She looked up slowly, her eyes scanning the underside of their shelter. "Where are we?"

"I'm not sure, exactly. We're sitting under one of the wings from the airplane, though."

4B took this in and flinched as she pressed along the edges of the bandage. The center of it was dark with dried blood. Nora thought maybe she should have changed it by now.

"That's a pretty nasty gash on your forehead. You've been unconscious for a while," Nora told her again, not sure if 4B remembered much of their previous conversations.

"How long?"

"It's Thursday afternoon. We went down on Tuesday."

"I've been unconscious for two days? Where are we? Shouldn't we be in the hospital?"

4B stopped talking. Nora watched her features pull into another grimace. She thought about concussion again. With 4B unable to remember her own name, amnesia seemed highly probable. Nora had no idea how to treat it, except to keep 4B calm. And wasn't she supposed to keep her from going to sleep? So far she hadn't done a great job on the sleeping part. What happened if she slept? Nora had no idea.

4B looked pale.

"Maybe you should lie back down," suggested Nora.

"I don't want to lie down," 4B snapped, brushing Nora's hand away. Chastised, Nora withdrew her hand, but 4B opened her eyes and searched Nora's face. "I'm sorry. That was mean. I just feel like I might throw up. God, I'm sorry... My head hurts so much and I just feel so disoriented."

"It's okay," said Nora. She still felt a little uncomfortable, not knowing what to do to help.

Finally, Nora pulled her backpack over and placed it behind 4B. "How about this? You can sort of lean back." She watched 4B's expression for acceptance, and when she thought she had it, she eased her into a semi-reclined position. She was grateful 4B didn't push her away again. She pulled up the blanket and tucked a couple of the small airline pillows behind her head. The woman sighed in relief.

"That feels so much better. Thanks. I'm really sorry about snapping."

"No worries," replied Nora. They were quiet for a few minutes. 4B shivered under the thin blankets. A sheen of sweat shone on her skin, even though the temperature was cool.

"Are you cold?"

4B nodded slowly without opening her eyes. Nora pulled the wool blanket up over her shoulders and threw more wood on the fire she had let go down during the day.

A few minutes later, 4B's shivering had subsided, and Nora tried not to stare at her. She wondered when she would stop worrying about 4B dying. When 4B opened her eyes a few moments later, she turned to tend to the fire to cover her relief.

"The fire feels good," said 4B through barely chattering teeth.

"You're still shivering. It's not that cold. You might be in shock."

"Are you a doctor?"

"No," laughed Nora, breaking a piece of wood and adding it to the fire. "I've had first aid training, but that's it."

Nora squatted by the fire, using a stick to arrange the burning wood. She felt 4B studying her and tried to convey confidence. She was pretty sure she was doing a miserable job of it.

"I'm feeling much warmer," said 4B. Nora could see her shivers had faded away again.

"One thing we have out here is plenty of wood," said Nora. She'd collected a small stack, which she'd stored in the narrow space where the inside wing rested on the ground. The sky looked angry again, and she decided she'd go out again soon to gather some more in case it started to rain. Nora had spent a lot of time staring at the sky, willing the low clouds to hold onto their rain. As if they sensed her distraction, a low rumble sounded in the distance and rolled down the mountain. Clouds moved over the late afternoon sun.

"If you had to guess, where would you say we are?" asked 4B.

"I'm not sure," responded Nora. "A little east of Valdez, I think. We were about a quarter of the way into the flight when we went down."

"Valdez, Mexico?"

Nora looked up at 4B, puzzled.

"Alaska. You aren't from around here, I take it?"

"I… I don't know."

"That bump must have really done a number on you. It'll come back." Nora studied her. "How do you feel now?"

"My head feels like it's going to explode. I'm nauseated, but I think… I think maybe some of it's thirst. And hunger."

"Well, you haven't eaten or had anything to drink except this in over two days," she agreed, handing 4B the water bottle.

Nora remembered the bag of crackers she had left over from her lunch and found them in the bag beside her. She handed them to 4B who examined the crackers and began to pop them, one by one, into her mouth.

Nora handed her another package of crackers after 4B tilted the little bag back to shake the last crumbs into her mouth.

"Thanks. My stomach feels a little better," said 4B opening the second package.

"How's your head?"

"It still throbs, but at least I don't feel like throwing up now."

Nora had a feeling 4B was minimizing her pain. When a brief expression of discomfort floated across 4B's face, her suspicion was confirmed. She wished she could do something about it. Then she remembered.

"I think we have some pain reliever," she said as she reached for the first aid kit she had found near the crash site. She balanced it in her lap. It doesn't have anything for serious injuries, but it contained more than her little travel kit did. She found what she was looking for and tore open the small package, shook out a couple of tablets, and offered them to the woman.

"Do we have more water?" asked 4B, finishing off what was left in the bottle as she washed down the pills. "I can't seem to get enough."

"We have plenty," said Nora, crawling over to the open metal drawer of the beverage cart. She had lined it with plastic and it held a blue chunk of melting ice that she had chipped from the face of the glacier. Requiring refrigeration, Aunt Mace's medicine floated in it, protected in a plastic baggie. "Direct from the nearby glacier. At least we don't need to worry about fresh water."

"It's so good. And cold," said 4B, after taking a sip of the refilled bottle Nora handed her. Nora noted that her color was improving already. "But I think I would feel the same way about drinking warm bath water right now. I don't suppose there's a cheeseburger in one of those drawers, is there?"

The unexpected joke made Nora laugh.

"I wish! But we do have a few bags of gourmet jerky."

"I suppose we need to ration it," said 4B.

"We're actually in pretty good shape as far as food goes, assuming we get rescued soon," explained Nora, not giving voice to the doubt that had recently started clouding her thoughts. She listed off the trail-mix, candy bars, and apples she'd found—not to mention the bonanza of airline peanuts and crackers. "Oh, and I can't believe I almost forgot—a dozen little bottles of wine."

"I think I'll hold off on the wine for the time being but please tell me you just forgot to tell me about the stash of coffee you have somewhere?"

Nora hated to disappoint her, but she was glad to hear 4B had a sense of humor.

"Sorry. I've been craving a hot cup myself."

"First, no cheeseburgers, and now no coffee? What kind of establishment is this?"

"I can offer you a soda," offered Nora. "Not nearly the same, but some of it has caffeine."

"A soda sounds good, please," responded 4B. "The caffeine will help the aspirin to work faster, too." Nora cracked open a can of cola and handed it to her.

"It's a little early for dinner, but I could eat now," said Nora. "You up for a little more than those crackers?"

"I was only halfway kidding about the cheeseburger earlier," sighed 4B. "I didn't know how hungry I was until the crackers hit my stomach."

"It's a good sign, I think. Especially if you have a concussion, as I suspect you do," said Nora reaching for the pack she'd stowed near her seat a little earlier. Normally, she didn't keep it in the shelter. She'd kept it hung in a distant tree to avoid attracting bears. But she'd taken it down for the lunch she'd forgotten to eat when 4B had distracted her by waking up.

"A concussion, huh? How do my pupils look?" asked 4B.

Nora lowered the pack she'd been going through and leaned closer to look at 4B's eyes. She'd learned to look for asymmetrical pupil dilation in first aid. But once she'd noted they were normal, she admired the beautiful green rings that looked back at her.

"My pupils?" asked 4B. "How do they look?"

Nora cleared her throat.

"They look fine," she replied with a smile.

"Are they the same size? Are the pupils really wide? Do I have burst blood vessels?"

"Um…" said Nora, and she studied them again with a more clinical regard. "They're the same size. Sort of dilated, but I think that's because we're in the shade. And not too bloodshot." As she appraised 4B's eyes, Nora became self-conscious of her own appearance. She leaned back and tugged the bill of the ball cap she wore down more snuggly and tightened the ponytail she had pulled through the back. If the front of her dirty clothes were any indication of everything else, she probably had streaks of dirt lining her face. She rubbed her hands across her chin. She didn't smell that great, either. "Whereas, mine feel like I have grit embedded in them, what with the smoke from the fire and the, well, grit out here. Outside. In the forest." Nora laughed self-consciously and began to pull food out of the bag again.

"Sounds like I'll live, then." 4B had a nice laugh. The woman had no concept of the fear Nora had lived with since finding her. She pulled out an apple, selected a couple of packs of crackers for each of them, along with a handful of small bags of peanuts. If 4B did well with the food, she'd give her some of the jerky.

"Linner is served," said Nora.

"Linner?"

"Lunch plus dinner. Linner," explained Nora as she sat down and spread her bounty next to 4B like a picnic. "We don't have a knife, so we'll have to share the apple." She didn't tell 4B she'd barely eaten in the last few days, what with the fear and worry that had made her stomach queasy. Suddenly, she was famished. They were quiet for a few minutes as they ate.

"You said this is an airplane wing?" asked 4B, extending an arm to touch the slanted metal overhead.

Nora nodded. "Most of the plane is at the bottom of a ravine not too far from here."

"Are we alone?"

"I've looked and I haven't found any other… survivors," said Nora, watching the woman's face for her reaction.

4B stopped eating. She stared at the apple in her hand. "I… I feel so disconnected. I know there was a crash. There must have been other people on the airplane. Are they all…?" 4B didn't finish the sentence. Nora hated the haunted look on her face, wishing she could comfort her.

"I don't know. I sort of feel disconnected, too. I mean, I remember, but it's hard to think about all the others." Images from the morning she'd climbed down into the ravine tried to invade her mind, but she didn't let them.

They were quiet for several minutes. Nora glanced at 4B a few times and watched her stare at the fire.

"Do you remember anything?" Nora finally asked. Maybe it was a good thing if she didn't.

"I'm not sure. I don't have any memory of how I got here. I'm sorry. I wish I could remember."

"You don't need to be sorry," said Nora. "I was a little out of it in the beginning, myself."

4B offered a small smile but her eyes went back to the fire. Nora wished she knew what she was thinking about.

Nora picked up the wrappers from their little meal and threw them in the fire. She crushed the soft drink can and put it in the pack with the remaining food.

"Have you had enough to eat?" asked Nora. She did a mental inventory of the food. With the bags of crackers and peanuts she'd found in the beverage cart, along with various food items she'd scavenged from the crash site, she figured they had several days if they rationed it. She hoped they wouldn't have to.

"I'm good for now," said 4B, rubbing her belly. "I feel a little better."

Nora nodded, picked up a stick, and poked at the fire before she tossed on a few more pieces of wood. The temperature outside was dropping as the day moved into evening. She rolled the sleeves of the flannel shirt she was wearing down to cover her arms and, not for the first time, wondered why help hadn't arrived yet.

"How long have we been out here? Did you say two days?" asked 4B. She pulled up the blanket resting in her lap and tucked it under her chin.

"Just over 56 hours," she answered.

"Where is the rescue team, then?"

"I'm actually kind of surprised they haven't found us yet. We're near the crash site. All I can figure is the cloud cover has hindered the search efforts. There are miles and miles of forest and coastline to search, all of which is pretty rugged. They probably don't know if we hit the water or the mountains. But I'm sure the plane has a beacon on it. They'll come soon."

Nora hoped she was right.

"Do we have enough food to last?"

"For a few days," answered Nora. "We'll be fine until they find us. I'm sure."

"Is that it?" asked 4B waving at the pack.

"We have another pack with more soda, candy bars, and a bunch more peanuts and crackers in it. I keep both packs up in a tree about three hundred feet from here to keep the bears away."

"Bears?" 4B peered out into the nearby woods.

Nora nodded and poked the fire with her stick. "Yeah. Alaska is crawling with them," she said, and then she noticed the startled look on 4B's face. "Don't worry. I haven't seen any signs of bear around here. We're on a ledge that doesn't have much food or reason for them to come up. Besides, I think bear-proofing a camp is something every young Alaskan learns at birth. They'll stay away if we don't give them a reason to investigate. They're more afraid of us than we are of them," encouraged Nora, trying to provide 4B with an assurance she didn't feel herself. Only a sidearm would have helped her confidence.

"You're from here, then? Around Valdez?"

"Close. Juneau. Born and raised. What about you?"

The woman appeared to think about it and that same strange look came over her face.

"I don't know."

"Nothing?" asked Nora. She wondered again about amnesia. She didn't know much about it, but it seemed to fit, what with the way 4B kept hitting blanks when she tried to remember even the most mundane item. She wanted to press 4B to see how deep it went, but something told her to be gentle about it, to ease 4B into her memory. It didn't make sense to get her worked up when they were out in the middle of nowhere. Survival should be at the top of their priority list.

4B shook her head. "It feels like it's just out of reach."

"It will probably come back as soon as your headache goes away."

They watched the fire in silence for a few minutes.

"You said it's just us? This wing is big, so it was a large plane?"

Nora nodded and her chest tightened as it did every time she thought about the crash. "Yeah. We were on a 737. I imagine they hold over a hundred people. It doesn't seem possible, you know?" She shook her head. "For a little while, I thought I was the only one. Then I found you."

"Thankfully," replied 4B with a smile. "What happened? Why did we crash? Did we hit bad weather?"

"I don't think so. The rain was coming down pretty hard in Anchorage when we took off, but we were above the cloud cover before it happened. Things were smooth. But then, one engine went out, and when the pilot turned around to go back to Anchorage, the other went out."

"Do you remember the actual crash? Going down?"

Nora shivered. The real question was, would she ever forget? The scariest part had been in the beginning, when the anticipation of everything had started, and then the feeling of dropping. The way everything had just ally-ooped and how it felt like it wouldn't end. It had been less scary when things had banged and bumped.

"Yeah, it felt like it went on forever, but really, it was so quick. I was thrown clear somehow, seat and all," Nora said, patting the cushion of the chair below her. "I ended up, still strapped into this seat, not too far from here, between two rocks. Somehow I landed without a scratch on me. I found you a few hundred feet out that way," Nora said, waving her hand in the opposite direction of the ravine. "You were nearly covered by a fallen tree I'd given up on finding anyone. I was walking along the crash path and I almost stepped on you. You were covered in dirt and pine needles. Your hair was the only thing I saw."

Nora watched 4B reach up and feel her hair. Half of it was matted with dirt and dried blood. 4B pulled a strand out and looked at it, rolling it between her fingers.

"You've been watching over me since then." It was a statement, not a question. Nora nodded her head. "Has watching over me kept you from looking for help? Should we try to hike out? Try to find a town or something?"

"The best thing we can do is stay put. There are miles of wilderness in every direction. Search and rescue will find the plane and rescue us." She said it with more conviction than she felt.

"You saved my life."

"Maybe. I honestly thought you were—" Nora paused. "I couldn't tell that you were breathing at first, and you weren't responsive. But you had a pulse, so I carried you over here, cleaned up your cut, and… well, I've been watching you breathe ever since."

"Saying thank you doesn't seem like enough," said 4B, dropping the dirty strand of hair and reaching up to take Nora's hand. Nora gave it a squeeze.

"You waking up is enough, believe me," said Nora. 4B couldn't know how taking care of her had kept her going.

They sat for a few minutes, each thinking her own thoughts.

"I'm tired. Do you mind if I rest a bit?" 4B didn't wait to hear Nora's response as she dropped Nora's hand and inched down to lie curled up with her back to Nora. Again, Nora worried about the concussion/sleep thing, but 4B clearly wanted some space to digest the conversation. So, Nora watched the even cadence of 4B's breathing and sat sentinel over her, just like she had the last two days.

♣♣♣♣♣

An hour later, as the afternoon turned to dusk, Nora reclined in the beat up airplane seat with her feet propped up on one of the rocks of the fire ring. It was a position that had become not so much comfortable, but at least familiar in the hours of waiting. The burning wood snapped, popped, and hissed, and she monitored the rise and fall of 4B's respiration as she slept. Sleep started to pull her in, too. She was exhausted, but she shifted in her seat instead and finished off the last few peanuts from the package in her lap. When she tossed the plastic wrapper on the fire, the package shrank and pulled in on itself. It probably wasn't good for the environment to burn the packaging, but her concern for the environment was overshadowed by concern of bears that could sniff out food from hundreds of feet away.

Even unconscious, 4B's company was a comfort to Nora. Nighttime was still bad, though, when the constant vigilance couldn't keep the doubt and dark memories away, and panic would try to set in. The first night had been the worst, when she didn't have the fire to help keep the dark away, and the thoughts that came with it. That's when the specter of the wreckage burning so far below, and fear of the predators that lurked in the night, tried to take over. But now, even with the fire, it was hard to keep at bay the horrors of the crash and the visions of the bodies she'd seen. So, she didn't sleep—at least not much. The fear of being stranded in the wilderness without protection or real shelter, along with the responsibility of taking care of someone who might die at any time, drove away any hope of sleep for her as soon as she tried to close her eyes.

Once again, nightfall was just a couple of hours away, and she braced herself for another sleepless, fear-filled night. Maybe this one wouldn't be so bad now that 4B was awake.

Nora pushed up from her seat and moved out from underneath the wing. Light was fading from the gray sky. She stood tall and stretched, trying to ignore the uncomfortable thoughts. It occurred to her again that 4B might be doing the same with the memory loss. Maybe, when she was safe and back with her family, 4B would remember. Nora hoped that would be the case.

4B continued to sleep, and Nora inventoried the remaining food. She carefully sealed the pack around what was left, hefted the bag to her shoulder, and took it back to the tree where she hung it again, beside the other one, high above the ground, safe from bears and other animals.

Instead of immediately going back to the shelter, she went to the lip of the ravine, crouching next to the tree she had clung to when she had watched the airplane explode. It seemed so long ago now, just a couple of days later. She draped her arms across her knees and rested her chin on them, looking out over the space before her, the shadows filling in the gorge. She couldn't see to the bottom from her vantage point—nor did she want to—but a thin dark stream of smoke snaked up from the abyss, just to be swept away immediately by a wind she couldn't feel when she was just a few feet into the tree line behind her. She could smell the plane smoldering below. The scent, acrid and industrial, was fainter than it had been, but she could still smell it, and it was different from the little campfire she had made.

She could feel the presence of the people who rested in the charred skeleton of the wreckage. After seeing it up close, she was no longer surprised she hadn't come across any survivors, though she still found it hard to believe she and 4B were the only ones. Was it just wishful thinking to feel others had to be out there somewhere?

She shuddered to think of the bodies and body parts she had stumbled across in her search. Although she had been trained for that situation, nothing could have prepared her for the horror she had experienced down there. The first two bodies had been awful, mostly because of the surprise of it. The first two turned out to be the least upsetting, though. Each body she had discovered—seven in total—was worse than the last. Coming across body parts had been the worst, seeming so out of place. Her stomach turned at the sights and smells she couldn't put out of her mind. She hoped they had died quickly.

She thought of them down there, now. She'd left them where they lay, unable to make herself move them to another spot. Should she have buried them? She'd hoped rescue would have come by now, making that unnecessary. It wasn't like her to be indecisive. She needed to do something.

Nora was getting good at locking her feelings away, so she shoved her dark thoughts aside once again. She just didn't have time for focusing on anything other than keeping her and 4B alive. Unless she learned to hunt—a skill neither her father nor the Guard had taught her—the food had to last them until someone came to find them. If someone came to get them. After two days, her confidence that they'd be rescued had started to wane. The charred wreckage of the airplane made it hard for her to believe that a tracking beacon had survived. And as the days crept on without a sign of help, Nora wondered what they would do. Strangely, she had no doubt they'd survive. She just had to figure out a plan.

With thoughts of survival occupying her mind, and darkness fully descended, Nora rose from her perch and returned to the makeshift camp. She threw some more wood on the fire, took her seat and watched her companion sleep. Once again, 4B's beauty struck Nora, even with the dirty bandage and blood-matted hair. As she watched, 4B stirred, still asleep, reached out, and then dropped her arms. Something disturbed her dreams. Nora wished she could help her, but she hadn't figured out how to fix her own nightmares.

🌲🌲🌲🌲🌲

Nora was dreaming.

She sat at the worn, green Formica dining table in Aunt Mace's kitchen. Steam from a freshly brewed cup of coffee grazed her chin as she hunkered over it, staring at the hand of cards she held fanned before her. She was one card away from calling rummy.

It was her turn. Her aunt, who sat across the table from her, gestured impatiently for her to draw the next card. Nora smirked, and watched her aunt push the sleeves of her housedress up and lean her chin on her free hand, signaling that she didn't have all day. But Nora didn't want the game to end. She drew a card. The exact card she needed. She considered tossing it on the discard pile.

"I know you got only one card to go, Eleanor, and I was dealt a shit hand. Don't you go throwing off to keep the game going."

"You don't know."

"You wouldn't be calling an old woman a liar, would you?"

"I wouldn't dream of it," said Nora. She fanned out the winning hand in front of her. "Rummy."

"That's my girl," said Aunt Mace with a smile and Nora's heart broke. Aunt Mace never lost without a string of curse words.

Nora woke and a wave of sadness surged through her. She yawned, and her surroundings—the crackling fire, the airplane wing shelter, and the smell of pine—re-established themselves in her awareness. The anxiety over their situation returned, and the sadness drifted away along with the dream. She shifted in her seat, and caught the e-reader as it slid off her lap. She set the device next to her chair and crossed her arms, dropping her chin back into her chest, ready to fall back to sleep. Night had just settled over the little camp, and Nora was tired from lack of sleep. Her eyes fluttered closed.

The woman across from her stirred in her sleep and Nora looked at her from through her lashes. The woman rolled to her side and looked at Nora. Nora watched through the shadows as the woman's eyes roamed over her. She must have thought Nora was asleep. Her gaze was unmasked, curious, as if she were trying to build a story from the intensity of her stare. Nora wondered what she saw: a somewhat attractive face, probably dirty, with a few lines, but not too many; dark, shoulder-length hair in a ponytail pulled through the back of a red ball cap; capable hands, nails trimmed short and no rings; a sports watch with a black band; loose blue jeans held up by an expensive belt; well-worn hiking boots; a brown and blue flannel shirt with the sleeves rolled up, a brown t-shirt underneath; a thick silver chain around her neck with an onyx pendent framed in silver; simple hoop earrings; a full mouth. Nora smiled and the woman started.

"Caught me staring." A blush crept up 4B's face.

"Just tell me I wasn't drooling," said Nora with a sleepy smile, sitting up and stretching. "Besides, I watched you sleep for two days. It was the best entertainment for miles around."

"I don't think either of us slept for long," said 4B, glancing outside where the darkness closed in around them. "I'm so thirsty. I think that's what woke me up."

Nora handed her a bottle of water and then looked at her watch. They'd slept about an hour. It was the longest Nora had slept at once so far.

"Is there something wrong with your hip? You yelped a little when you rolled over earlier."

The woman accepted the water, unscrewed the cap, and took a long drink. Breathless, she lowered the bottle with a grateful smile and reached down to feel her hip through her jeans, wincing as her fingers passed over the meaty place just where the thigh met the crease in her upper leg. "Oh, that smarts," she said, as she put the water aside. Nora was surprised when she unbuttoned her pants and pushed down the side far enough to take a look. The area, about five by three inches, was puffy and dark purple with bright red around the perimeter, but no abrasion. When 4B touched it, she hissed.

"Oh, yeah, I have a pretty good hematoma right there. No broken skin, though," she reported, carefully examining it before she pulled her pants back up. "I should probably ice it."

"We have plenty of ice. I'm actually surprised neither of us is more badly hurt," Nora said as she went over to the beverage cart and broke a piece of ice from the chunk of glacier she'd stowed in it. "I should have done a better job of checking you over for injuries when I found you."

Water sloshed in the metal container and Nora saw 4B sit up suddenly.

"Um, Nora? I have to go…" she started, struggling to get up.

"Gotta pee?" asked Nora, moving quickly to her side.

The woman nodded. By now she'd been able to get up on her hands and knees. Nora sensed the urgency of the situation even though 4B already looked exhausted.

"You'll need help."

Nora saw a blush creep up 4B's cheeks and found it amusing. She tried not to laugh, though.

"Easy getting up. You haven't been on your feet in a few days. Take your time. Mind the low ceiling under here."

She helped 4B rise in tentative stages, holding her arm as they paused in a crouch for a moment before easing to a semi-standing position under the wing. It looked like the effort eased the situation. They moved out from under the wing and stood up.

"I feel a little light-headed," 4B said uncertainly. She held tight to Nora's arm, taking her first unsteady steps. Nora was a good three inches taller than 4B, which helped as 4B leaned heavily against her. It was dark and the pause allowed Nora's eyes to adjust from the light of the fire. The moon was nearly full and even though it was dimmed by the cloud cover, it helped to illuminate the forest around them. It was bright enough that she didn't need to use the flashlight she had in her pocket.

"Oh god!" said 4B grabbing herself like a kindergartener. "We have to hurry!"

Nora shook with the effort of holding back her laughter.

"Stop laughing! I'm going to pee my pants!"

"I'm not laughing," said Nora, but the chuckle that punctuated the statement earned her a severe stare. It was enough to stifle further laughter and Nora concentrated on getting 4B to the area she'd turned into their informal latrine. It was far enough from the shelter to keep curious animals at a distance, but right now she wished it was closer for 4B's sake.

Unsteady at first, 4B soon gained enough confidence to walk with only an arm looped through Nora's. Nora finally indicated a spot behind a bush, next to a large rock.

Nora positioned her and backed up a step. "Just lean against the rock like that and squat. Do you need me to stay?" She wasn't sure she should leave her alone, even to pee.

"I think I have this. But thanks. I'll give a shout if I need help," said 4B, letting her know she wasn't wanted for this task.

"I'll be just over there," said Nora taking another step back, indicating the other side of the rock. The woman began to claw at the button on her jeans. "Just call if you need anything. Oh, and here," said Nora coming back, pulling her travel flashlight and a half-dozen square napkins from her pocket. "Um, they're for... well, you know."

4B hurriedly took them and waved her away. Nora retreated to the other side of the rock to give her some privacy. It took everything in Nora to stay where she was. She imagined 4B passing out from the unfamiliar exertion or tripping over something in the dark.

A few minutes later 4B carefully made her way over to the other side of the rock to Nora, who pretended to study some lichen, but turned when she approached.

4B leaned against the boulder next to Nora to catch her breath.

Nora leaned, too. "I forgot to ask you to wrap up the napkins so we could burn them. Leave no trace, and all that."

"Oh, um, I buried them," said 4B.

"That's okay. They'll decompose soon enough." Nora laughed. "Seems silly to worry about a napkin, when several tons of metal and plastic have basically embedded itself in this mountainside."

"Yeah, I guess so."

"It's probably a good sign you had to, you know, um, go," said Nora, thinking it meant all of her systems were functioning properly.

4B looked embarrassed.

"So, while I was unconscious... did I... I mean... how...?"

Nora was confused at first, and then amusement hit her when 4B waved her hand in front of her zipper. "Oh! You mean... um. No." Nora laughed. "You seem to be perfectly potty-trained."

"That's a relief. Two days, and I just thought... I must be dehydrated." 4B pinched the skin on the back of her hand and it didn't flatten out immediately. "Yep. Dehydrated."

"We'll get you hydrated. Under the circumstances, it's amazing neither of us is worse off than we are."

4B pushed her dirty hair behind her ears, considering the statement.

"Yeah. I guess not being able to remember my name is a relatively small issue considering how we got here. Though it is concerning."

Nora suddenly remembered the boarding pass.

"There's a boarding pass in your back pocket. Your name's on it," said Nora. "I hope you don't mind that I checked."

"Really?" 4B slid her hands into the pockets of her jeans. She pulled out the folded piece of paper and unfolded it with one hand even as she searched her front pockets with the other. She leaned back against the rock. "I didn't think to check my pockets for identification. Did I have a bag with me?"

"No. Just what's in your pockets. Oh, and this," said Nora holding out the tube of cherry Chap Stick. "You can blame me for your moisturized lips."

"I owe you for many things" 4B mumbled as she took the lip balm and then shone the light on the boarding pass. "So. I'm Grace Trackton."

Nora waited for some sign of recollection.

"Does it conjure up anything else?"

"Grace Trackton flying from LAX to JNU," 4B read, staring at the flimsy slip of paper. "Grace Trackton," she repeated. It sounded like she was trying to talk herself into it.

"I'm not seeing massive recognition," said Nora, disappointed. 4B sounded disappointed, too.

"Nope. Nothing new. I guess it's my name but it doesn't feel like it. It could be Grace, Linda or Bernice. Chuck or Louie, even. It doesn't matter. Still nothing."

They were quiet for a moment and 4B continued to stare at the paper.

"I kind of like Louie."

"I feel more like a Louie than I do a Grace, actually," said 4B. "Do I look like a Grace? I don't feel like a Grace."

"What does a Grace feel like?"

"I'm not sure, really. Not like this, though."

"Well, do you mind if I just call you 4B?" asked Nora. It was such a weird conversation to be having.

4B must have thought so, too. She laughed.

"That's what you were calling me when I woke up. Why 4B?"

"It was your seat number." Nora pointed to the number on the boarding pass. "My seat was 8D. You were a few rows in front of me."

"4B…" she said. "4B is interesting. It's good. I like it. For some reason it feels more like who I am than Grace."

"We can switch back later, if—" Nora caught herself, "—when—things change."

4B stuffed the boarding pass back into her back pocket.

"I don't know. 4B sounds kinda tough. I might just keep it."

"It'll sound good when we get rescued and all of the media asks about our ordeal. You know, the book deals, the speaking tours—"

"You already have all of that figured out, do you?" asked 4B.

"Honestly, besides worrying about you, I haven't figured anything out, or thought about anything except getting back to Aunt Mace. And my own bed," admitted Nora.

"I wonder what's waiting for me back home—wherever home is," said 4B. "A soft bed does sound great." Nora wondered what else was on 4B's mind as she watched her wrap her arms around herself. "It's creepy in the dark. We should get back," said 4B as she pushed away from the rock. She took a few steps and then stumbled.

Nora caught her before she fell and kept her hand wrapped around 4B's elbow as they made their way back to camp.

"You're actually steadier on your feet than I would have expected," observed Nora when they got there.

"You say this right after I nearly fell on my face," remarked 4B, with light sarcasm.

"You have to give yourself a break. Remember—you were unconscious for two days and haven't walked since falling several thousand feet out of the sky."

4B glanced at Nora with a smile.

"You have a unique way of putting things into perspective. Has anyone ever told you that?"

Nora just laughed and followed 4B back under the shelter. 4B crawled onto her little bed. The fire had burned down during their absence. "We really shouldn't leave the fire untended. Normally, I would've damped it a bit when no one was here to watch it," said Nora as she tossed a few pieces of wood onto the embers and then helped move the pack behind 4B. "But it was a bit of an emergency, I would say."

"If you mean that I nearly peed my pants, that would be a big yes," agreed 4B. She settled back and Nora draped a couple of the blankets over her legs, tucking a third one around her shoulders. Nora wondered how 4B felt about her taking care of her. She knew she could have done it herself, but Nora liked looking after her.

"Better?" asked Nora.

"Yes, thanks. Well, actually..."

"Yes?"

"This thing I'm sitting on—I think I'd rather sit on the ground."

"Kind of hard, huh?"

"Like sitting on a rock," admitted 4B.

"Let's see what we can do," said Nora, tapping a fingernail against a front tooth as her eyes roamed the area under the wing.

Nora took a blanket and ducked out from under the wing. A few minutes later, she came back with it thrown over her shoulder like a sack. She placed her cargo of pine needles on the ground and then she pulled the panel—4B and all—away from the fire, and started to dig a shallow indention in the dirt, where it used to be. The dirt was loose and easy to move, and when the indention was as long as she was and about three inches deep, Nora emptied the contents of the blanket into it, picking out any sticks.

"Be right back."

She came back with another blanket full of pine needles, and then another, until the indention was full. Then she spread the curtain she'd found over the whole thing, testing the cushion of it and smoothing out a few lumps.

"This might be more comfortable. Try it out." Nora gestured for 4B to lie down.

4B crawled gingerly over to test the new bed out.

"A little pokey in spots, but much softer," sighed 4B, reclining on the padded area.

Nora smiled and sat down in the airline chair. It looked like the short excursion out of the shelter had energized 4B.

They lapsed into a comfortable silence and Nora handed 4B a plastic bottle she refilled from the water in the metal drawer. She also handed her a square of plastic wrapped around a few chunks of ice. "For that nasty bruise on your hip," Nora said as she leaned over to resituate the blankets around her.

"You know, you don't have to baby me," said 4B, leaning back on her elbows. She pressed the ice pack to her hip. "Now that I'm awake, I should be able to take care of myself."

"I don't mind. It's something to do and keeps my mind occupied. But if it makes you uncomfortable, I'll stop."

"No, it doesn't make me uncomfortable… well, not that uncomfortable," said 4B with a little laugh. "I just get the feeling I'm not the kind of person who lets people take care of them. I'm not sure how I know that, but I do."

"I'll try to hold back my urges to play nurse, then. You do look like you feel a little better," said Nora, interrupting 4B's musings.

"I do. My head still hurts, but I'm not as dizzy or as nauseated as I was."

"Good. Because the pharmacy only has so much ibuprofen," joked Nora.

4B smiled. "It must be my awesome doctor."

"Maybe I've found my new calling," remarked Nora, breaking up a stick and throwing it on the fire. "Now, put the ice on that bruise. Doctor's orders."

4B complied.

"What do you do when you aren't moonlighting as a doctor? Wilderness guide? Outdoor survival training?"

Nora looked at 4B with a contemplative look and then smiled.

"Pretty much the exact opposite. I run a few websites, do a little trading in rare wines, fix computers, and work on home networks. But, when I was in college, I did a tour in the Air National Guard to help pay for tuition. Ironically, I was in search and rescue."

"Search and rescue I can see. But computers, huh?" 4B looked like she was trying to picture her working on a computer.

"It's my rugged good looks. It throws people off all the time," joked Nora.

"You are far from rugged. Is that your passion, working in computers?"

Nora picked up a stick and idly poked it into the ground.

"I prefer the software development aspect of it, but it pays the bills. Right now, it gives me flexibility to take care of my aunt."

"You've mentioned her, your Aunt Mace. Is she sick?" asked 4B. "Am I getting too personal?"

Nora stopped drawing circles in the dirt near her feet to look up.

"I believe surviving an airplane crash together lets us skip the polite acquaintances stage," said Nora, tapping her stick on the toe of 4B's tennis shoe. "Aunt Mace gets around by herself, mostly. But she's pretty sick. She has pancreatic cancer."

"I'm sorry. I hope she's beating it."

Nora kept her eyes on the tip of the stick she held and shook her head.

"We're starting to scrape the bottom of the barrel on treatments. She's about to start using an experimental drug. You didn't hear it from me, though. She doesn't qualify for the clinical trials. She's too old. And if you aren't part of the trials, you don't get to use it, at least not in the U.S. But it's all we have left to try. Her doctor knew a guy, who knew another guy... that sort of thing. I went down to Mexico, where anyone can get the medicine for the right money. I picked up a few bottles of what we call her last chance. They have to be refrigerated and the dry ice I was transporting them in evaporated, so that's what's floating in the water in the drawer over there. I was so scared the security monitors at the airport would find it and they would take it away. But I skated right through."

"Sounds like you took quite a risk," said 4B. "But I can understand why you did it."

"I don't know why I told you all this. My aunt's doctor would have her license revoked if anyone found out. All I keep thinking is she's probably sitting at home, not taking care of herself. Worrying about me."

The sadness of her dream came back in full force.

"Remember, we get to skip the normal getting-to-know-you stages," 4B reminded Nora. "And for the record, I won't tell anyone—even when the media makes us into the story of the moment. I promise not to include it in my book."

Nora smiled.

"Thanks. I knew you were good people."

"You're good people, too."

They were quiet for a minute, watching the fire. Nora poked at the burning logs and threw pieces of bark into the flames.

"Most people in Alaska are good people," said Nora. "The hard living does it to them—kind of makes it necessary. It's hard to survive in a place like Alaska on your own."

"Have you always lived here?" asked 4B.

"I was born in Juneau, but my parents moved us to Denver when I started high school. I lived there until four years ago. Moving back to Juneau was supposed to be temporary, but when my aunt got sick last year, I decided to stay. I'm all the family she has now."

"What about your parents?" asked 4B.

"My mom died just a year after we moved to Denver. It was a freak accident. She was backcountry snowshoeing with my dad. A snowmobiler jumped a rise and hit her. My dad had a really hard time with it. He wished it had been him instead."

"Oh, wow. That would definitely be a hard thing to deal with."

"He dealt with it by getting drunk," said Nora. She wondered why she said it. She didn't talk about that part of her life to people.

"God, I'm sorry, Nora. For your mom and your dad. For you." 4B looked like she didn't know what else to say and was one of the reasons Nora didn't talk about it. But 4B was easy to talk to. Maybe that's why she kept talking.

"Then one night, he drove off the road into the Platte River. I was in college at the time, and he and I weren't talking a lot. Actually, we weren't talking at all. He wouldn't get help for his drinking and I thought I had all the answers... anyway, Aunt Mace is the only family I have left now." Nora didn't mention she suspected her father's crash into the Platte wasn't really an accident. She'd never mentioned that specific detail to anyone.

"I wish I knew what to say."

Nora shrugged her shoulders and tossed more bark in the fire.

"It was a long time ago. I stayed in Denver for several years after that. Alaska has claimed me now, though. It seems to claim everyone who spends any time here. We take care of our own. That's what Alaskans do, especially Juneauites."

They were quiet for a little bit.

"You're a very interesting woman, Nora Kavendash. I wish I was as strong as you."

Nora laughed, embarrassed.

"Strong? I'm not so sure about that. Besides, how do you know you aren't?"

"First impressions are generally right," said 4B.

"Then you're a pretty strong woman, too," said Nora.

"What? I can't even go pee on my own!" laughed 4B. "I don't recognize my own name. How does that make me strong?"

"Exactly my point. Most people in your situation would be complaining about it. Maybe even freaking out. You're just sort of dealing with it as it unfolds. I think there's a strength in that kind of acceptance."

They listened to the campfire crackle for a few minutes.

"Does it get very cold at night?" 4B asked, pulling the blankets up under her chin.

"It's been dipping into the low 40s according to my watch."

"It feels colder than 40 right now. I thought they called Alaska the home of the midnight sun."

Nora looked at her watch. "Right now, at the end of September, day and night are about the same length. It's 53 degrees Fahrenheit right now. It's chilly, but not that cold. I wonder if the bump on your head has thrown off your thermostat."

"Maybe," said 4B, shivering.

"You are holding a chunk of ice to your hip, too," Nora remembered.

"True," acknowledged 4B, repositioning the bag.

"Oh, wait. I've got something," said Nora, leaning over to unzip the bag that 4B leaned against. She held 4B's shoulder to indicate she didn't need to move as she pulled out a hoodie. "Four hoodies for twenty bucks in Mexico City. Plus, I have this."

Nora held up a blue suit jacket, which had been lashed to the side of the pack. 4B took both of them.

"Thanks. You don't happen to have a cell phone with you, do you?" asked 4B, pulling the hoodie over her head, careful of her injury, and then slipping into the jacket. The blue jacket had gold stripes on the cuffs and wings on the lapels. Nora wondered if she guessed where it had come from.

"Yep. No service, though."

"Of course you would have checked the first day. The first minute of the first day, probably," said 4B, pulling the hood of the sweatshirt up and shoving her free hand deep into the front pocket.

"I don't think I consciously did anything the first day," said Nora, leaning back in her chair, peeling bark off of the stick she held. "I was on autopilot. Still am, sort of."

"You have innate survival skills, then. I mean, in addition to what you learned in the service."

Nora smiled and shook her head.

"I'm not so sure about that. All I can think to do now is sit and wait."

"But you searched the wreckage. You salvaged food and other stuff. You made a fire. You took care of me. Sounds like survival skills to me."

Nora just shrugged again, uncomfortable with the praise.

"How did you find your backpack? Was it near the wreckage?"

"It was a carry on and I strapped it to me when things started to happen," Nora said.

"That was smart."

"Just did it without thinking, really," shrugged Nora. "The only thing on my mind was holding onto Aunt Mace's medicine."

"Was the flight full?" 4B looked up at the metal structure above them.

"Yeah, it was full. At least a hundred people. Maybe more." A shadow fell over Nora's face as she thought about how many people who hadn't made it.

"And we're the only ones?" asked 4B.

Nora didn't answer immediately. When she did, her voice was tight.

"I've walked all over this area and I haven't seen anyone else up here. Down there... down where the wreckage is, I saw a few people who... who didn't make it."

4B was quiet and Nora wondered what she was thinking. Was it about the possibility of her family being worried about her? Nora couldn't stop thinking about Aunt Mace. The idea of so many people having lost their lives filled her with a cold sense of finality. She searched 4B's face to determine how she was doing with everything.

"You said you went down into the ravine and checked things out? How... how was it?"

Nora was quiet for a moment, staring into the fire, but seeing the blaze of the wreckage.

"Surreal. It was still on fire when I went down."

"You said you saw... were there... are there... bodies?"

A cold wave of emotion swept through Nora as memories of what she'd seen filled her mind. She didn't want to talk about it, but at the same time she didn't want to be alone with her experience.

"Yes. A few. No one... no one still in the plane could have survived the explosions." She was aware of 4B studying her face as she processed the memories. "It was awful. It's hard to think about. The hardest thing, though, is... there was a baby. That's... that's what I keep thinking about."

4B took her hand.

"Oh god, Nora."

Nora's eyes moved to 4B.

"You held her for a minute or two. The baby. She was sitting with the woman next to you."

"Were we together? Did I know her?" asked 4B. Nora saw the possibility haunting 4B's eyes. She was glad 4B didn't remember. It was probably a blessing.

"No. I don't think so. She and the baby boarded the plane after you."

4B nodded and wiped away a tear.

They lapsed into silence, both of them watching the small fire, thinking their own thoughts.

🌲🌲🌲🌲🌲

The next afternoon, thunder rumbled in the distance, and Nora launched an accusing stare up at the low clouds she could see in the narrow swath of sky visible through the thick canopy of pine trees above them. They were sitting near a group of rocks not far from the shelter. 4B was feeling a little stronger, so they had moved out from under the wing to sit in the open for a while. Nora was relieved to get out of the chair she felt like she'd been sitting in and sleeping in for days—which she had. The blue sky, which had been peppered by a few fluffy white clouds since the gray canopy had blown away after the first day, had transitioned to a solid dull gray. Nora expected the rain to arrive any minute now, and she wasn't surprised when she heard the sporadic tap begin in the foliage above them and then a fat drop hit her cheek. Hope for rescue sank a little further.

"I knew it wouldn't last," she said as she turned off her e-reader. The device was down to a quarter of battery. She didn't know what she would do when it was dead. It was one thing that kept her from obsessing about their situation.

"What wouldn't last?" asked 4B, stretching herself awake from the nap she had slipped into as soon as they had sat down next to the large rocks. The walk there had tired her.

"Dry weather."

"Oh!" exclaimed 4B as a drop hit her nose. She wiped it away and looked around. "Should we make a run for it?"

"I think we can walk. You shouldn't overdo it."

Nora let 4B lead the way, watching her protectively as they made their way back to the wing. She reached out once when she stumbled, but when 4B picked up a sturdy branch to use as a walking stick, she dropped back again, trying to honor 4B's need to do it on her own. Nora collected a few pieces of fire wood as they walked. When they passed the plastic section of cabin with the window missing, Nora decided to come back for it once 4B was settled under the wing. The large piece would make a good wind break if

55

the rain picked up. The weather seemed to sense her thoughts and the drops came more frequently.

They arrived at the camp and were about to crawl into the shelter when 4B paused to study the wing.

"I haven't really looked at how this thing is propped up. Do you think it's secure?" 4B tapped the flat metal structure with her walking stick.

Nora tossed the wood she'd collected underneath and slapped the rain-splattered metal. "It's wedged pretty securely. I don't think it'll go anywhere."

"It looks like it could just slip down the trees it's leaning against," said 4B with a doubtful look.

"Nah. The trees on the other side are propping it up. It's not going anywhere. Hold on. I'll show you."

Nora ran around to the far side of the wing and walked up the slopping metal like she had done on the first day when she'd tested it herself. With a smile she looked down at her and jumped up and down to show 4B it wasn't going to move.

"See? It's—as—stur—dy—as—a—" Nora's words came in cadence with her jumps—until her feet decided to slip out from under her on the rain-speckled metal surface. She lost sight of 4B's surprised face as she fell forward, and slid down the slick surface, landing unhurt, but in an awkward pile in the pine needles and damp earth next to the wing.

"Are you okay?" asked 4B, running around the wing to help her stand up. 4B's shoulders shook and Nora could tell she was trying to hold back laughter.

"Just a bruised ego," replied Nora, laughing at herself and brushing off the mud and pine needles stuck to her knees and backside.

"You've got something in your..." said 4B, not finishing her sentence as laughter bubbled out of her and she reached up and plucked some foliage from Nora's devastated ponytail. "I'm sorry. You should have seen your face!" 4B's words gave way to uncontrollable laughter and she wiped tears from her eyes.

"Aunt Mace says, "If someone ain't broke, bleeding, or dyin', it's fair to laugh."

"Sounds good to me," laughed 4B.

Nora forgot about her pride and laughed with her as she stood obediently while 4B circled her, brushing pine needles and dirt from her back. It felt good to laugh, even if it was at her own expense.

The rain started to pick up, and their laughter faded, but the smiles remained.

"I'm a lost cause," conceded Nora, indicating her dirty clothes. "Why don't you get under cover? I'll go find more firewood. There's no telling how long this rain will last."

"I saw some sort of plastic thing back there we can put up against the opening to block some of the wind," suggested 4B, giving voice to Nora's earlier thought. "I thought I'd go back to get it."

"You stay here. I'll get it."

"I'm fine. Let me help."

"You were unconscious for two days," reasoned Nora. "Please let me do this? It won't take long. If it's too heavy, I'll come back for you." A stubborn look molded itself to 4B's features and Nora could tell she was about to object again, even though she looked wiped out from the brief walk back to the shelter. "I'm already dirty and there's no reason for us both to get all wet. Why don't you get the fire started again?"

The task seemed to do the trick. 4B grudgingly crawled under the wing and let Nora retrieve the panel. But when Nora returned, dragging the piece of plastic on which she had also stacked a large pile of wood, she found 4B had been busy. Not only had she rekindled the fire they had extinguished before going on their excursion, she had widened the indention Nora had created for 4B's bed and redistributed the pine needles so it was now wide enough for two. She had also stood the fabric-covered panel Nora had used as 4B's stretcher against the open side, making a partial wall. Between that and the plastic piece she had retrieved, they could block several feet of opening from what had become a constant wind.

4B caught her assessing her handy work.

"It's colder now the rain has started. We're going to have to share the blankets tonight. There isn't enough room for both of us on your throne," teased 4B, gesturing toward Nora's airplane seat when she saw Nora's skeptical look. "I was cold last night. You must have been freezing."

Nora had to admit she'd been cold the night before, but what had really kept her up was worry. It had been 4 days, now. The supply of crackers and peanuts wouldn't last forever. During the days, the worry was manageable, but at night it messed with her mind.

"I was a little cold," mumbled Nora, kneeling beside the fire and stacking the load of wood she'd just gathered in the lowest angle of the shelter. She tried to keep her worry from showing. 4B looked pale, which added to her burden. It was probably just from the exertion of tidying the tiny camp, but she knew telling her to relax would be fruitless. So, she let her help stack the wood and made several more trips for more, which was plentiful in the old forest. Despite her hope that rescue was on its way, she only stopped when she thought she had several days' worth of fuel. By then her clothes were filthy and soaking wet from the rain that had steadily increased since she'd started her chore.

"I think this'll do it," she said, as she ducked under the wing. Drops of water fell from the bill of her ball cap and slid down her face. She wiped her cheek on her sleeve with an exhausted arm, realizing the sleeve was just as wet as her face. Tired and sodden as she was, the activity had been a welcome distraction from the relentless waiting of the last few days.

4B had her back to Nora, tending to the blaze she was managing, but she looked over her shoulder and smiled. Nora smiled back and was taken by how beautiful 4B looked in the firelight flickering against the waning light of the rainy afternoon. Nora cleared her throat and looked around, impressed with the neat campsite. Whoever 4B was, she was a resilient and capable woman.

"You must be a Girl Scout in your secret real life," joked Nora as she piled the last batch of wood beside the rest. She then tilted the long piece of plastic up and wedged it between the ground and a bent wing flap to keep it secure next to the heavier panel 4B had already leaned up. Immediately, the wind was diminished. The mismatched wall made the makeshift shelter feel almost cozy, blocked on three sides with the fire casting dancing light into the shadows.

4B finished arranging the fire and moved to kneel next to Nora to admire the ragtag wall. Nora barely stopped herself from reaching over to rub away a smudge of black ash on 4B's cheek. Even covered in dirt and soot, 4B was pretty. Nora was aware she was staring, so she scooted away, over to her chair, next to the fire.

"I was just about to move that," said 4B, as Nora dropped onto the seat.

"This? Move it where?" she asked, holding onto the single armrest. Her attachment to the chair flared and she hoped 4B attributed the squeak in her voice to the cold. The temperature really was dropping fast and her clothes were soaking wet, but all she cared about in that moment was the possibility

4B might want to throw her chair out into the rain. She immediately felt foolish.

4B studied her for a couple of seconds. Nora had the impression 4B was looking right into her, seeing her foolish concern and maybe some of her unspoken fears and thoughts. She squirmed. And then 4B smiled that smile.

"I'd like to move it for just a minute so I can do something."

"Sure. No problem," said Nora. Relieved but curious, she got up and helped 4B move the seat to the side so the newly erected wall was more accessible. Then 4B motioned for her to sit on a log next to the fire to get warm, which Nora gladly obliged. Shivering, she watched 4B unwind a swath of large plastic garbage bags from a roll they had found in the beverage cart. She unfolded the strand of attached bags to make a wide sheet of plastic, and then she wrapped it around the two pieces to seal out even more of the wind. She then tucked the top edges into and around the bent flaps to close the gaps at the top edge and in between the two pieces to block the rest of the wind. She leaned back on her heels again and studied the barrier. The area beneath the wing quickly became warmer.

"You're a genius. You totally just earned your fort building badge," said Nora, shrugging out of her wet flannel shirt. The t-shirt she wore beneath it was just as wet.

"Now we can move your chair back."

"I'm sort of attached to it," admitted Nora, draping her wet flannel over the back of the chair before she dragged it back to its original place near the fire and wiped bits of bark from the seat. She shivered in her remaining wet clothes. "Maybe a little too attached."

"I won't let anything happen to it," said 4B with another one of those smiles. Nora didn't get the impression 4B was mocking her and something in her stirred. She didn't know what to make of it, so she leaned toward the fire and rubbed her hands together.

"How much does it suck that I have to go pee now?" asked Nora a moment later, peering outside of the enclosure. The rain had really picked up and was pouring down in sheets.

"I'm glad I took care of that when it was just drizzling," said 4B moving over to where she'd piled most of their things in her tidying activity. "And I just used all of the plastic bags. I should have saved one for a poncho. Wait. There's the bag those pillows are in."

Nora laughed and shook her head as she watched 4B dump the dozen or so little pillows out of the plastic bag they came in. "I think I'm right about you and the Girl Scout hypothesis. But, no need, I'm still soaked, so a little more rain's not a big deal."

"Good luck out there," said 4B, shrugging at her and kneeling among the little white pillows.

Nora sighed and pulled the damp flannel shirt back on and ducked out into the rain. She quickly did her business and ran back to the shelter. Just feet away from the wing, she tripped on a root and found herself splayed out, face down on the soaking ground. She let out a mirthful laugh at her own clumsiness, grateful 4B hadn't witnessed her wiping out a second time. She pushed herself up and brushed at the dirt. Most of the pine needles fell away, but muddy smears replaced the dirt. Some had even made its way down the front of her pants. She tried to shake it out down her pant legs but it was no use.

She couldn't get much wetter or dirtier, so she decided to get their food while she was already out. She took a detour to the tree in which she'd hung their food bags, retrieved both backpacks, and ran back to the shelter. When she ducked back in, she found 4B arranging the airline pillows on the bed they'd dug out. It almost looked cozy.

4B didn't seem to sit still for any amount of time. Nora wondered if she was always like that, or if she was making up for all of the hours she'd been unconscious. At least she seemed to feel better, which indicated she was recovering from the head wound. Nora hadn't realized how much 4B's health had affected her until the worry began to ease.

Cold rain dripped down the center of Nora's back, reminding her she was sopping wet. She stayed near the edge of the shelter to avoid getting everything wet.

"It's really coming down out there."

"Yeah. I was beginning to worry you'd been swept away," said 4B, pausing in her bed making activities to look at Nora. "You're soaked through! What took so long?"

"I brought back our food," said Nora, slipping out of the straps of the backpack she wore and dropped both bags onto the ground in front of her. They were getting lighter and she thought about consolidating their supplies into one bag. She wiped the rain from her face. "We can't leave the food in here overnight, but I thought I'd save at least one trip in the rain."

"You're smart and good-looking. It doesn't seem fair," 4B quipped as she continued to smooth out the pillows. Nora blushed, and she was grateful for the dim lighting.

"I don't know about that. I think my growling stomach pretty much made the decision for me."

"What scrumptious morsels do our bountiful bear bags have in store for us this evening?" asked 4B, rubbing her belly. Her good-natured response almost made Nora forget her embarrassment and how much she was starting to loathe peanuts.

"Much to my disappointment, no steak dinners mysteriously appeared in the bags, I'm afraid," Nora shrugged.

"Dang," replied 4B. "How about some shrimp scampi or chicken cordon blu? Got any of that?"

"Unfortunately, we're all out," said Nora, genuinely sad to disappoint 4B. She pushed the bag with her foot. "We do have super scrumptious peanuts, though. The best you'll find for miles around."

"You sold me. It'll be peanuts for me, then." 4B rested her butt on her heels and reached forward to run her fingers over a place on the front of one of the backpacks. "Carly," she said, reading aloud, fingers tracing the embroidered name written across the front pocket.

Nora could see 4B imagining the owner of the bag and before she could brace herself for it, she was back at the bottom of the ravine, remembering when she had first found it.

The brightly patterned backpack had been the first item she had come across following the shock of seeing the first two bodies near the wreckage. It had rested against a rock several feet from the smoldering airplane, looking inconspicuous, like its owner had casually dropped it there during a break between classes to kick around a soccer ball or chat with friends. After seeing the bodies, she'd abandoned any hope of finding survivors, and in her desperation, she'd grabbed the bag and dumped it out before she could feel uneasy about rifling through someone else's belongings. But as the items tumbled out, she couldn't help it, visions of the faces that had filed by her seat before takeoff streamed through her mind. It occurred to her that she had barely acknowledged most of them. That's how it is in airports, where too many people in too close of quarters wander among one another without really seeing each other, lives transecting for less than a couple hours, before everyone was supposed to have moved on with their individual and anonymous lives. But even though she hadn't really seen them, there they were, just inside her head, as real as the bag now resting at her feet.

She remembered the textbooks and laptop, which had fallen to the ground when she'd emptied it. She'd tried not to imagine who the owner was based on the items that scattered onto the rocky dirt. Still, what had tumbled out told a tale. She'd bent to grab a bag of Skittles peeking out from beneath a notebook, but she caught her breath when she saw the cover. The spiral notebook was covered in adolescent writing, featuring a big heart with the words Carly + Nick in the middle of the cover. Too late not to wonder then. A past and future full of what ifs filled her head.

For several minutes, Nora had been held hostage by the grief, and if she was honest with herself, the guilt for being one of the only survivors of an airplane full of real people, with real lives, real hopes, and real loves. Unable to keep the pain at bay, she knelt, staring at the notebook, her back to the first two bodies, and she had cried until her throat grew raw. All of the feelings, experiences, and images she had tried to ignore until then had washed through her.

Now, stooped beneath the wing with the rain pounding down around them, she remembered how she had risen and picked up the items from the bag and piled them reverently next to a large rock. She had done the same with every personal item she had found during her search, adding them to the pile. Every time she had to go through another bag, a pang of guilt had struck her and she had to remind herself it was a matter of survival. If the roles had been reversed, if she had perished in the wreck instead of them, she would have hoped someone would have found use for the items in her bag. She had no choice. She had to keep telling herself that. Every search she made through someone else's bag, she had treated as a sacred duty, honoring the owner of the objects she collected. One of the lighters they used to light their fire had come from a purse with a wallet containing the smiling photos of five children and a keychain that boasted #1 Grandmother. A bottle they used to drink water from had been found in the purse of a young woman who liked anime and Hello Kitty. The second backpack they used for food had held gummy bears and Sudoku books. She had searched them all. Candy bars and snacks nourished them but also defined the lives of the people who would never see them again.

Triggered by the name on the backpack and the memory of a heart drawn in blue ink on a red cover, the slideshow of that day flashed through Nora's mind and her chest ached with memory. She imagined the inked heart running now in the rain.

"Are you okay?" asked 4B, and Nora struggled to repackage and store the memories away. She wondered how much of it was reflected on her face, grateful her tears blended with the rain dripping from her hair.

"Just thinking about where to store the bag," Nora lied, not wanting to explain. "Like I said, we can't keep it in here with us. I think I'll lower it down the edge of the ravine. It would keep away the predators and it should be okay even in the rain."

4B studied her face. "Good thinking," she said after a minute.

Nora couldn't look her in the eye, so she busied herself with taking food from the bag for their dinner, placing it on the seat of her chair, and then she ran out into the rain to hang the bag over the edge of the ravine.

She couldn't see the wreckage in the dark, which was a relief, but she could feel it looming. It bothered her that it was raining and no one was down there to—to do what? She didn't know, but not to just leave the dead and their possessions out there in the rain like that, vulnerable and uncherished. Thankfully, with the rain coming down hard, and the wind blowing into her face, it was all she could do to focus on not losing her balance and tumbling off the edge. By the time she returned to the shelter, her thoughts were all about getting dry and warm again.

The little area beneath the wing was warm with the roaring fire 4B had built. The light it emitted was welcome in the premature darkness that came with the storm. The heat felt good on her soaked skin, and she rubbed the rain from her face. She was exhausted. She looked around.

"You did a great job in here. Where did you learn to dig a trench to keep the water out?"

Lines appeared across 4B's forehead and she looked like she was trying to remember, but she finally shook her head. "I don't know."

"Maybe you're a forest ranger in your real life."

"That would be interesting," said 4B with a small laugh. The lines furrowing her brow cleared.

Nora rubbed her hands on her wet jeans and shivered. She moved closer to the fire. "Should we eat?"

"You look like you're freezing. Maybe you should get out of those wet clothes first."

"True. I'm soaked to the skin."

4B, who had been leaning against Nora's pack, sat up and pushed it toward Nora. Then she used a stick to reposition some of the burning logs and tossed another one on top. The fire was a blaze and Nora couldn't wait to get into some dry clothes and sit next to it.

Nora pulled fresh jeans and a t-shirt from the bag, placed them on the ground next to her, and took off her ball cap. Then she peeled off the wet flannel. Conscious of the small space and not having many options, she hung the wet garment over some of the firewood. She took off the t-shirt she wore under it and did the same thing. When she turned back, she thought she caught 4B looking quickly away. Nora didn't usually have a problem getting undressed in front of people, but it was a little unnerving to think 4B was watching her. Goosebumps rose on her skin and she didn't think it was all from the cold.

She pushed the food back on the chair and sat on the edge of the seat, kicking off her hiking boots, wishing she had done it before taking off her shirt, especially since she didn't wear a bra. She could see 4B taking furtive peeks out of the corner of her eye as she poked at the fire, which confirmed her suspicion 4B had been watching. Self-consciously, she peeled her wet jeans and panties down and reached for the fresh clothes. She brushed the dirt and leaves from her foot and realized she didn't relish putting clothes on over the dirt.

A massive boom of thunder shook the forest and the rain started to pour down with a renewed fury. She hugged her t-shirt to her chest and had an idea.

"I'm filthy. I'm going to take advantage of the rain and wash up. I'm already soaked," she said pulling her travel toiletry bag from a side pocket of her backpack. She took the small bottles of shampoo, conditioner, and body wash from it, leaving the toothbrushes and toothpaste. 4B had been grateful to hear she had an extra toothbrush, courtesy of the airline when the airport in Mexico had been locked down.

"You're going out in that?" 4B pointed into the darkness. "Naked?" 4B looked her up and down as the heavy downpour somehow increased in intensity.

"Sure. It'll be an adventure," said Nora with a grin. She was starting to believe it herself. And the appraisal 4B had just given her made heat radiate through her.

"Are you crazy? It's freezing out there. And dark. Aren't you afraid of the lightning?"

Just as the words were spoken, a flash of light illuminated the landscape just outside of their shelter.

Nora didn't even think about it. She'd already talked herself into it. It had been several days since she had bathed and the thought of clean hair was compelling enough for her to brave the cold, the dark, and even the possibility of lightning. This was nothing. She'd already survived a plane crash.

"I'm not sure what's safer—standing out there or being under this metal wing when lightning strikes," she said, and immediately wished she hadn't when she saw the look of fear pass over 4B's face.

"You're right. We've quite literally survived worse. I'm going with you," said 4B, pulling on a blood matted lank of hair, her fear seemingly forgotten.

When 4B started to strip off her clothes, Nora decided the situation was not appropriate for the thoughts that rushed through her mind. And when an expanse of skin appeared under the hem of the hoodie 4B pulled over her head, Nora found it was her turn to look away guiltily. She chose not to wait for 4B. She dropped her clean clothes into the chair and headed out into the rain.

Nora was grateful it was almost too dark to see anything when 4B appeared and began to wash beside her. Even so, she still got a couple of good looks at 4B's amazing body when lightning flashed and light filled the area in brilliant blasts. She didn't know if it was the cold or the fear of being struck by lightning that made 4B hurry, but she knew, at least for her, it was the way her body responded to the images of 4B's high round breasts and the sway of her hips, images that were now fixed indelibly upon the landscape of her mind. Nora felt a little guilty for her thoughts, what with 4B's injuries and their precarious situation, but there was something about 4B that made her pulse race.

They made quick work of it, using a stream of rain runoff from the wing to rinse out the shampoo. Nora was done first and she ducked under the wing to pull on the clean t-shirt and her last pair of semi-clean jeans, struggling to pull them up over her damp legs and fastening them with cold fingers when 4B appeared.

"Cold-cold-cold," chanted 4B as she came in from the rain, stepping carefully to avoid getting her feet dirty again. She started to pick up her dirty clothes, and Nora reached into her bag.

"Wait. Wear these," said Nora handing 4B a pair of clean pajama bottoms that she hadn't had a chance to wear during her delay-plagued travels, along with a relatively fresh t-shirt and a fresh hoodie. They'd all be a little big on 4B, but at least they were clean. 4B's hands were pale and shook so much when she accepted the clothes that Nora grew worried and put her discomfort aside. She rose to her knees, guided 4B closer to the fire, and then used the inside of one of their discarded hoodies to dry off 4B's back, before she helped her pull the t-shirt over her head. 4B's freshly washed golden hair, darkened by the water, was matted to her head, and her lips were blue.

"That's b-b-better," said 4B looking at Nora with appreciation. "Thanks."

"You won't thank me when you die from pneumonia," said Nora, pulling 4B's long hair from under her collar and patting some of the dripping rain from it, as 4B pulled the flannel pajama bottoms on. "Maybe the impromptu shower wasn't such a great idea for you."

"Believe me, it was worth it. If I die from pneumonia, at least the bears won't reject me as a meal because of my stench," joked 4B pulling on the clean hoodie and accepting a pair of tube socks Nora pulled out of the bag and handed to her.

"And you said I have a unique way of saying things. I don't want to even think about that," laughed Nora, sitting back on her heels and laughing as 4B tried to pull on the socks with shaking hands.

Finally, after they'd both used Nora's travel hairbrush, Nora stowed their dirty laundry and bath things, while 4B settled down on the log she had rolled closer to the fire earlier that day.

Nora joined her after draping a blanket over 4B's shoulders.

"Scoot closer. You're cold, too," said 4B, opening the blanket and pulling it around both of them as Nora obediently sat down next to her, leaving a couple of inches between them. 4B moved to close the distance. "Get closer. Body heat is the best defense against hypothermia."

"I can get another blanket," suggested Nora.

"Don't you dare move," ordered 4B. Her teeth chattered. "I'm already warmer. It'll be fine in a few minutes."

The rain continued to pour down and Nora noted the trenches that 4B had dug around the outside of the shelter were successfully diverting the water away. And as 4B had predicted, within a few minutes she was much warmer.

"I think I can feel my toes again," said 4B, trying to stifle a big yawn. She leaned her head against Nora's shoulder. Nora leaned away and smiled at 4B's questioning look as she freed her arm and then wrapped it around 4B's shoulders, pulling her closer. She was surprised at how well they fit together, how easy it seemed. Within minutes, 4B's breathing was steady and deep and Nora was jealous of 4B's ability to sleep. She hadn't slept more than ten minutes at a time since the crash.

The sound of the rain and the flickering firelight captured Nora's attention as she tried not to think too hard about how good it felt to be so close to 4B. But when her mind wandered to the quick shower they had shared, she didn't immediately push the images of 4B's body away. Instead she lingered on them, and used the distraction to help from focusing on her butt having fallen asleep and the increasing hunger pangs in her stomach.

"I'm starving," said 4B sometime later, making Nora jump. She hadn't felt 4B wake and she hoped she hadn't somehow exposed her thoughts.

"Me too, but you fell asleep and I didn't want to wake you." Nora rocked to get some circulation into her ass as 4B sat up and stretched. Nora immediately missed the warm press of 4B against her.

"I couldn't help it, once the fire warmed me up, I was out. It doesn't hurt you're a perfect pillow," said 4B. "But even so, my stomach wouldn't let me stay asleep. What have the chefs whipped up for us tonight?"

"Hmm… let's see what the specials are this evening," said Nora, reluctantly leaving the warm spot next to 4B, and dropping to her knees next to the food she had taken out of the pack earlier. "Looks like we have jerky and apples, with a side of peanuts," offered Nora, in her best snooty waiter's voice. "Or we have peanuts and jerky, with a side of apples. Gourmet crackers are the featured dessert with both entrees."

Neither option appealed to Nora. She was tired of jerky and peanuts, especially since she'd never been fond of peanuts in the first place. And jerky was kind of disgusting when she thought about it, which she tried not to. They'd been saving the last apple, though, and she was really looking forward to that. Then she remembered the wine, and reached over to the beverage cart, pulled out one of the tiny bottles, and waved it toward 4B. "And as a perfect pairing, we have a delightful Napa red."

"I forgot we had wine. Wine is good, and the jerky sounds delightful," answered 4B, "but on the side. I insist the jerky be on the side." Nora laughed and was grateful she had been stranded in the middle of nowhere with someone with a good disposition. The experience could have been so much different if one of them had been difficult or they hadn't gotten along.

As she moved back to the log with the food and wine, she thought about the way 4B had been watching her undress. Then she felt guilty. It had been so long since she had even cared about whether a woman found her attractive. And she wondered why now, in the middle of unimaginable circumstances, it would suddenly matter here. It didn't seem right. Somehow it felt like it minimized their situation. She should be thinking about their survival.

She sat down on the log, leaving a space between them, and handed 4B her portion of the food. She unscrewed the top of her bottle and tapped it against the bottle 4B held out to her before she took a long swallow of the wine. It wasn't great, but it wasn't bad. She liked the warmth it spread in her belly.

"Nice," remarked 4B, sipping hers. "Was that a deck of cards I saw in your pack when you were pulling out the clothes? Care to play after dinner?"

"Carrying a pack of cards around is a habit I picked up from my aunt. She's a nutter about rummy and likes to play while waiting at doctor appointments."

"Well, I wish you had broken them out days ago. It would have helped pass the time a little faster. Do you think you can put your deep thoughts aside for a little while, and teach me a game?"

"Deep thoughts?" dismissed Nora. "I'm not sure you can say daydreaming about a steak dinner would be considered deep thoughts. But I'll be happy to play cards with you."

"Definitely deep thoughts. I'd wager they're not about steak, either. I see you falling into your head sometimes. Some people wear their heart on their sleeve. You, dear Nora, wear yours in your eyes."

"Is that so?" asked Nora, wondering if 4B had any idea she had just been thinking about her naked. Then she wondered if 4B had guessed about her previous obsession, which was their narrowing chance of being rescued. Now that she thought about it, thinking about 4B naked was the least of the two sins. She took another drink of her wine.

"See? There you go again. I don't want to be nosey, but if you want to talk, let me know."

"It sounds like I need to work on my poker face," joked Nora, hoping to steer the conversation away from her thoughts. "Maybe I should teach you how to play a little Texas Hold 'em."

4B glanced at Nora, took another drink and popped a peanut into her mouth, but Nora could tell 4B wasn't going to be dissuaded with a bit of light banter.

"Just let me know if you want to talk. My schedule is open," said 4B.

"I will. I promise," said Nora, pulling the cards from the front pocket of her pack and getting them each another bottle of wine. "Maybe you're a psychotherapist in your real life."

"That's a thought," said 4B, but it didn't look like she believed it. "In the meantime, I think that kicking your butt at a little poker might keep your mind off of things."

"You're going to kick my butt, huh?" asked Nora, shuffling the cards.

"Poker it is, and we'll see who kicks whose butt."

🌲🌲🌲🌲🌲

The sound of steady rain broke through the mists of Nora's sleep. Her face was cold, so she pulled the blankets up a little higher, over her chin. The rest of her was warm and she pressed into the source of the heat and softness against her side. She started to drift back into sleep, but something moved and pulled her back. She shifted and woke, realizing she wasn't alone. Then she remembered. 4B was there. They'd played cards and finished off the wine the night before. Six bottles each, and they'd laughed a lot. Without discussing it, they'd made a single bed and had both crawled under the thin blankets when their yawns became too much to ignore.

4B was snuggled up against Nora's side, in the arc of Nora's arm, with her head resting on Nora's shoulder. Even though they'd both been a little drunk when they'd gone to bed, they'd started the night lying close but not touching. During the night, though, one or both of them had drifted closer. Nora lay still and glanced at the pale gray morning outside of the shelter. She'd slept through the night. It had been the most sleep she'd had since they'd been dropped out of the sky.

Nora knew she should get up to rekindle the fire, but she was so warm and the air outside was so cold. She justified staying where she was by not wanting to wake 4B. So she lay there, enjoying the possessive arm wrapped around her middle.

"I don't want to move," murmured 4B, just as Nora was about to drift back off.

"I thought you were still asleep," said Nora, hoping 4B wouldn't leave.

"I was until just now. I don't want to get up."

"Don't then. It's cold out there."

But 4B pushed herself up and looked out into the sodden light of the rainy morning. Nora missed her warmth as soon as she moved away.

"God, you're not kidding." 4B shivered, but slid out from under the covers and crawled toward the fire. She tossed a few sticks of wood on the embers and crouched over the flames that started to grow.

"That was the best night's sleep I've had in a long time," said Nora, stretching under the covers but not getting up.

"Stay there until it warms up out here," said 4B shrugging into the pilot's jacket and pulling the hood of the sweatshirt under it over her head. Her breath formed a cloud near her lips. Nora checked her watch. It was just past dawn and the temperature read just a few ticks above freezing.

Nora watched 4B, with her mussed up hair and sleepy face. 4B hugged her knees to her chest and hunched close to the fire. Another fine poof of white came from her mouth when she yawned and rubbed her face. "My head is a little fuzzy. I'm not sure if I should blame it on the bump on my head or the alcohol you plied me with last night," said 4B, with a wide yawn.

"I seem to remember it was you who insisted on finishing off our stash of wine. Not that I was complaining. But don't go spreading rumors about it being me getting you drunk when you know who did the plying."

"All right, all right. I accept the blame. Man, it's cold, though."

"Take your own advice and come back here and get under the covers until it warms up, then."

4B looked over at Nora with a contemplative look and then shook her head. Nora wondered if she had done something to make 4B uncomfortable. Or maybe 4B was embarrassed about their cozy sleeping position once she'd had a minute to think about it. Whatever it was, it felt like a huge wall had just gone up.

"Tempting," 4B finally said. "But I'm already up, and it's pretty warm by the fire."

"Suit yourself," Nora said as she rolled onto her side and shut her eyes. She hoped her voice didn't betray the disappointment she was feeling over 4B's sudden distance.

"I kind of thought I'd wake up this morning and have my memory back,"

said 4B, biting into a piece of jerky and gazing out at the rain that continued to fall in sheets around them. Nora was relieved 4B wasn't acting as distant as she had that morning. "I feel much better and my cognitive faculties seem to be functioning fine otherwise. Drinking all that wine with a possible concussion wasn't wise, but I don't seem any worse for it."

"Cognitive faculties, huh?" teased Nora, sitting across the fire from her and pausing in her mental inventory of their remaining food to smile at 4B. "You sound like a professor."

"Maybe that's what I am."

Nora squinted at her.

"Hmm… With a pipe and a tweed jacket. I can almost see it… in thirty years or so."

4B wrinkled her nose and Nora found it very cute.

"Strike the smelly pipe, but I think I could do the tweed jacket," said 4B with a grin.

"Still nothing?" asked Nora. She couldn't tell how 4B felt about her memory loss. Or about that morning. 4B's sudden distance still stung.

"It's a very strange feeling. I remember everything about yesterday, and odd things like knowing I don't like pipe smoke. But I have no memory from before waking up here yesterday. It didn't feel as strange at first, but now that some time has passed, it's weird to think back and hit a wall of… nothing-ness. It's like having a point of reference makes it more obvious."

"I can't even begin to imagine what it's like," said Nora, wondering what would be worse—having no memory or remembering the crash. Then she went directly to worrying about their food supply. She had a hard time swallowing her bite of jerky.

"There you go again."

"What?" asked Nora.

"Falling into your head again."

Nora tried to think of a response that didn't betray her dire thoughts, but 4B seemed to know what was on her mind.

"How much longer do you think we have until our food runs out?" asked 4B.

"The peanuts and crackers could last us several days if we continue to ration them, but as far as the rest of the jerky, I think we can make it stretch to dinner tomorrow or breakfast the next day. So, our variety is almost gone."

4B fiddled with the small bag of peanuts she hadn't yet opened.

"Maybe we need to think about hunting and gathering when this rain lets up. Do you know anything about what plants are safe to eat?" asked 4B.

Nora shook her head and felt like she was letting 4B down. She was embarrassed about her lack of survival skills. Being outdoorsy was almost a prerequisite for being an Alaskan, and although she had done her stint in search and rescue, Nora didn't really know that much about living off the land. Her survival training had come with plenty of military issued freeze-dried meals.

"I know how to fish. We're both smart women, I'm sure we can figure out how to hunt if it comes down to it. I just hope it won't," said Nora, sounding more confident than she felt.

"Necessity is the mother of invention. Maybe we can make a knife or arrows out of pieces of the airplane."

"I just had a vision of us going all Lord of the Flies out here," snorted Nora.

4B laughed and they were quiet for a moment.

"You know what's strange?"

"Besides this whole thing?" asked Nora spreading out her arms indicating everything around them.

"Yes, besides all of this," agreed 4B with a smile. "What I find strange is I am not more afraid than I am."

"You aren't? I'm terrified," admitted Nora. It felt good to say it out loud.

"I'm a little afraid, but not as much as I would have thought I would be," said 4B. "For whatever reason, I just have a feeling everything will be okay."

Nora looked into the fire. She felt just the opposite. She was scared she wouldn't be able to keep 4B safe. She was terrified they would run out of food and slowly starve to death. She worried 4B's wound would become infected and she'd die right in front of her for need of simple antibiotics. She was frightened that lack of food and infected wounds were the least of their worries, and that snow would come and they would freeze to death in their sleep. Or bears. She didn't want to think about bears.

"I hope you're right," she said, eating the last of her peanuts and reaching out to grab one of the plastic cups they had placed on a rock to catch the rain. "At least we have all the water we need."

♠♠♠♠♠

"Shit," said Nora, laying down her last card, dismayed that 4B had forced the queen of spades on her once again. They'd given up poker to play a two-handed version of hearts, and 4B's extraordinary beginner's luck had followed to this game, too. "I'd get upset at losing all the time, but Aunt Mace has numbed me to that delight already."

"Maybe I'm a professional card shark in real life," laughed 4B.

"Is it shark or sharp?" asked Nora.

"I have no idea, actually," said 4B handing over the cards she'd collected during the hand.

"Either way, you should seriously consider becoming a professional card player," said Nora, gathering the cards and shuffling them for a new hand. "We should take the first flight to Vegas when we get out of here." Realizing she had just suggested they get on another airplane, she stopped mid-shuffle and looked up. 4B looked up at the same time.

"Nah!" they said in unison and laughed.

Nora started to deal the cards and contemplated again how much more unpleasant the situation would have been had she been stranded with someone she didn't get along with—or even if her survival companion had been the woman sitting next to her in the plane before it crashed instead of 4B. An immediate wave of guilt washed over her for her thoughts. She started to beat herself up and had to remind herself that her thoughts hadn't caused any part of the ordeal they were faced with. The constant feeling of guilt kept rising in her, making her crazy. This wasn't her. She'd always been confident and easy going. The last couple of years had admittedly shaken her a bit, but all of that was behind her now, and she'd never wasted her time on guilt. Maybe the crash had changed her. She wondered if 4B had similar thoughts and feelings.

"You know, if I had to be stranded, I'm glad it was with you," said Nora, trying to put her feelings into words, putting positive thoughts out there instead of the self-deprecating ones that tried to steal her confidence. But hearing it out loud made her cringe. Seriously. Who says that sort of thing? And especially after the awkward morning they had. When 4B didn't respond immediately, she wished she had kept it to herself. "Yeah. Sorry. It sounded weirder out loud than it did in my head," said Nora, staring at the cards she was dealing.

4B's smile was hard to read.

"No. I get it," responded 4B, just as Nora was about to change the subject. "I'm glad you're not wishing you were stranded with someone else."

Nora was relieved but 4B hadn't said she was glad to be stranded with her. Maybe that's why she said what she said next, to test 4B's feelings about her. She wasn't exactly acting like her normal self. It seemed that putting herself out there was on par with everything else that had happened to them so far. "I like you. We barely know each other, but you're easy to be around and I can't imagine doing this alone. You keep me from dwelling on things, which helps more than you know. Also, it doesn't hurt that you have a killer smile. Oh, and you don't snore." She added the last to ease the unexpected seriousness she was heading toward.

4B laughed. "It's the same for me... except the snoring thing."

"What? I snore?" asked Nora, pausing in her dealing of the cards. She was a little embarrassed about her little monologue, but 4B didn't seem put off by it. She was glad they were talking about things. But, she didn't snore. Did she? "Really?"

4B held up a hand with her forefinger and thumb measuring out a quarter inch.

"Just a little. It's cute."

Nora shook her head and blushed. "No one has ever told me. Of course, it's been a while since I've had an overnight guest."

She finished dealing and they picked up their cards.

"I find it hard to believe," said 4B organizing the cards in her hand.

"Find what hard to believe?" asked Nora, leading with the two of clubs.

"That it's been a while," replied 4B, tossing out a card. "You know? The overnight guest thing."

"Oh," said Nora, picking out her lowest diamond to throw down on 4B's ten. She already knew 4B was going to rout her—again. "Yeah, I've sworn off women for a while."

They tossed out a few more rounds, and then Nora realized she had just come out to 4B. She'd been so focused on the stuff she'd said before that she hadn't even realized what she'd just said. Worry about giving 4B more reason to feel even weirder about the morning seized her. Nora peeked over her cards at 4B, who was staring at her cards and her brow was knit in concentration like it always was when she was trying to win the game. Or maybe absorbing the fact she was trapped alone in remote woods with a lesbian.

Nora couldn't tell how she felt. She was trying to decide whether she should ask, when 4B beat her to it.

"The woman who broke your heart didn't deserve to have it," said 4B.

"Wait. Did you really just throw that card? You know all of the diamonds are out there already, right? I have to give you the queen now."

"What?" asked Nora. She was having a hard time processing what 4B said. It was as if she had started to throw herself into an abyss, but just realized she didn't need to, and now she had to stop the forward momentum.

4B pointed at the cards lying on the rock between them.

"You threw the last diamond and you know I have the queen of spades."

Nora studied her cards. She had no idea what cards had been played while all the tumultuous thoughts had catapulted through her mind. She made a show of going back over the last few tricks as she reset her inner turmoil. She'd gotten distracted by her own thoughts and she'd made a stupid play. She did it all the time and that's why Aunt Mace always cleaned house on her at cards. It didn't bother her that 4B was doing the same, though. More importantly, 4B didn't seem bothered by Nora's comment, which was a good thing.

"I did, didn't I?"

"It's my fault. I distracted you. I shouldn't have said anything about the snoring. You really don't. It's more like heavy breathing, with an occasional teeny-tiny snort. Hardly noticeable. It's cute. I swear."

"That's it. You distracted me. Otherwise I'd be winning. So, stop it," admonished Nora with a mock glare and they both laughed. Nora relaxed. It felt like they had just settled a few things between them without a whole lot of effort. She had even more appreciation for having 4B in this with her rather than anyone else.

They finished out the hand and Nora took almost all of the hearts, losing soundly.

"Can I ask you something?" asked 4B, after she'd dealt the next hand.

"Sure," said Nora, leading again with the two of clubs.

"When we're like this, do you feel…? Oh, I don't know. Like it's wrong or something?"

"Wrong?" asked Nora. Maybe 4B did care about her being gay.

"Yeah. Like it's just not fair? Like how did we get lucky, and the others didn't? I know we're still in a pretty scary spot, and if we don't get rescued soon, we'll be in trouble. But we're still alive."

Nora looked up at 4B and wondered how she'd let herself get more concerned about 4B's reaction to her being gay than how she felt about surviving an airplane crash. Maybe she was avoiding thinking about it, even as they lived it. Psychology had always seemed like such an illogical concept to her, but now she wished it were something she knew more about. She was navigating unknown territory. Stuffing it away was her immediate reaction. But it seemed like 4B needed to talk about it.

"Yeah, the guilt has been hard. I know I should feel grateful I'm still alive, but…" she didn't know how to continue.

"I know. It's like… it's like… why am I alive and the others aren't?" offered 4B, sounding relieved to be talking about it.

Part of Nora wanted to change the subject, not knowing what to say, while the other part wanted to press forward. When she did, she found she had a lot to say. Not acting like herself was becoming a habit.

"Yeah. I feel like I'm not allowed to consider myself lucky, but then I feel guilty for not having the appropriate appreciation for not ending up in the ravine with the others. And then I remember we're still out here, not quite safe and sound, and I get scared. And something inside me tells me there's no room for fear, that I have to just push through and do what needs to be done. It's a vicious circle and I keep having these mental fights with myself about all of it."

4B lowered the hand of cards she had been arranging and studied Nora. "You just put into words an idea that has been lurking in my head all day. I didn't know how to say it. Except, I have this numb feeling inside me, too, a part that seems to be hiding from reality. Like I'm… broken, or something."

"Broken?"

"Yeah. It could be the memory loss. I'm pretty sure I have amnesia. At least I tell myself it's got to be amnesia. But I feel like there's something inside that's purposefully disjointed, preventing me from feeling the amount of scared I should be experiencing," 4B shook her head as if something in her mind was just out of grasp. "It's hard to explain. Maybe I should be grateful for it."

"I've just had a few more days to dwell on it," said Nora.

They were quiet for a few minutes, their cards forgotten.

"You're easy to be around, Nora. Easy to talk to. I'm glad it's you who found me."

"I am, too, 4B."

They sat quietly for a moment, staring into the fire.

"Why do you think we're the only ones who…" Nora looked at 4B, who continued to stare into the fire. She couldn't finish her sentence. Saying it out loud made it more real. It was one thing to talk about herself and her situation, but another to talk about the fate of the others.

"Survived?" prompted 4B, finishing her sentence.

"Yeah. I've been thinking about it a lot. Why did we get tossed out up here? Why aren't there others? How come we're not more badly injured?" The relief of talking about it battled with the pain of giving words to the thoughts she'd pushed aside.

"We'll probably never know," said 4B, confirming Nora's suspicions.

"I've been thinking about the whole physics aspect of it. The flight was full. There was a woman in the seat right next to me. Why am I here but she's not? You were up in first class and I was in coach. We weren't even on the same side of the aisle."

"Is there much wreckage up here? Besides this wing? Or is it all down in the ravine?" asked 4B.

"It's hard to say. The airplane was pretty broken up when I saw it. I couldn't really tell how much of it was down there but it seemed like some was missing. It seemed like some of the other wing was missing. I didn't recognize any of it as the tail. It makes me think some of it is up on the mountain above us. There's not much here, on this ledge. I think the plane, or a part of it, kind of bounced down here, barely touching down. The engine broke away from this wing and is close by," said Nora indicating behind them. "And some of the landing gear is past the rocks where the latrine is. I saw something that looked like a crumpled seat tray half buried. Other than that, and the stuff you see in here, plus a couple of airline magazines, which I burned, there wasn't much left up on this ledge. It all went into the ravine."

"So you think the plane hit something else before it touched down here?" asked 4B, and Nora could tell she was trying to piece things together.

"I think it did. I tried to hike back to where the plane might have first touched down by following the broken trees, but the trail ends at a rocky cliff going up the mountain. It makes sense that it might have hit somewhere above the cliff and then careened off, then hit here before it went into the ravine. The rocks up top look pretty jagged. It could have hit up there and opened up a hole in the bottom of the plane or broken a piece of it off. But I don't know. I couldn't find a way up to look, but I didn't try too hard either.

Maybe when the rain stops we can search for a way up together."

"Yeah, we should try to at least check it out. Maybe there are others. It's all so unreal," said 4B, absently reaching up to touch her head.

"How does it feel?" asked Nora. Her eyes were on the dirty bandage peeking from under 4B's hair. After four days, it could stand to be changed. A mental inventory of their first aid supplies ran through her mind.

4B's long fingers moved around the wound in ginger exploration.

"It's really tender and the area around it feels bruised." 4B put down the cards to their forgotten game and reached up with both hands to gently press the skull around her head. "I'm not dizzy anymore, my vision is clear, and I'm not overly sleepy. Best of all, my headache is finally fading."

"I was worried when you were out for so long. I wondered what I would do if you had…" Her words faded away.

"Died?" offered 4B. She said it so matter-of-factly, like it was a perfectly reasonable alternative. 4B's lack of emotion rattled Nora. Maybe that's why 4B thought she was broken inside. Nora, who seemed to be feeling for the both of them, nodded and swallowed as unexpected tears sprang to her eyes.

"I couldn't stop thinking about it, especially after—" she cleared her throat, "—after going down into the ravine. When I came back up, all I did was hold your hand to make sure you knew I was there. But, really, I think I was holding it so you wouldn't leave, too. I couldn't stop thinking about what I would do if… if…"

Nora couldn't finish her thought and wiped away the tear that slipped out against her will. She never cried. Now she couldn't seem to stop.

"How awful," said 4B, with a shiver. Nora was glad to see at least some sort of emotion from 4B on the subject. "Thank you for taking care of me."

"It was purely selfish. I wasn't alone. I didn't want it to change."

They were quiet for a few minutes, their card game forgotten. The rain poured down around them.

"Well, you did a good job of taking care of us both. You must have cleaned my wound before you dressed it. It doesn't seem infected. At least it isn't really sensitive. How did it look?"

Nora sucked air in through her teeth at the memory. "I could see the bone under the skin."

"Bone, huh?" asked 4B, grimacing. "Can you describe the wound?"

"It's kind of shaped like an inverted V and about an inch-and-a-half long. It extends into your hairline."

"Was it a clean cut? Was there a lot of blood?"

"Fairly clean. The skin flap settled down pretty smoothly after I cleaned it off. And judging by the amount of blood on your face, there was a lot at first, but it was just a trickle when I found you. It picked up again after I moved you here, and again when I poured water over it to clean it out, but it stopped when I put the bandage on it."

"It probably needed stitches. Do you think you got all of the dirt out of it?"

"I think so. There wasn't much on the wound itself. Most was just stuck to the area around it. There's probably going to be a good scar. You're right, I think it really needs stitches."

"It's a little late to stitch it up now. But it's under my bangs, so I guess that's a good thing," smiled 4B, pulling her blond bangs over the bandage. "Are there any more bandages? This one feels a little stiff."

"We have a couple. Are you sure we should mess with it?"

"I think we should take a look at it. How do you feel about playing doctor again?"

"Sure," said Nora, retrieving the first aid pack she'd found down near the wreck.

Nora washed her hands in rainwater, squirted some anti-bacterial gel on them, and rubbed them together in an effort to disinfect them as best she could before she gently peeled the bandage up. The most difficult part was not pulling the few hairs stuck in the adhesive, but she was happy to see the bandage hadn't stuck to the wound.

"How does it look?" asked 4B.

"It looks better. It's hard to tell under the dried blood, but it looks like it's healing. We probably should have done this when we took our rain bath."

"Does it look infected?"

"I don't think so. Just that it's been under a damp bandage for a while."

"There might be discharge, something other than just blood. Does redness radiate from the wound? Describe the swelling."

"There's none of that. There's a knot under the gash, which has a bruise around it, but no redness except around the actual cut."

"Does the knot look like it's filled with fluid? You can press it to check, if you want."

"I don't have to touch it. It doesn't look like there's fluid under it."

"Is there any evidence of fresh bleeding?"

"Not really," said Nora peering closely at the wound.

"When you found me, was there any blood or fluid coming out of my ears or nose?"

"Not that I remember. Not from your nose, for sure. I didn't check your ears."

"I wish I had a mirror."

"Me too. Maybe you missed your own calling as a doctor. You sure sound like one with all of your questions."

"Maybe," smiled 4B. "What I do know is it sounds like there isn't any infection and I probably don't have a severe brain injury. I'll settle for that right now."

Nora wiped away the old ointment, applied some more, and then affixed a large bandage over it.

"All set," declared Nora, as she tossed the trash into the fire and sat down, settling her back against the log. The heat near the blaze felt good. She picked up her cards and started to arrange them again.

"Ready for more abuse?" asked 4B, as she picked up her own hand.

"I see you've mastered the fine art of trash-talk, Doctor Card Shark," replied Nora, selecting a card to toss. "My training is a success."

♣♣♣♣♣

Nora woke in the middle of the night. Something had pulled her from sleep. She listened, but all she heard were the normal sounds of the forest. Under the shelter, the fire had burned down to crackling embers and the gentle breathing of the woman beside her eased the fear that had awakened her. The plastic barrier 4B had put up rustled gently in the wind and she wondered if a gust had snapped it to stir her. Then she realized the rain had stopped. Perhaps the comparative silence had roused her. She settled back into the warmth of their bed and would have drifted back to sleep if not for her awareness of the arm wrapped around her middle and the leg thrown over hers. Like the night before, she and 4B had gone to sleep lying apart, but somehow during the night they had drifted together. The contact was familiar this time, but it elicited a new awareness that kept her awake.

4B shifted in her sleep, pressing more firmly against Nora's side, and Nora pressed back, careful not to wake her. She felt almost claimed by the possessive hold 4B had on her, and she liked it. She wasn't sure she should, but she tried not to overanalyze it and closed her eyes.

She was almost asleep when something brought her back to full awareness. It was the same thing that had woken her before, and she lay quietly waiting for it to happen again.

There it was.

A scraping sound against the metal of the wing. Just two feet away from her head. She tried to think what it could be. It wasn't the familiar sound of the pine branches swaying against the shelter. It was too close to the ground. Nora stared into the darkness at the angle of the wing against the soil. It sounded like something was digging. It got louder. There was the sound of dirt being pushed away, then a snuffling grunt.

"Bear!" she shouted and sat up, grabbing the longest, thickest branch from their dwindling firewood pile. She hit it against the wing as close to the sound as she dared to get. She yelled unintelligible words. She beat the stick against the metal so hard, it broke and she grabbed the longest half and began to beat it again.

"Wh-what is it?" 4B sat up behind her, alarmed, still dazed from sleep.

"Bear!" screamed Nora, continuing to bash the stick against the metal, swiveling her head to watch the open sides to see if the bear came around.

"Git! Shoo! Go away!" shouted 4B, adding her own stick to the banging.

Nora kicked, beat, and yelled until her legs grew tired and her arms grew weak. 4B did the same. She had no idea how long they railed against the intruder as they kept their eyes peered for any sign of it coming around to the open sides. When nothing more happened, Nora stopped, motioning for 4B to do the same. They listened for any sign indicating the bear was still around.

Their heavy breathing and the wind whipping up from the ravine were the only sounds in the damp night air.

"Do you think it's gone?" whispered 4B, dropping to the ground and pulling the blanket up to her neck, looking around furtively. "Was it really a bear?"

"I'm pretty sure it was. It sounded big," replied Nora. Her voice sounded hoarse from the screaming. She crouched next to the fire, casting glances at all the open sides, and threw more wood on the embers in the fire ring. The fire roared to life, and she listened for further signs the animal was still lurking about. After a few minutes, she retrieved the travel flashlight from her backpack and, summoning the courage to poke her head out from beneath the shelter, she shone its pale beam into the dark. She felt extremely vulnerable standing in the ring of light cast by the fire, but she didn't want 4B to know how scared she was. The flashlight barely made a dent in the darkness, but she could almost make out shapes around her. Nothing stood out as she tried to discern rock from animal. When she was convinced nothing was moving, she ducked back inside.

"I think it's gone. It's pretty dark out there, but I didn't see anything. I think we scared it away."

"God, I hope so! What happened? How did you know it was out there?"

"It woke me up. I think it was trying to dig under the wing."

"Why would it try to dig under when it could have just walked around?"

"I have no idea, but that scared the crap out of me," she said with a tremulous laugh. Her adrenaline had left and she started to shake as she sat back down on her side of their camp bed and pulled the blankets over her legs. As she situated the blanket, she saw something near the log next to the fire.

"How stupid am I?" she said kicking the blankets off and leaning forward to pull it toward her.

"What?" asked 4B.

"It's my fault. I must have dropped this when I was putting the things from dinner away!" said Nora, looking at the plastic beef jerky package she held in her hand. With a disgusted grunt, she threw it onto the fire.

"Do you really think it was after a piece of trash?"

"Bears can smell food from hundreds of feet away. Leaving that lying around was like inviting him to dinner."

Nora scoured the area for anything else that might attract a bear.

"Hey, don't beat yourself up about it." 4B rested a hand on Nora's shoulder.

"I thought I was being so careful."

"You were."

"Can you imagine what would have happened if it had come around to the open side, instead of trying to dig under? You were lying right there," said Nora, indicating the open side of the wing. The only thing between her and the wild was a haphazard assortment of items blocking part of the opening. It wouldn't keep anything out that wanted to come in. She felt so vulnerable and visible where they were.

"I don't want to even imagine it. You shouldn't either. It didn't happen."

"God, I'm such an idiot," whispered Nora, as she sat back down on top of the blankets next to 4B. She'd endangered them both. She grabbed the sweatshirt she had left next to their pallet, buried her face in it, and fell back onto the blankets. "Ugh! Such an idiot," she repeated. She was cold, but didn't care. The adrenaline from the scare was still coursing through her veins and she wasn't about to try to go back to sleep. Not after such a terrifying experience. One that she had caused. She felt so stupid.

"Relax," whispered 4B. Nora felt 4B lie down next to her, and the sweatshirt was removed from her face. Nora kept her hands in fists over her eyes. 4B coaxed one of Nora's arms down so she could nestle close to her, like they'd been right before the scare. Nora breathed out and lowered the other arm, trying to relax for 4B's sake. She stared at the light of the fire dancing on the metal above them. Her self-recrimination didn't go away, but the distraction was helping.

4B's voice murmured close to her ear, making Nora shiver.

"It's fine now. The bear, or whatever it was, is a mile away now. The fire is blazing and will help keep it at bay. Don't worry."

Nora hoped that 4B attributed the shiver that ran through her to the cold, and she reached down and pulled the blanket up over them. She felt the rapid beating of 4B's heartbeat against her side. Despite 4B's reassuring words, Nora suspected she was still frightened.

"Yeah. Probably," said Nora, tightening her arm around 4B, as much to calm herself as it was to calm 4B.

"Bears are way more afraid of us than we are of them, right? As long as there's no more food in here, they'll stay away," said 4B, patting Nora's stomach. Nora focused on the hand resting on her stomach, the fingers of which were now rubbing small circles over the fabric.

"There isn't any more food in here. I promise," affirmed Nora, concentrating on the circles being drawn on her stomach. She could feel the warmth of 4B's hand through her t-shirt.

"Relax then," said 4B, and her words were soothing. Nora tried to release the tightness in her stomach muscles. She took a deep breath and let it out slowly. It helped, and she closed her eyes. The circles on Nora's stomach became slower and larger, and Nora felt a sort of hypnosis fall over her. She was acutely aware of the woman next to her, but the repetitive movement was making everything else begin to fade away. The rain had stopped, but drops fell in sporadic rhythm from the branches above them when the wind blew. The fire emitted its own calming litany of snaps, pops, and metallic clinks when the fiery embers shifted in the center of the pit and the wood burned. All of it receded as Nora concentrated on the circles being rubbed on her belly.

4B was motionless, aside from the movement of her hand, and Nora wondered if she was starting to fall asleep. Nora put the arm that wasn't around 4B behind her head and tried to relax. The motion caused Nora's t-shirt to slip up so a small swath of skin above the top of her jeans became exposed. 4B's fingers slowed as they touched the soft flesh. Nora's entire body responded as 4B paused, then slid her hand under the fabric of the shirt. Soon the circles were being drawn on bare skin. The warmth of 4B's touch made Nora crave more.

"Is this okay?" asked 4B, her voice barely a whisper against Nora's throat.

Nora was afraid to speak or move. She didn't want the feather light caresses to stop, so she squeezed 4B against her in answer, hoping she wouldn't take her hand away. Nora wasn't sure what to expect, but she was willing to let 4B set the pace. Sure her voice would betray her, she nodded her head and buried her face in the hair on the top of 4B's head.

"Nora, I… I want…"

Something in 4B's voice made Nora open her eyes and peer down at the woman pressed against her side. At the same time, 4B looked up, and Nora saw a dark need shining in 4B's green eyes. The expression pulled at Nora, compelling her to move. There was no time to wonder if 4B wanted it, but with their mouths so close together, she had no choice but to bridge the inch of space separating them.

When 4B's soft lips met hers, she was lost.

Their first kiss was an awakening, so deep and consuming, Nora wondered how it was they hadn't kissed before. 4B's lips were warm and soft, gently demanding and breathtakingly tender. Nora rolled toward her and moved her hand along 4B's neck, kissing her, breathing in the essence of her skin and body.

4B's hand inched up Nora's bare abdomen and rested on the place just below her breasts. Lost in the kiss, Nora was still highly aware of the hand as it pressed its heat deep into her skin. Nora's nipples rose as the caress slid further up, and then around, to skim the side of her breast. She experienced the tentative touch like an electric current across her skin, her sensitive flesh tightened in anticipation of where it would end up. She arched into the sensation and kissed 4B, trying to convey just what the touch did to her. When

4B's hand finally cupped her breast, closing over it, claiming it, her skin felt like it was splitting open with an exquisite ache. She'd thought nothing could feel as good as that kiss.

Breathlessly, they drew back, breaking the contact of their lips, freeing the moan building within Nora. She gazed into 4B's heavy lidded eyes, which seemed to dance in the shadows, bright with secret thoughts. Nora could almost feel the heat of the gaze that held her in its sights.

4B's mouth moved like she wanted to say something, but then her eyes moved back to Nora's lips. She seemed to lose her thought, and Nora watched, transfixed, as 4B leaned in and kissed her again, never giving voice to what she'd been about to say. It didn't matter. Nora knew her need. She parted her lips and 4B's mouth opened in return, sending a river of fire down Nora's body. The heat from the kiss before was nothing compared to what she felt now. She never wanted to stop. She held onto 4B, pulling her tightly against her, cradling the back of her head with her hand. Their bodies melded into one another, filling in the spaces. They wrapped around one another in a way that felt more familiar than Nora had ever expected.

4B's tongue brushed against hers, and the firm softness slowly traced the inside edge of her lips, setting Nora's senses on fire. The hand under Nora's t-shirt grew bold and rolled her nipple between exploring fingers. Nora's moan was plaintive and deep when 4B shifted to hover over her, pushing a thigh between her legs. Nora's hands moved across 4B's back and she moved against 4B's leg as the beautiful woman rose above her, holding her down, kissing her feverishly.

"I need to be close to you. I need to feel you," whispered 4B between kisses, in a voice so laden with desire, Nora would have done anything to obey it.

Nora wrapped her arms around 4B, and despite the layers of clothing separating them, the pressure of the leg pressed into her center drove her crazy. Her hips rose, seeking more contact, and she pulled at 4B, moving against her. Their kiss continued to deepen, and Nora could no longer tell who was leading who. The motion of their hips grew more fervent.

4B's lips slid to the corner of Nora's mouth and then across her cheek to rest in the tender spot below Nora's earlobe, raising an electric shiver down Nora's spine. Nora lifted her chin and gave 4B access to her neck. 4B took full advantage, kissing a trail across Nora's jawline and down the sensitive column of her throat, where she drove Nora insane by kissing and nibbling on the area where Nora's neck joined her shoulder. Nora was consumed with the heat of her desire, a desire that had erupted so suddenly, she had no time to consider how it had started. All she knew was she wanted to keep doing it, follow it through to where it went, where she hoped it would go.

"I need to see you," whispered 4B, sitting up as she thrust both hands under Nora's shirt, pushing it over Nora's head, exposing Nora's bare breasts to the cool night air. Nora didn't even register the chill as 4B's greedy eyes scoured her body with a hunger that seemed to etch a trail of heat over her skin. Nora arched under 4B, inviting her to claim her, and she watched as a look of insecurity clouded 4B's hungry expression. Nora smiled at her and used her hands to tell 4B that she felt it too, the hunger and the need, and 4B's eyes grew dark again as she bent to trace another line of kisses across Nora's neck.

Nora gasped and looked down when she felt 4B's lips encircle one of her nipples. 4B's eyes were closed, her pale eyelashes spread across her cheek and her brows knit in passionate attention. The sight of 4B's enraptured face sent a pulse through Nora's center. Every motion sent a reciprocal sensation to her swelling core, which she pressed against 4B's thigh. She ached for a more intimate touch. A slow, rolling pressure built low within her belly, and she ground her hips against the woman above her in a rhythmic motion, dangerously close to making her come. But Nora wasn't ready to give in to the demands of her body yet. She rolled 4B onto her back, and gazed into her eyes.

"You're going to make me explode," Nora explained through heavy breaths, dipping down to kiss 4B's neck, trailing her lips up so she could kiss her again, claiming 4B's talented lips and running her hand down 4B's side.

"Oh, God, that's exactly what I want. Please let me…" whispered 4B, as she wrapped a leg around Nora's leg, rolling them back over, so she was back on top. "I want to make you come."

Nora acknowledged a shift in 4B, a power that had, until that moment, been hidden in a serene and almost passive demeanor. The change thrilled Nora, who usually took the lead in her sexual encounters. Now, 4B set the pace and Nora was surprised to find she was more than willing to follow along.

When 4B reached down and slid her hand into Nora's pants, an explosion of need bounded through Nora's body. She helped by unbuttoning her jeans, and guided 4B's fingers to the hard knot of flesh begging for release. She gasped as warm fingers slide through her wet folds. No longer trying to hold back, Nora wanted more. She kicked away the blanket entangled around their legs, and pushed her pants down, so she was fully exposed, spreading herself wide to the cool night air and the warm caresses she soon felt reach deep within her.

4B's fingers worked magic inside of Nora, pushing her to dizzying heights. 4B was so deep inside, Nora thought she would burst, but she wanted even more. She found 4B's mouth and kissed her, trying to convey her crushing need. 4B returned the kiss with a heat that enflamed them both. She pressed against Nora, grinding her center down on Nora's taut thigh in a frenetic rhythm, and Nora could feel 4B's excitement through the damp pajama bottoms separating their aching flesh. The knowledge of 4B's need created a surge of pulsing thunder that started to spread across Nora's body. She felt it gather and flex, trying to override her senses and erase all but the moment they were in. But Nora needed to touch 4B, to let 4B feel what she was feeling. Just as she was about to lose her mind, she managed to reach down and thrust her hand into the loose waist of 4B's pajama pants. 4B was ready and open, and Nora's fingers slid deep into the wetness she found there. 4B threw her head back and moaned, arching into Nora. 4B's fingers dipped even deeper into Nora. All control fled. 4B's passion tightened around her fingers, and a maelstrom of sensation flared within her. Lightning blasted and waves of blinding energy washed through her, and each time 4B moved, the tumult inside of her intensified until she was a raging inferno. When 4B's orgasm exploded just seconds later, the sounds of 4B's cries and the feeling of the strong muscles pulsing over Nora's fingers in a warm flood of wet took Nora over the edge again with another shattering orgasm. Finally, 4B collapsed against her, breathing heavily into Nora's neck, her gasping breaths tickling the damp hair stuck to the sweat on her skin. With 4B's limp body covering her, Nora relaxed beneath her, holding 4B to her with one arm, as the other remained between them, her fingers still deep inside of 4B, luxuriating in the feel of the ebbing pulses caressing her fingers.

Soft lips teased a path up Nora's throat. A gentle kiss landed on her mouth, and Nora fell back into the warm bliss that had started everything.

"That was…" 4B murmured against Nora's lips. "I don't have words for what that was."

"Awesome?" smiled Nora, kissing the mouth hovering a hair's breadth from her own.

"Better than awesome," responded 4B, gently biting Nora's bottom lip.

"Incredible?"

"Better."

"Do I need to invent a word to describe it?"

"No. Let's let the absence of words define it," said 4B, staring into Nora's eyes for a long moment before she kissed her again.

And the kiss ignited another round of lovemaking that left them both gasping for air within a few minutes. When they relaxed, Nora pulled 4B to her and held her tightly.

"God. I don't know if I've ever come that hard once, let alone twice," moaned Nora into 4B's mouth as they kissed leisurely, basking in the after effects of their passion.

"If I counted right, it was actually three for you. God, you feel so good," sighed 4B, collapsing against Nora's chest, which was cooled by the sweat from their exertion.

"Yes, but who's counting?" laughed Nora, still trying to catch her breath. She hugged 4B to her and shivered.

"Are you cold?" asked 4B, rubbing her hands up and down Nora's exposed skin.

"Parts of me are a little chilly—others seem to need a cold shower," teased Nora, stroking 4B's back beneath the sweatshirt she still wore.

4B sat up and stripped off her sweatshirt. The pajama pants had been removed during their second round of passion. She then pulled the blankets over them as she lay down on top of Nora. She rested her head between Nora's breasts.

"Good idea. One of the best thermal regulators is another human body," said Nora.

"That sounds familiar," said 4B with a sigh as she settled back into her place with her head resting on Nora's chest. Nora loved the feel of 4B's weight upon her and buried her nose in the hair on the crown of 4B's head, inhaling her scent. Her skin tingled at the soft impression of 4B's breasts resting on her torso and she fought the urge to move against her, to feel their skin sliding together again.

As if reading Nora's mind, 4B moved to her side pulling Nora to face her, brushing their breasts together and running her fingers along every inch of exposed flesh she could reach without losing eye contact.

"Don't move. Just let me feel you," commanded 4B as she pressed her body into Nora's, and their legs entwined. 4B seemed to take care not to press into the very sensitive apex between Nora's thighs, which only made her crave it that much more. But she remained still, letting 4B skim her hand over her, tracing her lines and learning her skin.

4B's eyes preceded the movements of her hand and Nora watched her closely, receptive to the touching, anticipating the thrill of it more and more as each moment passed and the strokes became more urgent. Incredibly, she started to edge toward initiating the no-turning-back launch sequence of yet another orgasm. Their breathing became ragged, yet Nora obeyed 4B's command to lie still, and she remained mostly motionless, with only 4B's hand making its tracks across the expanse of her body. Words of a plea gathered on Nora's lips, and 4B's mouth pressed over hers to silence them, though her eyes remained open, connected to Nora's in an invisible conduit that let nothing else distract them.

Nora could stand it no longer, and she inched her hand, the one that had so patiently rested on the smooth skin of 4B's hip, down and between them, into the hot, slick valley between 4B's thighs. 4B's back arched at the contact, and her hand, which had teased but not touched Nora's sex, slid between them and into the pulsing heat, wrapping around 4B's seeking fingers. It took no other motion to bring them both to release, and their bodies heaved against each other as the powerful sensations rocked them into divine sensation.

"No fair. I wanted to watch you come without my own distraction," panted 4B, as she curled up against Nora once again. Nora's sweat-sheened body broke out in goose bumps at the feel of the chill night air. She pulled the blanket back over them, holding 4B tightly against her.

"I couldn't help myself," said Nora, brushing the hair from 4B's damp brow, and kissing her.

"I was almost there anyway. You have such expressive eyes," said 4B when their lips parted.

"My eyes have nothing on you, lady. God. I felt you touching me even when you weren't. You were killing me."

"Killing you would have made this a little counter-productive," replied 4B with a serious expression she quickly replaced with a playful wink.

"I'd say so," laughed Nora, stretching her well-used body in a sated crescent around 4B, who had no choice but to follow suit. They were both beyond physically sated, though a potent sexual energy hovered around them, promising more lovemaking would occur before the night was through. "I've determined that you must be a professional sex-machine in your mysterious real life."

A shadow passed over 4B's face and Nora wondered if she'd said something wrong. She reached out and caressed 4B's cheek.

"I didn't mean to…"

"Oh. You didn't say anything wrong," said 4B capturing Nora's hand and kissing her palm. "It's just that I sometimes feel disconnected, not having any memory beyond these last few days. It's so… isolating."

"I can't even imagine what it's like."

"I don't think I can describe it, really. It's weird. I know things, but I don't know how I know them. The only time I've felt like a whole person was… was just now, when we…" 4B didn't finish the sentence. Nora kissed her, telling her she understood.

4B looked at her and her eyes searched Nora's.

"When we're like this, it all feels right. I feel connected. I want to keep doing it until we're… until there's… ugh! I can't express it. I just want to be inside of you."

Nora knew what 4B was trying to say, even though she couldn't express it herself. And she kissed 4B, once again fueling the fire that had erupted so quickly between them.

🌲🌲🌲🌲🌲

Nora rolled to her side and felt a warm arm encircle her waist from behind. The soft silk of 4B's body shifted with her and pressed against her back. She pulled the arm tightly around her and settled into the cocoon of drowsy comfort surrounding them under the blanket. The covers were small and thin, and cool air snuck in around the edges as she moved. But the heat from the fire she'd kept stoked all night between bouts of lovemaking, along with their combined body temperatures, were enough to keep them warm and comfortable. She took a deep breath, and under the ubiquitous, tangy aromas of campfire and pine, she could make out the fresh and earthy scents of the forest as it woke from the long wet night. Even the intermittent dripping from the sodden canopy overhead had stopped, and from behind closed eyelids, she knew the sun was shining again.

She floated in the bliss between sleep and wakefulness and replayed her memories of the night before. A soft kiss on her shoulder told her 4B was probably thinking about the same thing and she pressed against her. Warm hands brushed over her body, arousing sensations that surprised and delighted her, not only for what they were, but for the fact that she would even have the energy for what her body was aching to do again.

"Good morning, beautiful," she said, as she rolled over to face 4B.

A sleepy smile and brilliant green eyes greeted her and she stopped to study the face of the woman beside her. She reached up and pushed back a strand of hair and 4B kissed her palm before she slid her hand behind 4B's head and pulled her toward her.

She saw 4B's eyes widen at the same time as a low, familiar sound drew near. An engine! A small plane engine, and it was close!

Nora jumped up quickly enough to bang her head on the wing above her. She barely felt it. Hunched over, she grabbed her sweatshirt and stepped over the suddenly wide-awake 4B.

"A plane! Someone came!" she shouted as she ducked out of the shelter, pulling on her top, and ran toward the edge of the ravine. "I see it! It just flew by, but it's turning back! We need to signal them somehow."

4B was already throwing the greenest, needle-laden branches she could find on the fire. "The smoke is already drifting toward the ravine, but we need something to wave more of it that way!"

Nora ran back over and pulled on her jeans before she began to wave a t-shirt behind the billowing clouds pouring from the green wood in the fire. The wind that had been blowing away from the ravine during the storm was now pulling the smoke toward it, helping them in their task.

4B put on some clothes and continued to feed the green fuel to the fire, but not so much she risked extinguishing it.

"They have to see this," said Nora, coughing at the acrid plume wafting back at her as she continued to wave the shirt at it. "One of us should stand near the edge so they see us when they investigate the smoke."

Even as she spoke the noise of the plane grew closer and they both whooped when the plane flew impossibly near the edge of the ravine closest to where they were. The pilot was at eye-level with them, and Nora knew that even if he couldn't see the two of them, he could see the wing of the plane and the smoke they were fanning toward the ravine. Nora ran forward, waving her arms, coming to a skidding stop just at the edge.

"Nora!" screamed 4B, coming up behind her and wrapping her arms around Nora's waist. "I thought you were going to run right off!"

"I'm okay. We're okay! We're going to be okay!" Nora laughed, feeling almost hysterical in her relief. She turned in 4B's embrace and kissed her. She picked her up and spun her around and 4B laughed too, pulling them both away from the lip of the drop-off when Nora put her down. Nora laughed again. It was her friend Tack's plane. In normal circumstances, she would have felt the effects of dancing so close to the precipice, but in that moment, giddy hope overrode all other emotions. "I know that plane! It's Tack! He saw us! He's coming back!"

Nora pointed at the small aircraft as it turned sharply and headed toward them again. When it got close, the wings dipped in a sign the pilot had seen them.

"Crazy bastard! He's flying too low. I hope he doesn't crash his own plane before he calls for help!" Nora laughed as she grabbed 4B around the waist and spun her around.

"You know the pilot?" asked 4B, laughing for the same reasons Nora was.

"Yes! We're getting out of here!"

Jubilation bubbled between them as they gathered up what little belongings they wanted to take with them and waited for the plane to come back. They debated how the rescue would happen, since there was no place for the plane to land, and they wondered if they should stay put or find a place where help could more easily get to them. Finally, they decided to wait exactly where they were. They'd keep the fire going and the smoke billowing so their rescuers could easily find them.

🌲🌲🌲🌲🌲

"Nora, I'm scared," whispered 4B as they were ushered from the helipad, past a throng of people, which had gathered near the emergency room entrance at the hospital in Anchorage.

During the thirty-minute helicopter flight, they'd been briefed that their rescue had already hit the news. The hospital had arranged for security, but the press of reporters surrounding them when they stepped from the noisy rescue helicopter was daunting. Hospital staff immediately surrounded them, ushering them from the aircraft to the hospital entrance. Wheelchairs had been brought to them but were ignored as both women waved them off and walked closely together, following the tall man who had been with them in the helicopter. The flashing lights of cameras assaulted their eyes and shouts rang out from every direction.

"Nora Kavendash! How does it feel to be rescued six days after one of the nation's deadliest airplane crashes? Do you think technology played a part in the delay?"

"Had you given up after so much time in the remote forest?"

"Who is the woman with you?"

"Let us see your face, Grace!"

"Were other survivors with you?"

"What did you eat?"

"Are you going to sue the airline?"

4B had her head down, pressed into Nora's chest, while Nora tried to ignore the questions. She'd been the focus of more than a few press conferences in her past as CEO of AdPrivacy, but she'd been prepared for those. She wrapped a protective arm around 4B and held her own head up against the scrutiny of the chaotic crowd that tried to penetrate the protective ring of hospital guards.

"I have you, 4B. I won't leave," said Nora, maintaining her hold on 4B as they swept through more guards stationed at the automatic doors in front of the emergency entrance, which slid shut behind them. The comparative hush of the inside of the hospital enfolded them. The smells of medicine and cleaning products replaced the odor of the helicopter fuel, which had replaced the scents of the forest and campfire. The olfactory changes provided a sense of moving from one surreal scene to another. All of it was so immediate, yet didn't feel quite solid.

Nora had scanned the crowd for anyone she knew on the landing pad, and then again in the emergency waiting room, as the tall man whisked them through the open area, and immediately past doors emblazoned with signs announcing they were in restricted territory. She looked for Tack, her burly pilot friend. She was dying to find out how he had found them and why it had taken so long. But she didn't see a single familiar face.

They walked through the busy emergency room, refusing to be separated, and were taken into a single examination room in the back. The nurse who entered with them took their vitals and promised a doctor would be in to see them shortly. She left two charts on the counter by the sink and quietly left the room. When they were alone again, the silence was thunderous.

The room was small, starkly lit with florescent lighting. It smelled of hospital antiseptic and latex gloves. Nora had insisted 4B take the only chair, while she sat at the edge of the bed. The plastic of the mattress crackled beneath her. As soon as the nurse left, 4B walked over and pushed into the circle of Nora's arms, resting her head on Nora's chest. 4B seemed small, pulled inward in her fear, and Nora held her close. She inhaled the familiar smoky scent of the campfire they'd left behind but she could make out the unique scent of 4B's skin, a smell she had basked in the night before. She closed her eyes and tried to memorize it, wondering how much longer they would be together.

"This is so unreal," said 4B. Her whisper sounded loud in the silent room.

"Don't worry. Things will be fine," said Nora, resting her chin on 4B's head.

"I don't even recognize my own name. I don't know who to call." 4B's voice trembled with emotion and Nora's heart constricted at the sound of fear coming from the strong woman she knew. When 4B's shoulders started to shake with silent sobs, Nora buried her face in the hair near 4B's ear and whispered soothing sounds, which seemed to help.

Nora lifted 4B's head and kissed her lightly on the lips.

"I'll stay with you. I'm sure the airline has information. They'll contact your family."

4B searched Nora's face.

"What happens when—?" started 4B, but a knock on the door interrupted the question she had been about to ask.

A woman in a lab coat walked in.

"I'm Dr. Warren. I hope I'm not interrupting anything."

🌲🌲🌲🌲🌲

Nora sat impatiently on the hard plastic chair in the hallway across from the examination room she and 4B had been in and out of all day. They had waited in the room together between tests and interviews, but the room was empty now. Nora had completed her last interview with the airline over an hour before, but she waited for 4B who had been moved to an office a few doors down. It was the last interview of the day; they'd been promised.

Nora picked at a seam in the new clothes she wore—a gift from the airline, the nurse had said, when she'd handed her the bag from an upscale local department store. They were stiff and not her normal brand, but they were clean, an improvement from the clothes in her pack, which all needed laundering. Because they hadn't been admitted to the hospital, she and 4B hadn't been given time or a place to fully bathe, though, and the smell of campfire still clung to her hair. And no matter how much she scrubbed her hands in the hospital sink, the dirt didn't seem to want to rinse completely from under her fingernails. It had been nice to wash her face and change into clean jeans, though. Fantasies of a warm shower filled her head. She couldn't wait for 4B to be released so they could head over to the hotel where North Star Airlines had reserved rooms for them.

Nora's examination had been quick since she didn't have a scratch on her. 4B's had taken longer and had consisted of numerous tests. But even after an MRI and a CAT scan, she had checked out fine, aside from the cut on her forehead, which wasn't serious but would leave a nice scar. Then there was the amnesia, for which the doctor couldn't provide a prognosis, saying they'd simply have to wait it out. It seemed amnesia was a wily affliction, affecting people differently, manifesting and disappearing with no rhyme or reason. None of it warranted keeping 4B in the hospital, though, unless she wanted to be put under voluntary psychiatric evaluation, which 4B had declined.

At 4B's request, Nora had remained with her during all of the examinations, but the agents from the airline had insisted they conduct their interviews separately. Thankfully, rather than conducting the interviews at the North Star Airlines offices at the airport, the airline had arranged to use an office at the hospital.

Nora's interview had only taken forty-five minutes. It had consisted of validating her identity, a description of events leading up to the crash, and a recount of what they had done to survive while awaiting rescue. Nora assumed 4B's interview would be much of the same, so she wondered what was taking so long. Nora's knee pumped up and down as she sat in her chair. She looked at her watch again. It had been over an hour. Just then, Dr. Warren left the office and Nora rose to intercept her, looking over the doctor's shoulder. The door whisked shut without anyone else following.

The doctor stopped and smiled when Nora approached her.

"It should only be a little while longer," she said before Nora had to ask.

"Is she doing okay?"

"She seems fine. She can't remember anything from before the crash, though."

"I expected it to be shorter because of that. Why did they allow you to go in with her when they wouldn't allow me to go in with her?"

"I think they just wanted to get your separate accounts of what happened."

"I hope she's doing okay. This has been pretty overwhelming for her," said Nora, remembering how scared 4B had been when they first arrived.

"She's fine. Really. Most people with amnesia react better to the loss of memory than the family or loved ones, actually. They don't know what they don't know. So there is very little stress as long as the people surrounding them are at ease."

"That's good to know. By the way, thanks for all the time you're spending with us today. I know you're busy."

"We're a little overstaffed today for once. When they said they were bringing in more survivors, we didn't know what to expect, so we brought in additional staff."

Nora wasn't sure she'd heard correctly.

"Did you say more survivors? There are others?"

Dr. Warren's brow furrowed. "No one told you?"

Nora shook her head. "This is the first I've heard of others. Where did they find them? How many are there?"

"I wish I had more information to give you. The others didn't come to this hospital and I don't keep up with the news."

Nora shook her head in disbelief. "I just assumed we were the only ones. I searched the wreckage. There was no one. I should have tried harder." She sat down in the chair she'd been sitting in earlier. Dr. Warren sat in the chair next to her and put a hand on her arm.

"I'm sorry. I wish I had more to tell you. I don't know much more other than they found the others a few days ago and they went to the hospital on Elmendorf. You're the only ones to come here."

Nora didn't know what to do with the information. She was elated there were other survivors. But they had been brought in days ago. How had that happened? How many were there?

"What happens next for 4B?"

"4B?"

"Sorry, I mean Grace. Have they contacted her family?"

The doctor shook her head. "She can't provide any information about her family or next of kin. I gather from the questions she paid cash for her ticket, so there isn't a credit card transaction to trace any of her personal information."

"How does this all affect her? She doesn't know where to go. Does she have to stay here, then? At the hospital until they figure it out?"

The doctor shook her head.

"Her injury isn't enough to keep her admitted, so, technically, she isn't my patient. I could possibly recommend she stay the night for observation, but beyond that, I don't have any authority in it."

Nora was surprised. "If she doesn't have a memory how does that work? Someone needs to take care of her. Where will she go? Who will help her regain her life?" Nora asked these questions knowing full well she would do all of those things.

"Technically, she's capable of taking care of herself, so unless someone contests it, or she displays exaggerated signs of incompetence, she has full rights and control over her own welfare. We can only help her as much as she requests it."

"So, as far as reminding her, trying to jog her memory, should we just let her remember things on her own?"

"I don't know. Every case is different. You might want to keep her access to the news and the media to a minimum for the next few days."

Nora remembered the crowd they had to get through when they came to the hospital. It seemed like it had been days ago, but in reality, it had only been a few hours. She hadn't thought about the next few days. She wasn't prepared for what they'd returned to. She knew 4B would be even less so.

A man Nora recognized from the airline approached them.

"Dr. Warren, may we have a word with you?"

The room they had taken 4B to was still closed.

Dr. Warren stood. "Certainly."

"A woman's purse was recovered from the crash site and we believe it contains the identification of Ms. Trackton," said the woman, holding a large plastic bag containing what appeared to be a singed and beaten up black leather bag in front of her. "The airline physician gave authorization to consult with you on how to present the bag to Ms. Trackton, because you treated her."

Dr. Warren accepted the bag from the official. "I'm not familiar with the airline physician. Is this normal procedure?"

"Normally the airline would defer to the passenger's personal physician. This case is atypical, since Ms. Trackton doesn't know who her own physician is and hasn't been admitted into this hospital. The airline physician might request your assistance with aspects related to insurance and other items that could be considered difficult to assess due to the amnesia. Of course, Ms. Trackton will be consulted, as well."

"May I open the bag to see what we're dealing with? It might help me determine how to move forward."

The female official nodded.

Dr. Warren opened the purse and pulled out a matching wallet. A driver's license slid out and fell to the ground. Dr. Warren picked it up and studied it. Aside from a little cash, there wasn't much else in the wallet.

"This sure looks like her," said Dr. Warren. She looked through the rest of the purse, which didn't have much in it, just a paperback book, a pen, lipstick, and a small box of decongestant. "I don't see anything that would cause her undo stress." Nora looked over Dr. Warren's shoulder and confirmed the photo on the Massachusetts driver's license was, indeed that of 4B, a.k.a. Grace Trackton. Now that they knew where she lived, it would be just a matter of time for the rest of 4B's life to emerge from the shadows.

When the officials and Dr. Warren returned to the room where 4B was being interviewed, Nora went to the cafeteria to get some coffee. The hospital had fed them soon after their arrival, but it had been a few hours since then, and even the limp broccoli in the steamer tray looked good to Nora when she'd passed by. She'd wait until 4B was available before eating again, though. Coffee in hand, she went down to the more comfortable front lobby to wait. She'd been waiting for about a half an hour and was considering going back to check on 4B when she heard a familiar voice.

"I never thought they'd stop asking questions," said 4B from close by. Nora turned and smiled as she approached.

4B wrapped her arms around Nora's waist and Nora returned the hug, relived to see her again.

"How are you doing? That took a while."

"I'm fine. Tired, but fine. They asked me questions about the crash, which I had no information about. And they asked some questions about what we did to survive while we waited for the rescue team. I left a few details out," said 4B with a shy glance away, and Nora blushed, which earned her a laugh.

"They asked me all of that, too," said Nora. "But you were with them twice as long."

"They had a thousand questions about my travel plans, my family, where I live, all the stuff I just can't remember. For a little while, I had the feeling they didn't believe I have amnesia."

"Were they being too aggressive?" asked Nora, a protective concern rising when she heard the last.

"No, they were just persistent, asking the same questions, only in a different way, over and over."

"Maybe they were trying to jump start your memory."

"Maybe. It didn't feel like an interrogation. They were gentle."

"I'm glad about that, otherwise I'd have to go talk to them about it," said Nora, the protective instinct raring up again. "I think they found a bag that belongs to you?"

"Yeah. When they brought it in, they stopped asking so many questions."

"They were probably just looking for ways to find your next of kin," said Nora. A feeling of apprehension filled her as she said it aloud, and she wondered again how much longer they would have together.

4B's eyes shifted over Nora's shoulder to the flat-screen television mounted near the ceiling across the nearly empty room. Nora turned to see what had caught 4B's attention. The sound was off and the closed captioning was scrolling along the bottom of the picture, which showed men and women in yellow uniforms sifting through a wreck.

"Is that—?"

"Yes," said Nora. It was the wreckage of their plane. She'd caught the loop from a national news service a little while earlier, and she'd watched, stunned to find out what had happened. She'd felt like crying with relief when she'd heard a thirteen-month-old baby girl had been found among the survivors.

"They're talking about us, Nora. That's the wreckage."

"It's the other half. They found it on the other side of the mountain. There are other survivors."

4B watched, stunned, and Nora wondered if she should be watching it after Dr. Warren's suggestion she stay away from the news for a while. Nora couldn't stop watching, though. It was compelling in a way she couldn't describe.

They sat together as the scrolling words described the rescue efforts, how the first group of survivors—thirty-one of them—had been found the day after the crash, once the cloud cover had broken up. And how two additional survivors—her and 4B—had been found six days later, after officials found the wreckage that had been separated from the rest due to the craggy terrain. A list of names of the survivors flowed across the screen. Followed by a longer list of the people who had perished.

One hundred and two passengers along with the two pilots and five crewmembers had died in the crash.

4B shifted in her seat and looked at Nora, who pulled her eyes from the screen to look back at her. Both of them had tears in their eyes.

"I don't want to watch any more of it. I can't," said 4B taking Nora's hand. Nora could hear the pain in 4B's voice and wondered what was going on in her head.

"Is it triggering anything for you?" asked Nora, feeling the anguish she saw reflected in 4B's expression.

4B shook her head. "So many people died, Nora. I can't imagine what the families are going through."

🌲🌲🌲🌲🌲

It was early evening, and less than a half an hour later, Nora and 4B stood in the lobby of a plush downtown hotel. They each held a plastic card key, a folder full of papers given to them by the airline, and a small bag containing their dirty clothes. Nora also had her backpack, and 4B—Grace—had the battered black purse that the airline officials had returned to her. She'd gone through the leather bag in the car on the ride between the hospital and the hotel, and although she'd stared at the driver's license for several minutes, she hadn't had a reaction to anything inside. With the presence of yet another new airline official sitting with them in the backseat, Nora had held back from asking 4B what she was thinking.

"Please don't hesitate to call me for anything," said the young man from the car, now standing across from them in the hotel lobby. He was wearing a neat suit and had a perfect haircut. He handed each of them one of his cards. His eager attentiveness was almost comical. "North Star Airlines is complete-ly available to you. Twenty-four by seven. If you need anything, anything at all, call the number right there and I'll make it happen."

"Thank you," said Nora, glancing at 4B—or Grace, according to the name everybody had been calling her since they had arrived. To Nora, she was still 4B and probably always would be. She saw 4B hide a small smile as the young man actually bowed when he took his leave. They watched as he backed out of the lobby and into the waiting black sedan that had dropped them off at the hotel. A small crowd of reporters was gathered outside, but hotel security wasn't letting anyone in unless they were registered guests. She wondered how the extra security was affecting business.

"God. I was afraid he'd follow us upstairs," said Nora, turning toward 4B. "Something tells me they're terrified of a lawsuit."

"They should be," said 4B. "A crew performed maintenance on the wrong aircraft and then took a break before it was complete when the rain started coming down too hard to continue. So the plane took off with part of the fuel line disconnected."

"It's amazing," said Nora, shaking her head. "I understand why they haven't disclosed the information to the public yet, but I was surprised they disclosed it so readily to us. And don't airplanes have sensors or something for that kind of thing? Something as critical as the fuel system should have monitors all over it. I don't get it. And aren't the pilots supposed to do some sort of visual check of the aircraft before getting inside? I know Tack does. Every single time. Commercial pilots should have the same pre-flight checks."

Nora's mind had been churning over the new details since she'd heard them, trying to piece it all together. She had a million questions. She would have gone through all of them with 4B, if 4B hadn't put a hand on her arm, calming her down before she got too worked up about it again.

"I'm sure we'll get better details about exactly what happened, and why they didn't detect it, but it's all quite overwhelming," agreed 4B. "It's possible they hope we'll be less inclined to sue if they provide details up front. If we feel informed, we're more likely to accept a settlement."

"Again, you amaze me with the things you know. Now I'm thinking you might be a lawyer in your real life—or an airline executive." Nora laughed when 4B just shrugged. She loved the way 4B seemed to accept that anything was possible. "Are you going to sign the papers they gave you?"

Nora's opinion was 4B was in no position to sign anything while she still had amnesia, but she didn't feel comfortable telling her what she should or shouldn't do. All she knew is she wanted to protect her.

"I don't know. They told me I had time to consult a lawyer. I guess I should wait until I get my memory back or they find my family, whichever comes first," said 4B, looking at the packet of papers in her hand. They had her name and an address, but so far had not been able to find her family. Nora wondered how it felt to be in that kind of limbo. "What about you?"

"I don't know. They moved so fast. We haven't even had a chance to clean the forest off of us yet, and they already had settlement papers in front of us. I won't sign anything until my lawyer has had a look. I'm sure he'd be happy to advise you as well, if you want."

"That would be great," said 4B with a look of appreciation, which made Nora feel more settled about at least this aspect of 4B's future.

They walked through the open hotel lobby toward the elevators. A huge double-sided fireplace crackled in the center of the room, and stuffed animal heads populated the expansive mantle. Nora was used to the rugged outdoorsman theme ubiquitous to Alaska, even in fancy hotels, but she noticed 4B staring at the mounted animals with a scowl.

"Something tells me you don't like something you see," she said, amused.

"I hate it when people display animals like they're trophies, like it's not morbid to have dead parts of animals hanging on the walls. Can they not see the sick irony of destroying and then displaying a life-like homage to the wild beauty of a once living creature?"

"You kind of get used to it in Alaska," said Nora. She liked seeing this spirited side of 4B. It was a new facet of a person she was finding more and more fascinating. "I'm okay with hunting as long as people eat the meat, but I don't really understand hunting for sport and I don't see the appeal of displaying the heads, either, even if you do eat them. It's kind of creepy, really. We're in the minority on that side of the discussion in Alaska, though."

"Sorry. It just makes me sad," said 4B looking away from the display. "Do you think the other survivors of the crash are staying at this hotel?"

Nora recognized the change of topic and shrugged her shoulders indicating she didn't know. "I'm still surprised they didn't tell us about the others right away. When I asked the agent who's been debriefing me all day, he told me they assumed the rescue team would have told us. From what I understand, most of the survivors are still in the hospital in Elmendorf. Some of them are pretty beat up. Only a few have gone home. The baby was flown down to a hospital in Seattle."

"I was so relieved the baby was found alive," said 4B with a sigh mirroring Nora's relief. "I wonder why they took us to a different hospital."

"I asked about that, too. I guess we would have been sent to Elmendorf, too, but they were doing military exercises at the base today and something about restricted airspace and they couldn't let the helicopter land."

"Are the ones in the hospital hurt badly?" asked 4B.

"Most of them were, from what I understand. Only a couple of them have been released. You and I were lucky." Nora's mind and heart swirled with emotions she had yet to process. "Would it be weird of me to say I want to go meet them?"

4B seemed to consider it.

"I feel connected to them, too. I guess it's normal that we would feel bonded by the experience." They both mulled it over as they walked. "Why do you think there was such a delay in finding us?"

They stopped in front of the bank of elevators.

"I only got to talk to my friend Tack for a minute, but he was part of the search team like many of the bush pilots in the area. He said the weather was bad and they'd stopped searching after they found the first part of the wreck and the survivors there. They thought the crash was confined to the other side of the peak we were on. They would have figured it out when the cleanup resumed this morning, but he was on a run between Juneau and Anchorage and he circled the site and saw the smoke from our fire. When he dropped down to check it out, he saw the wreckage in the ravine."

"We'd still be out there if it weren't for your friend?"

"Maybe. I don't know, but we owe him big time, that's for sure. I think they would have eventually pieced together that parts of the plane were still missing and widened their search perimeter. But who knows how much time it would have taken?" Nora shivered at the possibilities.

"I don't want to even guess," said 4B. "It's amazing there were any survivors."

"I know. I feel lucky. And numb. I'm afraid to question it too deeply. We'll probably find out more after the investigation is closed."

The elevator door opened and a businessman stepped out, nodding his head at them absently as he brushed past.

"I'm so tired. I can't wait for a hot shower," sighed 4B, as she stepped into the mirrored lift and leaned with obvious exhaustion against the handrail as Nora swiped her room key and pushed the button to the top floor. It had been a long, emotionally draining day.

"That's all I've thought about for the last ten hours," groaned Nora as she took a spot against the handrail next to 4B. The haggard and rumpled woman she saw in her reflection didn't look like her at all. In contrast, 4B looked tired but beautiful. She looked away from her reflection and down at their hands, which were centimeters apart on the rail. She could feel them, so close, like a buzz, the awareness of it was so strong. But, back to real life and suddenly shy, Nora discovered she had a hard time bridging the distance.

The doors slid open and they got off the elevator at the penthouse level. The hallway was elaborately decorated with only four doors, two on each side of the elevator, leading to what she imagined were more elaborately decorated rooms.

"I'm in P1," said Nora, unnecessarily checking the card folder the hotel manager had handed to her at the front desk. She didn't know how to say goodnight and she wasn't sure she wanted to.

"P2 for me," replied 4B, looking down the hall at her door, which was next to Nora's.

Nora followed 4B to the short set of marble steps leading up to the threshold of 4B's room and stood there, waiting.

4B turned toward Nora and looked like she didn't know what to say either.

"I'm starving. I'll probably order room service after a shower," said Nora.

"Me too. I'm dying for some real food. I hate to say it, but the hospital just reinforced the bad reputation of hospital food," said 4B, fiddling with the plastic card in her hand.

"Sad thing is they probably presented us with their best effort." Nora gave a shallow laugh. A long pause stretched between them. Struck by an unexpected bout of insecurity, she didn't know what to say, didn't know what came next for them. It felt like they stood at the thresholds of their old lives, pointing in different directions. "Well… I guess I'll see you tomorrow. Good night."

Nora started to turn.

"Um…" said 4B, and Nora turned back. "If you want, I can order dinner. For both of us. In my room… if you don't want to eat alone. But if you're tired, and just want to go to sleep, I'll understand…"

Nora finally found the courage to approach 4B. She transferred everything she held into one hand and grasped 4B's hand, which was nervously spinning the key card. She stepped closer and gently kissed her. "That sounds great. Order me anything with meat in it, and just call me when it gets there. Maybe by then, I'll have washed the smoke and pine resin out of my hair."

4B just smiled at her and watched Nora walk backward toward her own door. They smiled at each other as they keyed their locks and disappeared into their separate rooms.

🌲🌲🌲🌲🌲

Nora tossed the items she held onto the marble topped table in the wide entryway leading into a huge and luxuriously furnished room. She leaned against the door to shut it and wondered what 4B was doing in her room next door. Was she thinking about what had happened between them the night before? Thoughts of their night together had snuck into her head throughout the day, but the chaos of interviews and examinations had left her little time to really think about it at all. It seemed so long ago when they'd awoken, limbs entwined, deliriously sated in the aftermath of lovemaking. It felt like a dream. So different from where they were now, foreign to the lives they were going back to. She forced herself to move further into the room and not to dwell on the possibility that they might find the lives they lived back home—wherever that was for 4B—didn't match up with one another.

The room was a bit much for Nora, who would have been content with a simple bed and a clean shower. She'd spent many nights in similar rooms. As the CEO of a successful web design company, rooms like this had come as part of the package, but she'd just used them for sleep or work. Most of the time she'd been so immersed in writing code it wouldn't have mattered if she'd been sitting at a cherry wood desk or a rickety table at the local coffee shop in whatever fine city she happened to be visiting. All of that had been a long time ago, a different life.

She looked around. Soft piano music wafted from hidden speakers and a roaring fire billowed warmth from a large gas fireplace in the middle of the room, open on all sides. The airline had spared no expense on her and 4B. There was a spacious desk area, a fully stocked wet bar, a grand piano, and several couches and chairs arranged in two group settings; one near the fireplace, and another around a dark wood coffee table adorned with a huge fresh floral arrangement. An open double doorway led into another room featuring a plush, king-sized bed that had already been turned down, a gourmet chocolate nestled on the pillow. Across the room, a floor-to-ceiling window overlooked the city of Anchorage, which sparkled below in the clear night air. Nora walked over to the French doors that opened onto the wide balcony and she stepped into the late September evening. Chill night air surrounded her, and she shivered.

Nora went back inside, closing the doors behind her, and investigated the huge bedroom. The bed was bigger than most she had seen. It still wasn't her own feather bed, but it looked inviting, with a soft comforter and a dozen pillows creating a nest at the headboard. Her weary bones craved to feel the soft surface of the mattress after so many nights spent lying on the forest floor, though she already thought longingly of the pine needle bed 4B had made for them. Body memories from the night before tingled through her and she smiled. Yes, she'd remember that pine-scented pallet for far different reasons than the lack of comfort it provided.

Several bags brandishing familiar department store names sat on a low table at the foot of the bed. Curious, Nora went to see what was in them and found new clothing, pajamas, underwear, shoes, and a jacket. Aside from the underwear, which had been purchased at a famous chain known for frilly garments, rather than the more utilitarian ones she usually wore, all of it was clothing she would have purchased for herself. Whoever had shopped for them had even gotten her sizes right. Nora was impressed. In the bathroom, which was larger than most people's bedrooms, a similar set of bags was waiting with toiletry items.

Nora sniffed the ginger-lime body wash she pulled from one of the bags, and the marble and glass shower taking up one end of the large bathroom called her name. The shower would have to wait. Before Nora did anything else, she needed to call Aunt Mace. The circumstances of being stranded after the crash had distracted Nora, but now that she was on her way home, worry about her aunt had started to invade her thoughts more often. She had talked to her briefly, earlier in the day, but only to tell her she was all right, that she would be home soon. She'd promised to call her later. When she'd asked Aunt Mace how she was doing, Aunt Mace had diverted the conversation back to the rescue.

Nora went into the front room and grabbed her cell phone, which she'd recharged earlier at the hospital. She'd already gone through all of the voice messages, some of which were work related, but most of which were her friends calling to leave heartfelt messages of worry and hope after hearing about the plane crash. She had saved most of them without listening all the way through. She wasn't quite ready to deal with it all yet. She'd listen to them later and return the calls once everything settled down. Aunt Mace was the only one she wanted to reassure right now. She sat down next to the fireplace and pressed the speed dial. As she listened to the phone ring, the fire warmed her back.

"Ready on this end," quipped the voice on the line. Nora smiled at the familiar greeting.

"Hi there, crazy lady. It's Nora," she said, happy to hear her aunt's voice again.

"Eleanor! I've been waiting by the phone. When they lettin' you come home? Did the damn vampires drain you dry yet?"

Nora had called Aunt Mace earlier from the examination room. Despite her frequent need for tests, Aunt Mace had never grown used to needles, and voiced it quite loudly.

"They didn't take much blood, Aunt Mace. It was just a regular examination."

"Everything check out okay, then?"

"Yep. Fit as a fiddle, though a few pounds lighter. How about you?"

"You didn't need to lose any weight," said Aunt Mace, ignoring the rest.

"I know, but that's what a diet of peanuts and beef jerky does to you after a few days. How was—"

"We'll get that weight back on you in no time. Tell me everything. I wish I could have taken the ticket the airline offered and flown out to you today. But Dr. Shou said no. Too many germs, too much stress, blah, blah, blah! Is Tack there with you? I was scared shitless. There was no information from the airline. I kept calling. I'm not proud of some of the things I said to those yahoos who picked up the phone. And you know me. That's saying something. I'm so glad you're okay. We all are. I want to hear every detail."

Nora smiled at her aunt's monologue.

"I'll tell you all about it when I get home. But I want to know how—"

"When's that gonna be?"

Nora sighed. It was impossible to get a question in with Aunt Mace when she didn't want to talk about something, but Nora needed to know how her aunt's therapy was going.

"I have some more meetings tomorrow morning, but I'm going to try to come home as soon as possible," said Nora, and without taking a breath she asked: "How are you doing, Aunt Mace? And don't ignore my question. I need to know."

Aunt Mace let out a long sigh. "Circling the drain, Eleanor. Circling the drain." Nora's smile disappeared and she tried not to breathe her frustration into the receiver. The phrase was another favorite expression of her aunt's, and though it had been funny in the years past, it was too close to home for Nora now.

"You say that all the time, and it's not funny. How was your appointment this week? You went, didn't you? Even though I wasn't there? Ship took you, right? What did the tests say?"

In the several weeks prior to Nora's trip, the tests monitoring the marker for her aunt's cancer had remained at the same level. Still in the elevated zone, but just barely. They hadn't gotten any worse, which indicated the treatment was keeping the cancer from advancing. But it wasn't pushing it back. They had given up hope for that before Nora left. The answer, they hoped, was in the medicine Nora had bought in Mexico. They needed to start it as soon as Nora got it back to Juneau. They were now a week behind schedule.

"Ship, the old battle axe, made me go, even though I said no. It's never good news. Why go, I asked her. She dragged me anyway, and I was still right. Doctors live to suck the life out of you."

"You didn't give Doctor Shou a hard time did you? And you didn't answer my question. What did the tests—"

"The same! The same," said Aunt Mace, irritation painting her response. Nora knew her aunt had given as much as she would give in this phone call. "Dr. Shou lives to get a hard time from me. You know that. But enough about me. Are you okay, Eleanor? When are you coming home?"

"I'm shooting for tomorrow afternoon."

"Good. Good. I want to hear all about your adventure. You had me worried sick, girl."

"Sorry, Aunt Mace." Nora hated to have put undue stress on her aunt who didn't need anything more to weaken her immune system. She couldn't wait to get home just so she could hug her.

"No sorry necessary. As long as I can see you soon. I miss you," said Aunt Mace, her voice was softer.

"I miss you, too."

"Well, I gotta go. The crones' society is descending upon the house, waiting for me to hand them their asses in a friendly game. Call me when you know when you'll be back."

Nora pictured Aunt Mace at the head of the old Formica-topped kitchen table, Ship and Elphie at either elbow, each holding their cards close to their chests, sipping strong coffee—a little whiskey added to the brew in Ship's cup—as they harped at each other incessantly until one or more of them threw down their cards in disgust. Just another card game at Aunt Mace's place. Nora smiled.

"I will Aunt Mace. Give them hell. I know you will. Love you."

"Love you more."

Nora ended the call to the sound of Ship's loud laugh in the background. Despite the way Aunt Mace had led the conversation, she had sounded frail on the phone. Nora walked back into the bedroom full of worry and tossed her phone onto the huge bed. She'd never forgive herself if the stress of the crash caused her aunt to get sicker. She knew it wasn't her fault, but the blame would have to go somewhere.

Nora stripped out of her clothes and padded into the bathroom. The shower felt like a miracle. The spa-inspired scents of the shampoo and body wash rinsed away the smells of the forest, and the hot water penetrated her sore muscles. Getting the knots out of her hair made her feel human again.

When Nora emerged from the shower, she felt like a new woman. With the dirt of the past several days washed away, her head was clear and her spirits were a little better. She was still tired, though, and the bed looked inviting. However, despite her weariness, Nora couldn't wait to see 4B again. She just hoped 4B was still up for company. Even if it was just to curl around each other and fall into a feather comforter coma. She wasn't surprised she missed her, but the depth of it was a revelation. She really cared for 4B. And it went beyond responsibility. Beyond friendship. Beyond the simple attraction of new passion. She'd been there before with other women, but this was new, and the uncertainty of where their new relationship was going scared the hell out of her. A flood of what ifs tried to fill her head as she stood in her hotel robe and finished brushing her damp hair, contemplating the bags of new clothes, wondering what to wear. Jeans? Sweats? Pajamas? The airline really hadn't held back when they tried to anticipate their needs.

The room phone rang.

"This is Nora Kavendash," she said, putting on her business voice to answer the phone. She knew who it was. The caller ID displayed 4B's room number.

"You sound so… professional," replied the familiar voice.

"Habit, I guess." Nora laughed, feeling silly for her greeting. 4B didn't sound distant. It was a good sign. "In my real life, I answer a lot of phone calls."

"Do you make house calls in your real life?" asked 4B. Her voice dropped to a lower tone. Goosebumps rose on Nora's arms.

"Only for special customers," replied Nora, feeling the proximity of 4B on the other side of the wall. She wondered what she was wearing.

"I hope you didn't bother to get gussied up for me. I'm in my jammies," said 4B, reading her mind. Did that mean 4B was going to cancel their dinner plans?

"Sounds comfy. They didn't miss a thing, did they?" asked Nora, trying not to sound too disappointed. She pulled her own pair of classic striped pajamas from the bag sporting the fancy underwear store logo.

"Nope."

There was a silence and Nora wondered if 4B was still on the line. She wanted to ask her to come over but didn't want to appear too needy.

"Are you still there?" asked Nora.

"Yes. Why are you still over there? Come over. I miss you."

The words sent a shiver through Nora, and she heard a knock on a door that she hadn't noticed before on the other side of the front room. It was camouflaged by wallpaper. It connected her room to 4B's. When Nora pulled it open, 4B was standing on the other side, adorable with her damp hair and pajamas that had yellow ducks all over them. The other room was a mirror image of the one in which she stood.

Nora had thought 4B beautiful before, but with all of the grit washed away, and her damp hair brushed back, standing there all fresh and glowing, she took Nora's breath away.

Nora hung up and tossed the cordless phone onto the seat of a chair, followed by her pajamas. She didn't think she'd need them now.

"I was worried you would want to be alone tonight," she said, reducing the gap between them.

"Are you kidding? With you on the other side of this door? With all of the room there is in these incredible beds? Maybe you didn't hear me before. I missed you."

4B's green eyes flashed in the low lighting of the room, growing steadily darker the nearer Nora got to her. When they were within a breath of one another, Nora took the phone that dangled in 4B's hand and dropped it onto a nearby couch, closing the final inches between them.

"I missed you, too," said Nora, and she wrapped 4B in her arms, kissing her softly.

4B pushed her hands into Nora's robe, opening it, wrapping her arms around Nora's naked torso. Nora shivered at the feel of 4B's fingers skimming over her skin. She squeezed 4B to her, her kiss becoming more insistent. She began to walk 4B backward, toward the nearest piece of furniture, her only intent to be close to her again.

The long hours of the day had been draining, emotionally and physically. They had endured examinations, interviews, and the reliving of the accident and their subsequent survival in the wild. It had been torture to go through all of it again and again and not be able to touch. 4B's kiss drew her into another world, though, and Nora felt the return of the closeness that had been the center of their world the night before. She was impatient to let 4B know she missed her, too.

Even as she gloried in the feel of 4B in her arms, a thread of apprehension tried to steal her dream. What did 4B's unknown life contain? How would it shape their future? Not that Nora had thought much about a future. The circumstances of their union made it difficult to believe in permanency. But hope flared within her, even as the thought gave her heart a mean twist. She refused to think about it. The present moment was all that counted. Her hands became insistent. She unbuttoned the top of 4B's pajamas and cradled her breasts as their kiss became more urgent.

4B moaned into her mouth just as the back of her legs hit the edge of the sofa. She fell back. Nora held the back of 4B's head and fell with her. When they were lying down, her mouth moved from 4B's lips to the velvet tip of one of her nipples. 4B moaned again and Nora sighed as the pliant skin grow firm in her mouth. A pulse of desire tightened her core. Nora pressed against 4B's thigh, her need driving her actions.

The sound of a chime filled the room and Nora barely registered it above the rush of desire compelling her. The chime sounded again. 4B laughed. Gentle hands led Nora's lips from the warm breast that consumed Nora's attention.

"Dinner," whispered 4B, and Nora groaned against 4B's chest. The soft skin of 4B's breasts against Nora's face still claimed her attention, but the insistent chime sounded again.

"Room service," called a voice from the hall.

"Just a second!" Nora shouted distractedly at the unsuspecting intruder.

With an aching reluctance she stood and offered 4B her hand. 4B laughed again as she took it, and once up, she kissed Nora as she started for the door. It was Nora's turn to laugh. She pulled 4B back and pointed to her unbuttoned top.

"I think you need to do something about that. I'll get the door unless you want to give the food service person a different kind of tip."

4B looked down, and Nora witnessed the pink hue, which had started as passion on her chest, deepen and rise up her neck. Nora couldn't resist one more kiss before she answered the door while 4B buttoned up.

🌲🌲🌲🌲🌲

Dinner was wonderful.

After days of meager rations in the woods, followed by limp hospital fare, the food 4B had ordered from the hotel's four-star restaurant was like manna. The entrees of lightly seasoned and grilled-to-perfection New York strip and cashew-encrusted salmon were amazing. Unashamed, they ate every bite, sharing from each other's plates. In similar fashion, the sides of scalloped potatoes, sautéed mushrooms and braised asparagus tips were nearly gone when they pushed their plates away, unable to eat another bite.

Nora swung her leg up, crooked it so she sat with her back against the arm of the sofa, and faced 4B. She eyed the decadent chocolate dessert sitting untouched next to the half-finished complimentary bottle of champagne the hotel had sent up with their meal. It would have to wait. She had no more room left in her stomach.

"We should have started with dessert." Nora rubbed her belly.

"I can truly say I ate like I hadn't eaten in days," said 4B, patting her own stomach.

"I'll never take a decent meal for granted again."

"It all seems like a bad dream, doesn't it?" asked 4B, resting a hand on Nora's leg, leaning her head back and closing her eyes.

Nora studied 4B's profile. She admired the straight line of her nose, lingered over her defined jawline, and took in her smooth face, marred only by the much smaller bandage Dr. Warren had applied to the healing wound on her forehead. Nora was pleased when the Dr. had praised her treatment of the wound, predicting the scaring would be minimal. But it was the pulse at the base of 4B's throat that captivated Nora. She could almost feel it fluttering against her lips.

"Yes, it does," agreed Nora a beat later than she should have, barely remembering she was supposed to respond.

They were quiet for another moment and Nora enjoyed the warm imprint of 4B's hand on her thigh.

"I'm afraid of what I'm going to find out about… things," said 4B, breaking the easy silence.

"When you regain your memory?" asked Nora. She reached down to touch the hand on her leg and watched her own fingers trace the outlines of 4B's fingers.

"Yeah," said 4B, opening her eyes and looking down at their hands.

"If you had to guess, what do you think you'll find out?" asked Nora, venturing into the subject she was so afraid of herself.

4B withdrew her hand and sat up, pulling her legs under herself. She faced Nora.

"That's just the thing. I honestly don't know. I look in the mirror and I know it's me, and I know stuff about certain things, but I don't know how I know it, like the medical stuff when the doctor was examining me and talking to me about my wound, the MRI and ultrasounds. She didn't need to dumb it down for me, and I was aware of that. Thank you, by the way. You did a great job of preventing infection and excessive scarring," said 4B, reaching up and touching the small, white bandage. "And when I went to the bathroom earlier and two women were standing at the sink speaking Spanish I knew what they were saying and responded to them in Spanish like it was my first language. Maybe it is, who knows? But everything else is a great big blank."

"You speak fluent Spanish?"

"Apparently."

"That's hot," said Nora.

"Yeah, right," replied 4B sounding unconvinced. "I can speak another language, but I don't recognize my own name."

Nora ignored the self-derision.

"You're smart, no matter what you remember. It's obvious. And it is hot," said Nora, running a hand down 4B's calf. "I have to admit I have a hard time thinking of you as anything other than 4B, though. The name Grace just doesn't want to come from my mouth."

"I know. Grace Trackton. Grace Trackton," repeated 4B, sampling the sound as if it were strange even to her. "It doesn't sound familiar. It doesn't feel like my name. It doesn't jar any memories loose for me, either."

"You know, maybe you have someone else's boarding pass. You could have picked it up off the floor, or you could have been holding it for someone," suggested Nora, trying to come up with a plausible alternative.

"The ID in the purse they found proves it's me. It was definitely my face in the picture."

"I forgot about that. I wonder why they haven't found your family yet," said Nora.

"They'd tell me if they knew anything. Don't you think?"

"Yes, I think they would," agreed Nora.

They sat for a moment, each lost in their own private thoughts.

"Nora?" asked 4B, and Nora looked up from her musings. "What happens if I find out I'm someone I don't want to be?"

The question surprised Nora. She scooted closer to 4B.

"Like who?" asked Nora.

"I don't know… there are so many possibilities. But the one thing I keep thinking about is, what if… what if I already have someone?"

Nora's stomach dropped. Their ordeal had kept the real world at bay. She knew there was a possibility, but now that it was said out loud, it somehow made it more possible.

"Do you feel like you do?"

"Honestly? No. Not at all. But…"

"But…?"

"But, what if I do? When I'm with you, I feel right. It's weird. It's as if there's something so… I don't know… essential about it. About us. But at the same time, I have this sense that I have to look over my shoulder."

"For a lover or a husband or something like that?"

Nora asked it casually, but inside her guts twisted at the possibilities.

4B seemed to give the suggestions some thought, which didn't provide much comfort to Nora, who waited, barely breathing.

"No. It's more like I did something wrong and I'm not sorry, but I'm afraid I'll caught."

Despite the fear 4B might belong in someone else's life, Nora leaned closer and kissed her shoulder. She'd face whatever it was when it became a reality. Until then, she wanted to support 4B and take advantage of the time they had. She tried to lighten the mood.

"Maybe you're really some sort of conservative, right-wing, church-type. Someone who might be in for a whopper of a surprise when your memory comes back," teased Nora.

"How can you be so sure I'm not this conservative type you speak of?" asked 4B with a playful smile. Nora was happy to see the worry lines on her forehead smooth.

"I know for a fact there is no way it could be true."

"How so?"

"Well, for example, there's this thing you do with your tongue—"

"My tongue?" 4B leaned closer and her eyes darkened. Her hands snaked into the front of Nora's robe and opened it. Nora's sex clenched at the way 4B's eyes devoured her breasts.

"Yes, your tongue." Nora turned so she was sitting back against the couch and pulled 4B toward her so she straddled her lap.

"And what is it I do with my tongue that you like so much?" 4B's hands were now poised on the sofa back on either side of Nora's head and her eyes bored into Nora as her hips moved suggestively.

"You do this thing where you take me to the edge when you have me in your mouth and you wind me up until I explode into a million pieces."

"Oh, that thing. I thought you meant this," said 4B as she lowered her head and took one of Nora's nipples into her mouth. Nora dropped her head back against the couch and sucked air between her teeth.

"Oh, that, too," she moaned. "See what I mean? You are far too talented to be a novice at pleasing women, darlin'," replied Nora, lifting her head and running her hands up and down 4B's sides, slowing to trace the swells at the sides of her breasts. 4B sat up and pressed her center into Nora's lap.

"You think so, do you?" asked 4B. She leaned into Nora with a pleased smile and nuzzled her neck. "I am seriously happy to hear you say that. I hope you mean it."

"Oh, I mean it," said Nora, tilting her head to give 4B more space to work with. 4B had an amazing talent for hitting all of her favorite spots, and some new ones she didn't know she had. Every one sent a path of fire to her core. Her next words were breathless. "That thing you're currently doing? Expert workmanship."

"This just feels so right," murmured 4B, pulling Nora's head toward her to kiss her mouth. Nora couldn't agree more.

✦✦✦✦✦

The next morning began earlier than Nora wanted. 4B's bedside phone rang at 8:00 AM, waking them both from the kind of sleep that only comes from a long night of making love. Nora snuggled against 4B as she eavesdropped on her side of the conversation. It was the airline. They had been expecting the call, but both of them wanted all of the meetings and interviews to be over. Nora wondered if they had found 4B's family.

She rubbed the sleep from her eyes and listened to 4B make plans for the airline to send a car around to get them in an hour. As 4B hung up, the phone in Nora's room began to ring through the door adjoining their rooms, which still stood wide open. Of course, the airline didn't know they were sharing a bed, so they were calling her now. She thought about letting it go to message, but she reluctantly got up and went to her room to answer it.

When she came back to 4B's room minutes later, wrapped in another hotel robe, 4B was still in bed. She sat with her back against the headboard, sheet pulled up to her chest, and a sour look on her face.

"I want all of this to be over," she said.

"I know you don't mean this," said Nora, crawling up the bed from the foot, kissing a trail to 4B's throat, starting at the exposed skin at the top of the sheet just above her breasts.

4B responded by sliding down onto her back and pulling Nora on top of her.

"I want to make you come at least one more time before the real world claims us today," whispered 4B into Nora's ear, as she slipped her hand into the open front of Nora's robe, sliding her fingers over Nora's ready center.

"Please," moaned Nora, as she spread her legs over 4B and pulled the sheet down to expose 4B's breasts. 4B's fingers were deep inside of her, and Nora rocked above 4B, trying not to come immediately. But when she looked at 4B naked beneath her, any hope of holding back was lost and a sudden orgasm rolled through her, obliterating any ability for control. She was still shuddering from the unexpected release as she slid down 4B's body and skimmed her tongue through the silken heat between 4B's legs. When she took 4B's swollen clit between her lips, 4B came instantly with a loud cry and Nora buried her face in the pulsing wet until the waves of 4B's orgasm subsided. Afterward, Nora lingered with a sated stillness, her lips cupping 4B's center, kissing the swollen flesh. Only when 4B signaled she wanted

Nora to move back up, did she crawl up to lie against 4B's languid body.

"I'm sorry it was so fast. Let me take my time with you in the shower," smiled Nora.

4B lifted her hand to stroke Nora's face and then let it fall with a thump back to the bed.

"Okay, but I won't be able to walk today."

"That's my goal."

🌲🌲🌲🌲🌲

"I have to get back to my aunt," said Nora when they were alone again later that day. It was early afternoon. Another day of interviews had left her tired and cranky, and she longed to crawl back into bed and curl around 4B's wonderful, soft body. But she had talked to her aunt again that morning, and she sounded worse than the night before. "She's not doing very well and they don't need me here anymore. I've considered sending the medicine ahead, but it will get to her faster if I take it to her myself. Besides, I just need to see her. Make sure she's okay."

"When are you leaving?" asked 4B, picking at the salad she had ordered from the airport restaurant. The meetings today had been with the FAA as well as North Star Airlines, so they'd gone to the airport. Now, they sat at a table in the food court and watched passengers move like busy ants from place to place. The airline had given them cards allowing them to purchase almost anything they wanted from any of the vendors at the airport. They also had unlimited access to the VIP lounges in any airport North Star flew out of across the world. It appeared that surviving an airplane crash came with a lot of perks.

"I'm leaving for Juneau this afternoon. Tack is flying in to pick me up."

Nora wanted to ask 4B to come with her. But 4B still hadn't heard anything about her family, and Nora didn't want to further complicate her already complex situation by asking her to come home with her. On the other hand, when Nora left, 4B would be on her own, not only in a strange place, but also in a strange world. With no memory, she had no one, no place to go to, and it had to be scary. All of that, and there was the very selfish fear Nora had that there was someone waiting for 4B at home. What if 4B went back home and Nora never got to say goodbye? Nora's heart was in her stomach, but she had to leave. She had to get the medicine to Aunt Mace.

117

"So soon?" 4B set her fork down and pushed her mostly uneaten salad away. Nora's heart constricted at the sheen of tears she saw in 4B's eyes.

"I have to. I don't want to leave you, but I need to get back to her."

"I understand. I absolutely hate it, but I understand."

"What are your plans?"

"I don't have any. The airline still hasn't located my family so I guess I'm stuck here. They promised to put me up at the hotel until they find someone to claim me, or at least tell me where I live."

"It can't be much longer. What about the address on your ID?"

"There's something weird going on regarding that. They called and the address on it belongs to a house of studio apartments rented to students at the nearby university. The people who run it said no one by my name is or has ever stayed there."

"Really? That's weird. What school is nearby? Did they check there?"

"Yes, and they found the same results. Also, the state of Massachusetts doesn't have a record of the license they issued to me. They're still investigating the information on it, though. I get the feeling they have some other avenues to explore, too, but they haven't told me what those are yet. They did ask me if my ID was a forgery, though, if it was possible I was traveling under an assumed name."

"Are you on the lam?" Nora asked, trying to lighten the mood.

"What?"

"On the lam? You know, an escaped criminal or something?" explained Nora, feeling a little stupid for kidding about it, especially since 4B didn't laugh.

"Anything is possible, I guess," 4B replied. She actually seemed to consider it. "But I don't feel like a criminal."

Nora couldn't feel more stupid. It wasn't nice to tease someone with amnesia.

"I'm an idiot. I was just joking. There's no way you're running from the law," said Nora. And then, without thinking, she added: "Why don't you come home with me?"

4B looked at her for a moment without responding. Nora, who had surprised herself with the invitation, realized she could feel more stupid.

"I don't know..."

Nora had already said it, though, there was no taking it back. Besides, once she had thought about it, there was no way she could leave 4B alone, not when she had no one. Part of Nora was still in protector mode and part of her really didn't want to leave 4B without knowing when she'd see her again. If she would see her again.

"Is there any reason why you can't leave?"

"I don't think so..."

"So, give them my number. You can wait in Juneau just as easily as anywhere else." Nora scanned 4B's face to see if she could tell what she was thinking. "Only if you want to. No pressure."

4B chewed on her lower lip and Nora wanted to pull that lip between her own.

"It's a big imposition..."

Nora's heart sped up. She was thinking about it!

"No, it's not. I'm not ready to leave you yet, but I have to go. Please say yes. This is me being selfish."

4B's eyes glinted with promise and Nora held her breath.

"I don't know... what about your aunt?"

It was almost as good as a yes! Nora tried not to act too eager. She didn't want to spook her.

"I have my own place. It's behind her house, in an unattached granny flat, but it's mine. It was supposed to be temporary, but I've been there for almost four years. She wouldn't even know you were there if you didn't want her to." Nora took 4B's hands in hers. "Say yes."

"It's tempting..."

"What do you have to lose?"

"That's a good point. Okay... I'll do it."

Nora let out a happy hoot, making the people near them turn to look at them before she could control herself.

"I'm so happy. Thank you," she said grasping 4B's hands and smiling at her. "One other thing."

"Yes?"

"I'm going to keep calling you 4B. Grace still doesn't work for me."

"I'm with you. I like 4B better, too."

🌲🌲🌲🌲🌲

"You can't tell anyone," said Tack, glancing at Nora over his shoulder, shouting into his mic over the noise of the aircraft.

After an emotional reunion between Nora and Tack at the airport, where Tack ran up to her, picked her up and spun her around until she was dizzy, Nora, 4B and Tack, were flying through the cloudless sky on the way to Juneau. They had on headsets so they could talk to one another but the noise in the cabin was still distracting.

"Tell anyone what?" asked Nora. Nora didn't have a clue what her best friend was talking about. They had been in the air about twenty minutes and Nora had been focused on the hand she held, the one trapping hers in a steel grip. 4B's other hand was clasped around the arm of her seat in a similar white-knuckled grip.

"Under the tarp," he said, both hands on the controls, as he kept the small aircraft steady in the slight turbulence. He nodded toward the secured cargo just behind Nora's seat. His thick, untrimmed beard made it hard to read his lips, but the nod helped Nora to understand she should look behind her.

Nora stroked the side of 4B's face and placed 4B's hand on the armrest. 4B smiled thinly and took a deep breath. Nora smiled back, loosened her seatbelt, and reached into the cargo space behind their seats. She wasn't used to sitting in the back of Tack's plane. Normally, she rode in the co-pilot seat, but this time she wanted to be close to 4B. Good thing she was. The plane hit a bump and 4B grabbed Nora's wrist hard enough to leave a mark. Nora put her hand over 4B's and sat quietly until the small burst of turbulence subsided. It had been a bumpy ride so far. Aside from the helicopter ride to the hospital, it was their first flight since the accident. For someone who didn't remember the crash, 4B was very nervous. In contrast, Nora didn't mind it.

"Sorry. Instinct," grimaced 4B with a tight little laugh.

"You don't have to explain to me."

"How come it doesn't seem to bother you? You're the one who has actual memories of the accident," said 4B.

"I guess it's because I go up in this all the time with Tack. It's little more than a car ride for me. I'm not sure if it's true, but in my mind, this little thing will glide a lot farther than the great big hunk of metal we were in. Check in with me when we get on a big plane next time," joked Nora, and she was happy to see a smile brighten 4B's beautiful face. "Did I say when? I mean if we ever do…" Nora added.

When 4B's death grip loosened, Nora turned back to find out what Tack was so excited about. Knowing Tack, it could be anything. She had learned to be wary of his surprises. He had a habit of playing just outside of the rules. It wasn't that he was a troublemaker. Most of the time his little forays into breaking the rules were harmless. Most of the time.

She pulled the edge of the tarp back to reveal dozens of boxes filling the tight space. The small plane was packed. Tack hadn't expected an additional passenger. But he had just shrugged when she'd asked if he had enough room for one more. He somehow always made it work, no matter what the situation.

"I don't see anything," she yelled toward the front of the craft.

"Pull the cargo net back a little more."

She did, and still, all she saw was the back of a stowed seat.

"Seriously, Tack. Do I have to move shit around, or can this wait until we land and pull all this crap out?"

Nora relaxed into the familiar, and sometimes crude, way of communicating she and Tack used with one another. Her use of the curse words, mild as they were, made her glance at 4B, who had rarely used profanity around her. But 4B didn't look like she was even paying attention. She was pale, and she had her head held back with her eyes closed, her lips a tight line. Nora realized the flight was taking a toll on her girl and she stroked 4B's cheek. Another bout of turbulence shook the plane.

"Fuck!" squeaked 4B, and Nora suppressed a laugh.

"You're looking right at it." Tack's gruff voice intoned through the headset, tinny and hollow. A big hand reached behind the empty co-pilot's seat and pointed to the stack of stowed items packed tightly into the last third of the six-seater aircraft. The last row of seats had been pulled out and left at the terminal in Anchorage to make room for provisions. No trip was wasted when it came to transporting items from the larger cities into the more remote areas of Alaska.

Nora turned back again and scanned the stack of goods.

"It's just a seat… hey! That's my seat!" she said and laughed. "How the hell did you get this?"

"Your lady there told the rescue guys you were a little attached to it. I'd want to keep it as a souvenir, if it was me. So they pulled it up after they hauled you two up. I'm surprised you didn't see them load it in."

Nora didn't want to fight the noise of the aircraft to tell him that, at the time, in the helicopter, she had been trying to help 4B, who was on the verge of an anxiety attack—white knuckled, thin lipped, eyes open and glassy. 4B had been about to hyperventilate, and suspecting that the helicopter had triggered a flashback to the plane crash, Nora had held her and soothed her until her breathing had gone almost back to normal, which had taken most of the ride. 4B didn't look much better at the moment. Nora tightened her seat belt and took 4B's hand, pulling it into her lap.

"You're so awesome, Tack! Thank you!" she yelled into her microphone to be heard over the loud drone of the engine. She leaned closer to 4B, and covered the mic, so she could speak more privately. "You're even more awesome. Thanks for the seat. How are you doing? You look a little tense."

"Just a little jittery. Sorry."

"Don't be sorry. It's to be expected. Your color is getting better. Maybe if we just keep talking."

"Yeah. That's helping. Oh!" The airplane wings see-sawed as they hit a rough patch of air. 4B's fingers tightened around Nora's, and Nora rubbed circles over the back of her hand.

"We're almost there," said Nora in what she hoped was a soothing voice. She remembered the words she had used with the woman beside her on the previous flight she'd taken. A wave of guilt washed over her at the memory of lying to the woman.

"So, how long have you known Tack? You seem very close." 4B was going for small talk, probably to distract herself, and Nora was more than happy to go along with it.

"We grew up together. His mom died in childbirth when he was born, and his dad was a hunting and survival guide, when he wasn't getting ripping drunk down at the local bar. They lived a couple of miles down the road from us, in a cabin outside of town, but Tack would stay at our house more than he stayed at his own. At least until my family moved to Colorado. Aunt Mace tried to take him in, but by then, he was older and didn't think he needed anyone looking after him. He's followed in his father's footsteps on the wilderness guide thing. During the season, he flies groups into Juneau and then packs them out into the wild to hunt and live off the land for a week or more. The rest of the year, he works with Ship, Aunt Mace's best friend, who also owns the main supply store in Juneau. He flies supplies out to the remote cabins. He also takes on odd jobs that require a pilot. We rely on guys like him to get things to and from Anchorage in a hurry. Commercial flights are expensive. The drive is long and hard, when the road is even open, and no one but tourists take boats."

As she talked, Nora noticed 4B relaxing, even though the ride was still as bumpy. She was happy when Tack shouted back to them.

"We're dropping in for the landing. Buckle up if you took 'em off."

"Take it easy on the landing, Tack. Remember you have precious cargo," yelled Nora, squeezing 4B's hand.

"What are you trying to say?" asked Tack, grinning back at her.

"It wasn't a challenge, if that's what you thought! There's a bottle of Stranahan's whiskey in it for you if you set us down slow and steady."

"That's what I'm talking about!" Tack hooted and then announced his presence to the tower.

The landing was smoother than glass, but Nora noticed it wasn't until their feet were back on solid ground that 4B's color completely returned to normal.

🌲🌲🌲🌲🌲

Nora said goodbye to Tack as he drove away after dropping them off and watched 4B's reaction to the first view of her home. She was well aware of Juneau's charm and that the town was radiantly beautiful in the golden light of the last days of summer. There was still a lot of green, but fall was sneaking in. Leaves danced across the native grass lawn, and golds and reds were splashed among the trees lining the river behind the houses. But, 4B was staring at the landscaping art decorating the yard.

She watched as 4B took in the display as they walked past a hollowed-out tractor engine repurposed as a mailbox, a metal bedframe acting as a flower planter, a fountain made from a cascading line of porcelain water pitchers, wind chimes made from flattened spoons, and a variety of other landscaping decorations that adorned the front yard of her aunt's wood-sided A-frame. A wide porch spanned the front of the small house, and a spray of antique metal signs gave color to the front wall. The neat and tidy yard and house wore an assortment of whimsical and colorful art installations.

"This is amazing," said 4B and Nora smiled.

"My place in back," she said pointing to a miniature version of the bigger house they stood in front of. "But Aunt Mace is waiting in here."

Instead of walking down the side path, Nora led 4B up the worn front steps of her aunt's cabin and opened the red-painted front door.

"Ship? That you?" called a voice from the back of the house.

"No, but we saw her at The Strut when we flew in. It's me, Aunt Mace. And I have…"

A jangle of metal burst from the back of the house, like a handful of silverware had been tossed into a stainless steel sink. Seconds later, a tiny woman in a blue work shirt with the sleeves rolled up past the elbow, padded into the living room where Nora and 4B stood. She paused with a dishtowel dangling from her hands.

"Eleanor!"

Nora's throat felt tight, so she just nodded her head and opened her arms as Aunt Mace walked into them. Aunt Mace felt so fragile in the circle of her arms, but Nora couldn't bear to comment on it, though she'd never held back anything else from her aunt, who was more like a mother to her.

"Aunt Mace, this is 4… I mean, this is Grace Trackton," said Nora finally, after clearing her throat. "She's the woman I told you about."

"Heavens, gal! You didn't tell me how pretty she is!" said Aunt Mace, opening her arms to 4B in greeting.

Nora watched 4B accept Aunt Mace's hug and swallowed back a surge of emotion. Aunt Mace looked like she had lost several more pounds in just the week and a half since she had last seen her. Weight she couldn't afford to lose. Her hands were thin and claw-like, and the skin around her eyes seemed to have retreated, so the ever-watching orbs, which still shone with an internal light, had a sunken look to them. The scarf she wore on her chemo-denuded head just contributed to the frail appearance.

"It's nice to meet you, Ms…?" smiled 4B, and she looked at Nora and then back to Aunt Mace. "I don't know what to call you."

"People call me all sorts of things, but Aunt Mace will do," laughed the older woman. Nora realized she had missed Aunt Mace's quick wit. Tired or not, the woman could spit one-liners and sarcasm like a Gatling gun.

"Well, it's nice to meet you, Aunt Mace. Nora has told me a lot about you."

"That means I need to get caught up on you, since Nora hasn't told me a damn thing about you. Do you drink coffee?"

"A cup sounds nice."

"You gals go ahead and stow your gear and then come on back up here and tell me all about your adventure. Shit-fire!" the old woman added, and Nora dodged a flick of the towel she held. "You had me worried!"

"I'm so sorry you had to worry, Aunt Mace."

"Don't waste time feeling bad, Eleanor. You're safe and sound now. It's all that matters. Now go get settled while I fix us up some coffee."

Nora led 4B through the kitchen where Aunt Mace was already starting to pull out the things needed to make coffee. She'd already started the grinder and the rich smell of the fresh coffee grounds blending with the familiar smell of Aunt Mace's house reminded Nora that she was finally home. They went out the back door, and 4B threaded an arm through Nora's.

"Eleanor?"

Nora laughed. She was used to the question. She didn't look like an Eleanor, and never went by it. It had also taken her a big chunk of her life to appreciate the shortened form of Nora. She considered the names old fashioned and, at one time, had tried to get people to call her Lea, but it had never stuck. Now, she kind of liked Nora and only tolerated being called Eleanor from Aunt Mace and Aunt Mace's two best friends.

"My mom named me after Eleanor Roosevelt."

4B studied Nora for a moment.

"I don't see it."

"Me either. I've never gone by it. Even as an infant, my mom called me Nora. Aunt Mace is the only one who has ever called me Eleanor. Well, her and her friends Ship and Elphie." Nora explained the rest to her as they made the short trip from the main house to the small one behind it. "So, it's Eleanor or Nora, depending on who you are. That's the story, and I'm sticking to it," said Nora, opening the door and standing in the tiny mudroom opening into the small cabin.

"Well, Nora's my favorite name, now," said 4B, with a gaze into Nora's eyes that made Nora want to kiss her.

"Is it now?" she asked, refraining from doing any of the things that teased through her mind. "I'd give you the tour, but I'm afraid if we got near my bed, the coffee will get cold."

"I completely understand. I would want to take my time with you, anyway," said 4B, giving Nora a quick kiss and dropping her bag near the front door. Nora wrestled with the urge to grab her and take her upstairs anyway, but she just watched 4B gaze around the open area of the first floor, much of which was dominated by the living room. Then they retreated back to the front porch.

"You and your aunt certainly have different tastes," said 4B taking Nora's hand as they descended the front steps.

Nora's décor was minimalistic in comparison to her aunt's house, where every space was occupied with colorful art, knick-knacks, and crafts. In contrast, Nora's open living room displayed only a handful of well-loved pieces of art adorning the walls, and a half-dozen carved totems gracing the surface of a few shelves and tables. Books filled the floor-to-ceiling shelves of one wall, and a low table standing behind her work desk was stacked with computer equipment. Other than that there were a few other pieces of furniture, but the room was uncluttered and neat.

"My aunt is a famous homesteader," explained Nora, as they walked back to the house.

"Homesteader? Isn't the time of homesteading—even in Alaska—long over?"

Nora laughed.

"You're thinking of the homesteaders who settled our vast continent in the frontier days. Like Laura Ingalls Wilder and Mary Meyer. Today, it's a term used to describe a person who finds artful uses for things that would normally be discarded. You know—someone who makes a shelf out of a wine crate or a picture frame out of an old window."

"Oh. A recycler."

"Yeah, only a recycler on crack. A homesteader makes recycling into an art form. Aunt Mace is the queen of it."

"A local celebrity?"

"She's an international celebrity."

"She doesn't strike me as a traveler."

"She's never left Alaska. Hell, I don't think she's ever left Juneau. But she doesn't need to. She has a website."

"A website?"

"It started out as a blog and then went viral. The world knows her as Auntie Mace from Mace's Place."

Nora didn't have time to explain more, since they were already at the back stairs to Aunt Mace's house.

🌲🌲🌲🌲🌲

Nora moved around the small kitchen preparing a simple dinner for three while 4B played gin rummy with Aunt Mace. When 4B started to lie down her cards for the third hand in a row, Aunt Mace tossed down her own cards in disgust.

"I believe you have deceived me about your inexperience at rummy, young lady."

"I told you she can't stand to lose," said Nora in response to the helpless look 4B gave her. "Aunt Mace, I warned you she just has phenomenal first timer's luck."

"I think she's just pulling the wool over our eyes."

Nora shot a look at Aunt Mace, trying to tell the feisty woman to play nice. Aunt Mace was the most competitive woman Nora had ever known, and even though the teasing was in good fun, the woman's strong personality could be a bit intense at first. She didn't want 4B's feelings to get hurt. But 4B winked at her, telling her it was okay.

"There's nothing wrong with a little teasing. And to be honest, I could be the gin rummy world champion for all any of us know. But until you told me the rules tonight, I had no idea how to play."

Nora, with 4B's permission, had told Aunt Mace about her amnesia.

"Well, it's nice to see someone else win for a change," said Nora. "The ladies come over almost every day and Aunt Mace rarely lets them win. So don't let her beat you down." Nora turned back to stir the spaghetti sauce, but spun back with the spoon in her hand. "Oh! And, no matter what she says, don't play her for money!"

Aunt Mace was about to respond when 4B cut in.

"So, Nora told me you have a thriving web business, Aunt Mace." 4B looked innocent as she dealt a new hand, but Nora could identify a skillful subject change when she witnessed one.

"Thanks to her," said Aunt Mace, smiling as she looked at the cards she carefully arranged in her hand. She cackled to herself and Nora knew the look. It said that Aunt Mace thought she had the winning cards.

"I think the way you recycle things is brilliant. Like the flower bed you made out of a real bed frame near the back porch. It's clever and very pretty."

"That's one of my most imitated gardening ideas," said Aunt Mace with a smile.

Nora was grateful for the diversion 4B had created by bringing up Aunt Mace's work. She was quickly learning that 4B was able to fend for herself.

"The rowboat flower bed is a best seller, too," added Nora, stirring the pot of sauce on the gas burner. The delicious aroma of vegetables and simmering chicken filled the room as she prepared Aunt Mace's famous chicken marinara. "That one is really big in the Northeast and Seattle. The metal bed-frame flowerbed is huge in the Midwest, while in Europe people tend to go for smaller containers for their live flower displays—milk cans, teapots, dresser drawers."

"Too bad I can't make money off of ideas," grumbled Aunt Mace. "But I'm not complaining. I have more than I need. Thanks to Nora."

"Would it be crass to ask how the website works? You post ideas and people share them on social media. How do you earn money for your ideas?"

"Advertising revenue," said Aunt Mace pulling a card and grimacing. She tossed it onto the discard pile with a disgusted tick of her tongue.

"At first it was just the placement of click-through advertising on Aunt Mace's site," explained Nora. "Alaskan tourism is pretty lucrative, if you can figure out how to get your hands on it, which we did. Then it was through pushing traffic to linked pages. But now she makes the most money from consulting."

"Consulting?"

"Aunt Mace has a blog called "I have this thing…". As in I have this thing that I want to do something with, but need some help figuring it out. People pay ten dollars and submit a picture of something they want to convert into something useful and Aunt Mace sends them ideas. They get one idea described in an email for ten dollars, three ideas for twenty-five. She'll draw a picture and sign it, if they send her fifty dollars. I've been trying to get her to at least double the price for the drawing."

"Who wants to pay a hundred dollars for an old woman's crayon drawings?" asked Aunt Mace. Then she laid down her cards and cackled. "Got ya!"

"They're far from crayon drawings, Aunt Mace," said Nora, snapping a dishtowel at the back of her chair and leaning back against the counter to watch the two women play cards.

"They are exactly that—crayon drawings," said Aunt Mace counting the points 4B held in her hand. "Hey! You could have gone out already!"

"Oh! I suppose so," said 4B, looking at her cards. Nora suspected the innocent look wasn't completely genuine. "I guess I was distracted."

"Those crayon drawings, as you like to call them, are unique and a testament to the homesteading genre you've almost single-handedly grown into a cottage industry in the last twenty years. They go for hundreds of dollars on auction sites, the demand is so high," responded Nora. "You'd make a mint if you realized what you do is actually art."

"Pfft!" said Aunt Mace, discounting the comment with a dismissive wave as she watched 4B deal out a new set of cards.

"She makes all of her art supplies by hand. She reconstructs crayons melted down from the broken discards donated by the local school, and she even makes her own inks and paper. Her drawings are excellent. She uses a voice recognition program to dictate the ideas, so she can churn through several of them in an hour. But the pictures can take an hour to draw by themselves. She's a true artist. A bunch of her work is displayed in a gallery down by the marina, and another gallery in Anchorage sells out of them as fast as they get them," explained Nora. "They're all originals. She won't do re-prints."

"I'm the goddam Bob Ross of Alaska!" said Aunt Mace sarcastically. Then she pointed at 4B's cards. "Now, you! You need to concentrate. I don't want to win because your mind is somewhere else. Focus."

4B nodded obediently.

"She's been compared to Thomas Kinkade because of the 'bright whimsy' of her work," bragged Nora.

"Really?" asked 4B. "Can I see some of it?"

"I don't keep it here. That would be like displaying a portrait of yourself in your own living room," said Aunt Mace, as she discarded a king.

"She doesn't display her photographs either. It's all in her studio."

"Photographs?" asked 4B, picking up the last several discarded cards, up to a four of hearts. She laid down a run of hearts ace to five and then discarded. She still had several cards in her hand and Nora wondered if Aunt Mace was about to win another hand, the beginner's luck having worn off.

"Aunt Mace used to be a photographer before she started the homesteading stuff."

"What kind of photography?" asked 4B.

"Local wildlife, some studio work," answered Aunt Mace, drawing a card. "It's probably what gave me this rot-gut I got. The doc says all the mercuric acid in the development process seeped into my pancreas and festered. That was all before the digital camera, doncha know. But I loved taking photos. Capturing wild things on film. Developing my own prints."

"Do you do portraits?"

"I had a contract with the local school district for a while. But I stopped doing it right quick. I think I lasted three years. Those kids were assholes."

"Aunt Mace!" said Nora putting down the spoon she used to stir the sauce.

"They were!" insisted Aunt Mace. And then to 4B, she said: "Kids know I hate them, so they mess with me." Aunt Mace tossed the card she'd just picked up onto the discard pile.

"You don't hate kids," insisted Nora.

"I really do," said Aunt Mace looking up at 4B and then back down at her cards. Then she nodded her head at Nora. "She just doesn't like to hear me say it out loud. Thinks it's bad karma or something. It is what it is, is what I say. It doesn't make me a mean old bitch. It makes me honest."

"I have never called you a mean old bitch!"

"It's what you were thinking, admit it," replied Aunt Mace without looking up from her cards.

"It is not! I know from experience. Kids like you. When they act like assholes, as you so kindly refer to them, it's just because they're trying to get your attention. Besides, I was a kid once. You were nice to me."

"Well, truth be told, you were a little bit of an asshole, too," replied Aunt Mace, picking up the card 4B had just gotten rid of and winking at 4B.

Nora's jaw dropped at her aunt's declaration. She'd never heard this part before. Aunt Mace had never told her she hadn't liked her.

"You were nice to me, though!"

"Only because I loved your mother. I was nice to her spawn out of respect. It's only now you've grown up, that I can say I truly love you."

Nora saw the mischievous grin and the wink Aunt Mace gave to 4B when she thought she wasn't watching and she knew she was being played just as hard as those cards were.

"I love you too, you old crab cake!" Nora gave her aunt an impulsive hug.

"You two are cute," said 4B, holding her cards to her chest. Nora thought she caught a look of longing in her eyes and wondered if 4B missed her family. "Can I see some of your drawings and photographs sometime?"

"Sure. Nora can take you down to the studio. I don't leave the house much these days unless someone drags me out to see that vampire of a doctor of mine."

"Where's your studio?" asked 4B, drawing a card and laying the rest down before tossing out the two of spades.

"Dammit all! You had the card I was looking for!" groused Aunt Mace, laying down her cards to count up the points she was set back.

"Sorry," said 4B.

"Don't be sorry," said Nora. "Aunt Mace's reign as card queen won't be diminished by losing a game or two. She used to work out of the space I live in now. But when I moved back, she took a studio down near the airport. The city wants her to move it closer to the marina, where the cruise ships come in, to attract the tourists. But she likes it where it is."

"I can walk to work if it's at the airport. The marina is too far away," said Aunt Mace. "Of course, these days I can't walk to the bathroom without taking a break."

"I'd drive you," offered Nora, just like she had a thousand times before. Aunt Mace always exuded a brilliant energy when she spoke about her work, but she rarely spoke about it anymore. Nora wanted to see more of that old spark, the spark she was seeing now. If Aunt Mace moved her studio to the marina, where tourists and friends alike would congregate to see her work, maybe the spark would heal her. But for the first time, Nora wondered if Aunt Mace was too tired to deal with all of that any more. She was sick. And she was getting older. Nora wasn't ready to accept that the almost blinding energy her aunt had always exuded was starting to dim.

"I've been taking care of myself for seventy-two years, Eleanor. I don't need you to start taking care of me now. Besides, I'm sure you've told 4B about your work. What I do is a hobby. What you do is amazing. I don't even understand it, but I know it's changed the world."

Nora smarted from Aunt Mace's comment about being able to take care of herself. At the same time, she also felt the embarrassment of becoming the sudden center of attention. The mix of emotions she felt made her feel a little out of control so she turned away to stir the pot on the stove.

"Actually, she hasn't told me much about her work other than she works on computers," said 4B, shifting an expectant smile from Aunt Mace to Nora.

"You haven't told her what you do, Eleanor?" asked Aunt Mace, picking up the cards and executing a crisp shuffle.

"It's boring, and it hasn't changed the world," said Nora, adjusting the fire under the pot.

"It changed my world. I'd be living off of social security and my Alaskan Permanent Fund stipend if you hadn't used your technology on marketing my nonsense."

"Your work may have started as a hobby, but it is not nonsense," countered Nora. Then she turned to 4B. "Aunt Mace is the queen of creative inspiration. I guess you can say I created a way to market it. I built a marketing software program designed to identify and leverage a target audience to support her work, and it sort of took off."

Nora hoped the explanation would get the spotlight off of her. Although software development was fascinating to her, and she'd stood in front of countless audiences talking about her work at one time in her life, she knew it was boring if you weren't in it. And she didn't want to see 4B fake interest when she tried to explain it.

"'Sort of took off', my fanny! She invented something that almost every retail website uses to hawk their products. Tell her, Eleanor."

Nora sighed, embarrassed to be put on the spot. She'd spouted her elevator speech countless times for marketing reasons, but it was embarrassing when she was using it to explain who she was to someone, especially 4B. "The concept isn't unique. It uses a protocol that embeds information in images that sends information back to the originator so they can track the use of the image. The information is fed back to a program—"

"In English, Eleanor. Can't you see the girl's eyes are glazing over?"

"I am speaking English. I don't know how to explain it any other way." She sighed and put the spoon she'd been holding on the counter.

"Lay it on me. Who knows, I might be a big time computer nerd," said 4B. Her smile gave Nora a little encouragement to try to explain.

"I found a way to bridge the user privacy/targeted marketing gap for online retail. The program I developed uses an algorithm to parse certain information so the originator can predict behavior and then discretely market to them without spamming or stealing personal information from them. Like I said, the concept isn't unique. People have been doing it for a long time. But the predictive algorithm that protects people's identity is all mine, and it's what sets it apart."

"The damn internet is full of companies collecting and selling information about people that they have no business having!" declared Aunt Mace. "Or worse! Damned NSA! National Security Agency, my patootie! More like Nosey Scumball Assholes!"

Nora shrugged and laughed along with 4B before she continued.

"I had to do a project my senior year in college, where I majored in programming and engineering. Aunt Mace was uploading her ideas to a simple website I designed for her to display her homesteading ideas. Her work started to go viral as social media became more popular. She was getting major attention, but none of it was making her any money. She was spending more money on the servers she had to employ to keep up with the traffic hitting her website than she was bringing in. One day she joked that she could break even if she got a consulting fee for the ideas she came up with. So, I worked on it for my senior project."

"How does it work?" asked 4B. Nora wondered if 4B was just being nice by asking, but she tried to explain.

"By tracking unique image codes embedded in advertisements that, when triggered, will initiate an alg—"

"English, Eleanor!" Aunt Mace interrupted with an impatient wave of her hand. Aunt Mace rolled her eyes and turned to 4B. "There's some code on the pages, and somehow there is some matching of the whatchamacallits to the IP addresses, which tracks behaviors and files it away somehow. But the main thing is humans can't see it, and they can't take the information out of it," explained Aunt Mace. Nora was impressed by how much Aunt Mace retained of the technical detail, for all her bellyaching about the technical speak.

"That's pretty much it. It's also the unique aspect that sets it apart. The program can only suggest options to the user, who gets to choose to use it or ignore it. Depending on what the user selects, the program drives traffic back to Aunt Mace's website where the user can create an account, become a contributor, or buy something. Contributors get to trade with each other and Aunt Mace. Those who just want to purchase can do just that. The whole process is meant to be gentle and non-invasive. Users can accept the invitation or ignore it and they're not bothered again. They can be anonymous or be themselves. Privacy is a priority."

Nora paused to see if 4B was still with her.

"I think I get it," said 4B.

"See Eleanor? If you speak in regular people language, their eyes don't get that glassy look."

"Thanks for the lesson, Aunt Mace," Nora intoned.

"The end result is that people are more active when they feel safe, and active people spend more money and attract more users," added Aunt Mace.

"I don't claim to understand all of it, but it sounds very smart," said 4B, sounding impressed.

"Damn smart, actually. She founded an entire company on it," bragged Aunt Mace, dealing a new hand.

"I thought you said you were a computer doctor," said 4B, glancing at Nora. "This sounds a lot more complex than fixing computers."

"The fixing of computers is what I do now. I sold the software company before I moved up here."

"For a pretty penny, too," chimed in Aunt Mace. "She never has to work again if she doesn't want to. Neither would her kids, if she had any. Or her kids' kids. Or her—"

"I think she gets the picture, Aunt Mace," interrupted Nora, embarrassed. "And look who's talking. Your website community runs itself. She has the most loyal fan base on the internet."

"It's a hobby. I like to do it."

"I like what I do, too," said Nora.

"You wouldn't know it from the names you call some of those computers you bring home to work on," laughed Aunt Mace.

"Oh, those names are for the people who abuse their computers with some of the garbage they download onto them."

"You should see some of it," laughed Aunt Mace.

"Viruses?" asked 4B.

"She's talking about what they download along with the viruses." Nora laughed.

"Let's just say that we have a lot of lonely people up here in Juneau. The winters can be sort of long… and the people who produce some of the content those lonely people use for company aren't quite as privacy minded as our Nora," offered Aunt Mace with a wink.

"Oh! Porn!" laughed 4B, covering her mouth as she realized what they were talking about.

"Yep," said Nora. "Behind Utah and Hawaii, Alaska is the most active state per capita for viewing porn. Most of my work comes from cleaning up the malware people don't know they're downloading along with the porn."

"The first time Nora told me what she was doing and mentioned the word Trojan, I actually thought it was a safe-sex thing!" cackled Aunt Mace.

"She shows you this stuff?" asked 4B, looking slightly uncomfortable.

"I didn't mean to," said Nora, needing to explain, hoping 4B didn't all of a sudden see her as some sort of pervert, sharing dirty pictures with her frail and aged aunt, of all people.

"I heard some interesting sounds coming from her front porch one day as I was puttering around in the garden. I could see Nora sitting at her desk, but the sounds coming through the window were very… interesting. Nora didn't answer my knock, so I went in and what I saw over her shoulder… well, let's just say that what was displayed on the screen was not something my Nora would be into. Me either. Don't get me wrong. I'm no prude. Porn definitely has its place in a healthy—"

"Aunt Mace!" yelled Nora.

"Oh c'mon, Eleanor! I may be old, but I ain't dead—yet! But even I have my lines."

"So you see some gross stuff in the course of your work?" asked 4B.

"A little," admitted Nora, giving 4B a relieved smile. There was no telling where Aunt Mace would have gone, had 4B not diverted the conversation. "Mostly it's just fetish stuff. I figure it's 'to each his own', you know? Sometimes I see some pretty hardcore stuff that isn't okay."

"Nora busted up an international pedophile ring from up here a couple of years ago," interrupted Aunt Mace with a proud look on her face.

"Really?"

"Yeah. I was cleaning up the temp files on a laptop and saw… some stuff no one should ever see. I called the cops and we set up a sting. It was mostly a couple of folks who moved up here from the lower 48 thinking geography somehow protected them. That's the thing about the internet. You're only a data stream away from the furthest place. Stupid, sick idiots. Anyway. Hundreds of people, all across the globe, got busted the day the sting went down. I'm glad to say I haven't wandered across anything like that accidentally again."

"'Accidentally?' As opposed to what? You say it like you might wander across it on purpose otherwise," said 4B.

"It's another thing she does that's changing the world," said Aunt Mace proudly, getting up from her chair at the table. "Tell her, Eleanor, while I go wash my hands before dinner. Holding all of those shitty hands—"

"Aunt Mace!" laughed Nora.

Her aunt grinned mischievously as she shuffled to the restroom to wash up, and Nora was happy to hear her sound more and more like her old self. For the first time in a long time she had hope that Aunt Mace would pull through this awful sickness. Nora also had the medication, which was in the refrigerator. She had plans to start her aunt on it after dinner.

"So, what's this other thing you're doing to change the world? You're a surprising and remarkable woman, Nora Kavendash." 4B rose from her chair at the table and approached Nora, taking the dishtowel Nora had draped across her shoulder and putting it behind Nora, so she could pull her close with it. 4B kissed her. "It sounds like you're some sort of technical genius and a cyber cop on top of it all. It's pretty hot."

Nora smiled and kissed 4B again. She was proud of all of her work, even the mundane jobs she did to help her fellow Alaskans out, but she was proudest of her work to find and prosecute predators of children. She had no problem telling 4B about that.

"I created a program that searches for predators online. So, in a sense, I do go looking for it on purpose, but it's all contained in the program. When it hits, I just ship it to the authorities and I never have to see anything. The one glimpse I got the first time was enough to make me sick forever. I'm happy I get to help send those sickos to jail."

"So you are some sort of cyber cop, then."

"Only without the uniform or gun."

"That's pretty sexy. I always thought working in computers was a sexy profession—what, with all of the insertion, submission, RAM, GUI, hard drives..." joked 4B, batting her eyes at Nora.

"Oh. You know how to talk dirty to me," whispered Nora, turning down the fire on the sauce and stealing another kiss before Aunt Mace returned. "Then, let me tell you about the software side, and the bits and the bytes..."

"Okay, you two! Enough of the technical foreplay. You're going to ruin my appetite!" laughed Aunt Mace, sitting down at the table. They hadn't even heard her come in.

♣♣♣♣♣

Aunt Mace's energy faded quickly after dinner and she went to bed soon after they finished eating. Having insisted, 4B washed the dishes while Nora went through a stack of mail—much of it from the airline—and when they were finished, they went back to Nora's place. As they climbed the short set of wooden steps up to the front door of Nora's tiny A-frame, 4B walked slowly, staring at the clear, black sky blanketed with countless stars.

"The universe seems to go on forever from here. I've never seen so many stars," she whispered, holding tight to Nora's arm. "It's beautiful."

"I take it for granted now. When I'm down in the lower 48, I have to keep telling myself it isn't overcast when I can only see the brightest stars. But it rains so much here, we have more overcast days than not."

"There's something sweet and piney in the air."

"Ah, the sweet smell is the crabapple trees down by Glacier River. Aunt Mace used to pick them for canning, but this year she wasn't up to it. So they're falling to the ground and rotting. We might get to see some bears down there tomorrow gorging on them. The pine smell, well, that's obvious with the cedar and hemlock all around us."

4B closed her eyes and breathed in.

"I could get used to this."

Nora hoped 4B would have some time to do just that, but she didn't say it. There was no need to press it. Things would fall into place the way they fell into place.

Nora flipped a switch on the wall as they passed through the spacious mudroom and a lamp in the corner of the living room illuminated the cozy space inside of the cabin. The house was one large open room off of the initial mudroom. Gleaming wood floors throughout the house matched the rough-hewn pine paneled walls and high wood-beamed ceiling. A set of rustic glass-paned doors was centered on the back wall, which opened to a closed-in porch on the back of the cabin. A small kitchen with well-kept original appliances from the fifties took up the far right corner of the room, and an open office space, scattered with computer equipment in various stages of dismantle, took up the opposite corner. The entire front half of the space was a living room filled with soft leather furniture and built-in book-shelves, with a big wood stove in the corner. The front wall was composed almost entirely of windows. A huge rag rug that had been in the family for generations covered much of the floor and a scattering of smaller rugs dotted the rest of the floor space. A narrow set of varnished wooden stairs rose up from the left, ending at a loft landing outside of Nora's bedroom. The one bathroom in the house—if you didn't count the property's original outhouse, which was just beyond the back porch—was upstairs off of Nora's bedroom.

Nora looked around and was glad to be home.

"I love that I know where you live now. I can see you sitting in the chair over there near the stove on a snowy evening reading a book," said 4B, pointing to Nora's favorite chair with matching ottoman. 4B looked around. "But where's your cat?"

"How'd you know I have a cat?" asked Nora. She sniffed the air, mortified that Tack might have forgotten to keep the litter box clean while she was gone.

"Hairs on your clothes. Your backpack was full of them."

Nora laughed. Java, her longhaired, mostly black cat, liked to lie in the clean clothes fresh out of the dryer. All of her clothes were covered in a fine layer of the clingy hair. She had gotten used to carrying a lint roller with her on trips a long time ago, but it had seemed pointless to use it when she had ended up wearing half the forest in her clothes after the airplane had gone down.

"You're good. Maybe you're a detective in your real life." She smiled at the familiar shrug 4B gave at Nora's continuous guesses at 4B's profession. "She's around here somewhere. Java! Come here, girl," called Nora, looking up at the loft where she expected to see a curious head peeking down at them between the burnished wood railings. Normally, Java would have run to her when the front door opened, but 4B was new—not to mention the cat was probably punishing Nora out of spite for having been gone so long. It didn't matter that Tack always gave her more treats than Nora ever did.

"Hold on a minute," said 4B, stepping in front of Nora and encircling her waist with her arms. "I can't wait to meet Java, but it's been a long time since we've been alone, and I need a real kiss."

The kiss was slow and deep and Nora lost all sense of anything else except the way her body reacted to 4B's touch. It was a new feeling, the hyper-awareness 4B's kisses gave her. Every inch of her skin sang, and the soles of her feet seemed to be the only things tethering her to the earth while her heart soared into the stratosphere. She felt herself swell and flutter. Her lips became a focal point for the electricity that expanded throughout her body. Everything that wasn't 4B in her arms receded from her thoughts.

When their lips parted, Nora was out of breath. She leaned her forehead against 4B's and enjoyed the feelings coursing through her body.

"God, I love kissing you," sighed Nora.

4B's voice was breathless, too, and deep when she spoke.

"Would it be rude for me to ask you to take me to your bed right now? I'd love a tour later—and, of course, to meet Java, but I want you first."

In answer, Nora took 4B's hand and led her up the steep stairs to the loft and through her open bedroom door. Moonlight shone through the large bedroom window, illuminating a large brass bed covered in a cream colored duvet. Nora took 4B by both hands and pulled her to the high, soft bed situatiated in the middle of the room. When the back of her thighs touched the edge of the mattress, she turned 4B and kissed her, pushing her onto the bed.

"I enjoyed visiting with your aunt, but the whole time I couldn't stop thinking about doing this," said 4B, looking beautiful lying on the duvet, wrapping her legs around Nora. Nora, who was still standing next to the bed, bent forward so she could put her hands on 4B. 4B sat up and slid her lips along Nora's jawline. She left a tingling trail of kisses and nips down Nora's throat. Each sensation went straight to Nora's center, and Nora pressed into 4B as she lifted her head to provide unobstructed access.

"You do incredible things to me with your mouth," whispered Nora, as she slid a hand up the bottom of the long-sleeved t-shirt 4B wore under an unzipped fleece vest. Nora's fingers skimmed over twitching muscles as she caressed the silky skin of 4B's abdomen and ribs, reaching up to cup her breast. The thin fabric of 4B's bra slid beneath Nora's palm, and 4B's nipple responded. 4B gasped when Nora rolled it between her fingers, sending a shot of expectation down to Nora's center.

4B tangled her hands in the hair on either side of Nora's face and pulled her head down to her breast. Nora moved the shirt and vest up, pushing the bra over to put her mouth on the warm bare skin. The velvet texture of 4B's nipple brushed against Nora's lips and she moaned to feel the tip grow even firmer against her tongue. 4B arched into her and Nora wrapped her in her arms, holding her close as she kissed her breasts, only stopping when 4B untangled her arms from around Nora to pull everything off over her head. Nude from the waist up, 4B leaned back on her elbows and raised an eyebrow, nodding at her hips, indicating to Nora the rest was her job. Nora gladly performed the task, removing the remainder of 4B's clothing, kissing the skin she exposed. Her mouth watered as she slid 4B's panties down her thighs, wanting to taste the warmth that hid between them. But she wanted to go slow. She satisfied herself with kissing the crease at 4B's hip, inhaling the fragrance of what would come.

When Nora dropped 4B's jeans to the floor, she stood and studied the body before her. They hadn't turned on the lamp when they entered the bedroom but the moonlight illuminated everything. 4B was a silver-toned portrait, edged in soft light, taking Nora's breath away. Shadows defined her valleys, and light poured over the pale expanses of smooth skin. Nora stared as 4B waited, her abdomen lifting with each breath she took. Nora's fingertips pulsed with the desire to trace every inch of 4B's skin, to learn every line and memorize every curve.

"Now you," whispered 4B moving further onto the bed so her legs no longer dangled over the side. "I need to see you and feel you against me."

Nora made quick work of her flannel shirt and t-shirt, spending more time than she wanted to unlace her boots, but enjoying the hungry look in 4B's eyes as she watched, propped up on her elbows, her breath growing quicker as Nora shed her clothes. 4B idly trailed her hand over her own stomach and Nora couldn't wait to get her hands on that expanse of flesh. Nora didn't wear a bra and her small, firm breasts felt the chill of the air as she finally stood naked before 4B, who extended her hand to Nora. Nora moved to her, kneeling on the soft bed and crawling up so she could hover above 4B, watching her before she lowered her head to kiss her again. When their bodies touched, and Nora's chilled skin pressed against 4B's warm skin, the contrast was exquisite. The feel of their breasts pressed together, their bellies sliding over each other, made Nora shudder. Nora kissed 4B and groaned as 4B ran her short nails up her back, and then down, finally sliding her hands to cup her ass. 4B pulled Nora hard against her, and the wet, warm valley between 4B's legs pressed against Nora's thigh telling Nora just how ready her lover was for her.

They kissed and ground against each other in a rhythmic push that grew more fervent as their excitement mounted. Nora wanted to take 4B quickly, but she let her set the pace, and when 4B increased the tempo and pressure of her motions, Nora's anticipation pulsed, the direct contact of their bodies sliding against each other sending a cascading flow of throbbing electricity through Nora's center, bringing her so close, so fast. 4B's hands ran over her back, pulling them tighter together, which brought her closer still.

"I'm about to come. Can you feel it?" asked 4B, breaking their kiss, breathless, her eyes pierced Nora with their intensity, so dark, the brilliant flare of desire seeming to reflect the stars that could be seen through the uncovered window beside them. Nora shifted so her wet folds pressed against 4B's core, and her sensitive flesh felt the flutters of 4B's excitement. In tandem, their breaths hissed inward. The sensation caused her insides to contract, signaling the tide sending her into orgasm was about to come crashing over her.

"God, yes, baby. I feel you and it's making me..." Nora held 4B's piercing gaze as she felt the first explosion careen through her body. Her back arched and she wanted to throw her head back, but she held 4B's gaze, letting her see the fire shoot through her.

4B bucked beneath her as her own orgasm raged, and they moved against each other in a frantic dance, their moist centers pulsing together.

Finally, Nora felt the tension leave her body, and she collapsed against 4B, capturing her lover's mouth again, getting lost in the soft exploration. 4B sighed into her mouth and Nora wrapped her arms around 4B holding her tightly. She rolled to her side, bringing 4B with her and they curled up with their legs entwined, slow kisses conveying the emotional depth of their feelings for one another, the ones that they had yet to express through words.

"I don't think I have ever come that way before," said Nora after a while, trailing kisses into the area beneath 4B's ear. 4B shivered against her and Nora smiled.

"My only experience is you, as far as I know, so everything is pretty new for me," said 4B, rolling her head back and pressing her neck against Nora's mouth. "Everything you do, every touch, feels like fireworks to me."

"Oh. I like that," said Nora, gently biting 4B's neck where it connected to her shoulder, causing another shiver to move through the woman she held.

"You like having that kind of power over me, don't you," asked 4B, slipping her hand between their bodies and stroking Nora's flat belly. Her tone was half-teasing, half-serious.

"I don't know who has more power over who," replied Nora, as the strokes on her belly went lower and she felt fingers stroke her swollen center. A new gush of fluid spread over her thighs.

"You are so wet. I love that I do that to you," said 4B skimming her fingers through the moisture coating both of their legs. She trailed her fingers back and forth and then, without hesitation, pushed them deep into the source.

Nora groaned and rolled away with 4B's hand still inside of her. She spread her legs and shuddered at the sensation of 4B's fingers deep within her.

"Oh, yes. I want you to make me come hard and fast."

She was so ready, and her words in her own ears caused a deep pulse to radiate through her body, her need casting off all thought except being possessed by the woman beside her. 4B's knowing smile spread the heat further as she rose to her knees between Nora's legs and bent over her, her hand like a piston as she urged Nora to come.

"Come for me, Nora. I can feel how close you are. You're so open and hot."

Nora's hips rose from the bed and she grabbed handfuls of the duvet in her fists as she pumped her hips beneath 4B.

"I'm so close. So close," she panted as she felt her lower belly roll and the waves of ecstasy begin to build.

"I can feel it. Come for me, baby. Come on. Oh, that's fucking incredible. Yes."

4B's mouth was on her then, and that was all it took.

Nora looked down to see 4B's eyes watching her, her lips around her clit, the hard thrusts of 4B's hand moving inside of her as she came. She arched dramatically, opening all the paths of sensation to let the tsunami of rolling pleasure roar through her. 4B wrapped her other arm around Nora's waist to hold her up, causing a second round of waves to pound through her as 4B's mouth pulled at Nora's clit and urged the flame to grow. Explosion after explosion rocked her body and she gasped, trying to breathe, crying out, feeling 4B in every cell of her being. Nothing beyond the two of them together mattered, just 4B's breath against her heat, the bright star of sensation erupting. Finally, the storm started to subside, and 4B slowed her motions and, keeping her fingers buried deep inside, her lips soft against her clit, she massaged the inner walls, timing her movement to the subsiding pulses of the muscles within. Nora floated in her bliss, feeling everything, aware of nothing except the woman loving her. 4B kissed her again, running the flat of her tongue through her one last time before she rose to her knees and lay along Nora's body, which was now glistening under a veil of sweat. 4B's fingers remained inside of her, barely moving now, while her thumb circled the swollen and sensitive knot of flesh without directly touching it. Nora moaned and tried to catch her breath as she relaxed back onto the bed. 4B slowly withdrew her hand. Nora missed it immediately, but she couldn't take any more for the moment. She curled against 4B, smelling herself on 4B's breath.

"Amazing," she said, when she was able to talk again.

"You absolutely were," agreed 4B, wrapping her arms around her. 4B placed small kisses on Nora's neck. Goose bumps rose all over her.

"That was all you. One hundred percent you," said Nora, feeling completely drained, but managing to wrap her arms around 4B and drawing lazy circles along her back.

"It's a silly argument I refuse to take part in anymore, beyond the fact that it was all you, a million times no take-backs," said 4B, the last part coming out all in a rush, as if she were trying to beat Nora to some sort of finish line. A child's taunt.

"What's that supposed to mean?" laughed Nora, leaning back to look at 4B. The eyes gazing back gleamed with passion and mischief and seemed to be dancing in the moonlight. Nora was almost overcome with the tenderness rising in her chest.

"When someone declares no take-backs, the other person can't win. I know this as an irrefutable fact, but I have no idea how," said 4B. Her words were light, but Nora could feel the weight of something more in the gaze tracing her face.

"I guess it means you win, then. But once I get my strength back I will have to reciprocate the favor." Nora burrowed her face in 4B's hair, breathing in the smell of her skin, the shampoo she'd used that morning, and a musk that made Nora's pulse rise.

"You just bask. You deserve it after that."

"I honestly don't have a choice in the matter. My body is a marshmallow right now."

4B gave her a triumphant kiss and laid her head back down on Nora's chest. Nora enjoyed the long slow caresses 4B drew up and down her belly.

"Is it weird that I kind of like not having anything to compare this to?" asked 4B. "I like thinking you are the only woman I've ever been with."

"I kind of like it, too," admitted Nora. "Even though there is no way that what you just did came without plenty of practice. You are a phenomenal lover. I've never been with anyone like you."

"Wow. It's a lie, but I'll take it. Thank you," said 4B, and she rose up and kissed Nora until they were both breathless again.

"I speak the truth. I wouldn't lie about something like that," said Nora pulling back and looking her in the eye. It was the truth, but so much more. 4B had a way about her that Nora had never experienced with another person. Not just with sex, but with everything. It was most evident during sex, though. When other people tended to bring along some sort of baggage, 4B was open and intensely present, as if there was nothing else to diminish the experience. Every touch, every look, every wordless communication between them was pure and true. There were no hidden thoughts or feelings. Everything was just laid out there bare between them, and Nora knew exact-ly what she was feeling and thinking. It was contagious, too, because Nora, who'd always considered herself a direct and honest person, felt even more liberated and receptive to the blend of emotional and physical connection she felt with 4B.

4B kissed her again, this time slower and deeper, and then she smiled and lay back down in the crook of Nora's arm. They were quiet for a few minutes and Nora felt her skin tingle as 4B traced her fingers along the lines of her stomach and hips.

"Have there been many others?" asked 4B.

Nora knew the question would come up. It always did with new lovers—the sharing of pasts, the comparison of what once was to what was just beginning. Nora had had the conversation a few times before, but this time she was unprepared for it. She didn't consider what she had with 4B to be anything like what she'd had with women before her. The conversation didn't seem relevant.

"It depends on what you mean by many," replied Nora, knowing she was evading an answer. She didn't know what the notion of "many" consisted of, but she knew, even by most standards, she'd been with more than her fair share of women.

"That doesn't answer my question," prompted 4B.

"I guess you could say I've been with a lot of women," responded Nora, truthfully, wishing 4B would ask how many of them had really mattered instead. As soon as she thought that, she cringed inside. It made her seem callous, a womanizer. She wanted to explain that what she and 4B shared was incomparable to what she had experienced before. She didn't want to make her past encounters seem inconsequential—even though so many of them— the majority, really—had been exactly that—inconsequential. The one that had mattered hadn't ended well, which made even that relationship feel less meaningful in hindsight than it had been during its zenith.

"Oh," said 4B, and she sounded sorry she'd asked.

"You sound uncomfortable now."

"Not uncomfortable, just taking it in. I shouldn't be surprised. You're beautiful, smart, and fun to be around. Casual sex doesn't seem to fit your personality, but why wouldn't women throw themselves at you?" Nora wanted to protest, but 4B, kept going. Her tone grew lighter. "Mostly, I'm just pleased that I compare well against a large group of women, though." 4B smiled, which eased some of Nora's apprehension.

Nora rolled over to face 4B.

"First of all, it was a long time ago. I wasn't really a player then, and I am definitely not a player now. I think it was just the time and place more than anything else, and… well, my life was pretty chaotic."

"You don't have to justify anything to me," said 4B, stroking Nora's face.

"Yes, I do. I don't want you to think that this is casual for me. What we have, it's different than…" Nora found she couldn't bring herself to say what she was feeling. She wasn't sure why, but it seemed too much, too fast, and she wasn't ready to say it out loud, to make it real. Besides, 4B had so much to deal with already. It wasn't fair to saddle her with words implying commitment, when neither of them knew what waited for 4B in her real life. They were in a state of limbo, and maybe once 4B's life caught up with her, things would be different. Nora didn't want to think too much about it. For both of their sakes it was probably best to leave all their openness to what they shared without words. At least when they were making love Nora could be completely open. So, she settled on a partial truth. "You're the first woman I've slept with in a long time—since I moved up here."

"Are there no other lesbians up here?" asked 4B. Her expression was so sincere Nora had to laugh, easing some of the tension.

"Actually, Alaska seems to attract more than its fair share."

"You've been up here how long?"

"Four years."

"How on earth have you managed not to meet a woman in all this time?"

"I've met quite a few—"

"Let me be more direct, then," said 4B settling back a few inches. The almost fierce look in her eyes made Nora's belly flip. "You're beautiful. You're smart. You're fun. You're amazing in bed. How is it you haven't slept with anyone in all this time?"

Nora blushed at the complements, ecstatic 4B felt that way about her.

"It's a long story…"

"I'm not going anywhere," said 4B settling more closely against Nora's side, her fierceness gone. Nora lifted a strand of 4B's silky hair and let it slide between her fingers. A little of the uneasy feeling she'd shed just minutes before came back.

"It's so uninteresting…"

"Does it have to do with why you came up here in the first place? Were you running away from something?"

Nora marveled at 4B's perception, though she didn't think of it as running away, so much as getting some distance from a painful situation. She still owned an apartment in Denver, after all. She'd come to Alaska as more of a short break or a diversion, and somehow it had been extended, and thoughts about moving back had just become more infrequent over time. And once Aunt Mace had gotten sick, moving back had left her mind entirely. Maybe 4B's observation was just a good guess. Either way, she didn't want to bore her with the dull details of a broken heart. It had been so long ago, even she wasn't interested in it any more.

"The guess I made earlier about you being a detective? I think I nailed it," Nora teased, putting off discussing herself a little longer.

"That would be interesting. Oh! Or maybe I'm a cop. Some profession that requires a uniform."

"You like uniforms, huh?"

"I guess I do." Even though 4B's head was resting on her shoulder with her face out of view, she knew it was scrunched up in that cute way of hers, considering the question.

"Well, be careful who you investigate up here. It's common knowledge that criminals move to Alaska to avoid the law."

"They do? And you know this how?"

"Without naming names, I know some people," said Nora, intentionally sounding mysterious. In fact, she really only knew one person who'd admitted they had come to Alaska to avoid jail time for having a little over an ounce of marijuana on them when they were caught in a routine traffic stop in Nebraska. The crime had occurred a long time ago, before some states had started decriminalizing the possession of pot. The person in question wasn't anyone Nora would have ever suspected, either. Elphie was one of Aunt Mace's best friends, someone more easily imagined making cookies for a bake sale than toking up on a fat joint. She was hardly a hardened criminal. As a matter of fact, the confession had only come about because of a sweet wine, and before then, Nora had never even seen Elphie drink anything stronger than coffee. If truth were told, after the shock wore off, Nora liked her more because of it. The unexpected facet almost even made the religion Elphie frequently pontificated upon less annoying. Nora didn't know everyone's story up there, and there were a few others who she wondered about. But unless it was volunteered, people didn't snoop. It was an unwritten law in Alaska. People would give you the shirt off their back, but don't go asking about their personal lives.

4B rose up to look at Nora. Nora stroked her cheek.

"Is that why you're here? Are you dodging the law?"

"Me? No!" Nora laughed. "The only law I've ever broken is the speed limit… or maybe jaywalking. Besides, you're the one we decided was on the lam, remember!"

"True. But it's cool if you don't want to tell me why you're up here," said 4B, wiggling closer to Nora. "I'm just being nosy."

Nora felt bad. She and 4B had just been as intimate as they could physically get, so it was natural for her to want to know more about the woman in her arms.

"Oh, it's not that I don't want to tell you. It's just not very interesting."

"Everything about you interests me."

"Well, prepare yourself for the first uninteresting thing, then. I was running from a broken heart. Well, kind of…"

"Yours or someone else's?"

"Mine."

"So, you weren't running from a long line of broken-hearted ladies intent on revenge?" teased 4B.

"Not even close." Nora snorted. "Well, I guess you could say I was running from a long line of ladies, but none with broken hearts. It sounds gross. It kind of was."

"And…?" prompted 4B.

"Um, well, when I left Denver, it was because I was sick of being the kind of person I told you I wasn't. I was sleeping with a lot of women, none more than once, and no desire to get to know any of them beyond the bedroom. I just didn't want to be that person anymore. I needed to take a break and figure out what I wanted to do with my life."

"Did you fall in love with someone you shouldn't have?"

"No. Kind of the opposite. I don't know where to begin."

"How about from the beginning?" asked 4B, pushing up to sit cross legged next to Nora. Nora sat up too, leaning against the headboard. She pulled an afghan from the foot of the bed and wrapped one end of it around 4B's shoulders and draped the other end over her own legs. The sight of 4B in the moonlight stirred things deep within her. She was so damn beautiful. Nora would have been content to study 4B all night, but a pair of raised eyebrows asked Nora to start her story.

"Okay. From the beginning, but in broad strokes. I guess it will give you more context about why I felt the need to get away when I did."

"You don't need to do it in broad strokes. I like details. I need to fill my memory up again, anyway. Why not with you?"

Nora took 4B's hand and rubbed her thumb over the smooth skin on the back. "I don't think my experience is unique. There are probably a lot of stories like mine."

4B smiled. "Go on. I want to hear it."

"Well, tell me if you get bored." 4B nodded her head and she began. "I guess I always knew I was attracted to girls and I was different from my friends. Things were pretty typical when we were young. We played outside, rode our bikes, built forts, played house, all the normal kid stuff. But, sometime in late middle school things started to change. They all became boy crazy and I felt a little left behind because I wasn't. I still loved to hang out with my friends, joking, talking, having sleep-overs." 4B raised her eyebrows and laughed. "Not those kinds of sleepovers, dirty thinker," laughed Nora. "Physical thoughts came a little later, and by then, I knew what I had on my mind was not what my friends had on theirs. So, I half-heartedly played along. Mostly so no one would single me out. When they started to date boys, I sort of stood on the sidelines and watched. My friends thought I was a late bloomer. But I wasn't. I just didn't know any girls like me and, even if I did, I was too shy to pursue it. There was no one to talk to help me figure things out. I think I would have been able to talk to my mom, but she died before I could get up my courage to tell anyone. I'm sure she would have been great about it, though. My dad would have been cool, too, I think. At least before mom died. But afterward, he was just drunk all the time. After the accident, he went from being the best dad in the world, to... well, not the greatest dad in the world." Nora pushed her hand through her hair. She didn't like how the story was going. She'd never spent any time feeling sorry for herself about that time in her life. She didn't know why she was doing it now. She sighed. "This sounds like a pity party, and there are thousands of stories just like it."

"But they aren't your story. Tell me everything you feel like telling," said 4B squeezing Nora's hand.

"With my dad always drunk and me going through the typical teenage thing combined with feeling on the outside of things because of my secret, things weren't very good at home. So, when high school was over I couldn't wait to get out of my dad's house and go to college. The university wasn't far from where I already lived, but I needed to get away from my dad. We weren't getting along at all—he was always drunk and I was an angry teenager. So, I moved into the dorms, and—bang!—I felt like I was dropped into another universe." Nora, who had been staring at their intertwined fingers as she spoke, looked up at 4B. "Am I boring you now?"

"Not even close. I'm sorry you lost your mom and dad at such an early age. It had to have been hard," 4B squeezed her hand and Nora squeezed back.

"I didn't know anything different, so it sounds worse than it was." Nora wondered why she was minimizing her experiences. "Well, that's not true. I spent a lot of money on therapy to process all of this. It was just so long ago. I didn't tell you to make you feel sorry for me."

"I know you didn't, but I still wish you hadn't had to deal with it when you were a kid. Something tells me the story is about to get better, though. Go on. You moved into the dorms, and...?" Nora grinned at 4B's expectant expression. She had a knack for putting Nora at ease.

"I had never been around so many beautiful women in my life. Suddenly, they were everywhere and, surprisingly, many of them weren't shy at all about being attracted to other women. I think that's how it was for a lot of new students—girls and boys alike. You know how it is, kids get away from home for the first time and—" Nora paused and smiled. "Well, maybe you don't know it now, but when you remember, you'll get it. For kids—especially gay kids—going away to school can be pretty liberating. Some, like me, finally get the opportunity to explore who they are. It was like a candy shop. That's the best way to describe it. A big, gay candy shop. Despite my nerdy major—computer sciences. Being in the Air National Guard kind of made up for it. You know, the uniform. Some women kind of dig that sort of thing," said Nora, poking 4B in the side. She was rewarded with a squirm.

"Plus, I was in search and rescue, so I had to keep in shape, which was in my favor. At first, I kind of made a fool of myself thinking the first few girls I slept with wanted more than just a good time. But I soon learned how to sleep and run. And it was fun for a while. I admit I spent the better portion of my undergrad years playing the field. Thank goodness I didn't need to study too hard to get passing grades, because my mind wasn't really on academics those first few years. But, after a while, I got bored with it. That was about the time when I started to develop the software Aunt Mace told you about. It was easy to bury myself in my work and I stopped fooling around so much. Then, a reporter for a technical magazine came to interview me about the project I was working on. I knew it was a new idea. I just didn't know how interested the technical world would be in it. But, you heard enough about all that earlier."

"I didn't hear this part. Really—I want to know more. Keep going."

Nora sighed. She wasn't secretive. She just didn't think she was all that interesting. It had taken Nora over a year to tell her ex-wife, Christina, that her mother and father were dead. But Nora had told 4B within days. The big difference was Christina had been self-absorbed and had never asked Nora much about her past, while 4B seemed genuinely interested. She filed it away and kept on talking.

"I thought my interview was just a small part in a larger piece about student developers. But when the journalist showed up, I discovered my project was the main topic of the next month's edition, and I was the featured developer. Apparently, I had been identified as an up–and–comer in regard to innovation in the software development world. Being a woman was a bonus. Christina, the journalist who interviewed me, was very complimentary and attentive during the interview. It didn't hurt that she was beautiful, either. I developed an instant crush on her. I had no idea she was in a relationship at the time."

Nora remembered the day vividly. It wasn't until later that she'd discovered the photographer at the interview had been Christina's current girlfriend. It hadn't stopped Christina from flirting with Nora the whole time, though. And Christina hadn't mentioned her girlfriend when she'd called Nora a few days later and asked her on a date, either. Nora had gone back to that time—the start of their eight-year relationship—so many times in her head, chastising herself for not seeing the future in the first phone call. Even though Christina had later insisted the relationship had been on its last legs when they'd met, her girlfriend hadn't thought so. Nora had already fallen hard, though, and by the time she'd finally figured it out, it was too late. She'd been in love.

"The article Christina wrote hadn't even come out yet when a venture capitalist contacted me and offered to fund a company he wanted me to run. I didn't tell him I didn't have a clue about how venture capital worked—or about running a company. I later found out Christina had forwarded the story to him and had pitched me as the new best thing in technology. I was absolutely clueless. I was just blown away that they were interested in my idea and wanted to fund the development. So, with encouragement from Christina, I set up my first company. Before I knew it, I had a group of developers working for me, and soon, we were taking off and Christina was head of our marketing department."

Nora looked at 4B to make sure she was still listening. 4B nodded her head to keep Nora going.

"It was a pretty sweet ride. I had everything I thought I wanted. I was doing what I loved to do—writing code. I had a company that was growing faster than any other software company in its niche. We'd won almost all of the highest awards in the industry, which ensured the success of the company's growth, and I was invited to sit on the boards for other technology companies. All that, and I was barely into my twenties! I couldn't do anything wrong. My relationship with Christina was moving at the same rate, too, and about a year after we started dating, Christina and I went up to Whistler and had a quiet wedding. I even found time to attend grad school. I couldn't have been happier."

"It sounds like a storybook," said 4B.

"It was. As long as the company was in high growth mode, everything was great. Innovation kept us light years ahead of our competition. All I had to do was conceive and create. It was fun and interesting. It got a bit challenging when competitors began to really go after us, though. I had no idea how cutthroat the software industry is. I still have a hard time believing it, yet I lived right in the middle of it. Soon, I was forced to hire a team of lawyers just to deal with all of the copyright infringement that was going on. It was ridiculous. As a developer, I would have given my stuff away just to see it get used—you know, open source coding in a utopian tech world—the dream of all starry-eyed code designers. But as the owner of a company, I had to protect the research and development investment we'd put into it. I had to pay my employees. But no matter what we did, we'd do all the research and development, and then another company would basically clone our work and slap their own logo on it as soon as they thought they could get away with it.

"But even that didn't bug me. It was like playing a game of strategy. Sure it was annoying when customers would switch to one of the thieves who would throw together a cut-rate version at half the price. We always got the customer back, but it rankled me. It was when one of my own developers struck out on his own and started to use the software in ways that came close to abusing people's basic privacy rights. That's when some of the fun started to pale. If I could have just let it slide, I would have. But I had to protect the livelihood of all of the loyal people who worked for us and the innocent users of his application. I had to go after him, and it wasn't pretty. It was public. I won, and he was blackballed from working in the industry. I was in the right, and any other CEO would have done the same thing, but it made me sick to my stomach. He was an incredible developer, and he was a nice guy—still is, really—but he let the money get to him."

Nora remembered Christina's steely insistence that Nora retaliate against Pascale for his disloyalty, and how many fights they had gotten into over how Nora should pursue it legally. Nora had wanted to deal with him personally, talk it out with him, convince him to stop using her code for bad things. And she had tried to talk to him, but he had denied using her code, which was a blatant lie. In the end, Nora had left it to her lawyer, who had gone for blood. They had won. When the trial had finished, Christina had taken Nora out to dinner to celebrate and had followed Nora into the posh women's restroom of the steakhouse and fucked her in one of the two stalls. Women in pearls had used the toilet next to them and Nora got her first hint into what really drove Christina's passions. Still Nora stuck it out. She didn't go into any of that with 4B, though.

"I felt responsible, feeling I hadn't been a good enough mentor for him, that I hadn't been able to insulate him from the lure of advertisers who throw stacks of money at anyone who will get them personal data on a captive audience. Sometime around then, things stopped being fun. I kept going for a little while, hoping the fun would come back, but it didn't. I decided to sell the company. I was really specific about what I wanted and I eventually found a buyer who was supportive of my intent to never use the software in ways violating my basic principles of upholding user privacy. They signed the contract to protect the intent, and then I quietly stepped down. I'm still on the board, which was part of the deal. This way, I can monitor the privacy principal, but now, all I do is figurehead stuff. I fly into Denver once a quarter, sit in the shareholders' meetings, and fly out. So far, so good."

"Wow. You're amazing. I can't even begin to understand how hard all of that must have been. Is this where the broken heart thing comes in? Is it why you moved up here?"

"Well, it turned out Christina was more in love with the prestige than she was with me."

"What do you mean?"

"Shortly after I sold the business, things started getting a little tense at home. Christina wasn't happy living the quieter lifestyle. I thought having the time to go on long vacations, to travel and just spend time together would be a great way to reinvigorate our relationship. I was dead wrong. I had no idea how much she thrived on the industry parties and black tie events we were always invited to. I tried to make up for it. I bought her things—houses, jewelry, art—thinking it might help, but it didn't. She craved the limelight. She liked basking in the celebrity and all the things that come with it. That was the old me, though. I tried to go back to it for her, went to the industry events as a guest lecturer, attended the parties, rubbed the elbows. Ugh! But I hated it as much as she loved it."

"It must have been hard for you."

"It was. I tried, but I just wasn't made to live the hype. I never sought the attention, it just sort of happened, and I was glad when I could step away from it. Then one day, I went to the old office to attend the quarterly board meeting, and she was there. At first, I thought she was hanging out with the folks we used to hang out with, trying to soak up some of the old energy. But then I realized she was being a little more attentive than normal to the new head of marketing, Tessa Hightower, one of the women who used to work for me. When we got home that night, I asked her about it and she came right out and told me she and Tessa had been seeing each other for several months. And that was it. She took all of her things and moved in with Tessa. The company, which had always been private when I had it, went public shortly after that, and Tessa and Christina got to ride that whirlwind. They're still together, living the high life."

"Oh, Nora. I'm sorry."

"Yeah, I was too for a while. We divorced shortly after she moved in with Tessa."

"Was the divorce rough?"

"Emotionally, yes, but as far as those things go, it was pretty amicable. She didn't rake me over the coals, or anything like that. She's not a vindictive person, just shallow—her words, not mine. Aside from the infidelity, she is very open about what motivates her. And, oddly, the money wasn't her thing either. It was always the lifestyle and the prestige for her. She only wanted enough to keep her lifestyle going. Tessa gave her the lifestyle. All she asked of me was a modest settlement and the house in Aspen. I gave her half of everything, anyway. It was only fair. I still have more than I'll ever need."

"How long were you together?"

"Eight years, if you count the one before we got married."

"Then you came up here?"

"Not immediately. That's where the line of ladies thing came in," said Nora with an embarrassed shrug. "If I thought I was out of control when I was in college, I was off the charts after the divorce. The pain of Christina's cheating really did something to me. It was like I was trying to fill a void or something. I attended all of the kinds of parties I had despised going to before, and then some. I slept with more women than I could keep track of. Whatever it was I was looking for, I looked for in every bed I came across. I told myself it was casual, but it wasn't. It was a quest. I was with a new woman almost every night. Sometimes more than one." Nora snuck a glance at 4B to check her reaction. She noted a raised eyebrow, but not the look of disgust she expected. "I was the queen of one-night stands. It was pretty pathetic. I was pretty pathetic, actually. Then, there was the drinking and recreational drugs. Not my thing at all, but you wouldn't have known by watching me. After a while, everywhere I turned, I saw someone I had been with, reminders that I wasn't finding whatever it was I was looking for. I fell into a deep depression. I had to leave."

"And that's when you came here."

"I think Aunt Mace sensed I was floundering. She asked me to come up and stay with her temporarily to help her out with her business. I thought I'd be up here six months. It was supposed to be a way to check out for a while. Fours years later, I'm still here. It was one of the best decisions I've ever made."

"You seem happy here."

"It took about a year-and-a-half, but I kicked the depression. I stopped missing Christina. I stopped feeling angry about everything. Now I'm happy. I have friends. I keep busy. I love Alaska. I might never leave now. It's beautiful."

"You're beautiful," said 4B, and kissed her.

Nora awoke to clear sunshine flowing like liquid crystal over the mountains surrounding Juneau and in through the wide window above her bed. She was home again. And 4B was curled against her side.

She wanted to lie there and relish the happy buzz cascading through her but it seemed her internal habit of waking at 6:00 AM was back on track and a restless energy urged her awake. Rather than disturb 4B, who was sleeping like a baby, she uncurled from around her, immediately missing the comfort of her arms, and slipped quietly out of bed.

The morning air was chill on her nude body as she paused to stretch and gaze through the ceiling-to-floor glass window overlooking the slow moving Glacier River, which ran just behind her house. The trees along it had started to turn and sunlight glinted from the water she could see between the branches. It was a sight of which she'd never get tired. She closed the blinds so 4B could sleep a little longer, and paused by the side of the bed to watch her. 4B hadn't moved when Nora had risen, and she was still on her side, both hands tucked under her head. The crease that often appeared between her eyes when she was awake was smooth. Java, who had finally come out of hiding sometime during the night, was curled in the crook behind her knees.

Although Nora could watch her lover sleep forever, she pried herself away and took a quick shower before she went over to Aunt Mace's house for their morning coffee ritual.

She found her aunt at the kitchen table in the same chair she had been sitting in the night before. It was familiar, a sight that Nora had seen almost every day for the last four years. Some mornings there were friends at the table, too, laughing over a cup of coffee. Not this morning. Aunt Mace was by herself, sipping the dark brew and scanning the newspaper. If it weren't for the new frailty of the woman, and the scarf she wore to cover the wispy remnants of the few hairs spared from chemotherapy, it would have been the perfect picture of home for Nora.

"You're up early," said Aunt Mace when Nora let herself in through the back door.

"No earlier than usual," said Nora as she walked over to pour herself a cup of coffee. Her empty cup was already sitting next to the sugar bowl, along with another cup, no doubt for 4B. She poured the coffee, added sugar and cream and then slid into the chair she had claimed as her own four years earlier.

"I'd have wagered you and that beautiful thing you brought home would have been tuckered out."

"We had time to recuperate in Anchorage. The airline put us up at a nice hotel."

"That's not what I meant. You two were giving each other the sexy eyes

155

all night. I know you didn't get much sleep once you left."

Nora blushed but ignored the comment and took a sip of her coffee. Perfection in a cup. God she loved Aunt Mace's brew. She held her cup below her chin and shut her eyes, enjoying the tickle of warm steam as it wafted over her face.

"Ah! To be young and in love again," said Aunt Mace. Nora looked at her aunt who was staring into her half-full coffee cup.

Love?

"Has your coffee gone cold, Aunt Mace? Do you want me to get you a warm up?"

"No. I can't drink more than a few sips these days. Doesn't seem to please my wormy guts. Nothing tastes good. Bleh."

Nora had noticed Aunt Mace had barely touched the food she had prepared for her the night before, too. Chemo had that effect on her, but she'd finished her last round a few weeks ago. Her appetite should have returned by now.

"What does the doctor say?"

"Does it matter?" The unfamiliar sound of defeat threaded itself through her aunt's reply. It scared her.

"Of course it does, Aunt Mace."

"I'm tired of talking about what the doctor says. It doesn't matter what she says. I'm circling the drain, Eleanor."

"I hate it when you talk like that. You've been saying that for months, Aunt Mace."

"I've been circling the drain for months."

"No, you haven't. The chemo helped. It shrank the tumor. This new medicine will take care of the rest."

Her aunt just stared at her coffee.

"I'm sorry it took so long for me to get it here. But it feels like the Universe had a hand in making sure I did, otherwise I might not have made it at all."

"Or maybe you wouldn't have been on the goddamn airplane in the first place, Eleanor. Have you thought of that?"

Nora was surprised by the question.

"Since I don't believe in fate, no, I really haven't. The fact is I am here, and so is the medicine. Let's see how it helps us."

"How it helps me, not you," snapped Aunt Mace. "It's me who has to take it. No one else. Not you." Nora flinched from the comment as if Aunt Mace had screamed it. Aunt Mace was sometimes gruff, but she wasn't often mean, so the comment, tinged with rebuke, stung.

Nora fought her natural instinct to either snap back or withdraw. She couldn't face the gap either response might cause between them. Not now. She cleared her throat.

"Okay. Let's see how it helps you," she said.

Aunt Mace continued to look into her cup and they were quiet for a few minutes. Nora tried to drink the coffee that now felt like sand going down her throat. She knew her aunt was far more sensitive than she let on and would suffer for issuing the sharp comment, but there was no way to make it go away, and discussing it only made things worse when her aunt was in a mood, so Nora was surprised when her aunt spoke.

"Eleanor, I'm sorry. You know I don't mean it when the asshole in me speaks."

Nora reached over and put her hand over her aunt's bony knuckles, feeling the small, hard scabs dotting the paper-thin skin. She carefully ran her fingers over the hands that had always been so strong and able. Now they could barely lift a coffee mug.

"I know Aunt Mace. I just wish I had a magic wand, you know? The medi—"

"I don't think I will be taking the medicine, Puffinstuff," said Aunt Mace, placing her other hand over their hands. Aunt Mace's use of the nickname she had bestowed upon her when she was a toddler tugged at Nora's heart. Unconsciously, she blew out her cheeks in the gesture that had inspired it, and she tried to keep the tears from coming. "I know you went to a lot of trouble to get it, and I almost feel obligated to go through with it. I promised, I know. But I'd like you to let me out of that promise."

Nora remembered the talk she had with her aunt just before she'd left for Mexico. The doctors down there had refused to send the medicine in the mail because it hadn't been approved for use in the United States yet. Unlike some doctors, they were ethical enough to not want to flagrantly disregard the American law. If she came to them in their own country, it was different. They didn't need to know where she took it. As inconvenient as it was, it had been one of the things that had given Nora confidence in the experimental medicine. The doctors weren't quacks and it didn't feel like she was falling for fish oil. Aunt Mace hadn't wanted Nora to go to so much trouble, but Nora had insisted. And Aunt Mace had finally agreed to the plan.

"Why the change of heart, Aunt Mace?" asked Nora, already knowing the answer. Her aunt had given up. She could see it in her every move.

"I'm just tired, Eleanor. So tired. I just don't want to go through any more of the hoops that I've been jumping through all these months."

"Do you think that simply taking the medicine will be difficult? Are you afraid of the side effects? We can look it up and see if there's something we can do to counteract whatever it is you're concerned with. I'll do all the research." Nora asked the questions, and made suggestions, even though she knew she risked inciting her aunt's temper again.

"I've done the research. It's some of that. Some of everything else," said her aunt in a small voice that broke Nora's heart more than the worst lashing out could have. "Mostly I'm just so scared I might live longer but I won't know who I am anymore."

Nora remembered how hard the chemo had been, the forgetfulness, the mood swings, the day she had found her aunt curled in a ball next to her bed sobbing. Just sobbing. That hadn't been the Aunt Mace she knew. But her aunt had returned to her old self shortly after the last treatment, along with the wispy tufts of baby soft hair. If the medicine worked, there would be another round of chemo. They already knew that. Nora took a shuddering breath and decided she wouldn't try to get her aunt to take her last chance. It wasn't worth it to her to see her so defeated.

"Okay. No medicine, Aunt Mace. I won't try to convince you."

The relieved look on her aunt's face was worth the loss that Nora already felt slip into her heart.

🌲🌲🌲🌲🌲

"Are you sure you want to go out tonight?" asked 4B later that evening as they laced up their boots and got ready to walk the half-mile down to The Strut, a bar located near the airport, a place Nora had told 4B she sometimes frequented.

"Sure," said Nora. She was sitting on the edge of the bed, smoothing out the cuff of her jeans. She honestly didn't want to go out, but she didn't think it was fair to keep 4B cooped up in her small house, or subject her to the geriatric card party taking over her aunt's kitchen that night. After their talk, Aunt Mace's spirits had risen enough to ask her friends to come over.

"You had a rough day," offered 4B. Nora had told her about the decision Aunt Mace had made. "We can stay home. You have a million books here. It really isn't a problem."

"I need to get out, I think," said Nora, though she really would have preferred staying home. But not to read. The best distraction she could think of was in 4B's arms, but they had already done that most of the day, between visits from friends who were happy to see Nora home in one piece.

"Okay. But let's make it an early one. I have plans for you tonight," said 4B, standing up and pulling Nora to her feet. When they were standing toe-to-toe, she wrapped her arms around Nora's waist and treated her to a slow kiss.

"If that was your last ditch effort to convince me to stay home, it worked," said Nora, a little out of breath when they parted.

"Too late. I have my shoes on."

🌲🌲🌲🌲🌲

Before they left for the short walk to the bar, Nora and 4B stopped by to check on Aunt Mace. They were on the back steps, when they heard voices coming through the open window next to the back door.

"Because you're a freakin' cheater, that's why!"

"Shut your dern hole, Elphie! The Lord can hear you bearing false witness!"

Nora stopped 4B on the top stair and turned to face her.

"You're in for a treat. What you just heard was Elphie calling Ship a cheater and that was Ship firing a warning shot. Hold onto your hat. The Girls are here for card night."

"Aunt Mace has card night?"

"Actually, every night is card night. But Tuesday night is for money. And it can get ugly."

"Big stakes gambling, huh?"

Nora shook her head with a smile.

"Penny ante. But they're serious. Ambulances have been called."

"They hurt each other?"

"Well, it's never come to blows, but Elphie threw out her back one time, standing up to confront Ship. If I remember right, the claim was Ship purposefully forgot to burn one before throwing down the Turn, therefore cheating Elphie out of a flush."

"Are you still talking cards?" asked 4B.

Nora laughed. "Poker. Texas Hold 'Em"

"Oh, yeah. The one with Flops and Turns and Rivers and such."

"That's it."

"Maybe we should join them?"

"What? No way! You do not want to get involved. We're just going to pop in to say hello to the ladies, and to tell Aunt Mace where we're headed. Don't let them rope you in."

Nora opened the door just in time to see Elphie flip a plastic bowl of pretzel twists into Ship's lap. Ship stood up with fire in her eyes, pretzels scattering everywhere, but she stopped cold when she saw Nora and 4B in the doorway.

"You gals aren't going to make me call Sherriff Reynolds are you?" asked Nora, placing her hands on her hips.

Ship was tall—well over six feet—and handsome. Her steel gray hair was neatly clipped in a crew cut, and she was dressed in a long-sleeved work shirt, faded but sharply creased sleeves rolled to the elbow. Worn blue jeans and hiking boots completed the outfit. Ship dropped the finger she had been pointing at the woman sitting across from her and pretended to brush crumbs from her lap. She flashed an apologetic look at Aunt Mace and then smiled innocently at Nora. Nora had always suspected Ship of having a secret crush on her aunt, but to her knowledge, the woman had never even admitted she was gay.

"Hell, Nora. There's no need to call the law into this again. I can handle it. Elphie can't help it that she's an old bit—" Aunt Mace put her hand on Ship's arm, and Ship glanced down at it and blushed. "—an old bird. Just a mean, old, squawking bird."

The object of Ship's ire, a slight, old woman in glasses who wore a flow-ered pullover with beige polyester pants and a thick, gray braid down her back, pulled the cards and pennies piled in the middle of the table toward her, but stopped to wave a finger at Ship.

"If I'm an old bird, you're Satan's Asp, you cantankerous old—"

"Girls! Stop it now. Nora has a guest. We don't want to scare her away." Aunt Mace got up from her chair and shuffled over to where Nora and 4B stood just inside the door. Nora glanced at 4B to see what her reaction had been to the bickering. Nora was relieved to see amusement. Aunt Mace grabbed 4B's arm with both hands and faced her friends proudly.

"Ladies, this here is Grace, but we call her 4B. She's the woman I told you about. The one who kept Nora company after the crash while those incompetent testicle sniffers—"

"Aunt Mace!" interrupted Nora. Elphie and Ship always brought the worst out in her aunt.

Aunt Mace snickered and went back to the table. She lowered herself slowly into her chair, and Nora thought her aunt was holding herself like she hurt. It would have made her cry, if the situation around her weren't so comical. Aunt Mace slapped the tabletop. "Well, they took their damn time finding you."

Nora took 4B closer to the dining table, where Elphie guarded her winnings behind the deck of cards she dealt. "4B, the statuesque woman to your left is Ship. She's Aunt Mace's best friend from grade school. She also owns the Mercantile downtown."

"And she cheats!" said Elphie, sneaking a peek at her cards before she poured more pretzels into the bowl she had upended into Ship's lap.

"This lovely lady with the pretzels is Elphie. She used to be the music teacher at the grade school, and now she runs the children's choir down at the church."

"Speaking of which, I haven't seen you at services in a while, Eleanor."

"I was out of town for a while, Elphie, you know that."

"By a while, I mean in over a year, Eleanor."

"Uh, well, business has been pretty busy…"

"Are you two girls going down to the tavern?" asked Aunt Mace, saving Nora the trouble of coming up with an excuse for not going to church.

"Don't you mean the den of inequity, patronized by ruffians and whores?" asked Elphie. She shuffled the cards and looked at Nora over the top of her bifocals.

"That's the place, Elphie." Nora chuckled. "Do you need anything before we leave, Aunt Mace?"

"Naw. We'll be all right. You two have fun. I plan on being a couple of dollars richer and fast asleep when you get back."

🌲🌲🌲🌲🌲

The walk to the bar, which was near the airport, was half a mile down a

161

well-worn dirt road on an easy downhill grade. The sun hadn't yet set over the bay, and the weather was perfect. They carried light jackets with them for the trek back to the cabin later that evening. Nora and 4B strolled hand in hand, taking their time as Nora gave 4B a short history of the area where she had grown up. Her parents' old house was just down the road from Aunt Mace's and well kept by the current owner, a middle-aged woman named Tabitha, who wrote romance novels. Nora also pointed out where she had gone to grade school—in a small school house across the street from her old house. Before they reached the paved road that ran next to the airport, a pair of bald eagles swooped across the sky and perched in the skeleton of a dead tree on the bank of Glacier River. 4B stopped to watch them and Nora stopped to watch 4B.

A few minutes later, they arrived at The Strut, which was in an old Quonset hut close to the airport. Although there were only a few cars in the lot, there were about two dozen people in the bar. Nora explained to 4B that Sherriff Reynolds was a stickler on DUIs so if people couldn't walk it, they begged rides or took a taxi.

Patrons were scattered throughout the room. Some were sitting around a few of the dozen tall tables clustered in the center of the room, a few were squeezed into one of the booths near the back, and a handful were pressed up against the polished wood bar spanning the front of the room. A couple of guys were shooting pool at one of the two ratty felt covered tables in the back, and a woman with long dark hair, generously streaked with gray, swayed all by herself next to the jukebox. Her eyes were closed and she had a glass clasped in her hand, grooving to the sounds of The Grateful Dead. Heads swiveled toward Nora and 4B as they entered the bar, and when they recognized who had just walked in, several people rose to greet Nora, eager to hear about the plane crash the entire town had been talking about for a week.

Nora introduced 4B to the small crowd and then went on to describe their ordeal right up to the point when they saw the sweet sight of Tack's plane buzzing through the narrow canyon the morning of their rescue.

"Crazy fucker!" said Lawrence, the owner of the bar. He'd been sitting on his normal stool at the end of the bar when they'd come in, but had ordered a couple of pints and had wandered over to join the crowd. He handed the beer to Nora and 4B and listened to the tale.

Eventually, the crowd broke up and everyone went back to what they had been doing, and Lawrence walked Nora and 4B to the bar with their empty pint glasses.

"Crystal, give these ladies whatever they want all night. It's on the house. I want them good and drunk when they head home."

Nora thanked Lawrence for the drinks and when Crystal lifted her chin in a silent question, Nora lifted two fingers and pointed to one of the beer taps in answer. Crystal's eyes never left them as she poured two pint glasses of frothy beer from the tap. As usual, she was dressed in a tight black tank top, black jeans and a studded leather belt. A red bandana was knotted at her neck and a thick leather bracelet wrapped around her left wrist. Her bleach-blond hair was spiked perfectly, and the muscles in her well-defined arms twitched as she tipped the pint glasses to pour off the foam. She set the pint glasses on the bar, and in an impressive show of athleticism, she slapped her palms on the wood surface and vaulted the bar without kicking any of the customers or knocking over any of their drinks. She stuck her landing without visible effort right in front of Nora and pulled her in for a hug. A smattering of applause from the guys sitting at the bar broke out and Nora laughed. It was an unexpected greeting, one she'd never seen, let alone received, in the four years of her infrequent patronage of the bar. Nora took it to mean that Crystal was happy to see her alive and in one piece.

Nora returned the hug and then stepped back, pulling 4B to her side to introduce her.

"Crystal, this is 4… I mean, Grace. Grace, this is Crystal."

Nora watched Crystal, not sure how the introduction would go. The flirty bartender, a casual friend since grade school, but never her lover, had persistently pursued Nora from the day Nora had returned to Juneau, just months after Crystal had returned from a six-year stint in the Army. Nora had never been interested in Crystal—not in that way, anyway. Despite Crystal's obvious interest in her, she had kept her at arm's length with the truth that she wasn't ready to date anyone. Crystal hadn't pushed it, but she'd made it clear she would be there when Nora was ready. But now, Nora was here with another woman. She watched the greeting unfold.

"Hi there, "4-I-mean-Grace"," Crystal said with a wry lift of an eyebrow, as she wiped her hands down the front of her t-shirt, accentuating her high, firm breasts and toned abs, all of which were called out in high definition by the skin-tight fabric. Then she offered her hand to 4B.

"Nice to meet you, Crystal. You can call me 4B," said 4B, accepting Crystal's hand.

"4B?" asked Crystal, still holding 4B's hand and glancing at Nora with a raised eyebrow and a smile.

"It was her seat number on the airplane," offered Nora while she tried not to react to how Crystal still hadn't let go of 4B's hand.

"The nickname has sort of stuck," said 4B easily.

Nora was impressed with 4B's poise. The looks, the gestures, the hand-holding—none of it seemed to faze her. She was probably used to women showing off around her, paying attention to her.

"Interesting," said Crystal, finally letting go of 4B's hand. "We don't get many interesting women into The Strut." She grinned at Nora. "Present company excluded."

"That explains the vault," laughed Nora.

"Yes. It was very impressive," said 4B. She didn't seem intimidated by Crystal's antics.

"When Crystal isn't tending bar here at The Strut, she teaches gymnastics at the Rec Center," explained Nora.

"The ladies seem to like it," shrugged Crystal, giving Nora a meaningful look and Nora rolled her eyes. Crystal just chuckled and pasted her gaze on 4B again. "So, you were in the crash, too. It must have been fucking scary."

"I don't think the scared part has fully set in, to be honest." 4B naturally molded to Nora's side with Nora's arm casually wrapped around her waist. Crystal took it in and turned back to the bar to grab the beers she'd left there.

Crystal offered them the pint glasses she'd filled with amber liquid, winking at 4B.

"Thanks," said 4B, smiling back at Crystal, then she turned to Nora, handing her the full beer. "Excuse me for a minute? I'm going to visit the ladies room."

Nora took the beer and nodded toward the back corner of the bar. "It's in the back, down the hall, next to the grizzly."

4B hesitated.

"As in grizzly bear?"

"Yep. It's stuffed, though."

"Good to know. Be back in a jiff."

Nora stood next to Crystal and they both watched 4B walk toward the bathrooms. Several heads—men's and women's—swiveled to watch her pass. Nora waited for Crystal to say something. She didn't have to wait long.

"She's hot."

"That she is," agreed Nora.

"I can see you two are—close. A case of battlefield romance?"

"Battlefield romance?"

"You know. All hot and heavy when the shit is coming down, but then it quickly cools and you move on."

"Then, no," responded Nora tersely.

"Just kidding, buddy. It happens, though. Saw a lot of it in Iraq. Horrendous conditions bring people together. When the adrenaline wears off they usually go their separate ways."

"It's not—"

"Hey. I'm not judging. It is what it is."

"But you're wr—"

"What? I'm happy for you, babe. I'm just glad you didn't pick one of the hides around here."

"Be nice, okay?" Nora almost told Crystal that 4B was fragile, but she didn't. The amnesia was her story to tell. Besides, 4B wasn't fragile. Nora was beginning to see how strong 4B really was. "I like her."

"I can see that."

Nora didn't have a chance to respond as 4B walked back toward them. She wore an amused expression.

"Afraid I was gonna fall in?"

It was Nora's turn to look confused, and then she realized both she and Crystal were still standing side-by-side staring in the direction of the restroom.

"Just making sure Jerry didn't scare you," offered Nora with a smile.

"Jerry?"

"The bear."

"Ah! Yeah. He is quite the specimen," responded 4B with a smirk.

Crystal pointed her fingers like they were pistols at 4B and Nora and winked while backing around to get behind the bar. "Hey, I have to get back to work. But, tell her the story about Jerry, and don't forget to tell her the part about Rosie. Remember, it's on the house tonight. Take advantage of it. Lawrence doesn't give open bar to just anyone."

Nora thanked Crystal and then led 4B over to a tall table near one of the pool tables, where they stood shoulder to shoulder, alternating their gazes between the game being played and each other. Before Nora could tell 4B the story, more people came by to ask Nora about the plane crash. She found nearly everyone had already heard the details. News traveled fast in the small community.

Finally, when the last group had peeled away, 4B bumped her shoulder.

"Now tell me about the bear. He's, um, very well…"

"Hung?"

"I was going to say endowed, but hung is a good word."

"Oh, yeah. Jerry's a legend." Nora swallowed the last sip of her beer and smiled.

"It's easy to see why," replied 4B with a wry lift of an eyebrow.

"You notice Jerry is the only trophy animal in the place?"

4B took a look around the place.

"Yeah. Now that you mention it. I kind of like it. Every other place has a stuffed moose head, a wolf, or at least a fish of some kind. The airport is filled with them. Even the hotel we stayed at in Anchorage was plastered with them. I prefer the propeller over the bar here."

"So do I," said Nora.

"I trust you'll also tell me the story about the bra hanging from it?"

"I actually don't know the story about the bra. It just showed up one day. It's Crystal's trophy, and she won't tell."

"That's too bad. I have a feeling it's a good story."

"The bra is a legend unto itself just from the speculation alone," declared Nora with a smile.

"I'll bet," laughed 4B.

"But back to the bear."

"Yeah, what's the story about the bear?"

"The story of the bear starts with Lawrence."

"The guy we met when we walked in?"

"Yeah, the owner of the bar."

"So, does Lawrence always dress like a lumberjack?"

As if he'd heard them, Lawrence looked over at them and then raised his pint glass to them. They raised theirs in turn and smiled. Lawrence was dressed in a red plaid shirt with the sleeves rolled up to show off his ropey muscles and hairy arms. Suspenders held up his dark blue jeans, the hems of which were rolled to the top of his laced-up brown leather boots. The only thing missing to complete the costume was the knit cap. It was too warm for that. He took a drink of his beer and delicately wiped the foam from his manicured beard and mustache with the bandana he'd pulled from his back pocket and went back to talking to the man sitting next to him.

"I've never seen him wear anything else."

"Interesting," said 4B. "Now tell me about the bear."

"Okay. So, Lawrence is pretty much a rebel up here. Despite his he-man outfit, he's not the hunting type. But, one day, a few years back, that big old grizzly you saw in the hallway started to raid Lawrence's brew shed, getting into his stores of barley and hops."

"How terrifying."

"For sure," agreed Nora. "Lawrence tried everything to deter him, successfully running him off time and again, but the bear just kept coming back. Lawrence reinforced the shed, but the bear kept breaking in. He asked animal control to help, but they said they would have to destroy the animal if they intervened. Lawrence didn't want that, but eventually, he had enough. He borrowed a shotgun and filled it with salt shot. He didn't want to hurt it, but with the shot, he thought he'd teach it a lesson without having to kill it. So, he sat in wait for the bear to come back. He didn't have long to wait. But, even though the bear tore the shed door right off the hinges, he couldn't bring himself to aim the gun at the beast. Frustrated, and without thinking of how the bear would exit the building if he was standing in the way, Lawrence stood just outside the door and fired a warning shot straight up into the air. The sudden noise startled the bear, which reared up. Lawrence thought he was a goner. No more than a dozen feet away, the bear locked sights on him and roared. The way Lawrence tells it, ropes of bear spit were flying everywhere. It dropped to all fours to charge, but in it's fury, it knocked the legs out from under the largest fermentation tank. The two-and-a-half-ton tank toppled and fell right on the bear, killing him instantly. Lawrence's brother Jack, who lives on the stake next to Lawrence, had heard the shot and came running, only to find Lawrence sitting next to the bear, blubbering like a baby. Then the two brothers proceeded to get plastered, drinking toasts to the bear. Somehow during all of this, Jack, who happens to be a butcher, convinced Lawrence the honorable thing would be not to let the beast go to waste and offered to butcher the remains."

"You mean butcher it to eat it?" asked 4B, with an expression that made Nora laugh.

"Lots of people eat bear meat up here. The heart is a delicacy."

4B grimaced. "Interesting."

"Now, Jack is also an amateur taxidermist…"

"Oh, I see where this is going," said 4B.

Nora nodded her head.

"Fast forward several weeks later. Tack and I had just flown in from a drop, so he and I and a few of the regulars were all sitting at the bar having a beer one summer afternoon. Jack came into the bar and told Lawrence to close his eyes. Lawrence is a good-natured man. He did what his brother asked. Jack clapped his hands and his two oldest boys rolled the bear in on its pedestal, covered with a tarp. They placed it right in front of Lawrence, who was just a sitting there, eyes closed and grinning, waiting for his surprise." Nora started laughing like she did every time she remembered this part. "Jack told Lawrence to open his eyes while at the same time, he signaled for his boys to take off the tarp. When Lawrence opened his eyes, he nearly flew off his barstool and screamed like a six-year-old girl in terror. The first things he saw were those teeth and those eyes. He quickly got himself under control, but Jack about peed his pants laughing so hard. Lawrence stared slugging him in the shoulder as hard as he could. Everyone in the bar was laughing so hard it took a minute before any of us noticed the bear's, um, lower extremities," Nora pointed at her crotch. "When we did, the whole bar just got quiet—except Jack, who was still laughing about Lawrence's scream."

"What did they say?" asked 4B, laughing now, too.

"Well, Lawrence was the only one who said anything at first. 'What were you thinking, Jack? What in blooming tarnation were you thinking?' he blustered. And we all started laughing again."

Nora had to pause to catch her breath.

"What did he say? Did he explain?" asked 4B.

"He said, 'You told me that's how you liked it, Larry. You're always saying you like bears with big dicks.'"

"You mean…?" asked 4B, sneaking a look at Lawrence, who was at the end of the bar, chatting with a weathered old fellow in the stool next to him.

Nora just nodded. She couldn't hold it together any longer and laughed so hard, she cried. The kind of laughter that made her face feel like it was going to go numb. 4B, who had laughed at the story, started to laugh again just because Nora couldn't control her own laughter.

"That's not the end, though," wheezed Nora. "So, we're sitting there laughing and it's starting to die out, and there's the odd cough and renewed giggle, but Lawrence is just sitting there so humiliated. We're all looking anywhere but at him and the fully erect bear standing in the middle of the bar. But up strolls Rosie—you see that woman by the jukebox? That's Rosie."

4B turned to look at the dark-haired woman who was still leaning against the jukebox, moving along with a song about a sugar magnolia. "The drunk hippie, dancing by the juke box?"

"She's not drunk. Iced tea is about as strong of a drink as she goes. She just spends a lot of time inside of her own head." They both watched Rosie, who swayed with her eyes closed, blissfully unaware of their stares. "Anyway, we're all just standing there not knowing what to do with ourselves, and she walks up to the bar in the way she does, like she's floating or something— and she sets her empty water glass down for a refill. No one is really paying attention to her. We're all checking out the bear and trying not to look at Lawrence, when she rests her chin in her hand and glances down at the bear's—area," explained Nora gesturing to her own lap again and starting to laugh. "And she says, all dreamy-like, but loud enough for the folks closest to hear: 'I miss Jerry.'"

"Who's Jerry?" asked 4B, stealing a surreptitious glance at the woman by the jukebox.

"No one knows. There are stories—there are always stories—but no one really knows. Rosie is a bit of an odd duck. She lives alone and comes down here to listen to music and hang out more nights than not, but other than that, she doesn't really talk to anyone or go anywhere. But somewhere, sometime, there was a guy named Jerry who the bear reminded her of, and the name stuck."

"Fascinating," said 4B, taking a sip of her beer, and Nora wiped her eyes and grinned at her.

"And that's the story of Jerry."

"The Legend," said 4B, raising her glass in a toast.

"Yep, Jerry the Legend," said Nora, tapping the rim of her glass against 4B's.

They sipped their beers. Feeling eyes on her and 4B, Nora shifted her gaze to Crystal, who stood several feet away on the other side of the bar. She was drying and storing glasses, watching their every move.

"Do you want another drink?" asked Nora, stepping behind 4B, circling her waist with both arms and talking close to her ear. She had to get close to be heard over the growing crowd and the loud music, but she also wanted to make it clear to Crystal that 4B wasn't just a passing thing for her. The smell of 4B's hair and skin made her want to go back home.

"Why not? Neither of us is driving. How about another one of those with the moose horns? The first one was quite nice." 4B pointed to the tap handles.

"Moose have antlers, not horns," laughed Nora.

"What's the difference?"

"Animals with antlers shed them every year and grow back a bigger set in the spring. Horns don't naturally fall off." Nora picked up their empty glasses. "I'll get us some water, too."

"Good idea. I should slow down. I can already feel the first two."

Nora crossed the ten feet spanning between their table and the bar, and shouted to be heard over the music. "Two hefs and two waters, please?" Crystal nodded and went to work pouring their drinks without taking her eyes from 4B. Nora wanted to tell her to keep her eyes to herself, but she just smiled her thanks and tossed a few bucks on the bar for a tip. When she got back to the table with their drinks she felt a large hand fall on her shoulder.

"Well, if it isn't the luckiest ladies I know," said a booming voice from behind them, and Nora turned to see Tack's easygoing smile.

"Hi, Tack! It's good to see you again," said 4B, looking very happy to see someone else she knew.

Tack smiled and raised an arm toward the bar.

"Crystal! Put whatever they're having on my tab and let's have another round for the table!" shouted Tack in his gravelly voice. He pulled a stool over to the table and leaned in. Nora was about to tell him Lawrence was already taking care of their drinks, but Tack started to talk with a serious look on his face.

"I've been meaning to tell you ladies, you're lucky to be alive right now."

Nora and 4B looked at each other and then back at Tack. They laughed in unison.

"Considering we were in a plane crash, your point is…?" asked Nora, punching him in the arm.

"Besides that, I mean. C'mon, Nora!"

Tack blushed and swung his head. Nora felt bad for giving the gentle giant a bad time in front of 4B. They did it to each other all the time, but she knew he felt bashful around beautiful women, and 4B seemed to bring it on bad for him.

"What do you mean, then?" she asked.

"Well, for one thing, that wing you was camped under was full of airplane fuel, and you was burning a fire right under it. I don't know how you didn't go up in a ball of flame."

"Seriously? The fuel is in the wings?" asked Nora.

Tack nodded his bushy head. "That it is."

"Holy crap!"

"I took one of the guys who analyzed the scene down to Edna Bay for moose hunting this morning. He said most of the fuel must have drained from the line; otherwise, you two would have been toast. You didn't hear this from me, but the plane went down due to a botched maintenance. You two will be set for life because of this."

"The airline already told us about the maintenance," said Nora, who couldn't say more about it or talk about the settlement, since it was still in the works. "Your beer is on me, by the way. You're the one who found us. It's the least I can do." Nora knew it was a useless argument. Deciding who would pay was an ongoing fight between them. They always ended up splitting the tab down the middle.

"Not on your life. It isn't every day my best friend cheats death. You can't deny me the honor of buying drinks to toast to that!"

"I can't argue with that," said Nora, with a resigned sigh. And she was about to tell him they were already being taken care of, when Crystal reached around her and placed Tack's drink on the table. Crystal's breasts pressed against her back.

"These ladies' drinks are on Lawrence tonight, Tack, old man," said Crystal, with a quick rub against Nora's back before she leaned away.

Tack nodded his concession. "Next time is on me, then. Take your break and have a drink with us, Crysie."

"I told you about calling me Crysie. Do it again and you'll be sipping beer through a wired jaw." She glared at him and then checked the time on his watch. "My break is in twenty. I'll bring another round then and have a drink with you all."

"Roger that, Crys-Tal!" Tack lifted his pint glass to Crystal's back as she walked away. Then he leaned toward Nora. "She sure put me in my place, huh?" Tack rolled his eyes, but there was a gleam in them. "Table service? Taking a break? Looks like someone's interested in the new girl, or jealous over the old one. Just an observation."

"Did you just call me old?" laughed Nora.

"Who called you old?" asked 4B, leaning closer to Nora. "I can't hear anything over the jukebox.

"Tack did. But joke's on him. He's older than me by a month." Nora laughed.

"I can't tell how old he is under all those whiskers," observed 4B. "But you're just the right age for me, whatever age that is," replied 4B, looking Nora up and down. Nora felt 4B's assessment like it was a warm caress. Again, thoughts of going home came to mind.

"I'm thirty-five," said Nora, scanning 4B's face. Their respective ages hadn't even crossed her mind. If she had to guess how old 4B was, she'd have said late twenties.

"I wouldn't have put you at older than thirty," said 4B, and Tack pretended to choke on his beer. Nora punched him in the arm and 4B ignored him. "It makes four years difference, according to my license, if it's real."

"Does an age difference matter to you?" asked Nora.

"No. Besides, I feel like I've known you all of my life. I guess I have, actually, all things considered."

"What's she talking about?" asked Tack.

"Nora didn't tell you I have amnesia?" asked 4B, glancing at Nora, who shook her head.

"Amnesia means you can't remember anything, right?"

"Right. I have no memories from before the crash," 4B explained.

"Really?" he asked. "None at all?"

4B shook her head.

"My first memory is waking up to see Nora staring down at me when I first woke up after the crash."

"That would scare the memory out of me, too," laughed Tack, his adolescent humor coming through in brilliant color. Nora gave him a warning glare. He laughed again and rubbed his arm. "Just kidding! Just kidding!"

"I kind of like that her face is my first memory," said 4B, looking at Nora.

"I'm gonna get diabetes from all the sweetness over here," groaned Tack, tipping his pint back and finishing the last half in one gulp.

Crystal brought another round of shots to the table.

"From Lawrence," she explained as she doled out the short glasses, keeping one for herself. "Slippery nipples."

"Cheers! To being back with friends," said Nora, tossing her shot back, while the others echoed her salute and did the same.

Nora raised her empty shot glass with a smile at Lawrence, who was still at his seat at the bar, and raised his pint glass in return

"I'll be back in a few for my break," said Crystal, gathering the empties. When Nora felt Crystal's breasts against her shoulder again, she leaned away. Crystal had never been this obvious before. And her breasts may have been on Nora, but her eyes were all over 4B. Nora wondered whose attention Crystal was trying to get. Either way, Nora didn't like it.

"Yep. Definitely jealous, I'd think," observed Tack, watching Crystal walk away. When his eyes returned to the table, he slapped his palm down. "Oh yeah. By the way, I meant to tell you. You have another thing to feel lucky about. There was a couple of bears skulking around that wing you was camped out under."

Nora and 4B looked at each other.

"We chased one away the night before we were rescued."

"Well, it came back with a friend. The whole site had been trashed, when the crash analysis team showed up after you two was lifted out. Seems a tray of those in-flight meals they serve in planes was trapped under the wing. They must have smelled it and tried to dig under. Prints as big as my head was everywhere. They make Jerry seem like a runt."

🌲🌲🌲🌲🌲

A couple of hours later, Nora and 4B arrived at the house arm-in-arm, weaving slightly. Between Lawrence's open tab and drinks bought for them by their friends, they'd had lot to drink that night. The walk back from the bar in the chill night air, with the bright moonlight to guide them, had helped a little to sober them up, but not completely. Tack had offered them a ride, but Nora was delighted when 4B had told him she looked forward to the walk home. They were all the way up the front steps of Aunt Mace's house when they realized all of the lights were out. A small chalkboard hung from a hook near the door with a message on it saying Aunt Mace was sawing logs. Shushing each other's giggles, the two women left the porch and walked around to the side path leading to Nora's cabin. A basket of muffins wrapped in a dishtowel sat on the seat of an Adirondack chair on Nora's front porch. A note in Aunt Mace's handwriting was pinned to the cloth:

If the bears don't get these, they're all yours. Ship made 'em. They're delish. XOXO

They left the muffins on the table and 4B led Nora upstairs and slowly undressed her. They made love unhurriedly, and when they were done, Nora listened to 4B's breathing grow regular, until it was deep and slow. Nora was still a little drunk, and she held 4B for a long time, attempting to clear her mind of the thoughts that tried to take her peace. Thoughts of how sick Aunt Mace was. Thoughts of 4B leaving when her family found her. Thoughts of 4B having to choose between an old life and a new life. Thoughts of saying goodbye. Nora pushed the unwanted ideas away and focused instead on how the smell of campfire smoke would forever make her smile. She thought about 4B lying on her bed, eyes dark as Nora came to her. She thought about the way 4B had said her name just before she'd fallen asleep that night, nuzzling into the circle of her arm. She absorbed the warmth of 4B's body and luxuriated in the comfort of her embrace. Finally, she was at peace, but her mind still wouldn't completely quiet down, so she slipped out of bed, shrugged into an old t-shirt and a worn pair of boxers and went downstairs. Java followed her and meowed conversationally, weaving between her feet, forgiveness granted for Nora's long absence. Nora sat down at her desk and picked up the needy feline to scratch around her ears.

"You can't get enough love can you, little girl?"

Java answered by rubbing her face against Nora's cheek, greedily pressing her ears into Nora's scratching fingers. After a few moments of intense love, the cat jumped down, temporarily sated. Nora knew the furry beast would be back within minutes. She reached for the silver sheathed laptop on her desk, flipped it open, and powered it up. It had been so long since she had logged on, that she had to wade through several update prompts and a slew of calendar reminders, none of which were pressing, since anything urgent was automated by a script or application she had installed. She found a few things needing review, so she slid the items into the "To Do" folder on her desktop to deal with later. She wasn't ready to work. Right now, she was just doing some housekeeping to wind down.

Once the task of computer maintenance was completed, and despite her and 4B's discussion about avoiding the media, Nora did a search for news about the crash. Over a week old, and the rescue of her and 4B being a few days earlier, the most recent story was a short article explaining that the crash was still under investigation and a passenger manifest had finally been released. The list of survivors and victims whose family had been notified gave names, ages, hometowns, and, for most of them, pictures. Her picture and 4B's were among the survivors. There was also a picture of the woman who had been sitting next to her. Irma Santiago Vargas. Aged fifty-eight. From Long Beach, California. Her name was listed under the passengers who hadn't survived. Nora felt a sharp stab in her heart to see the woman's face again. She vowed right then to contact her family. She didn't know what she would say, but it was something she had to do.

There was a count of the victims whose families had not yet been notified. The names were being withheld until next of kin could be contacted. A phone number was posted for people to call in with questions or information about some of the unidentified victims.

Nora spent time looking at aerial images of the area where the plane had gone down. It was an untamed wilderness with dense forest covering exceptionally varied terrain, which included mountains, ravines, and coastal inlets with rocky coastlines, all of it uninhabited. Markers showed the impact zone, the slide range, and where the survivors had been located. She marveled that they had even been found, and that anyone had survived. Planes had disappeared in the region before. No commercial jetliners. But what real difference did the size of the airplane make, when you were talking about millions of square miles of wilderness? The plane was off-course because it had been in the process of turning around. It could have gone down anywhere.

She wondered what would have happened to them if they hadn't been found. After Tack's description of the site, now she knew the bear would have been back. Correction: bears. Would they have been successful at chasing them away again? If so, would she and 4B have stayed where they were? Or would they have left to find food and help? Would she have tried harder to find the others? She realized she was playing the what if game. The truth was none of that had happened and she and 4B and thirty-one others had survived.

They had been lucky.

Nora felt guilt edge into her thoughts. Yes, they had been lucky. Did she have a right to feel grateful? She thought, yes, she did. In fact, she felt obligated to feel grateful. It would be wrong to dismiss their survival in favor of the terrible alternative. It meant that she had to move forward and take what came with that reality.

It was the middle of the night, and as it often happens when a dark thing starts to wiggle in your head, other dark things begin to give it company. She

175

thought about what Aunt Mace had said, how Nora wouldn't have been on the airplane if not for the cancer that was eating away at her. She desperately wanted to beg her aunt to try the new medicine. But it wouldn't be fair. Aunt Mace didn't want to do it, and as hard as it would be, she had to respect her wishes.

Nora shifted in her seat and yawned. It was late, and there was a beautiful woman upstairs keeping her bed warm. She put her hand on the screen to flip the cover closed, but she didn't close her laptop. Feeling a little guilty because she had told herself she wouldn't do it, Nora typed the name Grace Trackton into her search engine and hit the "Go" button. The only strong hit she got back was the recent news article listing 4B's name in the list of survivors. She added Massachusetts to the search parameters. Other than the crash articles she'd already seen, there were no other Grace Tracktons from Massachusetts. The results were disappointing, yet expected. If there had been other information there, the officials from the airline would have found 4B's family by now.

Ads for a few private companies promising to scour files across the web for a small fee filled the sidebars of the web page. She smiled with the knowledge that the logic for those ads targeting her needs was the base for the company she had once built. Even back then, she did it better, she thought. Her finger hovered over the first one displayed. But it felt too sneaky. The FAA and North Star Airlines were on the case. If there was a family or a past to be found, Nora knew they would uncover them. And if they didn't, she'd figure out a search logic that would do it for them. As much as it scared her to unblock 4B's past, she knew she and 4B didn't have a future until she at least tried everything in her power to find out who 4B really was. But 4B hadn't asked her to help yet. In the meantime, she would let the officials do the legwork.

She logged off her computer and climbed the stairs, craving the warmth of the woman who filled her mind.

🌲🌲🌲🌲🌲

Nora stood back and gestured for 4B to precede her through the automatic sliding door at the airport terminal. They'd been called by the airline that morning and asked to come down for a meeting. After a couple of days away from all of it, the distinct smell and sounds of the airport provided a visceral re-emersion into their recent experiences. Nevertheless, they were in good spirits as they made their way into the terminal.

"Maybe they've discovered you're the famous heiress of a vast fortune," joked Nora. The apprehension she'd had the night before about finding 4B's family was still with her, but in the daylight it didn't seem so dismal. If it happened—when it happened—they would deal with it. In the meantime, she'd enjoy the time they had together.

"I truly doubt it. If I were famous, someone would have recognized me by now. But out of all the possibilities we've come up with, I like the heiress idea the most. Oh! Maybe I'm a reclusive heiress, and no one has seen me without a scarf and a hat. I'm unrecognizable without a disguise." 4B laughed, squeezing Nora's hand. She swung their hands playfully between them as they stepped through the terminal.

They had checked in at the North Star offices at the request of the home office in Anchorage the day they had flown into Juneau, but aside from meeting the local agents, there had been no need for them to go back. The agent who'd called that morning hadn't given a reason for the meeting request, and Nora suspected it was to go over their settlement papers again. She had heard many of the other survivors had already signed the generous offers, and she guessed they wanted to get the rest of the holdouts to do the same. She didn't blame the airline for wanting to get the whole thing behind them. Nora's lawyer had already approved the contracts, saying if Nora was comfortable with it, there wasn't anything to dispute, unless someone was out for the money, which Nora wasn't. Overall, the airline had been extreme-ly attentive, showing only deep compassion for them. So Nora didn't worry about what was motivating them, as long as the airline continued to do the right thing. As they entered the terminal, they joked that 4B's family had come to sweep her away.

"My vote still goes to you being a criminal on the lam from the law," said Nora. "It matches your bad girl vibe."

"That's me. Public enemy number one!" 4B laughed and bumped Nora's shoulder as they walked toward the corridor beyond the ticket counters to the private offices. This side of the terminal wasn't as busy as the rest of the airport, and most of the offices were behind discreet doors. Nora was just about to put her arm around 4B, when a very distinguished woman in a sophisticated suit amid a group of officious looking people rushed toward them followed closely by a well-dressed man holding her hand. Nora's first instinct was to get between 4B and the strangers, but their appearances threw her off. She and 4B had grown used to reporters trying to talk to them. These two didn't look like reporters. In fact, Nora saw a striking resemblance between 4B and the couple. Her stomach dropped.

4B's family had arrived.

"Elizabeth! My God!" they declared in unison, enveloping a very surprised-looking 4B in a double embrace. 4B held tight to Nora's hand and Nora stood there, uncomfortably close to the emotional scene, not knowing what to do.

Elizabeth?

When the woman Nora suspected was 4B's mother pulled away, her cheeks were wet with tears, and she held onto 4B's arms like 4B might drift away. A flurry of conflicting emotions whirled within Nora. She studied the newcomers, and a swarm of people in suits, some who Nora knew were with the airline, and some she'd never seen, surrounded the small group. Nora lost hold of 4B's hand and, in the rush, Nora was shuffled to the fringes of the crowd. She tried to get back to her, but the group pressed in around 4B and Nora felt awkward and unsure about whether she needed to rescue 4B or leave her to her family.

She was trying to make up her mind about what to do, when 4B's voice rose above the sound of many people talking at once.

"Nora! Where are you?"

Nora heard fear in the call and the sound tugged at Nora's sense of protectiveness, the one that had been there since the moment she'd first seen 4B. Nora caught sight of 4B's face through a small gap in the crowd. Just as Nora was reaching for 4B's hand, one of the men in suits stepped between them and Nora was once again forced to the sidelines facing a wall of backs. The small huddle of people tightened around 4B. Nora circled the group, trying to find a way back in. 4B needed her.

"Ms. Kavendash?"

Nora distractedly turned to the voice and with relief she saw Gina, their primary contact from the airline. Maybe she could help.

"Is that her family?" asked Nora.

"Yes. I apologize for the surprise. I would have warned you both when I called, but even I didn't know what this meeting was about. They didn't want the press to show up. It looks like it was still leaked somehow."

Nora looked where Gina indicated and saw a handful of journalists standing behind a roped off barrier, intent on watching the reunion. They must have been warned about taking pictures. All cameras were stowed, but most of them were speaking in urgent low tones into recording devices. Two tall men stood on the other side of the rope, facing the journalists.

"What is this all about? Why are they calling her Elizabeth?"

Nora was interrupted as a man in a suit with a red tie strode purposefully up and addressed the group.

"Senator, would you like to go somewhere a little more private?"

Gina flashed an expression of apology at Nora and 4B's mother turned around. Nora now recognized the woman as Senator Tollworthy. Nora didn't follow politics, but she admired Senator Tollworthy for her stances on civil rights, her work to help young families fight poverty, her anti-war stance, and her stringent views regarding Wall Street. As politicians went, Senator Tollworthy was a good one, Nora thought. And now she was here to claim 4B. The scene before Nora suddenly became surreal.

"That would be perfect, Andrew. Thank you," responded the senator, and Nora watched as the man led 4B's parents, who were guiding 4B, through an opening in the crowd. When they passed Nora, 4B's father had his hand on 4B's elbow. His eyes never left her.

4B reached out and touched Nora's arm as she passed, her eyes confused, but Nora thought it best to leave her to the people who had come to claim her. She hoped her eyes conveyed the strength she wished she could provide by being at her side, and she reached up to squeeze 4B's fingers before they slid from her arm. 4B's mother glanced at Nora but her eyes didn't linger. Her full attention was on her daughter.

"Elizabeth, love, you scared the hell out of us. Tell us what happened. Your father and I—" A door closed on the unfinished sentence. Nora was left standing. Alone. In the suddenly silent terminal. Gina had also disappeared into the back office with the rest of the crowd.

Nora stood where she was, debating whether to try to follow them. But the situation seemed to exclude her. Feeling cast adrift, she turned around, wondering if she should stay or go back home. Before she had a chance to decide, the door opened, and 4B came out. The senator hovered just inside the door, watching.

"Nora! Are you coming? I need you," 4B whispered, franticly waving her over. Nora saw confusion and fear in her eyes.

"They whisked you away so quickly," explained Nora, closing the distance between them, taking 4B's hands. "So, that's your family?"

"I don't remember them, Nora. I'm scared. Why am I so scared?" 4B squeezed her hands. All of the tension that had started to leave her expression over the last couple of days was back. The crease between her eyebrows cut a line through her otherwise smooth skin. A tear slid from 4B's eye and Nora reached up to wipe it.

Over 4B's shoulder, Nora noticed the man in the red tie consult with 4B's mother. He nodded his head and came out to them.

"Ms. Tollworthy? Would you and your friend like to join us? It's a little quieter in the office."

Nora looked over her shoulder at the people crowded behind the rope. Curious travelers had joined the group and the no-cameras agreement seemed to have lapsed. Several journalists and some curious on-lookers were aiming their cameras and cell phones at them. An airline representative approached the throng and most of the journalists lowered their devices, while the rest of the crowd continued to snap photos. Nora wondered what they thought they were seeing.

"Please come inside, ladies," requested the man. 4B's mother was still just inside the doorway, watching them.

4B took Nora's hand and guided her inside.

Nora closed her front door and leaned her back against the solid wood surface. She dropped her head and breathed in and out, pulling the air deep into her lungs before expelling it. Her chest was tight and the breathing helped. The smell of 4B surrounded her, filled her senses and tingled on her fingertips.

Now, Nora felt ripped apart and the reminders of 4B were more than just the scent of her clinging to her hand. She pushed away from the closed door and wandered aimlessly through the living room. She passed the sofa, where 4B had curled up with a book just yesterday morning while Nora worked, before the phone call, before 4B had been wrenched out of her life as suddenly as she'd entered it.

Look Homeward, Angel was still lying open, facedown, on the coffee table. Nora walked past it and stopped in front of the great glass window spanning most of the front wall of the cabin. She looked out, but didn't see anything—not the cloud of dust from the car that had just left, or the long grass in the meadow across the road bending lazily in the silver light of the late afternoon sun. What she saw was already a memory, a parade of images of 4B, permanently imprinted in her mind.

4B was gone, had left minutes ago, in the car her parents had rented at the airport. Now, Nora was left with an ache in her chest, and no idea of what would come next.

Part 2

4B

✿✿✿✿✿

4B STARED AT THE CEILING in the unfamiliar room, watching the shadows of plants cast by the outside security light move in a spooky dance. Hours after midnight, a cold rain was coming down in sheets, and all she could think of was curling up against Nora's body under an airplane wing as the rain came down in a deluge all around them.

Nothing about the reunion with her parents or being back in their house triggered her memory. Although everyone had been kind and sensitive, she longed to be with Nora, safe and familiar.

The meeting in the sterile office at the airport played through her memory.

From the moment her parents had appeared, she'd felt as if she'd been picked up and set in a scene in someone else's life. Grace? Elizabeth? 4B? Who was she? She'd sat in the bright white room, studying the grain of the wood in the conference table, trying to figure out who she was. Her only comfort had been Nora next to her. Nora holding her hand, squeezing it firmly beneath the table, conveying safety through the simple touch. On her other side had been the mother she didn't remember, attentive and sobbing. It had been difficult to see her cry like that. 4B had wanted to soothe the woman but she didn't know how, so she sat and stared at the table, sneaking glances at Nora, who was always ready with a reassuring smile.

The man, her father, had stood behind them, one hand placed on her shoulder, the other on her mother's. All while the airline discussed the details of the crash. 4B knew the story already, even though she was still disconnected from it. While they talked, she focused on what was going on in the room, witnessing everything as a spectator. She observed that she should have felt crowded, but aside from the initial rush of strangers that had terrified her and separated her from Nora, the nearness, even the touch of the strangers hadn't felt overbearing, just strange. The others—airline officials and her mother's assistants—had remained at a polite distance. There had been a quick round of introductions when they'd entered the office, but 4B hadn't remembered any of them. She'd focused on the two who said they were her family.

"Elizabeth, honey, we would have been here so much sooner. We had no idea until Miriam showed me your picture in the newspaper yesterday evening. We thought you were in Los Angeles. We…" Her mother had started to cry again. She noticed how her father had stroked her mother's shoulder. Who was Miriam?

"Your mother has been up all night, pumpkin," offered her father. 4B could tell the emotional reunion was uncomfortable for him. "Neither of us has been able to sleep since we heard."

Her mother wiped her eyes, careful of her makeup. "I should have known something was wrong. I hadn't heard from you in over a week. We never go that long without talking. I imagined you were just enjoying your visit to L.A. with Layce. But when we heard you were in the accident in Juneau— Alaska, of all places—we were so confused. And then we wondered why you hadn't contacted us immediately to tell us about it, to tell us you were fine. It wasn't until we arrived here this morning that we found out about the amnesia. Oh, god, honey!"

Her father moved to a seat next to his wife, draped his arm over her shoulders and leaned across her, taking 4B's free hand. So much was going on. She felt like she should be asking questions about her life before, but she didn't know what to ask. So she sat quietly, trying to bring detail out of the shadows of emotions she sensed floating below the surface of her mind.

"This must be a little overwhelming for you, pumpkin," her father said, an understatement.

4B studied her father's eyes, so similar to her own, full of concern. Innately, she trusted him. The protective gestures he'd displayed in the short time they'd been together—the hand on her elbow or her shoulder, standing near, always watching—made her certain of his love for her. In turn, she had wanted to make him feel better—wanted to make both of them feel better— but she hadn't known how. Somehow, all of this was about her, but it felt so separate from her. She felt the expectation from all of them, that she could explain or solve all of the unknowns. But she couldn't.

"I… I'm sorry," she said, owing him a response. "Yes, it's a little over-whelming. I wish… I wish I could remember."

"Do you remember us, honey?" her mother had asked and the gleam of hope in her mother's expression had made her feel insignificant and lacking.

"You do remember us, don't you?"

She hesitated. Her mother and father waited for her affirmation. Their eyes seemed to say, of course she remembered them.

"I'm sorry. I don't," she admitted. It had been a relief to say it out loud. The thick sense of expectation receded immediately.

"Not even a little?" her mother had prompted, disappointment dripped from her eyes while hope shone in her smile. 4B felt awful for getting the answer wrong.

"Roslyn, we mustn't push," her father had responded, gentle, but firm.

Her mother looked at him and nodded. 4B watched as she leaned into him and wiped away another tear. At least they have each other to rely on, she'd thought. Her father had smoothed her mother's hair. The next instant, her mother straightened up, composed herself, and her gaze had moved to Nora. She felt Nora shift beside her, sit up. Until that moment, neither of her parents had paid much attention to Nora. Selfishly, 4B was relieved to have their focus shift off of her for a moment.

"I'm sorry, dear," her mother apologized. "Where are our manners? Nora Kavendash? You were on the airplane, too. You were found with our Elizabeth."

"Yes, Senator. Your daughter and I were rescued together," Nora had replied, squeezing 4B's hand under the table. 4B had been grateful for Nora's assurance. It helped her feel a little more confident.

"How did… I mean, was Elizabeth… she was unconscious when you found her?" her mother had asked, looking distressed, almost like she didn't want to know the details. "You both look fine now, uninjured."

4B thought about how frightening it must have been for them when they had first heard the terrible news. Again, it seemed like she was peeking into another's life. Her father cleared his throat before he spoke.

"We're beyond grateful at the care you provided for her in the field. The airline hasn't disclosed much yet, even when I explained that I was a doctor, as well as Elizabeth's father." He glanced at the officials across the table from them. "As it should be, I suppose. But they only mentioned Elizabeth's amnesia today, when we arrived. To prepare us. You're both ambulatory. That's a good sign." Like her mother, he'd seemed rattled, looking for footing.

"Elizabeth was unconscious when I found her," Nora had responded, explaining 4B's condition and recovery. With it, she provided some detail about their time in the forest and the rescue. 4B was happy to let Nora do the talking. Nora had recounted the event to people numerous times since they'd been back in Juneau and could probably do it in her sleep. She had lifted her bangs and showed her father the healing scar on her forehead when Nora described her injury. He'd moved closer to examine the small bandage she still wore. His fingers had palpated the area around it and it hadn't been as weird as she would have expected. In fact, it had been comforting. She surprised herself by missing his nearness as he moved back into his seat.

"You probably saved our daughter's life out there," her father said, and his voice had cracked at the end. He'd had to pause before going on. "Thank you. We can never repay you."

Tears streamed from her mother's eyes again. While she wiped them away, her father turned his attention to the airline officials, and after that, the discussion had centered upon the airline's response and the settlement. The airline had seemed eager to please the Senator, so most of the conversation had been diverted to her mother and father asking questions and the airline answering them.

After the meeting, Nora had invited 4B's parents back to the house. The four of them drove back to Nora's in two cars, with 4B's parents following in a large rented SUV, while the senator's staff, also in a rented SUV, drove in the other direction, toward the hotel the airline had provided for them.

In the car, 4B's mind had raced with a flood of questions about who she was and how she was connected to the people who had come to claim her. In a very short time period, the bubble she'd been operating within had expand-ed, and an anxious fear had filled her. In the quiet of Nora's Jeep Cherokee, 4B's fear had needed an outlet.

"What do I do, Nora?"

Nora had navigated out of the airport parking lot while keeping an eye on the rearview mirror. Her lips had been drawn together in a thin line and when she had glanced at 4B, her eyes had held more questions than answers.

"What do you want to do?" Nora had asked.

"Turn time backward until we're back in your bed this morning, before the phone rang. Then we could have ignored it."

Nora had smiled then, and reached over to grab her hand.

"That sounds pretty good to me, too," Nora had said, squeezing her hand. "Assuming it isn't an option, though, what's your plan B?"

"I don't know. Not knowing what I don't remember makes it hard to plan. I don't know those people, Nora."

"They seem nice. It's obvious they care about you."

"Yeah," 4B had said, gazing at the houses they passed. Her gaze had caught her own reflection in the side mirror and she thought how seeing the woman who was her mother had felt a little like looking in a mirror. Nora had cleared her throat before glancing at her again.

"I think you should go home with them when they leave tomorrow."

4B hadn't expected that answer and fear and disappointment had threaded through her heart.

"Will you come with me?"

Nora smiled but her eyes had a cloudy look and 4B had known then Nora wouldn't go.

"I want to. I would. You need to know that."

"I understand."

"I can't leave Aunt Mace."

4B had felt like a selfish asshole for forgetting what Aunt Mace and Nora were going through.

"I'm sorry. I'm acting like the world revolves around me," she'd said.

"Hey. It's a lot to deal with." Nora reached over and squeezed her hand.

"I… I think I want to stay here. With you and Aunt Mace. Would that be terrible? If I told them I want to stay here?" 4B looked at Nora and a sudden bout of insecurity washed over her. "That is, if you want me to." Where did she belong? Nothing seemed solid anymore, her whole—

"It would make me happy," Nora had said, stopping the negative spiral 4B had just been about to plunge into. Nora had pulled the Jeep to a stop in front of Aunt Mace's house and had pulled the keys from the ignition. The ride had been too short. She needed more time. Nora had turned to face her.

"I would like you to stay here. More than you know. But, I think you need to go home. Your memory might—will—come back, and you'll have loose ends to tie up. Going home might help to push the process forward. And I'll be here waiting."

"I don't want to leave you." Tears had stung the back of 4B's eyes.

"Just until you figure things out."

"What if my memory never comes back?"

"I'll be right here."

"What… what if my memory does come back?"

"I'll still be right here."

They'd stared at each other for a moment, and Nora had held both of 4B's hands. Then they had gotten out of the car when they'd noticed 4B's parents waiting for them near the path to the front door to Aunt Mace's house.

Now, a day later, two flights, and an entire continent between them, 4B lay in her bed in Massachusetts and a tear leaked from her eye. She rolled over onto her side and remembered that last night at Nora's.

Before dinner, her father feeling restless, had gone into Juneau to get her a new cell phone, fixated on replacing the one she'd lost in the crash. When he'd returned with the newly activated phone, she'd been surprised by the number of missed calls and texts, all from people she didn't remember, so after reading a few she'd left the rest for later, until after she'd regained her memory. They'd eaten the simple dinner Nora had prepared for them, while her parents had succumbed to Aunt Mace's charm and her millions of stories. Everyone had seemed to relax throughout the evening, and 4B had been surprised at how comfortable she'd felt when she hadn't been thinking about what the next day would bring. For chunks of time, she had even almost forgotten about why they were all there. It seemed they all felt the same way. The discussion had stayed light all evening and they hadn't talked at all about what would happen the next day when her parents were scheduled to leave. 4B still hadn't decided whether she would stay or go, but she knew they expected her to leave with them.

She'd willingly returned the hugs when her parents claimed exhaustion early that evening, retiring to one of Aunt Mace's guest rooms. And she'd sensed Aunt Mace's relief when she'd said good night minutes later. Then Nora had led her back to the small cabin, had walked her upstairs to the bedroom, and had taken off her clothes. They'd slid between the sheets, and Nora had pulled the heavy covers over them before pulling 4B close.

"I don't want to leave you," 4B had said pressing into Nora's side. The internal debate that had waged within her all evening had culminated in an ache in her head and heart. She knew she'd leave the next morning.

Nora had held her close, her sigh deep and tinged with resignation.

"I want to be selfish. I want to tell you to stay here, but I think you need to go home," Nora had said as her hand had roamed the bare skin of 4B's back. Nora's hands were never still and often said more to 4B than her words did. They'd been telling her all day, with their seeking touches and lingering holds, that she'd be taking Nora's heart from Alaska when she left. She also knew she'd be leaving her own with Nora when she went.

"This feels like home to me," 4B had said, sinking her face into the space beside Nora's neck. The smell of Nora had given her peace.

"You might feel differently when you get there."

"But, what if I don't?" she'd sounded like a child, but she hadn't cared.

"Then you can always come back here. All you have to do is call and I'll even fly out to get you. Until then, we can talk on the phone."

"Phone calls can't give us this," 4B had said, pressing tighter against Nora's side. "I miss you already."

"I'm right here," said Nora, holding her tight. Desire had swelled between them then, at the smooth way their skin met, how their bodies merged so perfectly. It had made her ache. If she left, Nora's arms wouldn't be there when she needed them.

"Touch me, Nora. You're the only thing that makes me feel real," she'd said as she'd kissed Nora's neck and had guided Nora's hand between her legs. "I need you to make me feel real."

Nora's fingers slipped into her as they rolled over. With Nora above her, 4B opened up, letting Nora fill her, wanting all of her inside. Nora had been slow and tender, and 4B had watched her eyes as Nora touched her. More quickly than she'd expected, a great pressure tightened 4B's center while Nora's eyes bored into her. 4B rocked below Nora while the exquisite pulse built inside. 4B reached up and stroked the long muscle of Nora's thigh. She slid her hand around and ran her fingers through the warm, wet folds between Nora's legs. Nora shuddered then, but she didn't lose the rhythm. 4B plunged into the slick heat and matched Nora's pace. Their eyes remained locked on one another, and the pulses she'd discovered inside Nora matched the ones that originated inside of her, wrapping around Nora's fingers. She spread her legs further, a silent request for more, and she arched beneath Nora, her breath hitched, and she felt herself begin to explode. Nora's lips parted as a moan poured from her throat. And they came. Weakened by the storm, Nora's knees slid to the side and 4B withdrew her fingers. When their centers touched, 4B grabbed Nora's hips, pulling her closer, the soft heat sliding between them, and she soared to even higher places as another orgasm built. Nora's hands were on either side of her head as her hips moved in time with 4B's and another wave rushed between them, and then another. All the tension and unknowns that had filled them, creating this urgency, demanded to be released. And they'd flown with it. Allowed it to take them.

When the torrent of pleasure had started to subside, Nora had lowered herself to lie upon 4B, blanketing her with her warmth, their sweat and breaths combined, and still 4B hadn't been able to get close enough. Nora's mouth had moved against her throat and then her lips had been on her mouth. 4B had been crying then, and she'd thought maybe Nora had been, too. But she'd kept her eyes closed and had tried to lose herself in the kisses. As she'd drifted off to sleep, the memory of music floating through a forest wrapped around her.

Now, 4B was lying in her childhood bed, just twenty-four hours later, curled in a ball on her side, sore from missing Nora, and she felt like an outsider, disconnected. She remembered Nora playing the harmonica when they had been stranded on the ledge in the forest, and she tried to find the peace that listening had brought her when she was lost back then, too.

There was a certain familiarity in this house, with the people who called themselves her parents. She liked them. She felt safe with them. But she didn't know them.

The flight from Juneau had been a blur. Her father had given her an over the counter sedative to help her deal with her anxiety over flying so she'd slept through most of it.

When they'd finally arrived home that night, she'd been so emotionally and mentally drained, she hadn't been able to find the energy to ask the questions that had started to formulate in her mind. Did she still live with them? The room she stayed in, with its slightly juvenile décor, seemed like it may have been a childhood bedroom. Did she have a home of her own? Did she have siblings? Did she have a job? The question she didn't want to ask—because she was afraid of the answer—was whether she had anyone special in her life. When her mother had left her in her room, she'd fallen upon the bed and lain there awake, unable to sleep. An ache filled her chest. She longed to roll over and feel Nora's arms wrap around her protectively, pulling her snug against her side and into the warm, safe arc of her arm.

Time inched by, sleep still eluded her, and unable to shake the feeling of missing Nora, she sat up and swung her legs off the bed. Without turning on any lights, she navigated the long hallways and many rooms of her parents' home, along the path to the kitchen to get a drink of water. Unerringly, she went to the right cupboard, took down a glass, and filled it with water from the dispenser built into the front of the refrigerator. As she leaned back against the counter behind her, it occurred to her that her last motions were done out of habit. If her subconscious knew who she had been, it was just a matter of time when her conscious mind would, as well. Her memory felt closer to her now, just out of reach. She didn't know if that was a good thing or a bad thing.

She stared at the digital clock on the microwave and calculated the time difference. It was 2:00 AM in Cambridge, making it 10:00 PM in Juneau. Not too late, right? 4B thought. She had talked to Nora for a few minutes after the plane had arrived in Massachusetts, while she'd waited at baggage claim, but her parents had been right there and there were too many words between them to ever be done talking. God, she missed her.

A small sound from the deeper shadows at the end of the counter made her turn, and she started when she realized her mother was sitting on a barstool just a few feet away. She had probably been there the whole time.

"I didn't see you there," she said moving across the kitchen to lean against the counter standing between them. In the dim light, her mother looked younger with her hair slightly mussed and without her makeup. Until now, she hadn't seen her with a single hair out of place, even when she'd been crying at the airport, or after the lengthy flights to and from Juneau. Now, sitting before her in a cotton nightgown, the woman seemed softer, more relaxed, still beautiful. Affection stirred within 4B.

"Sorry. I tried not to scare you," said her mother over the rim of the mug she was holding. "I almost said something when you came in. I watched you navigate like you remembered," said her mother with a hopeful tone. "Do you?"

She was trying so hard, even though she seemed to be at a loss for how to cope with a daughter who didn't know her. 4B wanted to please her. But she didn't want to lie to her.

"Sorry. Not really. I'm not sure how I knew where the glasses were. I just did."

"It's a start, I suppose." Her mother lifted her mug and sighed. "I was just finishing some tea."

"Chamomile. You always drink it when you can't sleep," said 4B, and then realized what she had said. Another thing she didn't know how she know, but she did.

Her mother smiled. "You're right. It's the only thing that seems to help."

"I wish I could recall more. I feel like I'm being… disloyal to you and dad, not remembering," admitted 4B. She'd felt them watch her, skewering her with their expectant looks, here in this strange house, waiting for a sign indicating their daughter was whole once again.

"Oh, honey. I don't blame you for it. Neither of us do. We have faith your memory will come back soon."

"I hope so. I feel so... adrift."

"Adrift. That's an interesting word. If I may say so, I think you were feeling adrift before, though. I'm sure the memory loss is exacerbating it."

"You mean before the accident?" asked 4B. It was frustrating that other people knew who she was but she didn't. It made her feel less tangible, not knowing who she was, whether what she felt was even real.

"I don't know. I shouldn't have said anything. You never told me you were feeling that way. I just had a feeling. And maybe I was reading into it, but the last couple of times we spoke, you seemed distant, very thoughtful. I was going to mention it the next time we talked, but then, well, there wasn't a next time. And now..." Her mother shook her head, indicating she wished she could take it back. "I shouldn't have said anything right now."

4B didn't know what to say. Feelings drifted through her, among them, ones of confusion, frustration, even anger, but she didn't know why. She had no context in which to apply them, so she stood there with feelings she didn't know how to manage. It made her miss Nora even more and she wanted to cry.

"Do you want a cookie?" Her mother's voice broke through her confusion, easing the tightness squeezing her chest.

"Chocolate chip?"

"With walnuts."

"Is there any other kind?" they asked at the same time.

Her mother smiled, pulling the cookie jar from the middle of the counter and taking two large cookies out of it.

"Mmm... homemade," sighed 4B taking one.

"Miriam baked them when we were on our way back from Alaska," said her mother, as she took another glass out of the cupboard and poured some milk into 4B's empty water glass. She then poured some for herself.

"Who's Miriam? You mentioned her another time, when we were still in Juneau."

"Sorry. I keep forgetting you don't remember everything," said her mother.

Anything, thought 4B, but there was no need to say it. Her mother and father were still coming to terms with her amnesia and there was no need to press it.

"Miriam is our house manager. She's really much more than that, though.

She's been with us since before you were born. Her mother lived with my parents until she retired, and Miriam has been with us running the roost, as she likes to call it, since she finished her degree in hospitality management. She so very much wanted to be here when you arrived, but she had to be at her mother's convalescent home tonight. She'll be here tomorrow, though. She can't wait to see you. These cookies are her specialty and a special homecoming gift from her because she knows you love them."

4B tried to pull up a Miriam in her memory. Still nothing. Maybe a little flare of warm feelings, but nothing solid.

"I smelled them when we walked in," said 4B, taking a bite of cookie and then a sip of milk. A sense of security washed over her.

"I'll be honest. They say that smell is the most powerful sense connected to memory. You've always loved fresh baked chocolate chip cookies, so we thought..." Her mother's voice trailed off as she finished with a shrug.

"The olfactory receptors are part of the limbic system, which controls our emotions and the formation of our memories," said 4B, and then she looked up. "I have no idea how I know that."

"No?" Her mother looked like she wanted to say more, but she didn't.

"I know all this stuff, but I don't remember how I know it. Is it common knowledge? Educated knowledge?" 4B sighed. "Who am I?"

Her mother placed her glass on the counter. "Dr. Warren advised us not to do it unless you asked, but, she said it might help to tell you some stories when you're ready. Provide you with some details about what you've done in the past. Do you want me to tell you some stories to see if it helps?"

"You spoke to Dr. Warren?"

"This afternoon during the last layover. Her name was in the paperwork you gave us to look over. I gave her a call to see if there was anything I could do to help you through this. She's a good doctor and very concerned about you. She was very protective and wouldn't tell me anything about you I didn't already tell her first, even when I told her who I was. I hate throwing the Senator title around, but even that didn't work. Regulations, and all. But she did explain some ways to help with your amnesia."

"Like what?"

"She said a little storytelling might be a good way to nudge things along, although she advised us to be careful not to plant memories, so much as to ask about familiar things."

"What does that mean?"

"Well, she said memory was a tricky thing. That you have no short-term memory loss is a good sign. But there is a chance just by telling you things, you might try to synthesize the stories we tell into false memories, just because you want to remember."

"That makes sense. Why don't you start with facts? Like do I have brothers or sisters? Do I have a job?" 4B stopped short of asking about whether she was romantically involved with anyone. She wasn't sure she wanted to know just yet. Another sharp pang of missing Nora passed through her.

"Okay…" said her mother, looking like she was trying to figure out what to tell her first. "You're our only child. You grew up here, in this house. You love horses and rowing—you lettered in it in high school and were on your college rowing team. Your favorite color is blue. You just graduated from med school at Johns Hopkins University."

"That explains some things," mumbled 4B noting the medical knowledge that seemed to come to her when needed.

"With honors," added her mother with a proud smile, making 4B feel special. "After which you went down to Guatemala, like you do every summer, to do the immunizations. Except this year Layce couldn't go with you, what with the baby, and all."

"Layce?" Something pulled at her at the mention of the name.

"Layce is your best friend. You've known her since childhood. That's why you went to Los Angeles. To meet Layce and Andy's new baby. Andy is Layce's wife." Her mother looked at her as if she was looking for a reaction and 4B shrugged her shoulders to tell her none of it was ringing any bells. "You came back from Guatemala, packed up your apartment in Baltimore, and flew out to L.A. You were supposed to come back here for a quick visit before you went back to Baltimore to start your residency next week. The two times I talked to you—right after you got back from Guatemala and right before you flew out to L.A.—you sounded a little distracted. Like you had a lot on your mind. That's where I picked up on the 'adrift' thing." Her mother paused as if 4B might have additional information, but 4B didn't have anything to add, so her mother continued. "You go to South America every year with the med school to give inoculations. You went this year, like usual, and when you came back, you were supposed to go down and pick up the stuff you'd already packed at the apartment, so you could move into an apartment closer to the university hospital where you are scheduled to start your residency." Her mother studied her for a few seconds. "But I guess it's all up in the air now."

"I start a residency next week?" 4B had only an abstract idea of what that would entail, but even as her mother told her about it, it didn't seem like it had anything to do with her.

"If you'd like, I can take care of it when I go back to Washington for next week's session. Put things on hold for a little while until things… settle down. I can make a quick trip to Baltimore and explain things." Her mother's voice trailed off and 4B could almost feel her mother's eyes on her as she searched her face.

"That would be great. I don't even know where to begin dealing with all of that. None of this sounds familiar," said 4B, though a small amount of what she could only attribute to anxiety started to tighten in her chest at the information. She was getting used to not recognizing anything that she was supposed to know, but the ache accompanying the anxiety was new. She wondered if it had to do with not being able to fulfill the plans she had made, or if it was something else.

Roslyn paused and studied her daughter.

"I'm not sure if I should mention this next thing…"

"I guess I need to know everything," said 4B with a sigh.

"Well, this one is big. Dr. Warren said to try and ease you back into things. Not to overwhelm you. I had hoped this part would come to you on its own, being in a familiar place, but since you're still trying to remember me and your father…" her mother paused. "Do you remember Kev at all?" asked her mother, watching her intently. 4B searched her empty memory and shook her head. "He's in some of the pictures in your room."

4B had looked at the small grouping of photos displayed in her room, on her dresser, in various frames. Aside from her parents, she didn't recognize any of the people in them. They were all from a few years ago, based on how young she looked in the ones she was in. The absence of recent photos in the display confirmed for her that she hadn't lived at home with her parents in a few years. She shook her head.

"Are you going to say I'm married, or something?"

Her mother smiled.

"Soon, I hope, but currently you're engaged." 4B's stomach knotted up. Engaged? Her mother watched her face. Aside from the tightening in her belly, she had no other reaction, no flood of memories, no connection to the news. Kev was one of the names she'd seen as a missed call on her phone, along with some from Layce and a few others. Now she was glad she hadn't listened to the messages yet. She wanted to have a better handle on things before she did that. "He wanted to go with us to Alaska, but he's in the middle of a trial. It destroyed him to stay in Dallas. By the way, he's as mystified as we are about why you were in Alaska. I've spoken to him several times and he's anxious to see you. He was ready to abandon the trial and jump on the next flight out, but your father convinced him it might be better to stick out the trial. At least for now."

"Engaged, huh?" 4B recalled the photos on her dresser. She assumed the tall blond boy in one of them was Kev.

"You haven't set a date, but now that you've graduated we hope it will be soon." Roslyn let the comment trail off and just gave 4B a long look. "Of course you still have your internship and residency coming up, but I hope you don't wait long before you have the wedding. I know Kev is ready to get started."

4B tried to keep her face from showing the shock. She was engaged. She drank the last of her milk.

"Still nothing?"

"Nothing," she lied. Well, it wasn't a complete lie. It was true the information hadn't triggered any memories, but the shock she felt was certainly something.

❀❀❀❀❀

When her mother couldn't stifle her yawns anymore, they decided to try to get some sleep. Having a little more context around things, she went straight to the photos on her dresser and studied them. She took them out of the frames and found dates, names, and places written on the backs of them. Some of the frames contained more than one photo. It seemed she'd just put photos on top of others over time. There were about a dozen snapshots in all. One was of her on a horse. Some were of her and various friends. Most were of her and Kev or her and Layce. One had Kev standing behind her, leaning against a low wall, while she stood in front of him, wrapped in his arms. They looked happy. Another photo was of her and Layce. The back of the photo described them as best friends with a heart around Layce's name. Layce was a tall, beautiful, athletic-looking girl, and in the picture they stood side by side in front of a skiff that floated in the river behind them. They wore identical rowing uniforms, and Layce's arm was draped casually over her shoulders. Her arm was wrapped around Layce's waist. They looked happy, too. It was interesting to her, looking at herself in the photos, seeing the connection she had with others, yet she didn't feel connected to the moments or the people in them. She looked around her room again. She still didn't feel connected to the things she saw, the tasteful decorations and neutral colors. She put the photos back into the frames and turned off the light.

She curled up on the bed and called Nora. It was almost 4:00 AM in Massachusetts. Almost midnight in Juneau. All 4B needed was to hear her voice, so they only spoke for a few minutes. When they hung up, she could still hear Nora's voice in her mind, the rich calming tones, the smooth pace. She especially remembered the tingling anticipation of hearing what Nora would say next. They hadn't talked about anything major, but she wanted more. It seemed they'd never run out of words to share. When they'd hung up, 4B felt better, but she hadn't told Nora about Kev, the fiancé, her fiancé. How could she? He wasn't even real yet. Just an old photo on her dresser and a name programmed into her phone.

❀❀❀❀❀

She hadn't slept well that night. Unsurprisingly, the late talk with her mother had brought up all kinds of questions about who she was, her life, what she was going to do. But mostly, she felt guilty for not telling Nora about Kev. She woke, tired and fuzzy after less than two hours of restless sleep, immediately wanting to call Nora, to tell her she was engaged, to see what kind of advice Nora would give her. She stared at her phone, imagining Nora still asleep. Despite Nora's assurance 4B could call any time, Nora had told her she was going with Tack on a provision run that day, so 4B decided to call later.

The house was still and quiet when she got out of bed. The smell of coffee brewing filled her with a sense of comfort. She pulled on a thick robe and left her room to follow the scent. A thermal carafe sat on the counter, although there was no one around. She poured a steaming cup, and after adding cream and sugar, she stole out onto a patio overlooking a neat flower garden being groomed for the pending winter. A bed of vibrant calibrachoa encircling a mound of mums provided a late season splash of color. Beyond that, a long, neatly landscaped lawn scattered with falling leaves sloped away from the house and ended at a copse of thick woods. The damp air was chilly. Everything was wet, and clouds still mottled the sky, but the rain that had been falling since she had arrived had finally paused. She removed a plastic cover from one of the wicker chairs, and curled up on the cool, soft cushion, tucking her bare feet underneath her. Shivering, she clutched her coffee cup and enjoyed the sounds of the waking day.

Patches of sunlight and blue sky occasionally broke between the gray clouds being swept east by a light wind. Each time a waterfall of sunlight illuminated an area near her, she was transfixed with the resulting dia-mond-studded landscape. Drops of fallen rain clung to the edges of the stubborn remnants of summer and outlined the colorful leaves on the limbs of the trees around her. The smell of wet earth and cleansed vegetation floated in the morning air. Something in the moment felt like home. She closed her eyes and breathed deeply.

4B was filled with a nervous peace. It reminded her of the sense of antic-ipation she had felt in the days after waking from the accident. She'd spent her days studying Nora, watching her move around the camp, taking care of them, playing cards, laughing. They had been in a scary predicament, yet it had seemed so simple. There had been an underlying anxiety over being res-cued, but she knew most of it was what she had absorbed from Nora, since her own lack of memory brought the gift of being unconcerned with what she didn't know. But there had been a tingle of excitement all along. And then the bear had visited them, and in the aftermath of that, 4B had known she was attracted Nora. It had been so simple and uncomplicated. She shut her eyes and remembered. The firelight had bathed them. And for once, she was providing comfort to Nora. She'd lain beside Nora, trying to calm her, all the while, feeling like she couldn't get close enough to her. So she had touched her, and the restlessness had eased, replaced with a desire that still filled her when she thought about Nora. She longed to touch her now. She sighed and drifted in body memories that held no confusion or fear.

❀❀❀❀❀

Early afternoon brought another rainstorm and 4B's restlessness was growing. She was confined to a house she didn't know and there was no one to keep her company. Her mother was home, not wanting to go too far during 4B's first day home but she was working in her office located in the back of the house. Looking perfectly put together, 4B was amazed at her mother's energy the two times she'd seen her that day, once when she had checked in to see how 4B was doing and another for a few minutes when her mother had come out for a cup of coffee. 4B hadn't seen her father, who had gone to the hospital much earlier, according to her mother. Miriam was around, but she had disappeared into the many rooms of the rambling house after a tearful reunion, leaving 4B alone once again to putter about. Left to her own devices, and with no outlet to express the feelings that were bubbling up from a well of memories just outside her reach, 4B moved from room to room, seeking comfort in drinking too much coffee and eating too many chocolate chip cookies.

Finally, 4B settled in the informal dining area off of the large kitchen and stared out at the yard as the weather whipped at the remaining leaves on the trees. A notepad rested under her tapping fingers. She'd composed a letter to Nora in her mind, but when it came to putting the words on paper, she couldn't do it. There was too much to say, and the words and ideas competed in her mind. An enormous feeling built within her, but the words she conjured did nothing to describe it adequately. It was as if the very act of trying to define it pushed it away. She felt like she was chasing mercury, the small silver beads scattering and coalescing of their own will, slipping away as she reached for them, eluding capture. All the while, she wondered—if she caught anything, would it do more harm than good?

Her restless fingers began to doodle and then to draw. A portrait of Nora took shape beneath the tip of her pen.

A crack of thunder rattled the house and 4B's thoughts wandered to the storm that had raged while she and Nora had been in the forest. How comfortable they had been playing cards and talking, sheltering under the broken wing. And then her thoughts drifted to the night they had first made love. She remembered every touch, every word, every sensation that had rocked her body and heart, and as she lost herself in her memories, a little of the restless energy left.

A hand on her shoulder made her jump. She dropped the pen she'd been holding and it rolled across the table.

"Sorry, honey. I seem to be getting into the habit of startling you," said Roslyn, pulling out the chair next to her and sitting down. She placed a fresh cup of coffee on the table in front of 4B, and her nerves twisted at the thought of ingesting any more caffeine. At the same time, she craved the comfort of cradling the warm cup in her hands. Her mother smiled.

"Decaf."

"Perfect, thanks," said 4B, lifting the cup to her mouth. The steam from the hot liquid wafted up over her chin and into her nose. She sighed.

Roslyn turned the notepad so she could see the picture 4B had been absorbed in. "Oh, that's a lovely drawing of Nora."

4B looked at the picture. She barely remembered drawing it. The memories she'd been enjoying had demanded more of her active brain. As a result, the picture had been a product of her deeper mind, the part that felt more than thought. The image was of the first time 4B had seen Nora's face. She was above her, the sun shining through the edges of her hair. Now as she studied it, it could have been Nora getting ready to kiss her. The expression on Nora's face was one of elation and discovery, an expression that 4B had come to love.

4B nodded and her fingers traced the edge of the sketch.

"She's a very beautiful woman," said Roslyn, studying the drawing. "I didn't expect that in Alaska."

"What do you mean?"

"It just seems like such a hard place to live. Like it would weather the people."

"I like it there." 4B didn't mention that she had seen many beautiful women in Alaska. The women seemed comfortable in their skins. None of them had been more beautiful than Nora, though.

"Have you talked to her since you arrived home?" asked Roslyn.

"Yes, a couple of times." She didn't mention the calls had become her touchstone, and not having that link today while Nora was working with Tack had been harder than she'd thought it would be.

"You two seemed quite close. I imagine, under the circumstances, you were dependent on her. It would build a friendship rather quickly, I'd think."

"Yes, we're very close." 4B wanted to tell her mother they were more than just close, that they were lovers, but something stopped her. The fact that she had a fiancé was a good enough reason for her to be careful. Roslyn glanced at 4B as if she were going to say something, but changed her mind. She studied the picture a few seconds longer.

"Do you think you'll remain friends? Despite the distance? Like you and Layce have?"

She wanted to remind her mother that she didn't remember Layce, that she didn't remember anyone. But she didn't want to see the sadness settle on her mother's face when she was reminded of such things. So she shrugged and answered honestly.

"I hope so. I can't imagine not having Nora in my life."

"She did save it," agreed her mother.

In more ways than one, thought 4B, taking a sip of the decaf coffee, and then wondered why she had thought that particular thing.

They were quiet for a minute, while 4B watched the rain hitting the window and thought about Nora.

"I forgot what a talented artist you are."

Roslyn flipped through the pages in the notepad; past sketches of horses, trees, a dock with rowboats tied to it; past a relaxed hand, and a bird sitting on a fence; until she stopped at a half-finished picture of a girl, a few pages in.

Roslyn stopped to study the sketch. 4B had seen the drawing when she had found the pad of paper in her bedside table and had absently flipped through it. "I haven't seen Layce since she moved to California. How is she?" her mother asked.

"I don't know," said 4B.

"You were just out th—" began Roslyn, but she stopped. "How careless of me. You don't—" 4B listened as her normally implacable mother struggled with words. It was another thing she inexplicably knew—her mother's grace under any pressure—well, almost any pressure. The older women pulled back her shoulders and took a deep breath. "I'm sorry, honey."

"It's okay. It's kind of weird. I think I'm remembering feelings before remembering events. I mean, some things feel familiar even if I don't remember the specific detail. Then, other things I think I should feel something about, there's nothing. If that makes sense."

"It does, and I guess it's a start," said her mother. She paused and seemed to search 4B's eyes for something. "I'm not sure if this is the right time, but I wonder if you would reconsider talking with Kev." At the look of question on 4B's face, her mother added: "I spoke to him this morning. He said you haven't answered any of his calls. He's worried about you."

"I don't even know him," 4B tried to explain.

"You've known him your entire life, honey. When you talk to him, maybe it will—"

"But I don't remember him, Mom. Not at all." 4B hated the look of disappointment on her mother's face. She also wondered why she wasn't more curious about this man who was supposed to share her life. She felt more curiosity about Layce than she felt about Kev. She sighed and shrugged. "Can you tell me a little bit about him?"

Her mother smiled and settled back into her chair. She seemed to gather her thoughts.

"Your fiancé, Donald Kevin Kirkham, is the son of Daddy's best friend, Jackson. Do you remember Judge Donald Jackson Kirkham?" When 4B shook her head, she went on in that sing-song way of someone retelling a well-known story. "Daddy has known Jackson all his life. And Jackson's wife, Sandra, is one of my dearest friends. The Kirkhams are like family to us. We go on vacations together and celebrate holidays together. When Sandra and I had babies so close together, we joked that we timed it so you two could marry to merge the families. For a while, it seemed pretty far-fetched, but you surprised us. You can imagine our joy when you two decided to get married." 4B's mother looked like she was lost in happy memories. "Like his father before him, Kev goes by his middle name. He's a lawyer like his father, too, and now that Jackson is a judge, Kev is running the family law firm. You and Kev have played together at family gatherings since you were infants. Let's see..." Her mother touched 4B's chin. "He hit you with a croquet mallet when you were three. That's where this little scar under your chin came from."

4B ran her fingers over the small bump under her chin. A feeling of déjà vu swept over her, but no memory.

"You got him back a few years later, though, when you pushed him backward down the slide at the marina. He banged his head so badly on the way down, he needed twelve stitches just over his ear. I'll never forget your little face when you followed him down that slide, intent on finishing what you started. But when you saw the blood, all of the anger left your face, and you went right over and applied pressure to the wound. When your father tried to tend to him, you told him you would take care of it. I think that's when you started to talk about becoming a doctor." Her mother paused with a soft smile playing across her face. "Anything yet?"

4B shook her head. She was enthralled by the story, but it didn't feel at all personal.

"When he went away to boarding school in seventh grade, you two drifted apart. He's a year ahead of you and you started to run with a different group of kids who you met at the rowing club. Your new friend, Layce, didn't get along with Kev, so when he came home you didn't reconnect, like usual. Sometime around your junior or senior year in high school, it all changed, and you and Kev grew closer. While Layce and you were still very close, her..." Roslyn paused to find the right word, "...interests led her into different circles. By the time all of you went off to college, you and Kev were dating pretty seriously, and things just built from there." Roslyn paused again, and 4B, who was looking out the window, felt her gaze on her. "How about now?"

4B looked at her mother and shook her head one more time. A few emotions had bubbled under the surface as her mother spoke, but the prevalent feeling she had was one of hopelessness. All she could think about was how she was going to tell Nora about Kev.

"Not even when he asked you to marry him?" asked her mother. 4B shook her head. Roslyn's eyes grew soft with memory, and 4B felt even worse that she couldn't remember. A sense of irritation started to trickle in. "It was beautiful. He asked you during the 4th of July celebration at the Pritchards'. The one they put on every year down at the marina. The entire community and all of the members of the country club were there. Kev was so excited. He'd already talked to your father, so we knew about it weeks earlier, but you had no idea. In fact, you almost ruined it two weeks earlier, when you announced you were going to go on your first trip to Guatemala, which coincided with the week of the party. It turned out you had the dates wrong, though, and everyone was relieved. Even then, you showed up late to the party. You were so clueless. It was like one of those crazy movies where the audience is left wondering if all the plans would fall apart or come together. It wasn't your fault. You didn't know everyone was waiting for you. But, Layce," her mother's eyes narrowed. "She knew. Anyway, just when everyone thought you weren't going to show up, you and Layce arrived. It was worthy of any soap opera," laughed Roslyn. "We were just about to get things started, though, when Layce stormed off. You still had no idea about Kev's surprise and you were going to go after her. But, the band started to play and the fireworks went off, and at the end, Kev had about a million sparklers lit on the other side of the river." Her mother paused. "Anything now?"

4B shook her head yet again. She didn't remember. Kev was her fiancé, so she must have accepted, but something inside of her knew she wouldn't like someone putting her on the spot like that.

"The sparklers spelled out "MARRY EM ELIZABETH". You were so shocked you didn't notice the out of sequence letters, or him on his knee next to you with the ring. When he took your hand…" Roslyn, wiped a tear away. "It was so romantic. Everything leading up to that moment—all the starts and stops and wondering if you would even show up—it was all worth it. It's been a long engagement. You've been at school and he's been working out of state so much lately, but you two are just as in love now as you've ever been. No one can wait until you make it official."

Roslyn ended her story, wiping away a few more tears and 4B could feel her mother studying her, waiting for her reaction, wondering if any of it would jog 4B's memory. But she felt nothing. Not as it pertained to her, anyway. She did feel put off by the smarmy proposal, though. Who does that sort of thing? And who accepts that sort of thing? Was she the kind of person who did? Clueless and all caught up in appearances and hokey tradition? She wondered if she was going to like herself when she started to really remember. The idea scared her a little.

"That's such a… romantic story," she lied. Saying what she thought her mother wanted to hear. "I wish I remembered. I really do. But there's just this big blank."

Her mother's hopeful expression turned to dismay, and then just as quickly opened up, as an idea hit her.

"I know something that might help. I pulled some stuff out last night. It might jog your memory," said Roslyn as she stood. "I'll be right back."

A few minutes later she was back with a pile of oversized leather-bound binders in her arms.

"These are your photo albums," said Roslyn placing them on the table. "I was going to give them to you last night, but you looked so tired from the trip back. I'd hoped to go through them with you, but I have so much work to do before my trip to Washington tomorrow. I was supposed to be in D.C. yesterday. Flying out to Alaska set my schedule back a little." 4B felt terrible for the trouble she was causing. Her mother must have seen it on her face. "I wouldn't change a thing, though." Roslyn stood there and patted the stack of albums. Then she leaned down to give her a hug. "Look through these. See if it helps. Pictures of Kev's proposal are in there somewhere, too. I had a professional photographer capture everything. I don't leave until tomorrow. I'll be in my office if you need me."

Roslyn stood and kissed the top of 4B's head, lingering to hug her again. The perfume her mother wore was familiar and 4B took it in with a deep breath. The scent lingered long after she watched her mother disappear down the hall into the back of the house. She picked up the now tepid cup of coffee her mother had brought her, pulled the top album from the stack, set it before her, and opened the cover.

For the next two hours 4B flipped through the albums and watched herself grow up. The scenes were familiar in a way, but it wasn't like the familiarity that came with having experienced the moments. That kind of familiar was still just beyond her grasp. But it seemed to dance closer as she watched her childhood march toward adulthood.

When she reached her teenaged years, the pictures contained many with the girl she now knew was Layce. They seemed close. Best friends. She peeled up one of the pictures. Written on the back, in her own handwriting was, Me and Layce at the Branton Boat Club and the date. In the picture, they were on the water in rowing regalia with a few other girls their age. Their hair was pulled back, cheeks flushed from the sun and exercise. 4B was in front and was lying back against Layce. Layce's arm was draped casually over 4B's shoulder, while the other was propped on a scull. It was the pose of two girls who spent a lot of time together. They looked happy and carefree. A feeling of nostalgia welled up in 4B's chest.

She pressed the photo back into place on the sticky sheet and reaffixed the plastic.

There were five albums in total, the last two contained mostly loose photos dropped between pages, as if the pace of life had gotten in the way of organizing memories. 4B shuffled through the photos and occasionally found herself drawn to a picture, but she didn't remember them. She found the photos of the engagement party her mother had described. One showed Kev on his knee. It was posed and her smile seemed forced.

Early afternoon had rolled into late afternoon and 4B's disquiet was building. Her head was full of the many still frames from the photos she had looked at. Something was simmering underneath it all, but it wasn't ready to break the surface. Nora had said she would call when she got back from the trip with Tack, but 4B picked up her new cell phone and thought about calling Nora anyway. Just listening to Nora's recorded message would be better than not hearing her voice at all. Her phone had been on silent all day and two more missed calls from Kev showed in her status screen. She dismissed them and her finger was poised over the dial button when her phone rang. Nora's name came up on the screen.

"I was just about to call you," she said into the phone with a smile. She hadn't even heard Nora's voice yet, but her disquiet abated as soon as she lifted the phone to her ear.

"We just landed. I haven't even helped Tack tie the plane down, yet." Nora sounded breathless and 4B could hear the sounds of the airport in the background. "The plane was still taxiing to the hanger when I jumped out and ran in to call you."

"Do you need to go? You can call back when you're free."

"I couldn't wait to talk to you," said Nora, and 4B heard a smile in her voice. She rubbed the center of her chest. "But, I really should help Tack get the plane settled. I'll call you as soon as I get up to the house, okay? Give me forty-five minutes?"

"Sure. I'll be waiting," said 4B. The anxiety that had been building all day was replaced with a tingling expectation. She gathered the albums and notebook and went up to her room to wait for Nora's call.

❀❀❀❀❀

4B was lying on her bed, her back against the headboard, finishing the sketch she had started of Nora, when the phone rang again.

"I missed you today," said 4B, when she answered on the first ring, not bothering with the usual hellos.

"I miss you every day," replied Nora, making 4B smile. "If I could, I'd never hang up with you. I'd have you chained to your cell and chat your ear off until you were sick of me."

"I don't think it's possible—the getting sick of you part. I feel the same way. It's been hard not being able to call you today," admitted 4B.

"I'm glad it isn't only me, then," said Nora with a chuckle.

4B felt herself emerging from the funk she had been in all day. They talked about Nora's work and 4B described how she had been going through old photo albums. She described her childhood friends, Layce and Kev, but not that Kev was her fiancé. Part of her hoped that if she didn't think about it, it might go away.

"It's so hard being cooped up like this when I don't know what I usually do to pass the time. I don't even know what kinds of books I like to read. I drew a picture of you today, though. Apparently, I can draw." 4B looked at the sketch on the top sheet of the pad of paper lying in her lap. She ran her finger along the strong line of Nora's chin.

"Really? I wanna see. Take a picture of it and send it to me?"

4B stared at the drawing and wished Nora were with her.

"Right now?" she asked.

"Yeah. Take it with your phone and send it to me. I'll wait."

4B snapped the picture and sent it to Nora. Unlike her earlier non-chalance about showing it to her mother, the thought of Nora seeing the drawing made her nervous. She bit back the impulse to offer excuses about its quality. She knew it was good—it was the intimacy in what she captured that made her shy.

"Okay, you should get it in a second."

"Oh, there it is now, hold on." 4B heard Nora say "Wow" from far away and then there were a few sounds of movement before Nora got back on the phone. "You drew that? From memory?" Nora sounded impressed and 4B let out the breath she'd been holding. "It's really good, baby. So real." 4B loved the sound of appreciation in Nora's voice and a hot tingle moved through her. Nora's voice dropped with her next words and another, more intense feeling washed through 4B. "Is it a drawing of when we were, um…? The look in my eyes seems to be… very…" Nora didn't finish, but 4B knew what she was saying. She had seen it, too.

"It's the first time I saw your face. When I woke up. You get a similar look when you're about to kiss me."

4B heard Nora take a breath, but she was quiet for a moment. When Nora spoke again, she heard the longing in Nora's voice. "I wish I could kiss you now," whispered Nora. Goosebumps rose across 4B's skin.

"Me too. I ache for it." 4B rubbed the center of her chest again and she thought about how true it was that emotions resided in a person's heart.

They were quiet for a moment and 4B felt a ripple of tight need broadcast from her, tugging at the connection she felt with Nora, even though they were physically thousands of miles apart.

"How are you doing? Are you doing okay? Is being home helping?" asked Nora.

4B let out a short laugh. "Honestly, I'm going insane. It's only been a day and I don't know what to do with myself."

"Are you feeling pressure to remember?"

"My parents are patient. They're trying to nudge things along, but they aren't pushing me. A few people have asked to visit, but I'm not ready for that. I guess I'm bored, though. And a little lonely."

"I'm not sure you'd like living up here, then," said Nora. "The weather can get pretty extreme. It gets so cold in the winter. People tend to go into a kind of hibernation. We don't leave our houses unless we have to. Often, we can't even get out if we wanted to. It can get very lonely and boring up here, too."

4B thought about being snowed in with Nora and knew it wouldn't be much of a hardship. Ways they'd entertain themselves filled her mind. She felt her face get hot with some of the details that came to mind.

"I don't know. I kind of liked it up there," she said, wondering if her voice revealed her carnal imaginings. "I miss it, actually."

"You do?" asked Nora, and 4B could hear the smile in her voice again.

"I do. It's pretty there. There's so much open space," explained 4B. "But, I think it's the people that are the real draw for me."

"There are some pretty great people up here," agreed Nora.

"Yep. Some of them are more wonderful than others," teased 4B.

"Wonderful, huh?" asked Nora. 4B could almost see the little smile line appear next to Nora's mouth.

"Mind-blowing, actually."

Nora's next question surprised her.

"What are you wearing?"

4B glanced down at herself. She had pulled on the first comfortable clothes she had found in the dresser that morning; a Harvard sweatshirt, which had seen better days, and a pair of threadbare shorts. One of her hands rested on her stomach under the fabric of her sweatshirt. Her skin was warm and soft against her palm. She wanted to say she was wearing something sexy, but she chickened out.

"Soccer shorts and a sweatshirt."

"Oh…"

"What were you expecting?" teased 4B, pretty sure Nora's thoughts were closer to the sexy thing than the reality.

"Nothing really," replied Nora.

"Nothing?" asked 4B suggestively and then laughed.

Nora cleared her throat.

"Well, that too, but what I meant to say was, when I think about you, I picture you in jeans and a sweatshirt." There was a sight pause, and then she added: "Or nothing at all."

"What if I told you I wasn't wearing anything at all?" 4B was breathless all of a sudden.

There was a moment of silence.

"I'd like that."

A tremor passed through 4B.

"Really? Because I can make it true."

"Then do it," said Nora, and a shiver ran down 4B's spine.

"Only if you do, too," said 4B. She nestled the phone between her ear and her shoulder as she slid her shorts and panties down.

"Okay," said Nora, her voice was hardly more than a whisper, but it made 4B's heart race.

"Where are you?" asked 4B after she pulled her sweatshirt off. She was naked now, since she hadn't been wearing a bra. She settled into the pillows against her headboard. She wondered if she should lock her bedroom door, but didn't get up, lest she break the tenuous courage that would allow her to do what she hoped they were about to do.

"In my room. On my bed," said Nora.

4B pictured Nora, nude, spread across her bed. She could see the room with vivid clarity, but the body she saw in her mind was all she was interested in. Her heart hammered in her chest.

"Are you done yet?"

"We've barely gotten started," said Nora with a slow laugh.

"I meant, are you done removing your clothes," 4B laughed, drawing her fingers up her abdomen.

"Yes," said Nora, and 4B heard her swallow. "Are you?"

"Yes. I'm lying on my bed."

"And...?"

"... and I've got my legs spread," said 4B, opening her legs as she spoke.

"Are you touching yourself?" Nora's voice was husky and 4B's core throbbed at the sound.

"Do you want me to?" asked 4B, reaching down to feel how wet she was. She slipped her finger once through her slick folds and shivered at the touch.

"Yes, and I want you to tell me how it feels."

"It feels good. Warm and wet. Are you touching yourself, too? Will you make yourself come while I tell you how it feels to touch myself?"

4B heard a small gasp, and when Nora responded, 4B's heartbeat accelerated to hear the tone she recognized from when they made love.

"Yes. God, the sound of your voice is almost enough. I'm so ready. I want you to describe what you're doing."

4B slid her fingers between her legs and around the hard knot of nerves that were beginning to pulse.

"I'm very wet."

"I am too," whispered Nora.

"My lips are swollen, and my clit is getting harder. I'm spreading my legs wider…" 4B moaned as she slid down to lie flat on the bed, her legs spread, the cool air wafting over her heat.

"Are you touching your clit?"

"I can't. It's too sensitive. I'm circling it. And it feels good, really, really good," whispered 4B. Her voice hitched as she drew her finger near the spot that twitched when she barely touched it. "I could make myself come right now, if I rubbed it. If I thought about you touching me." She breathed in through her teeth. "But I want to… feel this a little longer."

"I'm thinking about putting my fingers inside of you as you stroke yourself," said Nora, and 4B's center clenched as she thought about Nora sliding her fingers deep into her wet need.

4B moaned again as her fingers entered the slick well between her legs. "Ah, you feel so good inside of me. I want you deeper…"

"I am, baby. I am. Deep inside of you. I feel you tightening around my fingers."

"Oh, yes…" 4B's voice was breathy, and she imagined she felt the moist expiration of Nora's breath against her neck as she envisioned Nora moving above her.

"Are you coming yet?" whispered Nora, and her voice trembled in 4B's ear. She could see Nora's eyes in her mind, dark with need, her hand working quickly between her legs. The first surge of orgasm drenched her hand at the thought.

"Close. I want you to come with me. I want to see you."

"I'm putting my fingers inside and then pulling them out. It's you… you're inside, so far, so deep… you're thrusting faster, and faster…" Nora's voice faded away as the sounds of her breathing vibrated in 4B's ear. She could see Nora fucking herself, her orgasm building. The sensation filled 4B's body and her hips rose from the bed.

"It is me, baby," she said hoarsely. "I'm inside of you right now. But now I'm putting my mouth on you, tasting you, sucking you. God, you taste so good, feel so good… I can feel your…"

"I'm going to come... I'm coming now, it's so... oh, god..." panted Nora into her ear, and the words were all it took to trigger an explosion of energy through 4B's center.

"I'm coming..." said 4B as her hand flew in circles over her clit. She could feel more moisture spill out as her hips jack-knifed off of the bed.

"Oh... oh! I'm coming, too. Coming with you..."

The only sounds on the line were their ragged breathing as 4B's orgasm rolled on and the strangled sounds spilling from their throats as they voiced their ecstasy to one another. Finally, their moans began to subside and 4B relaxed onto the bed, her core throbbing with the residual shudders coursing through her body. She moved her fingers slowly over the swollen flesh between her legs and longed for the feel of Nora's body settling over hers, heavy and sweaty. She wanted to taste Nora's throat and feel the kisses Nora would have trailed down her neck before she took her into her arms and held her as the storm subsided and they relaxed around one another. 4B rolled onto her side and felt an absence more profound than she thought she could bear.

"I wish you were here. I want to hold you," she whispered as she held the phone to her ear with one hand and wrapped her other arm around a pillow.

"Me too, baby."

❀❀❀❀❀

The phone was ringing when 4B stepped out of the shower in the bathroom adjoining her bedroom. She threw on her robe and wrapped the towel around her head before she answered it. She hoped it was Nora. Her pulse raced at the memory of their call from the evening before.

"Hello," she said into the receiver as she sat on the edge of her bed without checking the caller ID. She slipped her hand into the top part of her robe and rubbed the skin of her upper chest.

"Hi, Elizabeth," said a male voice. "It's me." He cleared his throat. "Kev."

"Oh," said 4B, pulling her hand out of her robe and tightening the tie around her waist. "How... how are you?"

"I'm good," he said, and there was a pause. "I didn't think you'd answer. Your mom said you were still sorting things out. But I had to try." There was a pause. "God, this is weird. How are you?"

4B laughed at his honesty.

"About the same," she admitted.

She heard him clear his throat again. "You sound good."

"So do you?" she said for lack of anything to say and then cringed at the question she made it into. She squeezed the bridge of her nose. What was she supposed to say to this person she didn't know?

"Um... this is kind of new territory, so I'm not sure how to act."

"That makes two of us," she admitted.

Kev laughed and sounded self-conscious. For the first time, and in a very clinical way, she wondered how close she and Kev really were. They were engaged, but why hadn't he come to see her? She had the excuse of her amnesia. He didn't. Being in an out of state trial didn't seem like a good enough excuse.

"Your mom told you I'm still in Dallas working on a case that keeps on dragging out, didn't she?" he said, as if reading her mind. "They have us backed into a corner, and we've had to work day and night responding to the surprise witnesses and evidence they've called up. It's been..." he seemed to catch himself. "It's no excuse. I should have flown out as soon as I heard. Even if it meant losing the case. Anyway. I'm turning the case over to the rest of the team. It's got at least another week, but I'm coming home tomorrow. I need to see you. See for myself that you're okay. God, I should have come as soon as I heard... Anyway, my flight gets in at 5:00. I'll come straight from the airport. Is that okay? We could go to dinner." He sounded tentative.

She wanted to tell him no. What would they talk about? What would he expect from her? What about Nora? She thought she should feel guilty, but she didn't. Not about Nora, anyway. Quite the opposite—she felt bad she hadn't told Nora about him yet. She realized her earlier condemnation of him was a bit hypocritical.

"Elizabeth? Are you still there?"

"Oh, sorry. Yes. I'm still here."

"So, we're on for tomorrow?" he prompted her.

She searched for an excuse not to see him and her mind came up blank. "Um, sure?"

"Great! We'll go to Scampi's," he said. "Oh. I gotta run. They're calling us into court. I love you."

She was relieved when he hung up before she had time to reply. Her fingers pulled up Nora's number, but hovered without selecting it. She wanted to talk to her, tell her about Kev and ask her what to do. Instead, she dropped the phone without calling her. Why get Nora worried about someone she didn't feel anything about?

❀❀❀❀❀

When the doorbell rang the next evening, she met Kev and stepped out onto the front porch so she wouldn't have to invite him inside. No one was there to help her entertain him. Her mother, who was thrilled they were going out to dinner and positive it would kick start her memory, had left for Washington, D.C. earlier in the day. Her father was still at work. Earlier, when Kev had called from the airport to confirm their plans, she'd suggested she meet him at the restaurant for dinner, but he wouldn't have it, insisting on picking her up.

They faced each other on the door stoop under the expansive carport that stretched over the circular drive in front of the house. Kev's car, a red Porsche, was parked at the base of the sweeping steps leading up to the door. He fiddled with his key fob, took a step toward her, and hesitated. He looked like he didn't know what to do with his arms.

"You look great, Elizabeth," he said, reaching out and taking the coat she had draped over her arm.

"You do, too," replied 4B, stepping into the coat he held open for her. All she had to compare him to were the lifetime of two-dimensional pictures that she had poured through over the last couple of days. Here he was in person and she didn't know how to act. She turned to face him. The man who stood before her was tall, handsome, and had a great smile. He'd matured and filled out since the most recent photos of him, none of which did him justice. His sandy blond hair blew in the cool damp wind, a reminder of the earlier storms. Most of the clouds were gone and the cold, cobalt sky was darkening as the sun started to set. The huge porch lights picked that moment to click on, and the small landscaping lights lining the drive blinked to life. The switch from day to dusk was complete.

She looked at Kev and felt nothing in his presence aside from curiosity about the role he played in her life.

"It's good to see you," he said and then leaned forward to pull her into an awkward embrace. His hand drifted up to caress the back of her hair and he pressed her head into his chest. 4B fought an urge to push him away. He dropped a kiss on the top of her head and, after a pause, pulled away and aimed another at her lips. She turned at the last minute when she realized

215

what he meant to do and it landed on her cheek. He gave no indication it wasn't what he intended when he let her go. His smile was warm. "I've really missed you, Elizabeth."

She gave him a smile and followed him to the low sports car, where he held the passenger side door open for her.

Thankfully the restaurant was nearby, because it was a nearly silent ride during which Kev held her hand between shifting gears, his thumb worrying the skin on her knuckles. 4B pretended not to notice his surreptitious glances, trying for an easy expression as she stared out the windshield.

There was no doubt that the restaurant was a favorite place for them after the emotional greeting they received from the owner.

"Cara! My Elizabeth! Come hug Isabella!" the bubbly woman shouted when they entered, and 4B found herself tucked into an exuberant, swaying embrace. Isabella was tall and thin and maybe in her late thirties, but the hug she enfolded 4B into felt like comfort bestowed by the plushest of grandmothers. "So many prayers! My knees are raw. An airplane crash? How does this happen? You are okay, though?" Isabella's eyes welled up and she crossed herself, looking to the ceiling with gratitude, the words flowing continuously. There were no pauses in which 4B could politely respond, so she just nodded as Isabella walked them to their table. Once they were seated, and after another hug, Isabella went back to her duties and the waiter brought them a bottle of wine—a gift from Isabella.

The waiter poured the wine and 4B looked around. Unopened wine bottles were stored on their sides, in multiple cubbies along most of the restaurant's walls. Low lighting, quiet music, and candlelit tables gave the place a very romantic vibe. It was early for dinner, and aside from one other couple, they had the place to themselves. She wished she were there with Nora.

"You remember Isabella, then," said Kev with what seemed a controlled expression as the waiter left them and he placed the linen napkin in his lap.

"Not at all," confessed 4B, looking around to make sure she wasn't overheard. "She seems very nice, but this is all new to me."

Kev looked a little relieved to know 4B's distance wasn't just toward him. He took a long drink of his wine. "It was hard to believe at first, that you were in an airplane crash. But once I realized it wasn't some stupid prank, it was one of the worst days of my life. I'd been so busy with the trial, and I hadn't heard much about the initial accident. Only bits and pieces from clips

I'd see in the papers. And then your mother calls, nearly hysterical—that was a first—to tell me she's flying to Juneau to pick you up after seeing your picture in the paper. Holy crap, Elizabeth. You can't imagine... And there I was, stuck in Dallas... What happened?"

4B told him what she knew, both what she remembered and what she'd been told. He asked many questions, but she was thankful he didn't ask much about Nora. It wasn't that she didn't want to tell him, more like it didn't seem to be any of his business.

"Maybe it's a good thing you have no memory from the actual accident. It must have been terrifying," Kev said, searching her face. "Your mom said you only had a cut on your head? That's amazing. It could have been so much worse."

4B lifted her bangs to display her wound. She wore a small bandage. Makeup and careful placement of her hair helped to camouflage the bruising, but the surrounding area was still quite painful, which was evidence that she'd hit the bone pretty hard. Kev's eyes showed his distress when he looked at it, demonstrating the depth of his affection for her. It made her uncomfortable. She tried to find something to say, to change the subject, but without a memory of their past, she was at a loss.

"You look great, Elizabeth. I've missed you," he said and took her hand across the white tablecloth. She watched as if she were a spectator as he bent to kiss it, sensing they both knew how awkward the evening was playing out.

"Um, thanks," she said, inching her hand from his clasp after the brief kiss. She tried to make it look like she was just reaching for her wine glass, but from the way he studied her face, she knew he could feel her discomfort.

"You don't remember me at all, do you?" he finally asked.

She blew out a breath and dropped both hands into her lap. A sort of relief fell over her. She hadn't acted as if she had recognized him, but she hadn't said otherwise either. It was nice to have it out on the table.

"I'm sorry. I don't. My mom told me about you... about us," she said, feeling awkward, but he deserved the truth. Just because she didn't remember him didn't mean he felt the distance that she did. It had to be tough on him, even though she still judged him for not having come earlier. If something happened to Nora, she would drop everything. Technically, she had been cheating on Kev with Nora, though it didn't feel like it. If anything, she felt unfaithful to Nora for not telling her about Kev.

"Do you remember anything?" he asked, taking another sip of his wine.

He didn't seem mad. Confused and sad, maybe even curious, but not mad.

She shook her head. "I've been looking at photo albums. I feel something simmering under everything, like it will all come to me, but right now it's just a big blank," she confessed.

"Do the pictures help?" he asked with a hopeful look.

"I think so. They make the bubbling feeling stronger," she said ambiguously. She didn't want to tell him that only the pictures of Layce made her feel anything, that the pictures of him elicited nothing, except questions on why he hadn't come to see her before now. It was so confusing, more so, because she really didn't seem to care except for the principal of it all.

"You sound the same. You look the same."

"Do I?"

"Yeah, it has to be a good sign. I've really missed you, you know. Not just because of this. But being in Dallas has been hard. Hard for both of us, even before. Harder now, after all of this." His voice broke on the last word.

It was the first real emotion he had displayed, and 4B realized he was trying to be strong. Her mother had probably told him to be careful with her. There was a pause, and 4B wished he would speak, because she honestly didn't have a clue what to say.

"Why were you in Alaska?"

"I don't know."

"It seems so random."

"Yeah," she agreed. "I have no memory from before I woke up after the crash," she explained.

"The last time we spoke was right after you returned from Guatemala. You told me you were going out to visit Layce and Andy in L.A. It was a last minute decision. I should have gone with you." He ran a hand down his face. "This trial has taken over my life. Two weeks ago I was up to my neck in mountains of research. Now it's strategy as we argue it in court," his eyes flicked from her to the glass he held in his hand and back again. "Sometimes I wish I had followed your advice and become a human rights lawyer. At least I'd feel like I was doing something worthwhile when I'm living out of a suitcase. This whole mess about figuring out how many particles of petroleum in seawater my client can get away with before it constitutes negligence is ridiculous. I'm an attorney, not a scientist."

4B watched him speak, but felt unmoved by his frustration.

"Sorry. I know you hate it when I complain about work, especially when

I use it as an excuse not to see you more often."

"The good thing is I don't remember it," she said with a hopeful smile.

He smiled back and took another sip of his wine. He was really a handsome guy. She wondered again why she felt nothing in his presence.

"I guess you don't remember we have that thing tomorrow night, do you?"

"What thing?" she asked. She tasted the wine. It was good, but she wished it were the Moose Antler beer she'd had with Nora in The Strut. Maybe she was more of a beer person than wine.

"The reception-slash-campaign fundraiser at the capital," he replied. "Our firm is sponsoring the event for your mother's office. I know you hate those things. I'd say we should skip it, but that's another reason why I had to come back. I have to speak. I can go stag if I need to, though. If you're not up to it."

Irritation rose in her. He'd come back for a fundraiser, not to make sure she was okay. Again, she reminded herself she didn't care.

"You're right, I have no idea what you're talking about."

"Your mom warned me. It's not a big deal. You don't need to go."

4B studied Kev. She was confused. He seemed very upset about the accident, but he hadn't rushed to her side. Instead, he seemed very obligated to a fundraiser for her family, but he was being very understanding if she didn't want to go. He seemed genuinely concerned about her. Was he just being nice by giving her an out? It seemed like he was letting her call the shots. Shots she didn't have enough information to call.

"Who'll be there? Would I have to speak or socialize with people I should know?" she asked, wondering what she was getting herself into if she decided to go. Was she really considering it?

"Not officially. People would want to talk to you, but mostly just because of your mother. You wouldn't know most of them anyway, so memory or no memory, it would be about the same experience. Even though your mother has kept it out of the papers, pretty much everyone in local politics has heard about your amnesia."

"In the papers?"

"You're a senator's daughter. It was all over the news when they realized who you were. Your mom worked overtime trying to explain why you were traveling under an assumed name. She explained it away by saying it was a security issue."

"Really? She hasn't said a thing to me. I don't even know why I was up there or why I was using another name."

"Don't worry. I didn't tell her it was the same name you used on the fake ID you had back in high school."

"A fake ID? Was I some sort of delinquent?"

Kev surprised her with a sudden laugh. "That's funny, actually. You were the least delinquent person I know. All I know is the Grace Trackton name you used on your tickets is the same name you used on the ID—an ID you never used, by the way. It's amazing you still have it."

"Like everything else, I have absolutely no memory of that. I can't wait to find out when it all comes back to me—if it ever does."

"I'm sure it will. Just give it time, Elizabeth. Layce might be able to fill in some of the gaps. The officials told your mother that you flew out to L.A. under your own name," he said as he took another sip of his wine. His voice was hesitant when he asked the next question. "Have you talked to her yet? Layce?"

"It would be awkward. If it makes you feel any better, I don't remember her either."

His eyes dropped to his glass, which he slowly rotated by the stem. "It's stupid, but, yes, it does make me feel better. I wanted to call her myself to see if she knew anything, but, number one, she hasn't talked to me since that huge argument before I asked you to marry me, and number two, I didn't want you to think I was nosing around in your business."

"My life is a bit of a soap opera, isn't it?"

"Not really. At least not until recently. It's been pretty much med school and being a senator's daughter. I'd say that's a lot in itself. All of this false name business and travelling to parts unknown is new. I can't wait for your memory to come back to find out what's changed."

4B was impressed with Kev's patience. He seemed like a remarkable person. But he didn't know about Nora yet. She wondered if it would change once he did. She wouldn't blame him if it did.

"Thank you for… well, I'm not sure what I'm thanking you for. But your patience is a relief," she said.

"Patience is my middle name."

Based on her mother's short history lesson, she knew what he meant by it. She wasn't ready to talk about their engagement yet.

"About the event tomorrow. I'm not sure what I would wear…"

He perked up. She knew then he wanted her to go, and she decided right then that she would. It wasn't a date. It would just be fulfilling a commitment.

"You and your mom already picked out that blue dress when you came home after Guatemala. You modeled it for me over Skype. It's kind of velvety, with swirls, and a little lower cut than you usually wear… which is why I love it so much."

4B ignored the last part and remembered seeing something like it in the closet, where she had found several dresses hanging in bags. There was a blue one matching Kev's description. Below it was a shoebox with matching shoes in it.

"What time is the event?" she asked. Her mom would be thrilled.

❁❁❁❁❁

The doorbell rang the next night, precisely at seven. 4B sat on the edge of her bed talking to Nora. She was in the blue dress, swinging her feet with the matching shoes dangling from her toes. She'd already sent a picture to Nora of herself standing in front of a full-length mirror. It was Nora's request. She tried to look poised and sophisticated in it. It felt like a sham, but Nora had actually gulped when she opened the picture on her phone, which made 4B feel more attractive than she'd ever felt in her life—at least as much of it as she remembered. She still felt like a little girl playing dress up, though.

They'd been on the phone for almost a half an hour and 4B had been trying to figure out how to tell Nora about Kev. Nora knew she was going to the benefit with Kev, but she hadn't asked more, and 4B hadn't offered more. Now, with Kev waiting downstairs she knew she was out of time. She still couldn't get the words out. She sighed impatiently.

"What's the matter," asked Nora.

4B almost told her and then chickened out again.

"How am I going to get through this night? I still can't believe I said I'd go. I won't know anyone. I won't know what to talk about." It was all true.

"No one will care, looking as phenomenal as you do," said Nora, always supportive.

"You're biased."

"And you're brave. Your courage is one of the things I like so much about you. You'll do fine, I'm sure."

"I don't know…"

"Your parents are comfortable with you going, right?"

"They are. My mom is tickled that I'm, and I quote, 'getting on the horse again.'"

"See? They wouldn't let you go if they thought it would be too difficult, or worse—traumatic—right?"

"You're right. You're always right."

"It's my superpower," joked Nora.

"Among other things," said 4B loosening up a little. Nora always made her feel better.

Nora chuckled and then cleared her throat.

"I guess you need to go meet Kev."

4B still felt like a liar. The information sat on the tip of her tongue, itching to be said. But even though she was certain it was only a matter of time before she'd break it off with him, she wasn't sure how to tell Nora without causing her concern. In her own heart, and after evaluating how she felt about her parents—and even about sweet Miriam—all of whom she still couldn't remember, but still felt innate warm feelings for—she knew Nora was far more important to her than Kev was. Something inside of her knew she'd feel the same even after her memory came back. She just didn't know how to express it in a way that would ease any concerns Nora might have. That's why she hesitated, she told herself.

There was also the small detail that she and Nora had never talked about what they were to one another. Truthfully, she was grateful that Nora had been so careful not to put any pressure on her or complicate things with expectations. It was clear, at least in her own head and heart about whom she wanted to be with.

Faced with the unusual position she was in, she decided right then to finish things off with Kev before she told Nora about their past. Because, whoever Kev may have been to her before was definitely in the past. Her feelings about Nora made everything pale in comparison.

"Yes, I suppose," she sighed. "I can hear him talking to my dad, who also told me I could pretty much just nod my head and smile all night. I just need to make an appearance."

"Do you have to stay long?"

"I definitely don't plan on it," said 4B. She heard her father calling for her from the foot of the stairs. "I'd better get going. My dad is summoning me for the carriage."

"Have fun tonight, Cinderella."

4B looked at the delicate blue velvet pumps dangling from her toes and, although she felt pretty in the glamorous dress she wore, she wished she were in Juneau wearing her favorite hiking boots and jeans, talking to Nora in person. Or better yet, not wearing her favorite hiking boots and jeans and doing something much more fun than talking. She sighed again.

"I'll try. I'll call you later and let you know how it goes."

"I look forward to it."

4B heard the smile in Nora's voice as they hung up and it calmed her nerves. Still, she sat on the edge of her bed, gathering her courage. Why had she agreed to attend this function? Her father came into the room, no doubt to see how much longer she would be. She stood up and nervously modeled her dress for him.

"You look stunning, pumpkin," said Dean Tollworthy, walking closer to kiss her cheek. 4B glowed with warmth at her father's compliment. Despite having no memory of him, being around him was a comfort she couldn't explain. His affection for her was evident in the way he looked at her, and she felt the same. If she had to define the word faith to someone, she would describe what she felt when she thought about either of her parents.

"Thanks, Daddy. With Mom away, I was worried about getting ready, but it all came to me as I went."

"I don't know how you women do it. When your mother drags me to these things, it's all I can do to shave properly and slip into my monkey suit. She has to remind me to get a haircut the day before and she picks out my cufflinks. You have so much more to deal with. Don't you tell her, but I'm relieved when your mother goes out of town and I don't have to go to these things."

"I'm sure I have some politically correct response to that, Daddy, but all I can think to say right now is you're right. It isn't fair," she laughed and kissed his cheek.

4B had discovered that, with her mother out of town, she and Kev were acting as her mother's ambassadors to the state Democratic fundraising dinner. Kev had the added duty of representing his family's law firm of Kirkham and Kirkham, who were one of the sponsors of the event. When 4B had called her mother to ask about it after she arrived home from dinner with Kev the night before, 4B's mother was thrilled she had decided to attend. Her mother, thinking it would be too much to ask of her, had tried to re-arrange her own schedule to make it back for the dinner, but she wasn't successful. She said they would have been able to make due one way or another, since so many political leaders were scheduled to attend, but it was a tradition for the Tollworthy family to host the event and it pleased her mother that the tradition would stand again this year. They discussed her responsibilities, and her mother echoed Kev's description that she would mostly need to shake hands and chat with the guests, but mostly it was just smiling and listening, since the guests would do most of the talking. Her mother eased her worry by telling her everyone there knew about the accident and if it came up she should discuss what she wanted to about it, or gently change the subject. The short speech 4B would have made was given to Kev, who she would accompany on the stage. Her mother admitted her plan had always been for 4B to follow in the footsteps of a long line of politicians from her mother's side of the family. The revelation was a shock to 4B. She didn't feel like a politician. If anything, the doctor thing seemed the correct path for her. It was how her brain worked. It may have been the schooling, but fundamentally, she didn't feel an affinity toward politics at all. She wondered if any of that would change when her memory came back.

Even though she felt a surprising lack of nervousness about attending the political dinner, her mother's disclosure about wanting her to go into politics, along with dinner with the fiancé she had felt no recognition for, left her feeling more disconnected than ever before. The only part of the day when she had felt grounded was when she'd discovered the stables during a long walk around the property. Behind the large building had been a pasture, and when she'd leaned against the fence to watch the horses, a beautiful gray mare had come to her. The horse had seemed happy to see her, even nuzzling her pocket for what she imagined was an expected treat. A feeling of peace and carefree happiness had filled 4B as she stroked the soft nose and ran her hands through the horse's mane.

After that, she'd wandered around the stables for a little while and had followed a well-worn path leading into the wooded areas beyond the buildings. It had felt good to be outside and as she'd walked, she realized the paths seemed familiar to her, and while she couldn't have described the landmarks prior to seeing them, she felt confident she could get back to the house without any trouble. At one point, she'd found a small clearing with a thick, low branch from one of the trees extending through a waterfall of sunlight. She sat on it for a few minutes. It had seemed familiar as if it had been a cherished spot for her in the past she did not remember.

4B tried to remember the feeling of peace she'd had during her walk as she followed her father down the stairs.

"Have a nice evening, pumpkin," he said with a kiss on the cheek as he left her at the door to his study.

"Thanks, Daddy," she said watching him walk down to the family room where she knew he'd turn on the baseball game. She'd only been home a few days and already she knew her father's routine.

The heavy wooden door was slightly ajar and soft yellow light spilled from the room. When she pushed it open, Kev stood with his back to her, studying the titles of books and medical journals behind her father's desk. When she entered the room, he turned and walked toward her, his eyes never leaving her face. The look of adoration in his eyes made her uneasy. She stood where she was next to the door as he approached, and sensed his internal debate on the correct greeting with her. After dinner the night before, he had merely given her a chaste kiss goodnight. She hadn't invited him in and he'd gotten back into his car and driven away. She was grateful now when he stopped a step away and settled on taking her hands in his.

"You look breathtaking, Elizabeth," he said with a warm smile, his eyes studying her face.

"Thank you," she responded with a polite smile.

His eyes scanned hers for a moment.

"Last night didn't bring anything back," he said. It wasn't a question.

She hesitated and then shook her head. She knew it would disappoint him, but it wasn't going to do either of them any good to minimize the gulf that still stood between her and her memory.

"I must admit I had this fantasy of being your golden key—that all of your memories would come back as soon as you saw me," he said with a look of disappointment. "Well, at least I don't have to apologize for what a terrible fiancé I've been lately. I can't blame it on the geographical distance. I've been so busy working on the case in Dallas I lost track of things. I promise to be more engaged in our relationship, Elizabeth. Maybe then you'll want to wear my ring again."

She saw him glance at her left hand when he said it. He wore a smile, but she could see the sadness in his eyes.

"I could tell I used to wear a ring on that finger. I think I may have lost it."

"Then I need to get you a new one—one twice as big," he smiled. "It will be my first act in becoming the perfect fiancé and the husband I intend to be for you."

Though she knew the efforts he described would be fruitless, she didn't think it was the right time to tell him. But what he said about the distance answered some of her questions about the lack of connection she sensed in their relationship. For many reasons, the knowledge gave her a small amount of relief. At the same time—and it surprised her to think along these lines—she wondered if she had a duty to invest in trying to rediscover the relationship they must have had at one time. Did she have an obligation? There must have been love and attraction at one time. Despite the certainty she had that Nora was the one for her, the question still plagued her. Would the connection she once had with Kev return with her memory? She suddenly felt guilty for the thought. She'd never once felt the responsibility to tell Kev about Nora. It had always been Nora who she felt honor-bound to. It told her everything she needed to know.

God, she was tired of analyzing everything.

"Why don't we save apologies and promises and see how it all plays out when I get my memory back?"

"I'm sorry for plunging into it so quickly. I didn't mean to overwhelm you. Your mom even warned me not to. But after dinner last night, after seeing you again…" Kev looked bereft and hopeful all in the same sad smile. It was obvious he had been holding back the night before. "I like your idea. And maybe while we see how it goes, I can shower you with enough devotion, you'll see the husband I can and will be for you."

"Sounds like a plan," she agreed. It wasn't really a plan at all, and she wasn't sure if it was fair of her to string him along like this. Wasn't that what she was doing? Since her heart now belonged completely to Nora? But it seemed to level the ground they stood on for now, at least until her memory came back. And when it happened, she could figure out how to handle everything.

❀❀❀❀❀

They arrived at the party and 4B was surprised by the ease with which she managed the evening. Kev and her mother had been right when they told her the small talk and mingling wouldn't take too much effort other than to listen, smile and respond with polite nods and unimportant discussion about the weather. Some people asked about the airplane crash, but she responded with honesty, telling them she didn't remember much about it. Kev stayed by her side for most of the night, and she was grateful when the discussion turned to more in-depth political talk, and he expertly diverted the conversation to other topics, essentially telling the guest the topic was best left to the real politicians, many of whom wandered through the room.

After they agreed they had put in enough time at the event, 4B excused herself to go to the ladies' room. Kev went to gather their coats and would meet her near the front entrance. On her way to the bathroom, a woman who she had talked to earlier in the evening stopped 4B and they chatted for a few minutes. It was a casual discussion unrelated to politics and 4B's confidence was high as she said goodnight to the woman and attended to her bathroom needs. Knowing she had taken longer than she had intended, 4B decided to take what she thought would be a shortcut to the front of the capital building. How she knew the building layout didn't even cross her mind. She had started to take for granted the innate knowledge that often came to her when she least expected it.

She was one hallway away from her destination when she turned down a side hallway and saw Kev at the other end talking to a woman. She quickly stepped back, out of their view. Something about their stances let her know it wasn't something she wanted to interrupt. They were several yards away, standing a few feet into a hall that split off from the main entrance. They didn't see her, and Kev glanced in the opposite direction occasionally, obviously looking out for unexpected company. He must have thought no one would be wandering the internal hallways, because he didn't seem concerned that someone would approach them from her direction.

She couldn't hear their whispered conversation, but she could tell it wasn't just a casual chat. The woman was up against the wall, and Kev leaned against it with one hand, the other in his pocket. He was dangerously close and they were smiling the smiles of flirtation and sexual insinuation. They weren't touching, but their body language suggested intimacy. 4B didn't wait for them to move. She retraced her steps and went back the original way she had come. When she arrived at the spot they had designated to meet, Kev was standing by himself with their coats draped over his arm. The woman he'd been talking to was standing with a group several feet away, engaged in conversation. She realized the situation didn't concern her. In fact, it assuaged some of her guilt.

When she approached him he looked every bit the attentive fiancé, waiting patiently for her arrival. His smile seemed genuine when he helped her into her coat and then into the waiting car. 4B wondered why she wasn't angry. If anything, she was curious. She chatted easily with him about the party as they drove back to her house, but he never mentioned the woman he had been talking to. He stopped the Porsche under the carport in front of the house where he had parked it the night before. It had started to rain.

He jumped out to rush to the other side of the car and open 4B's door. She was halfway out when he got there. "I see you haven't forgotten that habit," he said with an easy smile as he helped her the rest of the way out. "Is it too early to tease?"

"You're fine," she said with a little laugh. "Thank you for an enjoyable evening, Kev. I had fun."

He raised his eyebrows in question. "Fun?" he asked, clearly not believing her. "I'll hand it to you, though. You did seem to approach it with as much ease as you usually do. As I've said before, the women in your family must have the ability to handle any situation with grace embedded in their DNA."

"I'll take your word for it, but I'm telling the truth. It wasn't as bad as I expected it to be, and I did have a few interesting conversations. It was nice to talk about something other than my amnesia."

"I guess it's all about perspective," said Kev, leaning forward to give her a kiss goodnight. "Well, I had a good time, too, Elizabeth. I always forget how much I enjoy being with you when so much time goes between."

4B had dreaded this part of the evening, wondering what the protocol was for saying goodnight after a second meeting with a fiancé who you had no memory of—even if she had just seen him talking so cozily to another woman. She was relieved when he simply kissed her check.

She squeezed his hand and started to turn toward the house.

"Good night, Kev."

She was surprised when he didn't let go of her hand, and she turned back. He wore an expression of deliberation on his face, and she was about to ask him what was wrong when he leaned forward and kissed her on the mouth. The kiss wasn't long or terribly passionate, but there was a question in his eyes when he leaned away. She stood quietly, not knowing how to respond.

"I'm sorry, Elizabeth. I know you need some time to get your bearings. But I've missed you. I guess I needed to see if you remembered me that way. Do you?" he asked, searching her eyes in the dark shadows of the silent carport.

The only sound was the change in the idling car's quiet motor as it shifted when the heater kicked on.

It took 4B a moment to respond.

"I'm sorry, Kev..."

She was surprised when he took her into his arms and kissed her again. This time it was deeper and he pressed her against the low car. Instantly, she wanted to push him away, but she didn't get the impression he was trying to force her to do anything. His lips were warm and gentle against hers, but the stubble of his beard made it hard for her to find enjoyment in it even if she wanted to. He cradled her head in his hand and she tried to kiss him back. She allowed his tongue to find hers, and he pressed his body against hers. She could feel his desire grow firm against her hip. She was aware of every movement, every sound, every sensation—and none of them were sweeping her away. She squeezed her eyes shut and continued to kiss him back, willing herself to feel something, anything, except the deep feeling of emptiness that echoed within her. Finally, he pulled his head away, his breathing heavy. He closed his eyes and gently pressed his forehead against hers.

"You drive me crazy, Elizabeth. You always have."

He opened his eyes and searched 4B's face, looking for something. She stood there, hoping he would find his answer, whatever it was. Finally, he caressed the side of her face and stepped back.

"I'll call you from Dallas, okay? I fly back tomorrow," he cracked a small smile, but there was sadness in his eyes. "I won't forget my promise. The lavishing starts now."

With that, he walked around to the driver's side of the car and waited as she went into the house before he drove away. This time she had remembered to take a key, so she was grateful she didn't have to wait for Miriam to answer the door.

When she closed the door, she stood in the dark foyer and wondered how she felt about what had just happened. As she started up the stairs to her room, she realized she needed to clear things up with Kev sooner rather than later. It threw a wrench into things that he was going back to Dallas the next day. As much as she really didn't want to face him, she didn't want to break up with him over the phone. She needed to figure out this complication.

❁❁❁❁❁

4B took a shower and rinsed away the hairspray and makeup, but most of all, she wanted to get rid of the scent of Kev's cologne. Smoothing in the last of her moisturizer, she glanced at the clock and did the math on time zones. It was just after midnight in Cambridge, which made it just after 8:00 PM in Juneau. It didn't matter that she'd spoken to Nora already earlier in the day. She ached to hear her voice again.

Without having any sense of control over it, 4B picked up the phone and immediately felt better when she heard Nora's voice on the other end.

"Hi," she said in response to Nora's usual professional greeting. She smiled but didn't tease her like she sometimes did.

"Hey, you," said Nora, and 4B could hear the pleased smile in her voice. "I wasn't sure if you would call after the big shindig tonight."

"I just got back. I need to hear your voice before I go to sleep," said 4B.

"I'm glad," replied Nora. "How was it?"

"Not as bad as I thought it would be. There were people there to help me if I needed it, but I didn't rely on them too much."

"I'm glad it went well, then. It must have helped to go with someone you knew... or sort of know. I could tell you were way more nervous than you let on about it."

"You could?" asked 4B. She thought she had played it off better than that.

"Yes. When we were talking earlier, you sounded a little scattered. You normally don't sound like that, even when you're scared."

It gave 4B's heart a little skip to know Nora was so in tune with her, but she wondered what else she might be picking up on. She didn't ask. There were lots of things they didn't ask each other. Like, when would they see each other again? What did they mean to one another? Was there a future for them? The answers weren't available yet, and when they did become available, there was no guarantee they'd like the answers, so they avoided them—at least 4B did. She assumed Nora had similar reasons of her own. She wondered if Nora had questions about Kev.

"It turned out okay. I owe it to you. You helped me find my inner calm before I left."

"I did?" asked Nora and 4B was surprised to hear a little insecurity in her voice.

"Yes. You always make me feel better."

"I've done my job then. So, you were successful in getting back on the horse?"

4B gave a small laugh.

"I guess so. My mom will be pleased."

"Except for what?" asked Nora and the question surprised 4B.

"What do you mean?"

"I can hear it in your voice. Something didn't go well tonight."

4B paused. Nora was so gentle and intuitive. She didn't feel pressured to tell Nora anything, especially since nothing was going on between her and Kev, and she knew Nora would never push. Yet, she wanted to tell her everything, to lay everything out and to ask Nora to help her figure out her life. But it wasn't fair. She knew she'd be breaking things off with Kev, with or without her memory, despite his return to Dallas, but so far she hadn't been able to figure out how. And still, she wasn't ready to tell Nora. Mostly, because she didn't want to worry her, and she didn't know how not to.

"Hey, you don't have to talk if you don't want to. I know you have a lot on your plate and you don't have all of the words to describe what's going on. I just want you to know that I'm here for you. Regardless of what happens or how our lives play out, you have me on your side."

"See? You make me feel better just talking to you. I miss you. I miss you so much it hurts sometimes." 4B held her hand over her chest as if to help ward away the pain she was feeling there right then.

"I miss you too," whispered Nora, and 4B could hear the pain in her voice. It wasn't the first time they'd admitted to missing each other, but there was more to it tonight, an unspoken need left hanging there. "It's unfair to tell you that, though, what with everything you're going through," said Nora.

"I needed to hear it," said 4B. "You never make me feel like you expect anything from me." But if she were honest, she wanted Nora to expect things from her. She knew she wasn't in a position to deliver on anything, but if Nora had asked her for anything, she would try to give it to her, no matter what she asked. And it scared her.

"Then I'll tell you I miss you more often, because I do. I miss you more than you can know," said Nora.

"Same here," whispered 4B. And for a minute there was no sound except for their breathing. 4B thought she'd like to fall asleep to that peaceful sound.

"I hate to go, but Aunt Mace needs me," said Nora after a while.

"How is she?"

"About the same."

"Give her my love, okay?"

"I will. Good night."

4B listened to the silence after Nora hung up, unwilling to let go just yet. Her heart hurt more than it did before she had called, but she was glad for having shared those moments. She went to sleep with the memory of the smells of pine and smoke, and the soft sound of Nora's voice whispering her name.

❀❀❀❀❀

The next day, shortly after getting up, 4B went through some of the boxes and plastic containers stored on the shelves of her closet. Under a stack of boxes of clothing, and a bin filled with children's books, toys, and games, she hit pay dirt. A shoebox pushed into the furthest corner of the top-most shelf held a stack of journals, some loose letters, a handful of photos and a variety of mementos: a dried rose; a gold chain with half of a heart on it; a drawing of a girl who looked like Layce; a love poem; a mixed tape; a woven bracelet; and a collection of rocks shaped like hearts.

4B sat on her bed and spread the contents in an arc around her. There were seven journals in all, the oldest featuring cartoon characters on its cover, the most recent bound in a hard black cover. Curiosity rose within her, but something held her back. Feeling like a voyeur snooping through someone else's life, she reminded herself the books were hers. They contained her life. There was nothing in them she didn't already know on some level. She let her fingers slide over the stack of books. A thread of fear battled her curiosity. The books contained her past and might say more about her future than she was prepared to face. She left the journals for a moment to examine the random items sharing the box with them.

She picked up a folded yellow square of paper with blue lines, torn from a legal pad. Layce's name was written on one side. She opened the note, which was folded in the way of kids who passed notes in class, a small tight rectangle with the final corner tucked into a crease to hold it closed. She knew somehow she'd been an expert at that folding technique at one time. There was a short poem written in adolescent cursive on the page:

Layce-

I will give you my heart, as a friend
Until the world, it comes to an end
Though we do deserve so much more
But we both have figured the score
And since we can't 'marry'
Our secret we have to carry
Just know that if it could be
You'd be the only one for me.

I heart you, as my best friend, forever
(I hope that I can get up the nerve to actually give this to you!!)

4B cringed at the sophomoric rhyming scheme and the childish mushiness of the words, though she raised an eyebrow at the message. Since she was still in possession of the note, she figured she had never given it to Layce. And from the note, it was clear she had, at least at one time, felt more than just friendship for Layce. Had it remained a secret crush? After all, Layce was with someone else now and they had a baby. And she was engaged to Kev.

The confusing clue to her past forced her to examine who she really was. She'd written a love letter to a girl before she was with Kev. She felt so deeply for Nora now. Was she a lesbian? Straight? Bisexual? Kev appeared to be the kind of man most women would be attracted to. He was handsome, considerate, successful. He seemed to be a good man aside from the sexy flirting with other women. But she felt nothing in his presence. In comparison, just the thought of Nora elicited a warm rush of emotion within 4B, making her heart race and blood rush to sensitive places. Maybe her journals would tell her more.

She picked up the first one. A childish scrawl and dated entries documented the events of a young girl's life: school, friends, her horse, what she had for lunch, things she liked, things she hated. She laughed as she read her childish descriptions of her teachers and friends—some flattering, many not.

As she read through the journals, she decided she liked the young woman she had been. She was kind, sensitive, tough, smart, and she tried to see the world from other people's eyes.

As she entered her teen years, she saw a little of the classic mother-daughter stress, and she felt some of the frustration and resentment toward her mother. There was a fight over dresses—her mother insisted she wear them, and she wouldn't be caught dead in one. Based on the wardrobe currently hanging in her closet, she had obviously gotten over that. There was a passing mention of the general expectation she would follow in her mother's political steps someday. Her assertion was there was no way that would ever happen. Words of admiration for her mother peppered the texts for a period, along with her desire to never disappoint her, and then it was never mentioned again, as talk of becoming, first a firewoman, then an Olympic sculler, and then a doctor, filled her dreams.

In seventh grade, the journals became more detailed. Entire pages, and then several pages at a time, had been devoted to a day's experience and musings. Poems filled some of the pages, and the drawings interspersed among the entries began to get more elaborate and more carefully drawn. She imagined her thirteen-year-old self, sitting under one of the trees by the stables as she sketched the horses.

A drawing of a long boat skimming down a river preceded an exclamation, all in caps, each letter traced several times indicating high emotion:

I MADE THE SCULLING TEAM!!!!!!!

Excited entries described days spent down at the Branton Boat Club. And then they became even more excited as a new girl named Layce Dalton moved to town, joined the club, and then made the team.

Early afternoon found the adult 4B sitting in a wicker chair on the back porch of her parents' house enjoying the gentle warmth of the fall sunshine. A cool breeze made it necessary for her to wear a light sweater, and she had her legs tucked under her. One of the journals was open on her knee and two small stacks of books, one she'd read and one she hadn't, stood on a nearby table with an empty coffee cup keeping them company.

4B read the exploits of the two girls, her and Layce, as they quickly became friends, delighting in all of the fun times they had shared, and the description of Elizabeth as an outdoorsy, girly girl who wished she could be more like the wild tomboy, Layce. She even laughed when Elizabeth longed to have the untamed curls Layce complained about, describing her own fairly straight hair as "boring Rapunzel hair". The previous journal entries paled in comparison to the bright-toned activities described by the young Elizabeth from then on. Even the disappointments, few and far between, were vividly documented in the hyper-analytical fashion of a thirteen-year-old girl.

Emotions flew through 4B as she read her old journals. What had started out as a literary romp through someone else's life to satisfy her curiosity began to feel more personal. She still didn't read the journals with the familiarity of one who was recounting an experience, but more as a person who was visiting an old friend. The events were still new to her, but nothing surprised her and as soon as she read them, she could feel them weaving into the fabric of her past. She occasionally wondered if this was what her mother had warned her of—the synthetic assimilation of memories she wanted to have, rather than the organic real ones she should have. But it didn't matter to her. She wanted to know.

She was near the end of the second to last journal when the cell phone she'd tucked into the pocket of her sweater rang. She took a break from reading to answer it, hoping it would be Nora.

"Hi, honey. How did the dinner go last night?" asked her mother, who was still in Washington. She wasn't due back for another day. It was a nice interruption. 4B found she missed her.

"It was fine. I had a good time. I didn't expect to, but I did."

"I'm glad." Her mother sounded pleased. "Did you and Kev get a chance to catch up?"

"Do you mean; do I remember him?" asked 4B with a smile. She was discovering her mother was a diplomat in all things, not just politics. She knew a sensitive situation when she saw one. A direct question could be painful if 4B wasn't ready for it. "I still don't remember him, but we enjoyed each other's company. Every day, the feeling my memories will come back gets stronger."

"Well, as long as you're doing okay, I'm happy. What are you up to today?"

"Reading my old journals. I found them stashed in the back of my closet," explained 4B, picking up the journal she currently held, examining the cover.

"Oh, good! I'd forgotten about those. They should be a great nudge to get your memories flowing again. You have a whole stack of them, if I remember correctly. You used to write everything down when you were a kid."

"It's been interesting so far. It's weird to read about yourself as if I'm a character in a book."

"Is that how it feels for you?" asked her mother sounding both fascinated disappointed.

"Mostly. Sometimes I feel like I'm having déjà vu. I suppose it's a step in the right direction."

"I imagine you feel like your entire life is on hold until this shakes out."

"A little. But even if things don't come back to me soon, I think I'll still be comfortable with taking the next steps."

"What kind of next steps?" her mother sounded interested in what she planned to do. She felt guilty that at least one of those plans was to break it off with Kev, at least for her mother's sake.

"I'm not sure yet," she only halfway lied. She was going to do it. She just didn't know how she was going to do it.

"Has Kev been pressuring you? I know he feels sort of in limbo, too. I asked him to be patient."

"I didn't get the impression he and I had anything solidly planned out. Do we? I know we're engaged, but, have we set the date or started planning?"

"I've been trying to get you to set a date for years!" laughed Roslyn. "Everyone expected your graduation from med school last spring to set the whole ball in motion, to be honest."

"What are my career plans? Do you know?" 4B said to change the subject.

"Oh… that's a can of worms I prefer to discuss when we have a little more time."

"I've got time now."

"I'm sorry, sweetie, I'm due back for meetings in a few minutes."

"Okay," said 4B, adding her career into the list of questions she wanted to get to the bottom of. "Does your hesitation have to do with whether I go the political path versus the doctor path, by any chance?"

"Why do you ask about that?"

"Young Elizabeth discusses it a few times in the journals." 4B didn't mention her discovery that it had been a big source of frustration for her as a child. She wasn't able to provide more insight without her memory and her mother would probably want to know more about it. It was probably a conversation for later.

"Fascinating. I'd love to see what you said about it, if you want to share. I thought your father and I were so good about not applying pressure."

"I don't think any kid escapes childhood without feeling pressure—most of it being applied by themselves," laughed 4B, wondering if she would ever show her mother her journals. Like most kids she was far more critical of her parents than she might have been—at least from what she could tell as an unbiased observer, since it was still like reading a book about a fictional character. And contrary to her mother's intent, the pressure to marry Kev had been obvious since the first journal she'd written, when in second grade she'd already referred to him as her 'husband-to-be'.

"Oh, before we hang up, and along the career topic, I called down and asked them to defer the start date of your residency. They normally wouldn't do this, but under the circumstances…"

"And I'm sure it didn't hurt it was a call from Senator Tollworthy," interrupted 4B with a smile.

"Well, that, too," admitted her mother. "I hope you don't mind. It's difficult to know what to consult with you about while we wait for things to improve. You and I have a little bit of a history about my tendency to take over. It's a habit I'm trying desperately to control—at least with you. Your father seems to like it, and my constituents vote for me because of it. But I'm not so sure my daughter appreciates it all the time."

4B laughed. She was relieved that her mother had taken care of this particular commitment. In reality, she hadn't thought about it since a few days prior when her mother had first mentioned it. Again, it didn't seem like it was her life. "Considering the circumstances, I think you made the right decision. There's no way I could just show up and start being a doctor."

"My thinking exactly. But it was a bit disconcerting making the decision for you."

"Thanks for everything, mom. I know this is weird for you, too."

"It's what mothers do, honey—weird stuff and all."

4B spoke with her mother for a few more minutes before ringing off. The call put her into a state of deep contemplation. The realization that her state of limbo was putting other people's lives on hold wasn't a new thought to her, but she really hadn't thought about it having a deep impact on those around her. Sure, her mother and father were helping her get through it, and being her parents, they were invested in it. But the feeling of disconnect she felt with Kev had led her to assume the impact to him was moderate at most. Remembering the goodnight kiss, she wondered if she had it wrong. Hopefully she'd get it straightened out soon. Then she thought about Nora. Wonderful, beautiful, supportive, sexy Nora. She had purposefully not thought about what Nora meant to her, about how she fit into her future, but she knew that, whatever next steps she did take, she would have to make a decision about Nora. Nora had ever asked for a decision, but every day the unsaid became a louder topic in their phone calls.

As she thought about all of this, 4B stared absently at the journal in her hand. Her finger held her place, and her eyes, unfocused, had unintentionally centered on a specific spot. The journal was a generic blank-paged, black, hardcover book, the type found in any stationary or office supply store. It felt good in her hand and it made her itch to write new entries. A small gap in the pages caught her eye and she flipped forward to them. Several pages had been torn or cut out of the book. The gap in the dates suggested a span of several weeks had been removed. She went back to where she had paused in her reading and began to read the pages preceding the section.

When 4B read as far as the missing section, she found the last page before the gap described young Elizabeth's excitement over a coming youth dance at the boat club and a sleepover that had been arranged for afterward. The girls would stay in one of the meeting rooms, the boys in another. There was no mention of how it went, but when the journal picked up again, it described, in true adolescent angst, her deep unhappiness about a fight she and Layce had gotten into sometime during those days or immediately after. Whatever happened in those pages had resulted in a serious rift, which left the girls not talking to one another. The following pages described Elizabeth's grief after losing "the best friend she had ever had". As 4B read through those words, she sensed the emotional shadow of despair her younger self had felt. She wondered if the poem had anything to do with it. She kept reading.

4B's engrossment in the story grew deeper with the dramatic turmoil during that time in her life. She followed with interest how Elizabeth turned to Kev in her anguish. She read about how Kev had been her rock during that period. How he had listened to everything and was always supportive, even when Elizabeth wept to him about the black hole left in her chest at Layce's absence in her life. The drama continued, until, one day, almost out of the blue, Layce came back into the picture and things were almost fine. Elizabeth spoke of a subtle barrier, but in a strange shift in tone, she called it healthy. Life seemed to pick up in a happier fashion for a little while. Elizabeth found ways to include both Layce and Kev in her life, even when Layce started to date someone named Shannon. Elizabeth seemed relieved. She spoke of not wanting to have to entertain Layce while they were doing boyfriend/girlfriend things, so Shannon was a welcome addition. But soon, Elizabeth started to talk about small resentments and a feeling of disconnection. There were more fights where the girls would stop speaking and become friends again. But talk of college and graduating started to take up more of Elizabeth's writing, and talk of her personal relationships became one or two line notes.

One journal entry got 4B's attention. It was a very brief mention of Layce and her going down to the license bureau with doctored birth certificates to get fake ID's. A friend at school had produced the fake certificates, and she and Layce had boldly gone up to get the licenses so they could buy beer. The entry described how they both had used their middle names along with their mother's maiden names, and had included the address of a frat house where they had once gone to a party. This was the fake ID. The mystery still remained as to why she had been using it so many years later. 4B read on.

It wasn't until 4B had read the entries chronicling most of her senior year in high school that Elizabeth referred to Shannon as a woman. Until then, 4B had assumed Shannon was Layce's boyfriend. 4B paused to consider why she had automatically made the assumption, and realized it was because her mother had mentioned that 4B's trip to Los Angeles had been to go see Layce's baby. 4B laughed at herself. Of all people, she never thought she would fall into the trap of generalization. But, then again, she didn't know who she was, did she? She could guess, but aside from the journals and stories told to her, she had no idea who Elizabeth Tollworthy really was. Again, she realized she hadn't spent a lot of time analyzing her own sexuality in regard to Nora, and maybe she should have—especially since she had obviously been with Kev since she had started dating—but the ease with which she had made the transition made her think that the concept of straight and gay wasn't a huge issue for her. Nothing in her journals had indicated she had put much thought into it at all.

Late that night, 4B had moved her reading back to her room, and she finally closed the last journal, which ended the summer before she set off for Harvard, a student apartment, and a major in premed. She wondered if there were more journals somewhere chronicling her college years.

All of the reading had given her insight into the woman she had become, but still, the accounts were just stories, and she wanted them to be memories. She closed her eyes and envisioned the fog of forgetfulness receding. She willed the events she had read to become memory, and the hidden secrets containing the rest of her life to rise and fill in the cracks.

It didn't work.

4B looked at the digital display on her clock, which read 2:00 AM. She hadn't talked to Nora all day and she wondered if it was too late to call. She called anyway.

"Hey, you," said Nora, after the first ring, and 4B immediately felt better.

"Hey, you," replied 4B, closing her eyes and bringing Nora's face into her memory. She thought about asking her for a photograph, but she decided against it. She had her drawing, and she liked the more dynamic picture she stored in her mind.

"I'm glad you called," said Nora. She sounded tired. "This damn time zone thing caught me off guard today and I had a packed day. When I finished with my appointments it was after 11:00 PM your time. I didn't want to wake you if you had gone to bed already."

"You don't ever have to worry about the time when it comes to calling me. I want to talk to you whatever the time."

"Same here. What's the matter? You sound upset."

4B didn't know she was so close to crying until the tears started falling and she didn't answer because she didn't trust her voice.

"Are you still there?" asked Nora after a couple of moments.

4B cleared her throat.

"Yeah, I'm still here. I think I'm just tired."

"It's not just tired I hear in your voice."

"I don't know what's wrong. I was fine until I heard your voice," whispered 4B, no longer caring if Nora knew she was crying.

"I wish I could hold you right now."

The simple statement made 4B's chest ache. She wanted nothing more than the feel of Nora's arms around her.

"Me too," she whispered into the phone.

"Tell me what's on your mind. What were you doing before you called me?"

"I spent the whole day reading through my old journals."

"Ah. I imagine that's been an emotional ride."

"It was, but it wasn't. I still don't remember any of it."

"That's probably frustrating."

"It is. The weird thing is I feel sort of like the emotions are memories. I'm reading a story, but I feel like I remember the emotions I described back then, but not the details. And believe me, I described them in great detail when I was a young teenager."

"God, I remember those days. All of the ups and downs, the deep feelings. They felt like quicksand if I didn't get them out."

"I can't imagine you being anything like that. I was a quagmire of feeling."

"Are you kidding me? I was the worst. I wish I had written it all down so I could show you. I talked my friends to death with it instead. Some things I kept to myself, but others. Yikes."

"I did that, too, it appears," laughed 4B, wiping her nose on the sleeve of her sweater.

"Did you discover anything?"

"Not really. I mean, yes. But I didn't get my memory back."

"It will come, baby. Maybe it's a blessing not to have it all come back at once. Maybe the emotional memory is a soft way of landing back where you need to be and the memories will come after."

"You make me feel so much better. I wish I could see you right now."

"Me too," sighed Nora, and 4B could hear the longing in her voice.

4B woke from a dream she could barely remember. She and another girl were walking through the woods behind her parents' house. They came to a clearing much like the clearing that she'd found behind the stables. They sat on the low branch she remembered. 4B sketched the other girl's face. One of them spread out a blanket and they enjoyed a simple picnic, after which they lay down on the blanket and looked at the sky. It should have been a happy dream. The woods were unintimidating. The sky was blue and wide. The talk was lively and free. But when she awoke her chest was tight with anxiety and an unnamed fear. It was a little too early to call Nora, so she got dressed and went in search of caffeine.

The smell of brewing coffee led her downstairs. Expecting to see her father before he left for work, the sight of her mother reading the paper surprised her.

"When did you get home?"

"I took an early flight this morning. I can only stand Washington in small doses. Besides, your dad has a hard time sleeping when I'm out of town."

"Where is he? He's usually up by now."

"He went back to sleep as soon as we returned from the airport. Oh, that reminds me," her mother tilted her head to indicate something on the floor after she took a sip of her coffee. "Those packages were near the front door when we came in. They must have been delivered yesterday."

4B saw a stack of boxes near the kitchen table.

"For me?"

"The one on top has a return address from the airline and the other I recognize as the box I shipped from your apartment. When I went into Baltimore to settle up your living situation, I found you'd already packaged up your personal items, so I just shipped them here. I hired a service to put all the other stuff—mostly books, kitchen items, and furniture—into storage until you figure out what you want to do with it all, when or if you go back to start your residency."

4B ran her fingers over the top box. "I feel like I should have more of an emotional response when we talk about whether I start my residency or not. Isn't that the kind of thing people usually work toward during their entire education?"

"Pretty much," responded Roslyn. "You were elated when you were selected for this one. The attending physician is very disappointed right now. But under the circumstances, he agreed to hold onto your slot, at least for a short while. He doesn't want to lose you."

4B picked up the smaller box and shook it. There was no sound or discernable movement inside to indicate what was in it. She reached over the counter and pulled the utility scissors out of the knife block situated in the middle of the counter island.

When the box was opened, she pulled out a roll of bubble wrap with something secured in its center. She unwrapped the contents and found a simple Coach backpack zippered up.

"It's a backpack," she explained to her mother's interested expression and opened an enclosed letter. She read it aloud so her mother could hear.

Dear Ms. Tollworthy,

The following item was found at the crash scene. Please forgive that we are required to analyze every piece of aircraft, including luggage, as evidence in our investigation. Be assured, all of the contents have been inventoried and returned to you.

If you have any questions, please contact us.

A director-level administrator from the airline had signed the letter.

4B placed the letter on the counter and opened the backpack. It matched the purse they had already been returned to her. She had no idea if everything was still in it, as she had no memory of the bag or any of its contents. She pulled out a large plastic baggie with a list of the contents stapled to it. The bag contained a driver's license, her passport, two pairs of sunglasses, a Kindle e-reader, a couple of chargers for her electronics, a pack of gum, an iPhone, a couple of tampons, and some loose receipts—one of which was dated the day before the crash from a pizzeria in Venice Beach, California. She looked more closely at the license, which was different than the one returned to her with the purse. This one had her real name and a Baltimore address on it. It was most likely her official license, while the other she knew to be a fake now. It also indicated she was five years younger than she had thought. Oddly, the detail elicited the biggest reaction from her. She felt so much older than the twenty-six years her license said she was.

Nothing in the bag spurred even a faint sense of recollection, not even emotionally—except for her age on the license. Instead, she felt an even more vivid sense of disconnection than she had been. She placed the bag and its contents on the counter and moved over to the larger package.

"My life in a box," she said as she pulled the scissors across the tape on its top. "It's weird, I wish I could open this box and find my memory in it."

"That would be wonderful, honey. I actually don't know what's in it, since you packed it before I got there. Maybe something in it will trigger something."

"I'm not sure if it's possible. If my journals didn't do it, I can't imagine anything else doing it."

"Just give it some time," said Roslyn, as she sipped her coffee. "Maybe this is your mind's way of helping you to ease into things."

"Nora pretty much said the same thing," said 4B, pushing back the flaps of the box and peering into it. She pulled out a couple of sweaters from the top and saw a variety of items below them. Right away, she spied a small stack of three black books similar to the journals she had read the day before.

She pulled out a framed picture of Kev standing in his cap and gown at what looked to have been his graduation from law school. She pulled out another picture of her and a pretty woman who was a grown up version of

Layce. She studied the picture. They were in shorts and t-shirts, their arms loosely wrapped around each other's waists facing the camera. Lush vegetation was in the backdrop. She showed it to her mother.

"That was taken in Guatemala," said Roslyn. "If I remember correctly, it was taken in front of the command center of the medical unit you volunteered with. I have a similar one with just you in it on my desk."

"That's Layce, isn't it?" asked 4B, pointing at the other young woman in the photo.

"Yes. She certainly grew into a beautiful woman."

4B agreed and an interesting mix of emotions whirled inside of her at her mother's comment, though she couldn't define them.

"Have you told her about me? Does she know what happened?"

4B felt bad for not having picked up or returned the calls she'd seen from Layce. They were best friends. But what would she say? Hello, I don't remember you, but I'm fine?

"No. She might have heard about it in the papers, but I didn't call her. I guess it's the coward in me. But, I'm not sure she would speak to me if I did."

"Oh?" asked, 4B, surprised. "Why's that?"

Roslyn looked at 4B with a long look of consideration for a moment before she answered.

"It's funny. I was seriously wondering if I could get away with revising history with my answer, you know, telling you what I wished had happened, instead of what really did happen. But then I remembered you already know… or at least you will when things come back to you."

"What do you mean? Is it bad?"

Her mother paused and looked like she was considering how to respond.

"It's a matter of perspective," she replied finally. "But in the grand scheme of things, at the very least, it could be seen as a not very good thing. But, I don't skirt the tough issues in the rest of my life, so I'm not going to start here. Let's just say I wasn't the nicest person to Layce when you were girls. She hasn't spoken to me since you both went off to college."

"What happened?"

"I asked her to leave you alone."

"Why? What was she doing?"

Her mother paused. "Honestly? I'm not sure she really ever did anything. But, regardless, I reacted badly, and I was wrong. I'm glad your friendship has survived it."

"Survived what?" Anxiety tickled in Nora's chest. She wasn't sure if it was the way her mother wasn't answering the question directly or if she was afraid of the answer. It seemed like a big piece of fabric was about to be pulled away from a hidden object. She tried not to show her impatience.

"My maternal meddling. When you were in high school, I intercepted a note Layce left on your car confessing her feelings for you," said Roslyn, and 4B could sense her mother's shame. Nora started to say something, but her mother stopped her. "I didn't read the whole thing. I just didn't know what it was at first. It was Boating Days Weekend. All of you kids went to a dance at the Marina and then you all slept over at the Club House as the adults celebrated with an all-night bonfire. Your father and I were part of the host committee, so we had to stay to supervise the collection of all of the members and the kids the next morning. We were the last to leave, except you, who decided to go out on the water before going home. I noticed the note on the windshield of your car as I was walking by. I thought it was a flyer and pulled it off. When I got to my car I read the first lines, which explained she had feelings for you as more than a friend. Your father and I had always suspected something between you girls. You were always as thick as thieves. You thought the sun and moon rose and fell because of her. We didn't know if anything ever really happened between you, and when I asked you, you said no. I was relieved. Your father and I were going to let it take its course, whatever it was, but I was terrified she was confusing you. So when she came by the house a day or so after I found the note…"

"You thought I was gay? You suspected we were… that I…" 4B tried to find the words. She wasn't sure why she was having this response. Like she'd been caught doing something she shouldn't have been doing. It was true her parents thought of her as heterosexual, at least she assumed that, what with her engagement to Kev. And, other than the poem, which didn't have a date, none of the journals had indicated she thought of herself as anything other than straight back then, even if what she felt for Nora definitely challenged that. Since she'd been back, she'd deliberately not thought too hard on the subject, and it was easy not to dwell on it when so many other topics were competing for her attention—missing Nora; what to do about Kev; the residency; being a doctor or what she felt was someone else's career; finding her memory. But now that she thought about it, why wasn't there any mention in her journals? They spoke of her relationships with boys—first kisses, the first time she had sex with Kev. She hadn't gone into detail about the events—not like she did with other things—but she mentioned them. Now, talking with her mother, she was nervous, anxious, even.

"I know. Not my proudest moment. I've always been a big supporter of gay rights. But when it came down to the possibility that my own daughter might be gay, I had a hard time with it. When you and Kev started to date, it all became a moot point. I'm not proud of my reaction..."

"When you warned her off, what did you do?"

"She came by the house a few days after I intercepted the note and I handed it back to her. I asked her not to ruin your life. That was all. I didn't yell or cause a scene. But she didn't come by the house much afterwards, and when she did, she avoided me like the plague. Her reaction caused a rift with you two for a little while, but you both got over it. When you get your memory back, you'll remember you and I have already talked about this. Actually, yelled about it, would be more accurate. You weren't happy with me at all back then, and in hindsight, I don't blame you at all. I'm ashamed of my reaction. It was based out of fear and ignorance, and I know if you had turned out to be a lesbian, we would have worked through it. It's easy now to say I'm grateful you aren't—I know that being gay can sometimes be hard, and a mother can't be faulted for wanting her daughter to be protected from the pain that heartless people can inflict in the name of their religion or out of plain ignorance—but if things were different, I would be your biggest supporter. Hindsight is a powerful tool. If I could go back, I would have handled all of it differently and I would have been more supportive of Layce, too. She deserved more from me and I failed her."

4B didn't know what to say. Thankfully, her mother didn't seem to require a response. But, as her mother had spoken, nameless anxiety had tightened in her chest. And the feeling that was present so often when she learned something about her past, welled up inside of her. She acknowledged that she still hadn't told her mother about her and Nora. She just assumed it was because of her engagement to Kev. But maybe it had more to do with her worry about her mother's long ago reaction. Maybe it was both. She wanted to say something now, but uncertainty made her hold onto the information for a little bit longer.

The discussion turned to other things, and after a while, her mother went into her office and 4B poured herself another cup of coffee, and took the boxes up to her room. She went through the rest of the contents, and among the artifacts of a life she felt no connection to, she found a diamond ring, most likely, the ring Kev had mentioned to her the night of the fundraiser. She wondered why she wasn't wearing it.

Finally, she stacked the journals next to her on the bed and began to read. Her forgotten coffee grew cold, and a call from her mother downstairs about lunch went unanswered, so Miriam appeared and placed her lunch on her nightstand, where it too went untouched. The chronicles of her adult life were more sporadically entered, and far less angst ridden, but more interesting than her adolescent ramblings. As she got to know her emerging adult, some of the questions that had plagued her started to get answered.

She had gone to Harvard University to study premed, along with Layce, who studied architecture, and Kev, who had started the year before in law. While there, she had nearly aced the MCAT, and when she graduated from Harvard, since she had her pick of medical schools, she chose Johns Hopkins. Baltimore just happened to be where Layce went for her graduate studies in engineering. It wasn't clear whether one followed the other, or whether it had been a coincidence that they both ended up in Baltimore, but either way, Elizabeth had been ecstatic about being down there with Layce. She'd considered following Kev to Stanford, but she'd listed the pros and cons of either place, and Baltimore had won out. Though she never said it in her journals—her style of journaling had become terser—underneath it all, it was clear she had just wanted to be closer to Layce. She had taken Kev's devotion for granted, while she had always felt the need to reassure herself about Layce's friendship, as if it were a tenuous thing. There had been no mention at all about the incident her mother had told her about.

The journal spoke of an ideal period where the two women were always together, braving the arduous life of graduate school. During the summer between first and second year, they went on a school-sponsored mission to Guatemala, where they provided vaccines and helped build homes in remote villages. For a while, everything was perfect.

Then Layce met Andy. Andy was short for Andrea. And the dynamic of their friendship shifted. They still went on their summer trips to South America, but their closeness seemed to drift, and at about the same time, the journal entries started to get further apart. The last entry in the most recent journal had been from the summer before Elizabeth's last year in med school. Layce had already graduated and had moved to Los Angeles with Andrea, and Elizabeth was immersed in her studies, anxious about her final year of medical school, and uncertain about what she wanted to do when she finished. She had been grateful for a heavy course load, and full of guilt over not attending Layce's wedding. It had been a choice between going on what had become an annual trip to Guatemala or attending the wedding in L.A. And although Elizabeth expressed a sincere hope that her best friend would find a lasting happiness with her new wife, she had chosen Guatemala, with a thin justification that she didn't want to leave the organization short two of its regular members. She'd sent a thoughtful present instead.

The last entry read, 4B closed the journal, placed it on her nightstand, and curled up in a ball. A deep depression settled over her, and though it was early afternoon and she fought the urge, all she wanted to do was slip into a forgetful sleep. More than anything, though, she wanted Nora. They hadn't spoken that day, and Nora missed her terribly. She picked up her phone to call her, but was frustrated when her phone wouldn't turn on. She remembered she hadn't plugged it in the night before. With a disgruntled sigh, she got up, plugged it into the charger, and lay back down on the bed, waiting the few minutes it would take for it to get enough juice to make the call.

❀❀❀❀❀

4B woke late the next morning dressed in the clothes she had been wearing the day before. She didn't remember falling asleep, but she remembered her mother coming in to check on her, murmuring something about a golf tournament and a dinner afterward, pulling the covers over her, turning out the light. Remnants of her dreams floated in her mind. Visions of a falling baby, but this time it began with her almost being swept away by a raging river as she tried desperately to hold onto the mother and the infant. Her stomach felt the lurch from the dream she'd had so often, at the moment when the baby began to fall from the mother's arms into the river below. She closed her eyes and tried to forget, but more and more details of it filled her mind.

A storm raged so hard, it penetrated the canopy of a dense tropical rainforest. Drops, heavy and fat battered her. She was soaked through, and her clothes clung to her, water streamed from the bill of her well-worn Orioles cap. The ground was muddy, sucking at her sandaled feet as rivulets of water ran over them, and she grabbed at plants to keep her footing as she slipped down a gentle slope. She shouted a warning to a woman holding a baby, begging her not to cross the stream, which was swollen several times its normal size from the rain that grew stronger as it continued to fall. The woman couldn't hear, or didn't listen; two of her children were already across and they were calling to her, their voices drowned out by the deluge around them, but the fear on their faces was plain to see.

Elizabeth finally caught up to the woman, who was about to try to ford the stream using a cable stretching across the water. The cable already dipped below the surface in the middle, when normally, it hung a foot or more above the water. The raft that was normally there to traverse the stream via the cable was nowhere to be seen. Elizabeth tried to stop her, but the woman waved Elizabeth off and waded into the torrent up to her knees, one hand on the cable and one arm clutching the wrap tightly swaddling the baby to her body. Horror filled Elizabeth when the woman slipped, and she sprang forward, grabbing the back of the woman's tee shirt with one hand, the cable with her other. The rushing stream nearly swept her off her feet, but she held on to the cable and tried to keep her feet under her as she held on to the woman.

The stream, now a raging river, continued to rise in the pouring rain. The woman's struggles twisted the shirt in her fist, but still she held on, her feet struggling to keep purchase on the rocks beneath them. The children across the river ran up the embankment, fleeing the rising water. She lost sight of them as she focused her attention on clinging to both the cable and the woman. Then, the cable she clung to was under water and she had to let go, or go down with it. A broken branch made the decision for her when it side swept her, knocking her off her feet. She let go of the cable, but kept her grip on the woman's shirt. She was a strong swimmer. She positioned herself feet first down the river with the woman between her legs, keeping her and the baby afloat in the raging water, debris sweeping past them.

The woman fought against her, struggling to keep her infant above the water. They were swept toward a footing of a washed away bridge, a miniscule island in the middle of the racing current. Elizabeth's feet hit the concrete piling and a wave of water arced over them as the rushing water battered them. The strength of the current kept them pressed to the piling, and Elizabeth grabbed onto one of the metal bars that acted as steps up the side of the concrete. She pulled the woman and baby toward the steps and helped the woman climb up, and then pulled herself up with rubbery arms and leaden legs. The rain had stopped, but the water continued to rise, and her wet clothes tried to suck her down, but she made it up and collapsed on the small, rough platform above the water.

The woman yelled at her, tearing at her clothes as she pointed at the water below them. Elizabeth was too tired to respond and the noise made it difficult to hear. Then the woman was pointing skyward, and Elizabeth had enough strength to open her eyes. A helicopter, unexpected, appeared above them. Impossible in the rain. Un milagro. A miracle.

The woman crossed herself. Elizabeth did too, even though she wasn't religious. A rope was lowered. It blew in the wind, but Elizabeth, with a surge of adrenaline, was able to catch it, and somehow, with arms that felt like jelly, she fixed the harness attached to it around her and the woman, and they were pulled up just as the water overtook the concrete island. The helicopter was buffeted in the wind and the rope began to swing. The woman lost hold of her baby and it rolled in slow motion out of the material in which it was wrapped. Elizabeth reached for it and caught it, pulling it back. At first she thought it was only the fabric and her heart froze, but she had a hold of the baby too, and she pulled it to her. The woman flailed trying to take the baby from her, and the harness loosened, but did not come off. Elizabeth nearly dropped the baby again, but still managed to hook her arm under the woman's armpit, and held on to both of them for dear life, even as she tried to keep the harness from loosening more. She held her breath and gritted her teeth, willing the harness to hold. They were finally pulled into the helicopter.

Elizabeth collapsed on the floor and someone had to pull her legs in for her, because she had no more strength to swing her legs up the last few inches. Someone else unhooked the harness. She rolled over in time to see the woman grab the wailing baby from the arms of one of the men who had pulled them to safety. The woman began to cry. The man in fatigues who had pulled them in started to cry. Elizabeth realized she was crying, too. She had cried in the dream and she cried right there, lying in yesterday's clothes, soft from sleep, surprised her wet hair wasn't clinging to her face or her sodden clothes weren't chaffing her puckered skin.

It wasn't a dream. Elizabeth knew that now. It was a memory. Heavy, un-stopping rains had plagued the mission during her last trip to Guatemala. It was supposed to be the dry season, but El Nino had brought the heavy rains that hadn't stopped. Instead of falling each afternoon for a couple of hours and stopping, they'd persisted, day and night, until the ground could hold no more and the rivers and reservoirs were full. Instead of building houses, she and her team had fortified existing shacks and dug diversion ditches to guide the never-ending water away from structures and livestock.

In addition to vaccinations, she'd treated colds and lacerations. She'd worked day and night to help the locals. Then the dam upstream started to fail. Water levels in the normally placid stream next to the village rose. She'd saved the woman and her baby, while floods had claimed the lives of many of the villagers she'd gone down to help. The woman had been reunited with her other children, and the infant and her small family had survived in real life, but in her dreams, the baby always fell.

When the rain eventually stopped. Elizabeth was grateful for the nearly around-the-clock work details she was given, along with every able-bodied person in the nearby villages—except when the cleanup entailed digging out bodies. But, even that was better than not working. It was muddy and difficult, but the work kept her from remembering. However, when exhaustion claimed her, the dream started, the baby began to roll out of the sodden fabric, and in her dream, she didn't catch it. The baby always fell. Exhausted from lack of sleep and anxious, Elizabeth was forced to leave her trip early. She made excuses, but she hadn't told anyone the real reason why she left—that the dreams of a baby falling from her arms were haunting her even when the work of finding real bodies did not. She didn't even really know why herself.

Now, safe and dry in her childhood room, 4B ran to the bathroom and threw up. When her last heave subsided, she collapsed where she was, curled up on the tile floor and cried. She wept as she hadn't wept in years, until her sides ached and her throat felt raw. And still she cried some more.

❀❀❀❀❀

Hours later, 4B awoke on the bathroom floor. The house was dark and silent. Her eyes felt sandy, her mouth was dry, and she had a sinus headache. She pushed herself up and sat wearily, cross-legged on the nubby bathroom throw rug that smelled of rubber from the anti-skid underneath. She pulled herself up using the counter and drank water from her hands at the sink. Her hair was a mess, her face was blotchy, and finally, she knew, at least in part, who she was.

She wandered over to her bed, noting it was dark outside and an entire day had slid by. Still, she sat down on the edge of the mattress, wanting to lie back down, exhausted. The journals were stacked on the bedside table, and she picked them up one by one. Small pieces of her past started to link together. She stopped with the journal with the missing pages, the only one with a removable leather cover, and she peeled the leather away as if she had done it before. Hidden between the leather and the book, as she knew they would be, were the missing pages, along with a folded piece of white paper with the name Eliza printed neatly on one side. Layce was the only one who had ever called her Eliza. 4B put the folded square to the side and began to read the loose journal pages.

Something happened tonight. Something big. I kissed Layce. Yes. I wrote it out loud!!!!! I kissed her. And she kissed me back. I didn't mean to. It just happened, but I'm glad it did. I think it settles some things. But before I get into that, I just need to say it was fantastic!!! Better than fantastic! It was incredible! Actually, there are no words for how it was. It felt like I stepped out of my own body and was floating. No one ever told me a kiss could feel like that. It never has with Kev or Josh. They just try to stick their tongue down your throat. It's enough to make you gag! But Layce kissed me so softly, and she put her arms around me, and I thought I would melt away. I was the first person she has ever kissed. I know this for a fact, because we talk about those things. I always thought it strange that she made it to her senior year without ever kissing a guy—even Josh, since everyone has kissed Josh. I wish I had waited, too. I'm sure she never expected she would kiss me. She didn't kiss like someone who never has, though. God. None of this makes sense. I don't know what I feel. Good and a little scared. What does it mean? My mother will NOT approve. I know she's supposed to be gay friendly, being a Dem. Senator, but I've heard her talking to dad. I know they wonder about Layce. Just because she's athletic and doesn't want a boyfriend. I almost laughed when I heard my mom tell my dad she's too pretty to be gay. She would die if she knew I started it. Besides, what about Kev? Even his parents expect us to get married and have 2.5 children. Just pop out the perfect family. I can't do it. I won't do it. Especially now that I know what it feels like to kiss Layce. There was more, too. I almost don't want to write it down. I don't want it to sound cheap or dirty, but there was touching. I know it's not real sex, but it sort of is. We had to be quiet because the rest of the team was sleeping right next to us. I'm positive no one knew what we were doing. No one looked at us weird the next morning at least. Even if they did, I wouldn't care. Not now, when I know Layce feels the same way I do. At least I think she does. You don't kiss someone like THAT and not feel the same way. Anyway, we kissed and touched each other all night and it felt so nice to sleep right next to her. I want to ask her to spend the night, but I wonder if she'll think all I'm after is more of what happened…and I am…kind of…but not like a guy would be. I really care about her and it's natural to want that kind of closeness, right? Ugh! God, I could scream!!!

I finally got up the nerve to ask Layce to come over. Not to spend the night, but just to hang out. It's been three days since THAT NIGHT. I was starting to get scared she hated me or something. But she doesn't. I was so nervous. I think she was, too. She wouldn't come inside the house and kept asking where my mom was. We haven't mentioned what happened since the night it happened. I'm worried she's ashamed or having second thoughts or something. I'm not, though. We took a blanket out to our secret meadow and we hung out there, and I almost couldn't get my nerve up to say or do anything. At first, we just lay there and talked a little and watched the sky. But I had to kiss her again. There was no way I could have not kissed her again. It was all I could think about. And when I did, it was like an invisible force pulled us together. There is no other way to describe it. When I looked at her, we just floated together as if there was no way to prevent it. And I didn't want to. I couldn't. And we had sex. The guys are always talking about how two women together can't have "real" sex because "real" sex consists of penetration. Well, they don't know what they're talking about. If what Layce and I did isn't sex, I don't know what sex is. Not that I have done it with anyone else yet. But I know what I'm talking about. Wait. You know what? We didn't have sex, we made love. That's what it was and it was perfect. Oh my god. Oh my god. Oh my god. I can't even describe what it feels like to touch her and to let her touch me. It's indescribable. And, besides, I don't want kissing or sex to define us anyway. God, it was great, but even when we just sit quietly not even talking and feeling comfortable it's good, too. I am so happy. I never knew I could feel this way.

I can't fucking believe it. Fuck! Fuck! Fuck! Layce called me tonight to apologize for what happened. She acted ashamed and told me it wasn't right. I thought maybe we would talk about it, but I never expected her to apologize. Not after what happened. Not after how we were together. She acted all noble and said she accepted responsibility…blah, blah, blah. What the eff? She didn't even take into consideration my feelings. She said we should try to hang out with other people. Not apart, but with other people around us so it doesn't *happen again. What is she? My prison warden? Does she think I can't control myself? I feel like an idiot. I honestly thought she felt some of the things I did. I told her to eff off. I didn't mean it. Well, I did, but I didn't. I was hurt and I reacted badly. I can't even think clearly. It hurts so much I can barely breathe. I can't breathe. Death would feel better than this. How could she be so stoic about it? How could she look at me so softly one minute and so coldly another? How does someone do that? She is seriously fucked up. Or is it me? This hurts so much. I can't breathe.*

Layce won't talk to me. I apologized for telling her to eff off, but she doesn't care. She must be really grossed out about what happened. I'm surprised, but if it's how she feels… I'll wait for her to figure things out if I have to. God I love her. As a friend and more… but if she can't handle it, I can't make her. Besides I've been thinking, there is no way my mom will accept it. Especially if I go into politics, which who knows, I still might do. Being gay is political suicide. And who wants to go to a gay doctor? But if Layce comes to me and tells me she loves me, I will be with her in a heartbeat. I don't care about my career. She is way more important than anything else. We could run away to Bolivia or Peru or something. We could live in a box for all I care. But until/if she decides, I will be her best friend. I just wish she would talk to me again. I wish I could kiss her and hold her, too. But if I can be her friend again, I'll gladly take it. Anything is better than this silent treatment she's giving me.

My mom is making me go to the dance with Kev. He and I have been hanging out a lot more these days. I finally told him about Layce. It's been weeks since Layce and I did that stuff and I really needed to talk to someone. He was so shocked, but he didn't say anything shitty. I can tell him anything. I think he sort of suspected anyway. I wonder why I never suspected myself. Anyway. I have to go to the dance and I don't want to, but if I have to, I'm glad it's with Kev. I hope Layce goes with us, but it's unlikely.

Layce and I are friends again. It's weird but I'd rather have the friendship than nothing. I won't even hope for more… well maybe a little. OK a lot. But it's up to her.

4B read the entries and felt the manic-depressive ups and downs of her teenaged self. Just reading the passages made her heart ache in memory.

Yes!

Real memory!

She remembered the old ache for the one thing she wanted more than anything else, and was afraid to ask for. She hadn't read those pages since she had torn them out all those years ago, after it became apparent to her Layce didn't want her. She remembered how embarrassed she had been, how scared she'd been about the possibility of her mother finding the pages, but she couldn't bear to throw them away. So, she'd tucked them behind the leather, along with the whole event.

Another memory assailed her then, a memory she'd rather not have recovered, a moment in her life she would never have written down. This memory came from a darker place than the hidden spot behind the leather cover.

Time had passed and high school was almost over. She and Kev had been dating for several months, and she and Layce were in their last year of high school. They'd found a comfortable peace and had settled back into a close friendship—mostly. There were still some odd moments of discomfort and sometimes they fought about little things because they didn't talk about the unspoken thing that hung between them. But mostly, they tried to be careful to not tread on sensitive territory.

One day, Layce and she had been sharing an embrace after one of their many fights. It had been over Thanksgiving break because Kev was home from his first year in college and she remembered how cold it had been outside. They were standing between their cars in the driveway of Elizabeth's parents' house and Layce had been leaning with her back against her car while Elizabeth leaned against her. Her head was buried in Layce's neck. Suddenly Kev was there and he grabbed Elizabeth's hand, pulling her toward his car. He didn't say a word. He just put her in the passenger seat and sped away. It was dark. He found a quiet road and he drove.

Elizabeth just sat there looking out the windshield. She wasn't scared. Kev wasn't a scary guy. But she was a little angry at the way he'd just come and grabbed her, treating her like she was his property or something. It wasn't cool, and not like him at all. Knowing it wasn't like him diminished some of her anger. Not all of it, but some. She wondered what he wanted to talk about. When he turned to her in the dark and looked at her, she just kept looking forward.

"What the hell was that all about?" he demanded.

"I don't know what you're talking about, Kev. What the hell is the matter with you?"

"She's what's the matter with me. You're supposed to be my girlfriend, but you barely touch me. And then you go hanging all over her in public. That's what's the matter with me."

"You don't know what you're talking about. My driveway isn't in public. We had a fight. She was just hugging me because I was upset. It's what best friends do."

"Do best friends fuck each other?"

"What?" asked Elizabeth finally turning to him and seeing the anger in his face. She also smelled alcohol. "Are you drunk?"

"I had a few beers with the guys. They think you and Layce are fucking each other."

"Take me home. I don't want to become a statistic in a drunk driving public service announcement." Kev seemed to hear her concern, but instead of heading home, he pulled the car to the side of the road, turned off the ignition, and turned off the lights. The sudden silence pressed upon them as they each stared out the front windshield. Elizabeth listened to the ticking of the cooling engine and the creaking of Kev's fists working against the steering wheel as he gripped and ungripped the leather-encased plastic. The waves of oppressive judgment coming from the other side of the car filled her with anger. "They talk about us? You talk about us to them?"

"Sure they do. Everyone does. They say she's a dyke and that she's fucking you."

"They're ignorant assholes who don't know what they're talking about."

"Are you fucking her, too? If you aren't fucking her anymore, then why aren't you fucking me more often?"

"Is that what all of this is about? Is it because I won't jump your bones as soon as you walk into town on your school breaks? I wish I hadn't told you about her and me. I thought I could talk to you. I thought you'd be cool."

"What is it then? We've officially been going out for over a year, and I can count on both hands how many times you've slept with me. Shit, most of the time, you won't let me get past second base."

Elizabeth couldn't believe what she was hearing. He'd turned to face her and was staring at her and she looked away. He knew how confused she'd been about Layce and how devastated she'd been when Layce had told her they should just be friends. He'd known how hurt she'd been. After she'd told him all of it, after she'd let their relationship progress to boyfriend and girlfriend, she wondered why he felt like he could say the things he was saying now.

"Why, Elizabeth? Are you giving it all to that dyke?"

"Take me home."

"Answer me, Elizabeth."

"I said take me home."

"I need to know!" he said, and before she knew what was happening, he had climbed over the console between them and was on top of her. He lay upon her and kissed her roughly, the scent of his cologne and beer assailed her. She tried to turn her head away, to get away from the nauseating smells, but he held her face between both hands, hurting her ears, his mouth pressing against her, his sparse stubble scratching her face.

"Stop it, Kev! Get off of me!"

"Not until you tell me if you're fucking her!"

"I already told you I'm not!"

"I don't believe you," he said as he put his hand up her shirt and grabbed her breast.

"No! Kev, don't do this!"

He suddenly stilled and pulled his hand out of her shirt. His head dropped and he panted against her neck. He held himself away, removing the hardness she'd felt grow against her trapped legs.

"I'm sorry. I'm sorry," he whispered. "Why won't you let me be with you, Elizabeth?"

Elizabeth didn't know what to say. They had never talked about it. After she had allowed him to make love to her a few weeks after they had officially started going out, she more often than not moved his hands from her breasts when he'd tried to take things beyond kissing. She just wasn't into sex like all of her friends. Despite his frustration, he'd always been a gentleman about it. He'd never tried to force anything.

Elizabeth put her arms around him and kissed the side of his head, and when he lifted his face from her shoulder, she could see the pain in his eyes. She pulled his head down and kissed him. When she reached down to rub the subsiding thickness in his pants he had been surprised, but he had let her unzip his pants and take him in her hand. He had even lifted himself off of her so she could slide her own shorts down. It had been fast, and she had initiated every move until he collapsed against her. But when he reached down to touch her, to give her relief, she had lied and told him she had come when he had. After that, she had let him have sex with her any time she sensed he wanted to, which really wasn't that often. If she couldn't be with Layce, she might as well be with the one everyone had chosen for her.

Later, when Layce had finally admitted she had feelings for her, it had been impossible for her to go back. She'd made her decision in the car with Kev, and by then, she'd known that Kev was going to ask her to marry him. She knew her parents expected her to say yes—everyone expected her to say yes. She had the perfect life mapped out for her. She was terrified of disappointing any of them, terrified of losing Layce's friendship if she couldn't handle the pressure of going against the grain. So, she'd stayed on track, going the route expected of her, burying her wants and her heart along the way.

Old memories and feelings swept through her. She put the pages on top of the stack of journals and picked up the folded note. She turned it over and over in her hands before she slowly opened it, pulled the tucked corner from its slot, unfolded the single page and smoothed it open in front of her. A sense of anticipation rose in her, even though she'd memorized the words long ago. The paper bore a map of faded wrinkles, as if it had been crumpled up and smoothed out, once upon a time. There were some torn edges. The scars worn by the paper were the only physical evidence of the pain she'd experienced back then, but based on the longing and hurt surging within her, the paper had weathered much better than Elizabeth's heart. She read the letter Layce had written to her the day after their kiss at the boat club.

Eliza-

I don't know what to say. I kissed you. Wow. I never expected it to happen, but I've dreamed about it for years. You're always on my mind. You're everything I want. So, now you know my secret. What happened didn't seem one-sided, but maybe it's wishful thinking. I hope you'll let me know. Above everything else, I hope you're okay.

I love you, and I hope that whatever happens between us from here on, that no matter what, we always remain friends- hopefully more- but always friends. I'd die if I didn't have you in my life.

Please call me.

Love,

Layce

Below the note, on the same page but in a different ink, the same neat boxy script formed a postscript. A chill ran through Elizabeth like the one she'd felt all those years ago when she'd first read it.

(Eliza- I left this on your windshield the day after the sleepover. Your mother answered the door and gave it back to me a couple days later when I got up the nerve to go see you when you didn't call. She didn't say a word, just handed the note back to me. I left without seeing you. But then you called me and then we went to our meadow and…well, wow. I've relived that time in my head a thousand times. I really thought we'd figure things out. But when I came by the next day, your mother looked at me with such hate, like she knew what had happened and was repulsed by it. She told me to leave you alone, to not ruin your life…. I've kept it all this time, thinking maybe I'd give it to you in person. Maybe we could figure it out together. Anyway, I know that's not gonna happen now. So don't tell me you were the only one to suffer. You have no idea. No idea.)

4B read the note another time and thought back to the day Layce had given it to her—no, thrown it at her. It had been after yet another argument. They always seemed to start the same, with Elizabeth accusing Layce of being insensitive by not showing up when she said she would, or showing up drunk with some girl and making a scene. This fight had been the worst though. This one had almost killed their friendship forever.

It had been the 4th of July right after she and Layce had graduated from Harvard. The summer had started off shaky because Kev had been pissed that Elizabeth had chosen to go to med school at Johns Hopkins instead of moving to California to be closer to him at Stanford. But Elizabeth had listed all of the reasons she wanted to go to Johns Hopkins—except the real one, that it was closer to Layce—and Kev had finally seemed to accept it. He'd even stopped being an asshole when Elizabeth and Layce made plans to do things that didn't include him during their break.

Before going down to the marina that evening to watch the annual fireworks display with the rest of the town, she and Layce had spent the day swimming at Layce's house. Kev, for once, had other plans, so it was just them, and Elizabeth had been glad for the alone time with Layce. But Layce had been picking fights all day. Finally, after ignoring it for hours, Layce had made one crack too many and Elizabeth had thrown the sunscreen she'd been holding at Layce. Layce had responded by throwing it back and glaring at her from one of the chaise lounges by the pool. When Elizabeth had asked her what her problem was, Layce finally told her Kev was planning on asking Elizabeth to marry him during the fireworks display that night and she wasn't okay with it. Elizabeth had been shocked. She'd been clear about not wanting to even talk about getting married until after she was done with med school, which was years away. She'd told Layce she was wrong. She said Kev knew she had no intention of getting married in the next few years. But Layce had told her Kev had bought the ring at her father's jewelry store earlier in the week and he'd even told her dad he was pretty sure she'd end up changing schools to go to Stanford once she was wearing it.

Elizabeth had been beyond angry. Angry at Kev for dismissing her desire to wait until after med school to even discuss marriage. But the more interesting thing was that she'd been even angrier at Layce for making her feel like it was her fault Kev was going to ask her to marry him in the first place. What did Layce care? Layce of the never-ending line of women she flaunted in her face. Layce who had dumped her all those years ago. As far as she was concerned, Layce had absolutely no say in the matter. Even so, she decided then if Kev really did ask her to marry him, she would say no.

Pissed off, but still sensitive to Kev's feelings, she didn't say any of this to Layce. Instead, Elizabeth had asked Layce why she even cared. Elizabeth had been tired of dealing with Layce's attitude all day. She'd had half a mind not to even go to the marina that night. She'd rather take a long drive by herself. Everyone could fuck off with their unwanted proposals and bitchiness for all she cared.

Unexpectedly, the conversation had brought up a whole lot of old feelings for Elizabeth. She and Layce had never really talked about the time at the sleepover or the time in the meadow—except for when Layce had told her how wrong it had been and that they should forget it. Elizabeth had been too embarrassed to press Layce about and she'd tucked it away. After that, they had gone on with their lives as if nothing had ever happened. But months later, after Elizabeth and Kev had started dating, Layce had started dating other girls. A bitter sense of betrayal had filled Elizabeth, but since they had never spoken about what had happened, she had to kept it all inside. She had watched Layce with the other girls and her heart broke with each new one. Each one had proven to Elizabeth that Layce just didn't feel the same way Elizabeth felt about about her.

Until that 4th of July.

Layce had begun acting like she had a say in the matter. And she definitely did not.

"You have no right to tell me who I should or shouldn't marry. You can't even stay with one girlfriend for more than a month!" she'd said, squaring off with Layce, daring her to respond.

That's when the fight had really escalated. They'd said a lot of things to one another, but never once had they said what was really bothering them. Then, tired of the fight and raw from the subject, Elizabeth had looked Layce in the eye and told her what she had been holding onto for so long.

"You fucking don't get it! You never have."

"You're right, I don't," said Layce, and Elizabeth remembered how frustrated she'd been at the smirk on Layce's face.

"I have been the one suffering all of this time, watching you go from girl to girl, listening to how great this one is, how awesome that one is. Even telling me details about your sex life..."

"What?" Layce had spat out, clenching her fists. Elizabeth had never seen her so angry. "You've told me every excruciating detail about you and Kev! Oh, wait! It's okay because you're straight? Is that it? Are you a closet homophobe just like your mom?"

"What does my mom have to do with anything? And you know I'm not a homophobe."

"Yeah, right."

"You know it! All these years you've been parading all your girlfriends by me as if it didn't matter. And all this time all I've ever wanted was for you to acknowledge..." Elizabeth couldn't say it.

"Acknowledge what?"

"Nothing."

"Really. Acknowledge what? That you and Kev are made for each other? You're not. There. I've said it. You don't belong together. You're settling. You don't love him."

"I do."

"Not the right way."

"What do you know about it? But you're right. I don't. All this time I've only wished he was you." Elizabeth had been shocked to hear herself say those words out loud. She'd hardly admitted them to herself. But now that they were out, and she knew they were true, even if she didn't know the extent of what it meant, she figured she should admit the rest. Get the rest off her chest. "But you never gave me the chance, Layce. You told me to forget what happened. You're the homophobe. You! You know what? Never mind. You'll never get it, anyway," said Elizabeth as she stormed away from Layce's house, from Layce's surprised eyes.

She drove around for a while, trying to figure out where she should go. And finally, when the sun started to set, she went where she was expected. She was late getting to the marina, but she went, just like everyone knew she would. Layce had been there, though. Even though Elizabeth hadn't thought she would be, even after the embarrassing things Elizabeth had admitted to her, Layce had waited at their secret parking spot, the one no one ever thought to use, intercepting her as she parked her car. Elizabeth had still been angry, but she was tired of fighting. She was ready to put the fight to rest and was just about to tell her she wasn't going to marry Kev anyway. Layce had even seemed to drop some of her bitchiness as she had approached Elizabeth, helping her out of the car.

But Kev had found them.

He'd been exuberant when he approached Elizabeth. She saw his smile dim a little when he saw Layce was with her, but it stayed on his face as he guided them to the picnic area, where he said everyone was already celebrating. Layce got shitty again. She'd made some remarks about how Kev always got his way and about people being forced to do things they didn't want to do. Kev had lost his temper. He'd told Layce to mind her own business and go find some other girl to fuck. Elizabeth had yelled at him, then, she had yelled at them both. She'd told them that they were out of line. She'd almost left, but her mother found them and they'd all stuffed the anger down and pretended everything was fine.

The surge of emotions had left Elizabeth fuzzy and in the next moments, she'd found herself shuffled over to the marina where she lost track of Layce. Someone told her that Layce had left. She wanted to go find her, ashamed at having yelled at her, but people were pulling at her and she didn't know where Layce had gone, anyway. That's when everyone had mysteriously backed up a few feet. They were looking at her with big smiles and nudging each other. She'd looked around, confused, and Kev had been on his knee. There had been a big flash across the water, and a huge array of sparklers flamed a misspelled proposal. And, as if they hadn't just been screaming at each other, Kev had asked her to marry him. In front of the entire town. She had almost run away when she saw the sparklers, but Kev had been on his knee and how could she embarrass him like that? She wasn't even sure she had said yes. Kev had just slipped the ring on her finger and the town had exploded in congratulations. And they were engaged.

Layce had refused to speak to her after that night. Elizabeth hadn't even known how to approach her after what she'd said. It had been a terrible summer. It had taken the rest of July and most of August to convince Kev that being engaged didn't mean she was going to change schools and that she still had no intention of getting married before she finished med school. Thankfully, he'd eventually stopped trying to convince her. It seemed just wearing his ring put him in an overall better mood. Maybe that's why she stopped trying to figure out how to give the ring back. And as the hot days of that summer wore on, she and Layce continued to avoid one another. She'd begun to wonder if she needed to make new living arrangements down in Baltimore, since it didn't seem like she'd be sharing the apartment she and Layce had picked out.

Then Layce had shown up at her house. It had been the first time in a long time since Layce had come to her house.

They went for a drive.

"You weren't the only one suffering, Eliza. I was suffering, too."

"Why didn't you say anything?"

"Your mother told me to leave you alone."

"What?"

"I left a note on your windshield after you went rowing the day after the sleepover. You didn't call and I was going crazy wondering if you were okay, worried that you were flipping out. So the next day, I went by your house and she answered the door. She had the note."

"I never got a note."

Layce reached into her pocket and pulled something out. She threw a crumpled note at her. Elizabeth smoothed it out and read it. A tsunami of emotion swept through her.

"This is from then, right after we…?"

Layce cleared her throat.

"Um. Yeah. The first part. I wrote the last part while everyone was watching the fireworks. I was a little pissed off that night."

"I wish... I mean, if I'd seen this..." She didn't know what she would have done if she'd seen it back then. But she knew things would have turned out different. Anger erupted in her. "She just said to leave me alone? And you listened to her? You never even told me!"

"She said you weren't like me. That it wasn't healthy for me to fill your head with stuff. 'Painful confusion' she called it. I was embarrassed, confused, scared. You hadn't tried to talk to me. I didn't know what to think. It was all new to me, too, Eliza. So, I left and pretended it never happened."

Elizabeth stared at her hands in her lap, clutching the note. Her anger was gone and a dark emptiness filled her. She didn't know what it all meant and so much had changed.

"It's not fair," she whispered. "All this time..."

"But, now you know. I've always loved you. I always will. But you're with Kev now, and you're going to marry him."

"I'll break it off."

"Is it what you really want? Don't do it for me, if that's what you're doing it for. You need to do it for yourself."

"Of course I'd being doing it for myself. If I could be with you..."

"That can't be your reason, Eliza. It can't be for me. What do you want for yourself? I couldn't stand to be your experiment. Not now. I don't want to be your secret either. I want to be friends with you forever. If I had to choose between being your lover for a while or your friend forever, I would choose you as my best friend. If you break up with Kev, it has to be for something other than just to be with me."

Elizabeth thought about breaking it off with Kev. She had wanted Layce for so long. But could she be open about it? Would her mother understand? What about Kev? He'd stood by her during her darkest times. She'd even told him about her and Layce—the times at the sleepover and in the meadow, but not the fight before he asked her to marry him. It would have been too much for him to carry. Could she do that to him? Could she break his heart after he'd stood by her through so much?

She felt Layce's eyes on her as she considered everything. Her chest felt tight, feeling so many questions in her gaze. She wanted to tell Layce that she wanted to be lovers and best friends, that it didn't need to be a choice. But she wasn't sure she could live up to it. She wanted Layce more than anything else in the world. But, was she strong enough to disappoint every other person in her life? Maybe even lose some of them? She was relieved when

Layce sighed and started the car without asking what she'd do.

Layce dropped Elizabeth back home after they agreed they would see how things played out. Elizabeth made no promises to change the direction of her life, and Layce made no promises other than to be a good friend. They did agree to one thing, though—they would live together in Baltimore, but they would keep their relationships with others separate. Kev wouldn't come to visit, and Layce wouldn't bring her girlfriends around. Somehow, they both assumed things would carry on as if nothing had ever been said.

That day, Elizabeth watched Layce drive off and an enormous hole in her heart opened up. All the time they'd had, all those chances, and she had missed them. Now she wasn't sure she could change the image of herself she had worked so hard to build. An anger, dark and oily, began to swell within her.

Her mother was in her office—she was always in her office—and Elizabeth walked in. She slammed the door. Startled, her mother looked up from the stack of pages she was reviewing.

"Elizabeth, what's wrong?"

"Did you really warn Layce off?"

Her mother paused and considered the question.

"I have no idea what you're talking about. I haven't seen Layce Dalton since you girls were in high school."

"That's because you told her to leave me alone."

"I didn't tell her to leave you alone."

"What did you tell her, mother? She just told me her side, now I want to hear yours."

"I found a letter she had written to you. A love letter." Her mother's eyes bored into her with meaning. "I saved you both some embarrassment and told her you weren't interested."

"How do you know I wasn't?"

Her mother relaxed her shoulders.

"Don't be ridiculous, Elizabeth. For one, you were still in high school, if I recall. You were already dating Kev. You're engaged, for goodness sake. You aren't like that."

"Like what?"

"Elizabeth Grace, what has gotten into you?" asked her mother, lying down the pen she'd been holding. "You are not a lesbian."

"How do you know?"

"I just do. Honey, I don't understand this. I would know if you were gay. And I thank God you're not. What mother would wish for their daughter to be unhappy and reviled?" A look of alarm crossed her mother's face. "Are you worried I may have hurt your friend's feelings? It was years ago. Layce can't still be harboring ill feelings. I'll be happy to talk to her."

"Mom…"

"Seriously, if she's still upset I'll talk to her. People like her need to know they have people on their side."

"As long as they aren't trying to convert your daughter, is that it?"

"Elizabeth, what is wrong with you? Gays don't convert people. They are born that way."

"Is that what you really think, or is it just your canned senatorial response?"

"It's not a canned response."

"How do you feel about gays?"

"You know how I feel. They're important in my life, though their orientation doesn't define their relationship with me. They're my friends. They're some of my most brilliant staff members. They are valuable community members. I don't know what this has to do with…"

"What if I were gay?" interrupted Elizabeth.

"But you aren't."

"But what if I were? And don't try to do the politically correct thing. I've heard you talking to dad about it. I've heard you tell him you'd be disappointed."

"If we're being honest, I would be. The gay life is hard. There are so many people who disagree with it and condemn it. I get to see death threats made to my staffers from mean and sometimes violent anti-gay groups and people. Why would I want you to live with the constant stress and fear? Why would I want such difficulty in our family? Beyond that, the limitations under the law are a burden. And selfishly, I want grandchildren. I want you to follow in my footsteps and be the next generation carrying our name into Washington. Neither of those would be likely if you were a lesbian. So, if it's wrong for me to be grateful you don't have to face any of those hardships because you aren't gay, then I'm wrong."

Elizabeth didn't know how to respond. It was true. Her mother wasn't hateful. But something didn't sit well, and she didn't have the words to describe what it was. The confusion kept her from trying and she knew she would continue to choose the path that was chosen for her until she knew how to define what she felt.

She left her mother's office still not knowing what she should do about her feelings for Layce, her promise to Kev, and the hopes that she represented for her parents. The one thing she would do, she knew, was be the best friend Layce needed her to be. Maybe she'd figure out the rest in time.

So, she and Layce moved to Baltimore. They lived together and they protected each other from their romantic lives. They made a trip down to Guatemala every year during summer break and provided shelter and immunizations to the locals.

But neither of them thought the impasse they had tacitly agreed upon would last. And it didn't. One day Layce told Elizabeth about Andrea, and Elizabeth could tell Andrea wasn't just another girlfriend. Layce was in love and the dynamic had to shift. Layce still made time for Elizabeth and they still went on their trips. But Layce started to spend more time away from Elizabeth and more time with Andrea. And Elizabeth knew Layce's heart had found a home.

Curious about the new girlfriend, because Layce had honored her promise and had never brought Andrea to the apartment, Elizabeth convinced Layce it was time to meet her. And against her will, she liked Andrea. Andrea was smart and funny, but most of all, she was good to Layce, and that was the most important thing.

It broke Elizabeth's heart.

She and Layce got drunk one night, something they never did, because there was a chance that they'd edge back toward the place they had both walked away from.

Although Elizabeth had two more years of med school, Layce had just graduated from engineering school. They were celebrating.

Three bottles of champagne sat on the coffee table; two of them empty, one was still half-full. Layce sat at one end of the sofa and Elizabeth had her head in her lap. She was curled up on her side, facing away, and Layce scratched her back through her t-shirt.

"Someday you're gonna build me a house, Layce," said Elizabeth, first closing one eye, and then closing the other, watching the champagne bottles line up and then move apart. She pointed a finger at one of the bottles to hold it there and squinted. A flock of bottles fanned out in her vision and her finger wasn't pointed at any of them.

"I have always known this. It will have high glass walls and lots of wood."

"How'd you know?" asked Elizabeth, dropping her outstretched hand and glancing back at Layce before she dropped her head back onto her warm lap.

"You told me."

"When was this?"

"We were on our blanket in the secret meadow."

"Ah. Our secret meadow," sighed Elizabeth. A sadness fell over her at the thought of it, like it always did these days.

"Remember when we used to do that? Talk all day while watching the sky?"

"It was a long time ago."

"Yep. But I remembered. You described your house one time and that night I drew it so I would remember."

"You did?"

"Yep. Down to the stainless steel countertops and the fireman's pole dropping from the bedroom balcony into the pool."

"Oh my god! I remember!"

"It's why I became an architect."

"To build me a house?"

"Pretty much."

Layce stroked her hair and Elizabeth closed her eyes. If she could, she would have purred like a cat.

"Are you happy, Layce?"

The pause was so long, Elizabeth thought that maybe she forgot to ask out loud. She was about to ask again when Layce finally answered.

"Yes. Are you?"

"I'm not sure I know what happy is," said Elizabeth and she was kind of surprised she'd said it. The response had just come out of her without her thinking it and her own words struck her as kind of deep and melancholy. It was as if she was feeling someone else's feelings. Suddenly, she felt very alone.

Layce rolled Elizabeth over and Elizabeth looked up into Layce's eyes.

"Sure you do."

"I know how to be comfortable, but I don't know how to be happy."

Layce studied her face for a moment.

"I think I know what you mean, Eliza."

"But you're happy. That's cool. What makes you happy, Layce?"

"This. Talking with you makes me happy. Being done with school makes me happy. Feeling like I'm about to start my life makes me happy."

"Being with Andrea."

Layce paused, but her eyes grew soft.

"Yes, being with Andy makes me happy."

"I don't have any of that…"

"Hey…!" laughed Layce, pretending to be offended.

"Yes, talking with you makes me happy. Hanging out with you does. But it makes me sad sometimes, too. So, that cancels it out."

Confusion filled Layce's face.

"Hanging out with me makes you sad?"

"Yes. Because I know it won't always be like this."

"Yes, it will. If we want it to be."

"No. It won't. We won't always live together like…" Elizabeth tried to explain, but Layce interrupted her.

"But we'll always be friends. We can…"

"Things will change. Maybe you'll go live with Andrea. And when I come over—because I will come over—a lot—I won't be able to get you drunk and lay in your lap."

"Yes, you will."

"No. I won't. It wouldn't be fair to Andrea… or whoever it is you end up with."

"If they're not cool with it, they won't be in the picture. Andrea included."

"Layce. You don't mean that."

"No. I get it. Our relationship will evolve. It will be okay. But the other stuff… Kev, you being a doctor…"

Elizabeth rolled her eyes. And the hiccups started. She laughed.

"I can't even make up my mind what to specialize in. You know why? Because I know my mother expects me to go into politics."

"You hate politics. You aren't even registered to vote."

Elizabeth reached up and put her hand over Layce's mouth.

"Shhhh! That's a secret!"

They giggled and Layce let Elizabeth's hand rest against her lips for a few seconds before she reached up and removed it.

"But seriously, you hate politics."

"I know. It's what she wants, though. It's always been The Plan. Oh, I'll finish my schooling, and get my medical license, fighting the political path all the way. But I have no idea what I want to do after that. My life is in limbo and I don't know how to get out of it."

"But Kev—doesn't he make you happy?"

Elizabeth stared at Layce, then rolled her eyes.

"I can't believe you, of all people, would ask that question, Layce."

"So, why are you still with him?"

"Because… because… what else is there?"

"Love. Romance. Passion. Just to name a few things."

"I get as much of all of that from him as I'm bound to get with anyone else."

"You just haven't experienced it, Eliza. You'll see it and feel it when you come across it. Maybe you need to get away from Kev to allow yourself the possibility."

Elizabeth almost said that she had, once upon a time, on a floor in a club house filled with sleeping teammates, and again a few days later she'd risen to higher heights in their secret meadow. But she wasn't drunk enough to go there. She knew her eyes would say it, though, so she rolled back onto her side, facing away from Layce, and stared at the champagne bottles again.

"I'm afraid of what I would find."

"What are you afraid of, Eliza?" asked Layce, gently rolling her back to face her again.

Elizabeth just looked into Layce's eyes and saw that Layce knew. She didn't have to answer. So she just closed her eyes and cried. She'd fallen asleep crying, and she'd woken up the next morning, covered in a blanket that Layce must have tucked around her, with a head that felt like a truck had run over it.

Two weeks later, Layce accepted one of the offers she'd been given, from an architectural firm in Los Angeles. And before Elizabeth had gotten over the shock, she and Andrea moved out to California. Elizabeth pretended to be supportive, but inside she had died just a little. It helped that, even in all of the rush to move, Layce had still found time to go on their annual trip to Guatemala. They acted the same, they still shared a tent, but there was a sadness lingering over everything.

Over the next year, Elizabeth found herself too busy to make it out to Los Angeles to visit, but she and Layce talked on the phone several times a week. When the invitation to Layce's wedding came, scheduled for the same week as their annual trip to Guatemala, Elizabeth had to decline, even though Layce begged her to be her best woman. Elizabeth's justification was she couldn't short the team two of the regulars they counted on, but she and Layce knew it wasn't that at all. They didn't talk about it, and though their friendship cooled down a little bit, it still didn't disintegrate.

The final year of medical school was tough, and Elizabeth found the mind-numbing pace of her coursework a welcome distraction. She still talked to Layce, but she didn't have time to dwell on her own happiness or get too upset hearing Layce plan her family. One day she realized that, while she had managed to talk to Layce at least twice a week on the phone, she hadn't talked to Kev in over a month, and when she looked back on the last year, she had only seen him twice—when they both went home for Christmas, and a couple of days over spring break. And she'd talked to him less than twice a month the rest of the year. She began to understand that she couldn't follow through with marrying him.

By the time medical school was over, Elizabeth still had no idea what she was going to do with her career, other than she would stay at Johns Hopkins for her residency. Once again, she had let life just happen to her, taking the path laid out for her.

On the day she was leaving Guatemala—three days earlier than planned because the nightmares of the baby falling from her arms had kept her awake each night and she was beginning to feel a little delirious between the fatigue, the heat and the humidity—she received the call from Layce that Andrea had given birth to seven pound, three ounce Elizabeth Simone. With a baby named after her, and an elated Layce on the phone, Elizabeth had run out of excuses not to visit, so she made plans to fly out to meet her little namesake. She'd had almost two years to get used to the fact that Layce's life was with someone else. She missed Layce, but it was time to evolve. She went back to Baltimore and packed up her things, took off her engagement ring, sucked up her courage, and went out to Los Angeles to see Layce and her family.

"God, it's good to see you, Eliza—I mean, Doctor Tollworthy," said Layce, holding her at arm's length, before pulling her in for another long hug. "I was starting to think I'd have to contract some rare disease that only you would know how to cure just to see you again."

They were standing in the bright sunshine, on the Arrivals sidewalk in front of LAX. It smelled of cigarette smoke, jet exhaust, chlorinated smog, and the vague idea of suntan lotion and salty air.

"It's good to see you too, Layce," said Elizabeth, not wanting to let go. But she did. "Whoa. Look at you. All Los Angeles hipster with your hair and elegantly casual attire."

"Shut your mouth. Hipster? Ugh."

"Your hair is cut like a Showtime lesbian and, what? No more jeans?"

Layce looked elegant in tight houndstooth pants, a tight buttoned-up vest with no shirt under it, and a funky scarf.

"Are you kidding? I'd be in jeans twenty-four by seven if I could. These are my work clothes. I just left the office to pick you up. They take architecture very seriously in the City of Angels, and it's not what you know here, it's what you wear."

"Well, I like it. You look all grown up."

Layce looked at her with a bright smile and playfully yanked the hood of Elizabeth's sculling team sweatshirt over her head.

"So do you. I'm not sure what's different... I think you've been wearing that particular sweatshirt since junior high."

Elizabeth laughed as she pushed the hood back and smoothed her hair.

"It's called malnutrition and stress. Otherwise known as the medical school diet, combined with Montezuma's Revenge. Those L.A. celebrities you have out here, with all their juice and color-coded diets, can't even compete. Send them to med school and a month in Guatemala, then they can talk." Sleep deprivation and mild depression factored into it, too, though Elizabeth couldn't bring herself to say it. Not right then, surrounded by swarming arrivals and the constant movement of cars jockeying for room at the curb.

Layce hugged her again and then pushed away, spinning her around toward the trunk of a shiny black BMW.

"I've missed you so much, Eliza! I still can't believe you're here. Come on. There's a little someone I want you to meet," said Layce, picking up Elizabeth's suitcase and swinging it into the trunk of the idling car.

"I can't wait to meet my namesake," said Elizabeth, telling the truth. She ran her hand over the roof of the car. "Nice ride, Layce."

"It was a wedding present from my parents. I posted all the pictures on my social profile."

Elizabeth didn't tell Layce she hadn't visited her profile since a night over a year earlier, right before Layce and Andrea got married and after a horrible day of exams. She had gotten drunk all by herself and, thankfully, had passed out before sending a private message to Layce that she had typed out in a drunken haze. She didn't even know she had it in her to write such things, but, boy had she! Disjointed and difficult to read, it had described what she was sure Layce and Andrea did in the privacy of their bedroom. She'd read it the next morning, mortified by her vivid imagination. She'd erased the note thanking the Universe she hadn't sent it. She'd stayed away from the social site ever since.

On the drive to Layce and Andrea's house Elizabeth distracted herself with the scenery, questions about the new baby, and describing her final exams. She had passed all of the necessary boards with a lot more ease than she thought she would. But then again, she had been abnormally focused in her Quest to Avoid and studying was a great tool.

When they got to the house, she expected to see newborn chaos: a baby crying, a frazzled mom, and the place in disarray. But the serene scene they walked into was just the opposite. Andrea looked just as good as the day Elizabeth had first met her, one of the lucky few to whom baby pounds didn't seem to stick. The baby was beautiful and happy and the house was not the disorderly mess she had envisioned. To Elizabeth's surprise, it didn't pull at her heart to see Layce give Andrea a quick kiss hello. The scene actually made her smile. Layce seemed so happy, which in turn, made her happy.

Three days later, she was certain she had gotten past most of the things that had made her avoid seeing Layce all these months. She enjoyed the company of Layce and Andrea, who were good about not being too affectionate in front of her, but the small gestures she did see didn't seem to affect her as they once had.

One night, they decided to order out for pizza. The restaurant Layce and Andrea raved about didn't deliver, so Layce and Elizabeth drove down for pick up. The pizzeria was an unassuming shop directly across the street from the beach. Surf competition memorabilia decorated the small interior, and the smell of baking bread in a wood-fired oven enveloped them as they walked through the door. They placed their order and took a seat on the patio and watched the sun set over the Pacific Ocean as they waited for their pizza to be ready. Pale pinks were already starting to tinge the sky near the horizon and the sun reflected a narrowing path of diamonds across the indigo water.

"You should have let me pay, Eliza. You're a guest in my town."

"We always trade, and if I remember correctly, you bought last time."

"If so, that was a long time ago, Eliza, and I actually think you're lying."

"No! No! I remember! It's definitely my turn—a million times no take-backs."

"No fair!" cried Layce, slapping her arm. Elizabeth just laughed and felt her heart grow warm at the successful evocation of the familiar refrain they had used since middle school. Its deployment, if uttered before anyone else, was a guaranteed win for any argument. Some things would always be just theirs. A pang struck her heart at the thought and she tried to find a way to change the subject.

Layce saved her the trouble and handed Elizabeth a pair of fake IDs they had made several years earlier.

"Remember these?"

Elizabeth laughed when she saw the IDs still had a couple of years before they 'expired'. They looked authentic.

"I can't believe you still have these," said Elizabeth, looking down at the ID card displaying a picture of a much younger her on it, but had a different version of her name. It featured a birthdate making her several years older.

"I found them in one of my old wallets when I was going through things the other day. We spent a fortune on them, and you would never use it. You made me keep it for you."

"I was terrified we'd get caught. My mother would have skinned me alive for doing something as stupid as that."

"You were always so cautious. Kev used one of his dad's old licenses all the time to get beer at that rundown gas station just out of town. If he got away with it, I'm sure you would have been fine. These are good. I guess that's why they cost so much. We'd have committed the perfect crime if you weren't such a chicken."

"I know. I'm pathetic. Always afraid of getting in trouble."

"We still had fun," said Layce, sliding her own fake ID back into her wallet while Elizabeth held onto hers, studying the picture on it. "I keep meaning to ask you, where's your ring?"

Elizabeth looked at her hand.

"Oh, yeah. I left it back in Baltimore."

Layce crossed her legs, resting her ankle on her knee and picked at a string on the cuff of her pants.

"How does Kev feel about it? Speaking of which, you haven't mentioned him since you got here."

"I haven't talked to him in over a month," said Elizabeth. She knew it would be news to Layce, but it was par for the course for her.

"A fight?"

"No. We don't normally talk all that much."

"Is this a new thing?"

"Not really. This last year has been worse, mostly because of my exam schedule and all the cases he's been working at his dad's firm, but we've never been much for talking on the phone."

"So, what's with the ring?"

Elizabeth gazed out over the darkening ocean, watching the silhouettes of the last diehard surfers bobbing past the breakers, waiting for the next perfect wave.

"I finally realized I was never going to marry him."

Layce was quiet for a moment.

"Does he know?"

"I don't know. We haven't talked about it in so long. I should never have accepted his proposal in the first place. I knew back then I would never marry him."

"Hmmm…" said Layce, her eyes trained on a couple of surfers in wetsuits, rinsing off in a nearby public shower.

"Hey," said Elizabeth, getting up. She'd spotted something at a vendor cart parked on the sidewalk in front of the pizzeria. She picked up a soft toy. "I'm going to get this for little Elizabeth. Is that okay? I want to be the auntie who showers her with elephant toys. It will be our thing."

"Sure. It sounds great," said Layce.

Elizabeth paid for the toy and slipped it into her bag. A few minutes later, their order was up and they took the pizza back home.

Later that night, after Layce and Andrea went to bed, Elizabeth stepped out into the beautifully landscaped backyard. She pulled out a deck chair and sat by the dimly lit pool, as she had every night since she had arrived in L.A. She'd been sleeping better at Layce's, but the dreams still haunted her, and she avoided going to sleep because of it. Since Layce and Andy slept around little Elizabeth's schedule, they turned in earlier than her, and she enjoyed the alone time she found in the quiet setting. She went through the moments of the day in a sort of mental journal, having given up the actual writing in them when school had gotten too intense. She kept meaning to pick it up again.

Several minutes later, the sliding glass door opened and Layce appeared, wearing pajama bottoms and a tight tank top showing off her athletic build, and, in the evening chill, her perfect nipples. Elizabeth stifled a sigh. It was a look that had driven her silently crazy for years. Layce probably never even noticed how Elizabeth's heart raced at the sight of her in the outfit.

"Hey," said Layce, pulling out another deck chair and curling her legs under her as she eased herself down. She pushed her shoulder length auburn curls back with one hand in a gesture Elizabeth had always found sexy. Elizabeth turned away from Layce's perfect arms and tousled hair.

"Hey," she responded staring into the pool water, the lights casting a blue glow against the underside of the nearby foliage. They sat quietly for a few moments.

Layce cleared her throat. "So, earlier… about the ring…"

"Um huh…?" said Elizabeth, watching the ripples on the water's surface.

"Tell me more about that."

"There's nothing more to say," said Elizabeth, glancing at Layce and then back to the water. She was pretty sure she knew what Layce had on her mind, but she wasn't sure how to discuss it. Layce had a new life, and here she was, still trying to figure out what she wanted from her own life—actually, she'd only just figured out what she didn't want from her life. There was still so much more for her to figure out. "I just realized that I didn't need to marry Kev."

"Earlier, you said you shouldn't have said yes in the first place."

"Yeah. You were right. He's not for me. Besides, I know that I'll never be happy with a man."

Layce was quiet for a minute.

"When did you realize it?" asked Layce, after clearing her throat again.

"I've known all along."

Layce was quiet for another minute. When she spoke again, the anger in her voice surprised Elizabeth.

"You fucking amaze me."

"What…?" Elizabeth looked at Layce, who sat stiffly, with her arms crossed and her jaw set.

"You've known all this time and never once said those words to me."

"I don't understand."

"Obviously. I'm your best friend. We went through all of that… that… bullshit, and you don't think it would be important to tell me? Instead, you sink into a little pre-defined rut and coast along until I'm in a good place and lay that kind of shit on me?"

Elizabeth was taken off guard by Layce's anger.

"What do you mean, lay it on you? How does this affect you at all? You have the perfect life. You've always done what you wanted to do…"

"Is that how you see it? You're right. I do have a perfect life right now. But it took a long time for me to be in a place where I could be open to it. It took me telling you…" said Layce, nearly shouting now. She took a deep breath and lowered her voice. When she spoke again, it was still shaking with emotion. "Remember that night? Remember just after I graduated and we got drunk and you were complaining about not knowing what happiness is? That night was the night I realized I had to stop waiting for you to get your shit together. That night was the first time I realized you might never be able to crawl out of whatever little hole you had made for yourself."

Little hole? Elizabeth started to get angry now.

"You moved to California a few weeks later. Don't tell me you were waiting for me. You left. Not me."

"Andy had had enough. She had a job offer out here and had decided to take it to get some distance from what she saw as my obsession with my roommate." Elizabeth was shocked. She'd never suspected. Andy had always been kind to her, not once had she hinted at any sort of animosity. Elizabeth's respect for Andy grew exponentially right then. "It just worked out that I had an offer out here, too. I was going to stay there. In Baltimore. But that night, I decided to follow another path instead. I couldn't just keep waiting for you."

"Are you happy?" asked Elizabeth.

Layce didn't hesitate. "Yes, I am."

"Are you glad you left?"

"Yes, I am. But, now I get to wonder if I gave up just a little too soon."

Elizabeth felt Layce staring at her, studying her. She swallowed hard because there was something stuck in her throat and she realized it was all the words of love and yearning and asking that she had never found the courage to reveal. But now it wasn't fair to say them. Now would just be too cruel. And now she finally realized they were just ghosts of a pain that she'd simply gotten used to. She couldn't tell if the hurt she felt was the opening of a new wound, or the closing of an old one. Tears streamed from her eyes, but she wouldn't turn to Layce. She couldn't. It was just too late.

After a few minutes, Layce got up and walked toward the house. She stopped a few steps away and looked back.

"I'll always love you, you know. That will never change."

The door whisked shut, and the care that Layce took to keep from waking Andy reminded Elizabeth of all the things she'd never have. She sat in her chair and didn't move for what felt like hours. Eventually she went back into the house and crawled into bed, but she didn't sleep. Then, in the hour just before dawn, she heard the baby cry and knew Andy was in the living room nursing and rocking her.

She gathered her suitcase and wrote a quick note telling them thanks for letting her stay with them and she'd call when she got settled in her new apartment in Baltimore. She handed the note and the elephant toy to the bleary-eyed Andy, kissed her and the breastfeeding baby on the foreheads, and went out to get into the taxi she had already called.

When she arrived at the airport and got into line to rebook her flight back home, she stared at her return ticket to Baltimore. She still had a week before anyone expected her and she wasn't ready to just fall back into whatever waited for her there. She felt aimless, untethered. The conversation with Layce had released her from an unknown tie, but she needed to end things with Kev before she could really move forward. And then there was her career. She loved medicine, but what was she going to do with it? She needed time. She had nothing figured out by the time she reached the ticketing counter.

"Welcome to North Star Airlines. What's your destination?"

Elizabeth glanced at the departures sign and picked the first flight that looked tempting.

"I'd like a one-way ticket to Juneau, Alaska, please." It was an impulse, but it felt right. She'd always wanted to visit Juneau. It sounded peaceful and remote. It would be a perfect place to spend a few days thinking and figuring out what came next.

"May I see your identification?"

Elizabeth handed the agent her identification and felt a surge of energy. A week in Juneau. It would be a great place to get her life together. She could do some hiking, check out the scenery, and figure some stuff out.

"A one-way ticket to Juneau, Alaska departing in an hour and fifteen minutes from Terminal 6. How would you like to pay, Ms. Trackton?"

Ms. Trackton? Shit. She'd given her the fake ID. If she traded in the ticket to Baltimore the agent would see the different name. If she gave her another ID, she'd probably get in trouble. The irony of Layce's teasing her about her adolescent fears of getting in trouble over the ID didn't escape her.

"Do you take cash?" she asked, thankful she had enough to cover the ticket.

Relief rushed over her when the agent nodded her head and extended her hand to take the bills Elizabeth had taken from her wallet and held out to her.

While the agent was busy checking her single bag, Elizabeth slid the removable insert from her wallet holding the real license and credit cards into a secret pocket in the black leather backpack matching her Coach purse. In her present state of mind, knowing her, she'd accidentally give the real one and screw everything up. She'd keep the fake ID in the wallet. If they searched her at security, it would probably be discovered, but she hoped she'd go right through, like usual.

She relaxed only after she made it through security without incident. By then, she'd also realized the benefit of the error, because even her mother wouldn't be able to use her political strings or Homeland Security to find where she went if it took longer than a week to figure out what she wanted to do. Not that she'd intentionally do anything to worry anyone, but the thought of doing something that wasn't tied to anyone else's expectations gave her a momentary sense of freedom.

By the time she got to her gate, the conversation she had had with Layce started to hit home and the sense of freedom she'd felt was replaced by anxiety. The lack of sleep and Layce's reaction to their conversation pounded her like an emotional bludgeon. Graduation and the prospect of her future, along with the flood in Guatemala and her decision not to marry Kev, had already worn the walls controlling her emotional state to barely there. Layce was just the final straw. Elizabeth went into the nearest bathroom, locked herself in a stall, and had a good cry. When she emerged, she felt better, but her head—all stuffy from crying—was pounding. So she popped a couple of Benadryl she bought at a newsstand and sat in the plastic chair at the gate to wait for her flight. By the time she got to her first class seat on the plane, she had taken a third pill to address the stubborn stuffiness and was yawning. With any luck, the Benadryl and exhaustion would let her doze during the flight. She didn't have to change planes in Anchorage, so it would be perfect. In Anchorage she woke for just a few minutes to hold a little girl in her lap to let the mother in the seat next to her get settled, but that hadn't kept her awake for long, and she was back to sleep just minutes after the plane took off for the hour and half flight to Juneau. She remembered nothing else until she woke up to Nora's beautiful eyes.

4B sat on the edge of her bed, having remembered her entire life in the time it took to read half-a-dozen pages and a handwritten note. She thought she would have felt different, fuller, heavier, maybe. Her skin felt stretched tight with memory. But she didn't. She felt the same as she had before. At least physically. Emotionally, it was a different story. All of that time, all of those events, all of those emotions, all of it assailed her, raged against her very core. Her world felt like it was collapsing around her. Unable to sit still, she got up, and though it was the middle of the night, she took a shower. After that, she tried to lie down and go to sleep, but she couldn't shut down her mind. So she did the only thing she could think of.

She found the keys to her mother's car and drove.

She pulled up to an upscale townhouse in a gated community a few minutes later and rang the bell. She had her own key, but it didn't seem right to use it. She waited for the door to be answered and she used the time to figure out what she needed to do to clean up the mess she had made of her life.

"Hey," she said when Kev finally answered the door. The flickering light of the television in an otherwise dark house framed him in the doorway. He wore pajama bottoms and a blue and white striped robe hanging open. He wasn't wearing a shirt. He was a handsome man, and most women would have enjoyed the view of his defined abs and nearly hairless chest. It was wasted on 4B.

"Hey," said Kev, rubbing his eyes with one hand and holding the door open with the other. It was obvious she had just awakened him. "How did you…?"

"My dad ran into your dad down at the boat club and mentioned you were still in town," she explained.

Kev dropped his eyes.

"I didn't want to lie to you. With your memory and all, I thought it would be easier on both of us if I told you I had to get back to Texas right away."

"It's okay. You're probably right," she said running her hand down his arm as she walked past him into the house. Their fingertips held for a second before she dropped her hand to her side.

"What's up? Not that I mind you dropping by, but it's after midnight," he said, standing by the closed front door, his eyes following her to the couch. His body heat still warmed the cushions as she sat. The TV was playing low in the corner of the room. She smiled at his predictability.

"I have my memory back," she said.

"That's a good thing, right?" he said studying her from the doorway.

She hadn't considered that question yet, and honestly, she didn't know how to answer it.

"Yes, I guess. And no. Yes, and no."

"I'm not sure I understand," he said, striding over to where she sat.

"Yes, for obvious reasons. No, because some things were better off forgetting."

"Explain," he prompted, stifling a yawn.

"Sit down. You're hovering all above me," she patted the seat next to her and looked up at him. "I'm sorry."

"For what?" he asked, as he sat down close to her, but didn't touch her. She could always count on Kev to read a situation and react to it in the right way. He was perceptive, which made him a good attorney, but he was empathic, which made him a great guy. She hoped he would find a woman who deserved him some day.

"Stringing you along for most of a decade."

"You haven't strung me…"

"Yes, I have. We both know I've been in love with Layce."

There was a short pause.

"Still?"

"I probably always will be, but it's different now. We'll never be more than friends."

Kev was quiet and 4B thought about what else she needed to say.

"When I told you about what happened between Layce and me way back then, why did you still want to be with me?"

"Because I love you, I always have," he said without hesitation.

"Really? Or was it out of duty?"

"It was never out of duty, Elizabeth. I have always loved you. I have always wanted to be with you," he said, again without hesitation. "Even if I was a second choice."

"How did you do it? How did you never get angry? Why didn't you say anything?"

"I did get angry, remember?" asked Kev, looking away.

"The night at the marina?" she guessed. The argument right before he'd proposed had been uglier between him and Layce than it had been between him and her. Had he held on to it all this time?

"It wasn't a proud moment, but no. Before that."

At first, 4B struggled to recall what Kev was talking about. It was the shame on his face that brought it back for her. It was the moment both of them wished had never happened. The moment in the car when Kev had had enough and Elizabeth had decided her path.

Now, all these years later, she sat on the couch and looked at him, seeing the boy in the car, wishing she had set him free way back then.

"Oh, Kev, have you been holding onto that all of this time?"

"Not really, but sometimes I remember, and well..." he sat on the edge of the sofa with his elbows on his knees, hands dangling. He stared at the carpet between his feet.

"Nothing happened that shouldn't have."

He looked at her with sorry eyes.

"I disagree. I shouldn't have scared you like that."

"Well, true, but you stopped when I told you to."

"That night kind of defined our whole relationship, you know."

"How's so?" she asked, but she knew. She'd picked him that night.

"After what happened, I relied on you to set the pace and tone for everything."

She didn't expect that answer.

"How do you figure?" asked 4B. She looked back on their relationship and tried to see what he meant. She certainly never felt like she called the shots on anything, except maybe the long engagement. Other than that, she'd done what everyone else expected of her. She'd picked a path and went along with what was expected of her.

"I didn't want to push you away. So, I waited. I always waited until you were ready or initiated things. It wasn't just sex, but also when we saw each other, planning things, everything. I knew, after a while, I often came across as inattentive, but I didn't know how to bridge the gap from my desire to be with you and the chance of pushing you away. It was self-preservation, I guess. I knew if I pushed, it would force you away." He dropped his gaze, but not before she saw the sadness in his eyes. "It seems that my inattention has actually succeeded in pushing you away anyway."

Suddenly, everything made sense. Why they were together. How things had gone the way they did.

"I never saw it that way. I just thought it was how we were. I thought we were both comfortable with the way things were."

"After a while, it was comfortable. We had our own lives, but we had the same goals. At least I thought so. Maybe I was wrong. Maybe I should have been more demanding."

"No. You're right. Being demanding would have made it happen sooner. I almost wish it had."

"What do you mean?"

She tried to find words for what she meant.

"If you had pushed me away earlier, maybe you would have found someone who deserves you. Who knows, maybe I would have had a chance with Layce."

4B mumbled the last sentence quietly, finally realizing the truth of the words.

"What was that last part?" Kev asked.

"Nothing."

He tensed up.

"I think I heard you. Elizabeth, you can't blame me for—"

"I'm not blaming you, Kev," she said, shaking her head and resting her hand on his leg. She wanted him to believe her. "I will never blame you for anything. This was all my doing. I gave you mixed messages. Hell, I gave myself mixed messages."

"What happened? Layce has always been out and proud. If you wanted to be with her, why weren't you?" She heard the derision in his voice when he said "out and proud" and part of her cringed. What would he say about her once she told him? She had to tell him. She told herself his reaction was understandable. She was changing the direction of his life right now.

4B paused and wondered how she could explain the constant yearning she had had for her best friend, the inability to act on it because of her own confusion about what her parents and society expected her to be. She didn't want to hurt him with the details.

"Layce moved on, and I was just a couple of years too late."

There was a long pause as they both absorbed what was happening.

"I'm sorry, Elizabeth."

She looked up at him and wished she could love him the way he needed her to. He was such a good man.

"You're too good to me, Kev. I don't deserve you."

"You're right, you don't," he laughed and reached down for the hand she still had on his leg and pulled her toward him, settling her against his chest as he sat more comfortably into the couch. Kev smelled warm and sleepy, and she yawned. They were quiet for a minute. 4B closed her eyes.

"So? What now?" asked Kev, picking up a few strands of her hair and running his fingers idly through them.

"I've met someone."

"You have? Who?" His hands stilled and his voice was measured.

She felt him tense, and she tried to read the emotion in his voice. Jealous? Angry? Resigned? Irritated? She had gotten the impression he was as done with the façade of their relationship as she was. Had she read it wrong? Had she rushed it?

"Is it okay for me to be talking to you like this?" she asked lifting her head to look at his face.

He nodded slowly and then answered.

"Yes. I've known for a long time we were never going to get married."

"Why didn't you say something?"

"I was into my work, things seemed to be okay as they were. Our parents had stopped pushing us. I don't know. It was easy to go along with the status quo, I guess." He blew out a breath. "And there was always the chance I was wrong."

"Have you already moved on?" she asked. She realized she didn't know, out of all of the possible answers, what answer would make her feel worse.

"No…" he said and let the word draw out.

"You can tell the truth." She patted his chest and hoped he felt safe enough to be honest with her. The stolen glimpse of him with the woman at the party came to mind, and part of her hoped he'd been drifting away from her, too. It would make things easier.

"Really?" he asked, and she heard the contemplation in his voice. "No. Not emotionally, anyway. But I know it's time and knowing it doesn't hurt as much as I thought it would."

"I'm so sorry, Kev."

"We've already established we're both sorry. Let's make a pact that we don't have to say it again."

"Deal," she said as she settled back down to lie against his chest. He pushed his fingers into her hair and gently massaged her scalp. She closed her eyes and enjoyed the massage.

"So who is she?" he asked.

"How do you know it's a she?"

"It better be a she," he said, and 4B felt him tense up again as his fingers stilled.

"It is a she. Her name is Nora."

"Good. Because if it was a guy, then all bets are off." His fingers started to work their magic on her scalp again.

"There will never be another guy, Kev." She meant what she said.

"Do you love her?"

"Yes… I do," she said, and realized she had been hiding from those words for a while. Ever since she had left Juneau.

"Have you told her?"

"No. Not yet. It didn't seem fair to—"

"Stop trying to manage other people's hearts, Elizabeth. Work on your own."

She contemplated his words and something about them resonated with her.

"How did you get so smart?"

"It just comes natural."

"I don't deserve you."

"Another thing we need to agree to not say."

"Deal," she said and laughed, but a yawn cut it short. "God, I'm tired. Do you mind if I stay here tonight?"

"I thought you'd never ask," he said mischievously, opening his robe.

"Pig!"

"I was just kidding!" he said, putting up his hands to fend off the weak smacks she pummeled him with. "Of course you can."

She settled back into the curled up position in the circle of his arm, and her eyes started to slip closed as Kev ran his fingers through her hair. She listened to the steady beat of his heart and felt herself drift away. Sometime later she awoke just enough to know he had lifted her and tucked her into his bed. She felt him hover over her for a few minutes as he smoothed her hair and then he gently kissed her lips. She pretended to sleep. She listened to him leave the room and she fell back to sleep.

"Good morning, Sleeping Beauty. Or should I say good afternoon?" said Kev, pausing in his project of slathering on mustard over a thick piece of bread as he gave a meaningful look at the digital display on the microwave. He was in his workout clothes and she knew he'd already taken his regular run down to the marina, done a few passes on the river, shared coffee with some of the regulars, and run back to his place.

"What time is it?" asked 4B, stretching as she walked. She had spent many nights at Kev's place over the last several years, and she still felt comfortable waking up there, despite the change in their relationship.

"Eleven-thirty," he replied. "AM."

"My sleep schedule may be out of whack, kind sir, but I'm coherent enough to understand that, when the sun is shining, it means it is in the AM."

"I was just kidding. Anyway, no worries. I went down to the boat club and did my rowing already. I kind of expected you to be gone already."

"I've overstayed my welcome, I see. You don't even have coffee ready."

"I may suck at being a fiancé, but you can never call me a bad host," said Kev, turning to get the thermal carafe and coffee cup he had ready on the counter behind him. He poured her a cup of coffee and the rich scent filled the room. He added the perfect amount of half and half and sugar, and she hunched her shoulders in appreciation as she took her first sip.

"You are a wonderful man. Thank you."

"No one wants to see you deprived of your life's elixir," he said dryly and then went back to building his sandwich. "I saw your dad down at the marina this morning. He said he saw the car parked out front. He must have told your mom, because she called this morning."

"She did? I kind of just took off last night. I didn't tell anyone where I went."

"I told her you were fine. She told me to tell you to call Nora."

4B felt her pockets, then remembered she didn't have her phone. She had left with nothing but the car keys.

"Oh. I must have left my cell phone at the house."

"She told me that, too," Kev said, paying inordinate attention to his sandwich.

"I haven't told her anything yet, Kev. She doesn't even know I have my memory back."

"No?"

"You were the first person I told."

"I don't know why that gives me as much satisfaction as it does, but I'm glad."

"I love you, Kev."

"I know, Elizabeth."

❀❀❀❀❀

The house was quiet in the early afternoon, and 4B tossed her mother's keys on a table in the foyer. 4B went upstairs to get her phone so she could call Nora and talk to her about everything she had discovered in the last two days. It felt so long ago since they had last talked and she desperately wanted to hear her voice. She also wanted to start figuring out her next steps.

4B walked over to her bed, where the loose pages from the journal were lying along with Layce's note. She remembered putting them on the night-stand on top of the journals that were still neatly stacked where she'd left them. Someone had moved the pages and the note. Had they read them? She picked up the papers along with her phone, which was still plugged in right beside the journals.

There were four missed calls, one from her mother and the rest from Nora. Nora had only left one message. She listened to the voicemail, which simply asked 4B to call her back. The weariness she heard in Nora's voice sent a tremor through 4B's heart. She hit redial and listened to the phone ring to voicemail.

"Hey, Nora. It's me. It feels like forever since I've heard your voice. You sounded tired in your message. I hope everything is okay up in the great white North. Call me back when you can. Um, well, I… I have… some things to talk to you about. I have my memory back. It's different than I thought it would be. Anyway, I can't wait to talk to you. Give my love to Aunt Mace. Bye."

She stared at the phone and wished she'd told Nora she loved her. But it wasn't something she wanted to do in a voice message. Still, it was burning a hole in her heart. She debated on calling again and leaving another message.

"Elizabeth?" came Roslyn's voice from behind 4B. "I thought I heard you come in."

4B turned toward her mother's voice, looking at the time of the calls. The first had come at 4:00 AM Massachusetts time, making it midnight Nora's time, when Nora had left the message. The next message was a couple of hours later, and the one after that, was just two hours earlier.

"Sorry I didn't leave a note. I knew you were out, but I should have told you where I went," 4B said absently, not looking up, checking her phone to see if Nora had sent a text. She hadn't.

"When Daddy and I arrived home after the golf thing. I checked in on you. When I didn't find you, I noticed the car keys were gone. I was worried, but not terribly. When I tried to call you, I heard it ring in your room, which did worry me. But, then this morning, Daddy saw the car in front of Kev's house when he went to play golf this morning and then talked to Kev at the marina afterward. I knew you were safe then."

"I'm sorry I just took off like that. I shouldn't have worried you," said Nora sitting on the edge of her bed. Her mind was preoccupied with Nora.

"Normally I wouldn't have worried, but you've been through a lot lately," said Roslyn, sitting down next to her.

"I know. I'm sorry."

"No need to be sorry, honey. I just worry."

"So… you read some of my stuff?" asked 4B, indicating the papers and the note.

Her mother's face visibly blanched.

"I was tempted. I saw the note on top, and well I… I recognized it. I stacked it all up and left it there. In the end I couldn't bring myself to read your private stuff."

4B believed her mother and she almost wished her mother had read her journals. It would have made it easier to broach what she needed to tell her.

"I have my memory back," she said.

Roslyn took her hand and squeezed it.

"You do? That's great! When? How do you feel?"

"Last night… part of yesterday. It started to come to me as I was sleeping. I thought it was a dream and it wasn't. Then it just kind of filled in after that."

4B told her mother about the dream that wasn't a dream, how all of her memories were just there now, and how she was trying to reconcile the life she used to have with the life she had right now. "It's so weird, Mom. Everything that was gone is back and I expected to feel some sort of… I don't know how to describe it. Maybe a sense of things clicking together? A rush of understanding, or something? But I think the thing I feel most of all is a sense of anxiety. Anxiety tinged with sadness."

As she said it, the feelings that she guessed at became clearer. The sadness overshadowed the anxiety.

"I imagine it's hard, honey. Is there at least some sense of relief?"

"Like I told Kev, part of me is relieved, part of me is... a lot of me is just, well... overwhelmed."

"It's understandable. And then I go and rifle through your stuff. I shouldn't have... I was worried. But it's no excuse."

"I understand, Mom. I probably would have read them."

"Believe me, it was a true act of will to just stack it all up and leave it there without reading it," said Roslyn, shaking her head. "If you're not stewing over that, though, what has your forehead all creased? It only gets like that when you're upset or terribly worried about something."

She rubbed her forehead. Her mother always knew when she was upset.

"I think you probably already know," said 4B, picking up the journal pages, absently shuffling through them. Her mother let out a long breath.

"Maybe I have an idea, but why don't you tell me?"

4B took a deep breath.

"I'm a lesbian, Mom."

"Is this about the note? About Layce?"

"Yes, but it's more than that. Much more than that."

"Having feelings for your best friend doesn't make you a lesbian, honey."

"Believe me, these kinds of feelings do, Mom," said 4B, flapping the pages in her lap. "I've known for a while. I was just afraid to admit it. To you. To Layce. To myself."

"So, you are attracted to women? Does it extend beyond Layce?"

4B nodded her head. She felt a tear slip down her cheek. Her mother reached up and wiped it away.

"Why on earth would you be afraid to tell me?"

"Do you remember your response when we talked about Layce all those years ago? I would have told you then. But you told me how relieved you were that I wasn't. After that I just couldn't."

"Relieved? I don't think so..."

"Yes, relieved was the exact word you used."

"Oh, honey. I don't remember the exact words we spoke, but I remember thinking there was a good possibility you were gay then. I wanted you to know I loved my gay friends and coworkers and I would love you, too. You know that, right? No matter what, I will always love you."

4B took a moment to let it sink in.

"But you said you were relieved that I wouldn't have to deal with all of the issues of being gay."

"I am relieved. I mean I would be if you weren't gay. Ugh! This isn't coming out right," her mother breathed out a frustrated sigh. "What I mean is, there are a lot of pressures and pain that go along with being gay, honey. Of course I would be relieved for you if you didn't have to deal with all of that. But it doesn't make me think there is anything wrong with you just because some of society is so narrow-minded and filled with hate—" Her mother paused and took hold of her hands, holding them tightly. "Honey, I want to protect you. But who you love will never change my love and acceptance for who you are. God, I hope you know that." Her mother dropped her hands and hugged her.

"I do now," said 4B accepting her mother's hug and clinging to her. She never knew what a relief telling her mother would be. She cried against her mother's shoulder.

"Were you talking to Nora on the phone when I came up?" Her mother asked. "Did Kev tell you she called? Have you told her you have your memory back?"

"Yes, he told me, but no, it wasn't her. The call went to voicemail. I told her about my memory in the message."

"Is she... are you two...?"

"Yes, Mom." 4B watched her mother's reaction. All she saw was acceptance. Another huge weight lifted from her.

"What about Kev?"

"He knows. It's a long story, but he's okay."

"Oh." 4B could see her mother's mind churning with all of the new information. "She seemed like a very nice woman when your father and I met her up in Juneau, and she sounded so polite this morning on the phone. I hope to get to know her a little better. But she lives all the way—"

"Did you talk to her?" interrupted 4B. Maybe her mother knew more about the strange tone of the message.

"Yes. About an hour or two ago. I thought I should answer it since you left your phone here and she had called more than once."

"Is she okay? She didn't say in the message and she sounded weird."

"She didn't say anything other than to ask me to tell you she'd called. I told her you left your phone when you went to Kev's house last night, and I'd give you the message when you got—Oh, dear."

"Oh, Mom," said 4B as she dialed Nora's number again.

❀❀❀❀❀

It was a few hours before 4B was able to get a hold of Nora, and when Nora finally answered the phone, 4B was relieved, but there was a distance in Nora's voice she'd never heard before.

"Oh, god, Nora. Finally. Where have you been? Did you get any of my messages?"

"Yes. I was at the hospital."

4B felt a sheet of icy cold descend upon her. Aunt Mace.

"Why were you at the hospital? What happened?"

There was a long silence and 4B could hear Nora's uneven breathing.

"Nora? I can hear you breathing. Are you—?"

"I'm happy you have your memory back."

"So, you did get my messages. I've been—"

"Can I ask you something?"

"Sure. Anything. I'm—"

"Who's Donald Kirkham?" asked Nora. Her voice sounded weary rather than confrontational. 4B wasn't surprised at the question, and she finally wanted to explain who Kev was to her, but Nora's tone was so strange and it made her nervous. Why had she been at the hospital? Dread continued to make her skin feel cold.

"Donald is Kev. I told you about Kev. He goes by his middle name. He's the friend I told you about. Why were you at—?"

"What kind of friend?" Again, Nora's voice sounded more tired than angry, and 4B was sure Nora had already somehow discovered Kev was her fiancé. She wanted to explain it all to Nora, but her tone of voice made her hesitate. There was something very different about Nora and it scared her.

"Just a really good friend. At least he is now. I'll tell you all about him, but why—"

"There were pictures taken of you and Donald Kirkham at the fundraiser the other night. I saw them on the internet."

"Pictures?" asked 4B. Of course. There had been photographers at the event. She immediately wished she had told Nora about her and Kev. "I'm not sure what you saw on the internet, but there is nothing to be worried about. I promise."

"I'm not worried. I'm confused. At first I wanted to believe he was just a friend, because that's what you told me he was to you. I thought you would have told me if it was something else. But the pictures of you, well, he looked at you like you were more than just friends, that maybe the event was more like a date." Nora sighed and 4B wanted to do something, anything, to fix the sadness in her voice. "I guess I don't have any right to care."

"It wasn't a date, Nora." Not really. At least for 4B it hadn't been.

"Your mother said you'd spent the night. The internet called him your fiancé."

There it was.

"Oh, Nora! He was my fiancé. He isn't anymore. It seems I had some entanglements to unwind. It's a long story. I didn't want to worry you before I could figure out a way to—"

"I would have understood, Elizabeth. I wouldn't have liked it, but I would have understood. I just don't get why you didn't tell me when you found out. I kept waiting, thinking you'd bring it up. I totally get it. It's hard. I get it. But not telling me about your fiancé, and still talking to me like... like... well, I get the feeling that maybe you weren't going to tell me."

"No wonder you sounded so weird in the message. You have to believe me. You do believe me, right?"

Nora didn't answer at first. 4B heard her breathing, and there was a hitch in her voice. "Nora, honey, are you okay? Are you crying?" asked 4B quietly.

"4B... Aunt Mace... Aunt Mace died this morning..."

The news hit 4B like a blast. Aunt Mace? Dead? She needed to get to Nora. She needed to be with her, comfort her.

"Oh, No! God, Nora. I am so sorry. Where are you?"

Nora drew a deep breath, like she was trying to pull herself together.

"I'm at the hanger. Tack will be flying in any minute now."

"Good. You have someone to be with. Oh, Nora. I just want to be there with you so badly right now. I want to explain all of these things that have you worried. It's all so convoluted, but if I was there, I could prove to you..."

"I understand. You have your life, your entanglements..."

4B grasped her phone, wishing she could crawl through it right then.

"You're more important than all of that. You know that, right?"

292

Nora didn't respond and 4B could hear her trying to get her breathing under control. It scared her that the woman she knew as strong and confident was having such a hard time pulling it together.

"Hey, anyway, Tack just rolled up. I gotta go."

"Nora! Wait! I have something to tell you… I… I love you."

There was no reply. 4B looked at her display and saw the call had ended. Had Nora heard what she said? She tried to call back several times but only got Nora's voicemail. She hung up each time without leaving a message.

For the second time in less than twenty-four hours, 4B went downstairs and grabbed her mother's car keys. But as she was walking out the door, her mother stopped her and asked her where she was going.

"Juneau." She didn't say why or provide any other information, but her mother seemed to understand.

"I see you have your phone, at least. You'll probably need this, too." Roslyn grabbed 4B's wallet and tossed it to her. "I took that pesky fake ID out of there. I can't have my daughter forgetting who she is again, or getting picked up by TSA with something like that. The last thing I need to worry about is giving those damn Republicans something to chase around in the media! And call me as soon as you arrive!"

4B was already opening the car door.

❀❀❀❀❀

"Welcome to Juneau, Alaska, the capitol of the largest state in the union, where it is currently forty-three degrees Fahrenheit with a high probability of a foot or more of snow in the next twelve to twenty-four hours. I hope you all packed your parkas and your mukluks! On behalf of North Star Airlines, thank you for flying with us. We know you have a choice, so thanks for choosing us. For those of you ending your journey here…"

The flight attendant continued her spiel as the plane taxied to the gate. The first thing 4B did was send a text to her mother telling her she'd finally landed in Juneau. Then she checked the weather app on her phone to compare it to what the flight attendant had just said about the snow. It looked like it was going to be cold. Not just cold, frigid cold. It had been lovely in Juneau just over a week earlier. It didn't matter, she'd left with nothing but her wallet and cell phone, and unless she wanted to freeze to death in the yoga pants and sweater she currently wore, she had to find a place to purchase some clothes to wear during her stay, however long it ended up being.

The flight attendant's cheery voice continued to chime through the overhead speakers with information about connecting flights. The activity level in the airplane cabin rose as occupants started to get out of their seats despite the attendant's warning to wait for a complete stop. When the door latches were popped, 4B stood to stretch in the wide first class aisle. It had been a long night and an even longer flight. The total time she had spent traveling was lost on her, what with the long layover in Seattle along with the time change between the East Coast and Juneau, and it was hard to digest that it was now mid-morning of the day after she had set off. She was tired and stiff from the trip, which, thankfully, had been uneventful. Also, she had been one of only two occupants in first class on the long second leg of her journey from Seattle, which had given her plenty of room to stretch out. Even so, halfway through the flight, she'd moved to seat 4B just to see if it would spark any response in her. It hadn't. Maybe it was because she had taken the Benadryl, but she still had no memory of the crash, and therefore no nervousness about flying again. She was glad she hadn't taken the over-the-counter sedatives her mother had suggested when she'd called from the airport to tell her that she'd booked the flight.

She had purchased a paperback novel at the airport before she'd departed, but it had gone mostly unread, her memories more interesting than the words in print. Worries about what awaited her in Juneau had tried to sneak in, so she had focused instead on reliving the days she had spent with Nora in the forest of Valdez, as well as their short time together in Juneau. The trip was long, but went by quickly with the help of the internal picture show she played behind her closed eyes.

Heeding the flight attendant's warning about the pending snow, she tried to find a parka in the shops at the airport, but was thwarted by the airport's small size and limited shopping opportunity. Shivering in the morning chill when she got into the first available car in the line of taxis waiting at the curb in front of the airport, 4B asked her cab driver to take her by the place where locals purchased their winter gear. He looked at her and winked.

"Forgot you were headed into the wild, did you?" He nodded at her thin sweater and yoga pants.

"Something like that," she said, feeling like an unprepared girl scout showing up to her first camping trip without a sleeping bag. At least she was wearing tennis shoes instead of her normal flip-flops.

The Mercantile had a good selection of parkas, and she selected a white one with faux fur lining. She felt like she looked like a polar bear when she tried it on but it was warm and fit well. Then she picked out some jeans, a couple of western shirts, and some very utilitarian cotton underwear. Instead of the suggested mukluks, she bought a pair of hiking boots, hoping the choice in footwear would help her to blend in better with the locals. The clerk didn't bat an eye when she came out of the dressing room with a handful of tags and her travel clothes rolled up in a ball. 4B scanned the store to see if Ship was there, but she didn't see her.

The cab driver, whom she had asked to wait, nodded his approval when she got back into the car and gave him Nora's address.

"We're sure gonna miss Old Mace," he said when she told him her destination. "She was one wickedly funny old bean, that one. And she never let her fame change her."

"I guess she's a celebrity up here, huh?"

"Oh, yeah. She's like royalty around here. Known on every continent and in most every country. She spiked our tourism just from the folks that come to see where she lives. Computers sure have changed the world, I tell you. We have a few famous folks up here—artists, writers, Olympians. There are two internet celebrities just on this road alone."

"Is that so?" she asked just to be polite.

"Yup. Aunt Mace is one of them. The other is a lady who is famous for showing folks a good time, if you get my inference."

4B responded with what she hoped was the right amount of ambiguous interest, not knowing if the taxi driver was proud of their infamous internet sensation or not. She was glad Juneau was as small as it was, because they pulled up in front of the whimsically landscaped house before he could regale her with more fun facts. She would have liked to hear more about Aunt Mace, but she wanted to hear it from Nora.

Although it hadn't yet materialized, the threat of the promised snowfall was heavy in the air when 4B stepped out of the cab. She paid the driver and gathered the bags holding her purchases. Turning up the gravel path to the house, 4B suddenly felt the brashness of her impulse to travel halfway across the world without letting anyone know she was coming. The sky was low, the day was dark, and the large front window of Aunt Mace's A-frame was lit from inside, displaying a room full of people, though there were few cars parked in front. It was a testament to the pedestrian lifestyle of the native Juneauites. 4B stood on the path and watched the people inside move and interact, and she wondered if she should go up to the house first, or go directly around back to Nora's place. Her decision was made for her when an old woman walked up behind her and ushered her up the porch steps.

"I know, honey. It hurts our mortal hearts to lose such a wonderful woman, but the ecclesiastic kingdom is celebrating its newest member. God willing, we'll see her soon enough, some of us sooner than others, I dare say. I, for one, hope St. Peter will take me to see her soon."

Elphie's pious remark sparked a memory of Aunt Mace's scrunched up face when Elphie had stooped to pick up pretzels the night she and Nora had interrupted their poker game. Elphie had said a little prayer for their safe return from what she'd called "the viper's nest", and when she turned her back, Aunt Mace had pretended to cross herself and pray. The memory provided 4B with sweet nostalgia and it helped to propel her forward. Nora was inside there somewhere, and she needed her.

As soon as they crossed the threshold, Elphie scurried into the living room to take over direction of the small group of musicians who had assembled. The gathering was the closest thing to a wake that 4B had ever experienced. The liquor flowed and stories were spun, all while a lively quartet of musicians played music in the corner of the small front room. A man who looked a little like Santa Claus, with his white beard and red thermal shirt with black suspenders holding his jeans up under a big round belly, pressed a plastic cup that was three-quarters full into her hand. He shuffled away before she had a chance to ask him what was in it. She watched him fill other cups before he disappeared into the kitchen.

4B took a sip of the drink, shuddered at the strength of the concoction, took another, and began to wander slowly through each crowded room in search of Nora. She would never have guessed the house could fit so many people. There were pods of people in every room, taking up every seat, occupying most of the open space. Finally, there was only the kitchen left and, with no sign of Nora, she leaned against the sink and looked out the back window. There weren't any lights on in Nora's little house. Was she huddled all alone in the dark, clutching her grief, mourning the loss of her beloved Aunt Mace? 4B's heart stung thinking about it and she put her empty cup down ready to go find her.

"4B? That you? Well, fuck me! It is!"

A heavy hand fell on 4B's shoulder and she turned around, her eyes coming to rest on an ample bosom contained within a baggy workshirt. She looked up and into the rheumy eyes of Ship, where she witnessed an agony of pain swimming in their watery depths. 4B was certain that under normal circumstances Ship would have been uncomfortable with any close physical gesture, but right then, she didn't care. She leaned in and pulled Ship tight. Ship accepted the hug and clung to her like a child—a child who was twice as big as she, but needing comfort just the same.

"Oh, Ship," she said, her voice muffled against the warm softness of the old woman's chest. "I'm so sorry. I came as soon as I heard."

"Christ. You know, we all knew it was coming, and I gotta be happy for her it was quick. Right? But, shit, it hurts in your heart, you know?" asked Ship, pulling away and rubbing the center of her chest. She held herself steady with a handful of 4B's shirtfront and that's when 4B knew Ship was drunk. Beyond drunk. She was barely standing. 4B put her hand on Ship's elbow and led her to a chair at the table, where Ship sat down, nearly missing the seat. Then the large woman buried her head in her arms and sobbed. It was heartbreaking to see the tough butch weep like that. The woman's grief was deep. She had lost her oldest friend, and probably the only person in her life who truly understood her. 4B could see why she would want to numb herself with alcohol. She hoped one day someone would feel that way about her passing.

She stood with her hand resting on Ship's trembling back. She stared at the dark house in the yard, torn between staying with Ship and going to find Nora. Nora. An almost physical pull compelled her, but fear kept her in her place. Nora had sounded so distant on the phone. Now that she was here, would Nora want to see her? 4B wavered. She didn't want to leave Ship alone with her grief anyway.

Elphie approached and clucked her tongue.

"Two days in a row, Ship. You're too old to do that to yourself. Come on, tough guy. I'll walk you home before you fall asleep where you sit."

To 4B's surprise, Ship stood up and let Elphie lead her out of the kitchen toward the front of the house.

"Just you don't start your praying, Elphie. Lightning's likely to strike me down before your very eyes if you get me down on my knees," said Ship, and as she passed 4B, she winked, though her cheeks were still wet with tears.

"Hush up, Ship. The Lord would provide you with comfort if only you would open your heart to him."

"Open my wallet to him is more like it."

4B lost the trail of the two women's conversation as they moved into the living room and she marveled at the unlikely friendships that were forged in the wilds of Alaska.

The man who looked like Santa Claus approached her again, and seeing that 4B no longer held a cup, wordlessly gave her a new one and upended two liquor bottles into it until it was nearly full. Then he pulled another bottle from his back pocket to add a dash of something else. It was too quick for 4B to see what they were, but since he stood in front of her after he was done, watching her with an expectant smile, she lifted it in a cheer, smiled back, and took a sip. A surprising taste of black licorice filled her mouth. It was delicious. Much better than the first drink. She raised the cup in another cheer to him and he smiled before he shuffled away.

4B took the Mercantile bags and her drink out through the back door and headed over to Nora's house. She could smell the damp earthiness of Glacier River running in the channel behind the houses. In the short time she had been gone, the smell had gone from late summer to that of mid-fall edging into winter.

She climbed the wooden steps, and when there was no answer to her knock, she tried the doorknob. It wasn't locked. She didn't think it would be. She stuck her head in and called Nora's name. There was no answer but Java came running down the steep stairs from the loft at the sound of her voice.

The little house was dark and silent as she entered, and the small black cat weaved between her feet. The smell of the house reminded her of Nora and a poignant yearning filled her heart.

There was no sign of Nora downstairs, so she climbed the steep stairway to the bedroom, hoping to find her there, but Nora wasn't there, either.

She left her bag at the foot of the bed, went downstairs and out to the front porch. She opened her phone and called Nora's cell for the first time since arriving. There was no answer. As the call rolled over to voicemail, 4B noticed Nora's Jeep was not parked out front where Nora had parked it the last time she'd been there.

She left her empty plastic cup on the porch railing and started to walk. As she left the front yard of Aunt Mace's house, three more people arrived, toting heavy bags emitting the clanking sounds of glass bottles. The already full house was going to be packed soon and it looked like the party had just begun.

4B walked down the dirt road toward town. Sooner than she expected, she was on the paved road, where she missed the accompanying sound of the gravel crunching under the soles of her new hiking boots. The days were shorter in Alaska, and she was struck by how early the sun seemed to be setting. The low sky enhanced the dimming of the late afternoon.

The parking lot of The Strut was empty when she arrived, but she was still surprised to find herself the lone customer when she went in. The jukebox was silent, and the only sound in the place was the low sound of the one television set turned to a soccer match. After 4B's last visit there, the quiet was eerie. Crystal stood behind the bar spinning a damp towel, watching the game. She turned when the door slapped shut.

"Well, well, well. I wondered if you'd be back." Crystal tossed aside the towel she'd been holding and used the remote control to turn down the sound of the TV. The only sounds now were the steady stream of water that issued from the sink Crystal was filling and the tap of her fingertips against the bar.

"Hi, Crystal," said 4B, looking into the back corner to see if she'd missed anyone in the empty tavern. Crystal leaned her hip against the polished surface of the bar and crossed her arms over her chest.

"It's just you and me. She and Tack went out on a provision run this morning," said Crystal, before 4B could ask. 4B was comforted to know Nora might be arriving soon. Her stomach fluttered in anticipation.

"When will they be back, do you know?"

"Soon, I think. Shoulda been back by now, actually. They were dropping off orders from the Mercantile to some folks out past Turner Lake. They got most of it out yesterday, so there were only a couple of stops today. Besides, the snow looks like it might be early."

A thread of apprehension snuck into 4B's mind.

"I suppose it's not good for them to be out in the snow?" asked 4B, thinking about the one or two flakes she'd seen drop right before she entered the bar.

"The job of an Alaskan bush pilot is one of the most dangerous there is. They watch the weather pretty closely. It's not common practice to go flying in it, so no." Crystal answered her question with an impatient shrug.

"What happens if the snow beats them back?" asked 4B, needing to know, not caring if Crystal was annoyed by her questions.

"Most likely, they get stranded at the last camp or stake they visited until the weather breaks and they can get the strip cleared. They have a radio. They'll call in." Crystal didn't seem too concerned, but 4B got the idea that Crystal was looking for her reaction.

"And if they had already left the last place? If they're in the air?"

"Depends. Worst case? Well, you know a little about worst case on an airplane."

"You don't think…" began 4B, not able to finish the sentence.

Crystal blew out an aggravated breath.

"Tack is an experienced pilot. He knows the area better than anyone around. I don't think it will come down to that. And before you ask, I already tried to radio them. I know they'll call in when they can."

They were quiet for a few minutes as 4B tried to rein in the surge of fear she'd just been faced with. Crystal shut off the water and picked up the towel to wipe down the already pristine bar. 4B tried to figure out why she felt panicky. It was probably just the way the last phone call had ended. Crystal seemed calm. She would try to be, too. She leaned against a barstool and put her foot up on the kick bar.

"Once it snows, does it stick for the rest of winter?" asked 4B, trying for conversation. She wanted to know why Crystal seemed so much colder with her this time. Wasn't it less than a week ago that the bartender had been undressing her with her eyes?

"The middle of October is a little early even for here, so anything we get now will probably melt off. It starts to hang around in earnest starting in November. The mountains will probably keep it."

4B watched the television, thinking about the darkness that had grown more impenetrable as she'd walked down to the bar. Crystal picked glasses from the shelf behind her and polished them.

"Do the pilots usually fly after sundown? What with the dark and the snow, isn't it dangerous?"

"If you ask me, it's dangerous to fly anytime." Crystal laughed and tossed her towel in the air and caught it. "You should know."

The response was a little lighter than the rest, and 4B wondered if Crystal had just been responding to her stress when she walked in.

"Yeah, I guess so."

"Out past the lake isn't that far out. Tack's plane has no instrumentation, though; so technically, he isn't supposed to fly if he can't see, and that includes after sundown."

"Technically?"

Crystal shrugged her shoulders. "You know Tack. He does what he wants."

"Oh," said 4B, picturing the first time she had seen Tack, daredevil flying through the ravine. It had been perfect weather that day and watching him had terrified her then. Crystal must have seen the fear in her eyes.

"But he won't put Nora in danger... at least I don't think so. They'll be back soon."

"You're very reassuring," said 4B with an uneasy laugh.

"You want a drink while you wait?"

4B nodded and climbed onto a barstool. Crystal reached into a space beneath the bar and flipped a frosty pint glass into the air and caught it in the same hand as she pulled the tap toward her with the other and expertly filled the glass with golden liquid. She placed it on the bar and pushed it to 4B. There was none of the previous flirtation or long stares Crystal had given her the first time, but 4B was glad she wasn't as icy as she had seemed minutes before.

"Thanks," said 4B taking a long drink. The buzz the two drinks Santa Claus had given her had worn off on the walk down to the bar. Crystal tossed her towel up in the air like pizza dough and caught it on her finger.

"So... you heard about Aunt Mace?"

4B nodded and for the first time she wanted to cry. She swallowed hard. Crystal turned away to straighten the bottles on the shelf behind her, but 4B saw the expression of grief before her back was turned.

"Nora told me you have a fiancé," said Crystal, clearing her throat and turning back.

4B nearly choked on her ale.

"I suppose she told you this before she took off this morning?"

"Nah. A week or so ago, right after you left."

4B was surprised. She thought about all of the calls she'd had with Nora in that time. Nora hadn't said anything.

"I didn't even know."

"She did an internet search. Your mother's a senator. It wasn't hard to do."

"I wonder why she waited so long to say anything to me," said 4B. Then, she wondered why she hadn't thought of googling herself. But the truth was, it had never even dawned on her to do that. She'd been so deep into her physical environment and delving into the artifacts of her past, that it just hadn't occurred to her to check the internet. Besides, she didn't remember the last time she'd gone near a computer. After the doctor warned her to stay away from the news for a while, she'd avoided them.

"She figured when your memory came back, you'd eventually tell her what you wanted her to know," Crystal said, using the towel to polish the brass bars near the well. "She has more patience than I do."

4B stared into her beer and wondered what other things Nora had talked to Crystal about. She didn't want to bring Crystal into a conversation that should be between her and Nora, but she didn't blame Nora for needing to talk about it with her friends. She felt awful about how she'd left Nora hanging, especially with everything going on with Aunt Mace. Of course she had needed to talk.

"Crystal, can I ask you something?"

"As if you haven't already asked a dozen somethings without my permission already?" joked Crystal.

"Yeah, I guess," answered 4B with a hollow laugh, and she paused while Crystal waited for her to ask the question. "Why didn't she ask me about Kev before now? Why did she wait?"

Crystal regarded her for a minute before answering.

"She was holding onto hope you'd chose her when your memory came back." Crystal studied 4B's reaction to the statement for a few seconds. "I, on the other hand, figured you would either flip out when your memory came back—if you really did have amnesia, that is. Because, I have this theory that maybe, just maybe, you saw an opportunity and were trying to figure out how to keep her on the side while you continued to build the All American Family back home."

"Seriously? What you just said couldn't be further from—"

"Yeah, but this morning, when she and Tack came through before they took off, she seemed less worried. And when I asked, she told me I was wrong. I asked her how she knew, and she just said that's what you told her." Crystal swiped at the surface of the bar. "Just so you know, I think she's I to trust you, and I told her so."

"Why are you so certain I'm trying to build this elaborate ruse?"

"Too many things add up."

"Like what? What would my motive be?"

"At first I thought it was her money—"

4B hadn't considered that, but immediately dismissed it.

"I had no idea who she was until after we got back here. By then, I'd already fallen for her. Her money doesn't mean anything to me." 4B had been raised to not talk about money. It wasn't polite. But she continued on because it mattered to her what Crystal thought. Especially if Crystal had any sway over Nora. "My family has plenty. You're the one who pointed out that my mom's a U.S. Senator. She comes from a long line of them. And my dad is a surgeon. I just graduated from med school, and while I haven't amassed my own fortunes, I do have a large trust. I don't need or want her money."

"Eventually I figured it out on my own. But then it occurred to me. You are a Senator's daughter. You're gay. You're hiding that."

"What?"

"Political deception." Crystal pronounced it like she was one hundred percent certain of her version of the truth. 4B started to speak, to tell her she was wrong, but Crystal held up a hand to stop her. "It's convenient. You can't be openly gay. None of the articles I read about you—and I read plenty—not one of them remotely suggests you're gay. Like any politician—"

"I'm not a politi—" 4B tried to interrupt.

"—you've hidden it well," Crystal kept speaking, never missing a beat. "Not even the picture I dug up of you and Nora standing in the airport here, practically kissing, insinuated you were gay. The article only mentioned Nora was a friend. So, you keep your little All American Family tied up with a little bow back home, and you have Nora, your hot secret girlfriend, to satisfy you on the side. It's Alaska. We're practically another country up here. No one would ever know. Now you just need to get Nora to go along with it."

4B could only stare at Crystal, who stood there with a look of victory in her eyes. Her hands were busy, winding the towel around and around, the muscles in her arms flexing. She probably didn't know how intimidating she looked. But 4B wasn't afraid. Because she knew the truth. She just needed to make sure Nora knew it, too.

"That's incredible. And not even close to being accurate," she sputtered. "You don't know me." 4B, usually a conflict avoider, didn't even try to keep the frustration and anger out of her voice. She was pissed, and she didn't care if Crystal knew it.

"You say it like it isn't easy enough to verify these days," scoffed Crystal.

"It isn't true, so there isn't anything to support it," she spit out.

"I'll admit you've done a good job hiding it. But I know."

"You don't know anything. But why would she talk to you about it instead of me?"

"Maybe because she was trying to protect you?" suggested Crystal. "Maybe she was hoping it wasn't true? Caring for someone makes people do crazy things. She tried to call you. You didn't answer. You're the daughter of a senator, and politicians keep their skeletons securely hidden—especially when it involves their homosexual children. And you, my dear, own that skeleton. She was dealing with all of this on her own, and I think she would have continued keeping it to herself, hoping it wasn't true, but I was there with her at the hospital, when Aunt Mace started to fail, and she'd been holding back so many things, it all came pouring out. I didn't even know about the supposed amnesia until she told me. She's been trying to be strong for everyone—for you, for Aunt Mace—but she's been through the wringer, too, you know. She doesn't deserve to be jacked around."

"I'm not jacking her around. I—" 4B stopped herself. She'd almost told Crystal she loved Nora, but she needed to tell Nora first. "I wouldn't— couldn't—do that," she said instead. Even though she was touched by Crystal's loyalty toward Nora, the accusations were pissing her off.

"Well, intended or not, it's what you're doing."

4B stared at Crystal and she wanted to be angry. Instead, she was ashamed.

"We talked every day. She never even hinted she had these doubts. But I've been such an ass, so wrapped up in my own head, that I was blind to everything going on around me. Until yesterday, I never even thought about how many people had their lives on hold because of me," admitted 4B, almost to herself. She watched the tiny bubbles in her beer rise to the surface and thought about how her calls with Nora had been her link to sanity over the last week. She wanted to be there for Nora now. "I need to talk to her. I need to tell her none of this is what she thinks it is," said 4B, staring into her beer. Tears of impotence and sadness filled her eyes and she wiped them away.

Crystal twisted the towel and seemed to be considering something. Some of her toughness seemed to recede.

"She'll be back. And she'll stop in before heading up the hill. She always does. In the meantime, why don't you practice explaining to me how it isn't what it seems?"

"I don't even know where to start," said 4B, shaking her head. Why would she want to talk to Crystal? Crystal thought she was some sort of manipulator.

"How about at the beginning? It doesn't look like the evening rush is going to make it in tonight." Crystal gave a sweeping look around the empty bar.

"I don't know," hedged 4B. "Why would you want to hear my pathetic story anyway?"

"Hey, I'm a bartender. People spill their guts to me all the time. Think of me as a free therapist. Shit, half this town does. And for some reason, I want to give you a chance. Give me the real story. I'll tell you if it's believable."

Crystal pushed a fresh beer across the bar and, ignoring her doubts, 4B started to talk. She didn't know why she talked. Maybe because she hadn't had a chance to talk it all out with anyone yet. But something compelled her and she opened up. All of the introspection she'd avoided all of her life was completed over a couple of beers. Crystal listened with rapt attention until 4B finished.

"And this Layce? You're not still pining for her?" asked Crystal. She started to pick up 4B's empty glass to refill it, but 4B put her hand over the top to signal she'd had enough.

"No. A couple of loose ends needed gathering, but it's been over for a long time."

"You mean about the fiancé?"

"Mostly."

"Hmm. Well, I guess I owe you an apology, then."

"Are you saying you finally believe me?" asked 4B, relieved.

Crystal regarded her for a moment.

"Yeah. I think I do. It was so easy to believe you were living out some sort of dual life because the opportunity presented itself. Maybe I've watched too many movies."

"Now I just have to convince Nora. I can see why she might have jumped to some conclusions. I probably would have, too. I just wish she had talked to me about all of this."

"She tried, even though I told her not to bother."

4B sighed and lowered her forehead into her palms. "She did, and I wasn't there." She dropped her hands into her lap and looked up at Crystal. "She's been there for me from the start, and I wasn't there for her the one time she needed me. Now, all I want to know is that she's okay. The rest will fix itself. At least I hope so. It has to."

Crystal reached across the bar and placed her hand on 4B's arm. "You'll be able to fix it. If you convinced me, convincing her will be simple. Like I said a while ago, she already told me she chose to believe you."

"I hope she still does. I need to tell her—" 4B stopped.

"Tell her what?"

4B shook her head.

"It's something I need to tell her first."

Crystal was silent for a moment. She twisted the towel in her hands and watched 4B.

"I'm pretty sure some stuff is pretty obvious," she said finally.

They waited and watched the women's soccer team on television. Not a single customer came in during the three hours 4B sat there, and while a small plane landed in the nearby airpark, it wasn't Tack's, and he still wasn't answering Crystal's radio checks. Crystal called a friend of hers in the flight control tower and found that they hadn't heard from them, either. When Crystal got off the phone, she relayed that the tower had submitted a missing aircraft report, but it was just a formality, since Tack was known to do what he wanted, when he wanted, and often deviated from his flight plans. But because Nora was with him, she was being cautious. And although Crystal continued to claim it wasn't out of the ordinary for Tack to change his flight plan in the middle of a trip, or to stay the night at one of the drop points along his route, 4B had studied her closely during the phone call. Crystal was worried even if she said otherwise.

Finally, it was evident the plane would not be landing that night. 4B turned down Crystal's offer of a ride back to Nora's and she started the lonely walk back to Nora's house. When she stepped outside, a thin layer of snow had dusted the ground, and a thick darkness enfolded her both physically and emotionally once she left the circle of illumination provided by the single light post in the parking lot. The low clouds blocked the moonlight and she had to use the flashlight app on her phone to see the tall reflective poles dotting the side of the road. Though the snow was barely falling, she could feel the low pressure of the threatening blizzard and hoped she'd make it back to the cabin before it really started to come down.

The snow accumulating on the ground cushioned her steps on the gravel, muting the crunching that had kept her company on the way down. The dead quiet was a bit unnerving with the sound of her breathing the only thing marring the silence. Halfway there, she had convinced herself that Nora had somehow come back and hadn't checked in at The Strut. With desperate hope, she increased her pace, but when she arrived the little house in back was just as dark as she had left it and the Jeep was nowhere to be seen. Her anxiety doubled at the thought of Nora stranded again in the forest, huddled under some sort of pieced together protection, all alone, scared. She couldn't think about Nora having not survived an accident. That was too much.

Grappling with her fear, 4B walked past Mace's house, making her way down the side path to the back. Sounds spilled out in to the night. She paused and stood in the light shining from a window that had been cracked open in the kitchen. And as the snow fell on her, she listened to the strange and beautiful sound of tears and laughter wrapped around each other. She wanted to go in and let the party wrap around her too, but she needed to be alone with her fear. Even in the darkness, though, she reflected on the idea that she hadn't known Aunt Mace very long, but she suspected the woman would have liked the gathering that was going on in her name. Nora would, too. The colorful spirit of Aunt Mace had touched so many lives, as well as hers. Her heart ached for the people who had known her well. She hoped that Nora would come back soon and take comfort in the warmth of her friends who had come to seek solace for their own pain. Most of all, she wanted to be able to take care of the woman who she loved, and help ease the heart that was surely breaking. She didn't normally pray, but she did right then.

❀❀❀❀❀

4B woke alone the next morning in Nora's bed with Java curled up behind her knees and a pillow pulled to her chest. The pillow smelled of Nora and she clung to it, trying to invoke the real woman from the sheer want of her. 4B hadn't slept very well, waking at every gust of wind or creak of old wood, hoping it was Nora coming home, falling back onto the mattress when she realized she hadn't. Every time she woke, it took longer for her to go back to sleep. In the morning gray, the frustrated sadness of the night before had become an anxious thread of fear. If Nora wasn't home, it meant the plane was stuck, either having been snowed in somewhere, or due to some sort of emergency. Nora didn't like either possibility, but she was far more worried about the later.

Crystal had explained how the provision drop-off worked. That people who lived far out of town needed provisions brought to them, so they often had short landing strips for airplanes, pads for helicopters, or lakes for the airplanes called "puddle jumpers" to land on. They hired people like Tack to bring them the provisions they couldn't make or hunt for, like aspirin, books, gunpowder and spices; and sometimes luxuries, like soft toilet paper, ice cream and new underwear. It was a harsh life, but they liked it out there, and 4B could even see a sort of allure in living so simply. She didn't want to try it, but she could appreciate how some people would want to.

4B pictured Nora waiting for the snow to stop so she and Tack could shovel a landing strip wherever they had been snowed in. An image of Nora came unbidden—sad, anxious and heartbroken, missing her aunt, missing her. 4B's entire being ached to make it better. Most of all, 4B hoped Nora wasn't out there feeling worse because of her. She pulled the pillow to her again and shut her eyes. Maybe she could sleep until Nora made it back home.

❀❀❀❀❀

Early afternoon roused her, though it seemed much later due to the darkness of the day. Snow pelted the windows, and the weight of the lethargy that wound itself around 4B grew stronger the longer she stayed in bed. She couldn't make herself get up. She could barely summon enough energy to roll over. She buried her face in the pillow that smelled like Nora and shut her eyes again.

It was the meowing of a hungry cat that finally pulled her from her morose lie-in. She stumbled out of bed, took a long shower, pulled on her new jeans, along with one of Nora's thermal shirts that went under one of the new country-style shirts she'd purchased from the Mercantile, and went down to dish up some kibble. All the while, Java wound around her ankles. When the cat was fed she made herself some coffee and toast. She wasn't hungry, but she couldn't remember how long ago she'd last eaten. As the coffee dripped, she paced until she came to stand at the great front window, her arms wrapped around herself, watching the snow come down heavy and fat.

The house across the yard was just a hulking shadow in the gray and white day. Under the blanket of snow, it was dark and still. 4B wondered if the mourners from the night before had all gone home. A feeling of solitude slipped over her and she imagined Nora spending her winters here. She tried to think of the active woman snowed in and had a hard time imagining her idle. Nora had said she and Aunt Mace played a lot of cards in the winter. But Aunt Mace wasn't there anymore. Remembering made her heart break again for Nora. The coffee pot finished its cycle and she fixed herself a cup. She sat down at the tiny breakfast table, sipping the hot brew, ignoring the toast. Alone and with nothing to keep her occupied, 4B missed Nora with an acute and painful longing.

Trying not to acknowledge the fear she felt about Nora's absence 4B scanned the open room. She'd never been there by herself. The place felt different without Nora. Unable to stay seated, she got up from the table, cradling her coffee mug, and began to explore the cabin to see and touch the things she hadn't had time to investigate before. She walked through the small house and tried to see it through Nora's eyes, starting with the books. An entire wall downstairs was covered with shelves, and books covered every inch of them, some shelves two stacks deep. There was another smaller bookcase under the stairs and small stacks of books were neatly perched on flat surfaces throughout the house. Nora's tastes in reading were diverse.

4B sat down with a book about Alaska, but like the last time she'd tried to read at Nora's house, she couldn't concentrate. Before it had been because she couldn't keep her hands off of Nora. This time it was because she couldn't keep her mind off of her. Everywhere she turned, she was reminded of Nora, and she missed her with a fierceness she couldn't control. She returned the book to the shelf where she'd found it, and started to explore again, trying to feel close to Nora.

In the space below the stairs, in a small nook 4B had never noticed, there was a rack containing a dozen harmonicas. 4B could almost hear the plaintive notes of Nora playing and it took her back to the time they had spent waiting to be rescued. Near the shelf was a short door. 4B opened it, expecting storage or a pantry, but only saw darkness. She pulled the string hanging from a bare light bulb and a short set of stairs was illuminated. She crouched and stepped down, and then around, stopping in a low cellar under the cabin. It was a large area. The space was the size of the bottom story of the cabin. She was standing under the living room, in what she found was a fairly large wine cellar and every rack was fully stocked. A stack of folded wine boxes was lying in a corner along with packing tape and a label maker. 4B remembered Nora had mentioned she traded in wine, but she had expected a few bottles here and there. It looked like she was running a decent-sized business. 4B remembered getting drunk on tiny bottles of airline wine with Nora and waking up wrapped around her on a pallet of pine needles. Longing shot through her again and she started to cry.

It seemed, every time she turned around, she was discovering another aspect to the woman she had fallen in love with, and a brief bout with regret that she hadn't gotten a chance to find out more tried to sneak into her thoughts. But she pushed it away. She was determined to find out all of the little secrets that made Nora who she was. She just needed her to get back to fill in the missing details.

4B emerged from the wine cellar and wandered over to Nora's desk. Nora hadn't worked much in the days following their rescue. She'd explained what she'd been doing when she checked in just long enough to look at Aunt Mace's website and to scan her email. 4B smiled at the memory of watching Nora work. She'd tried to be patient, but she hadn't been able to refrain from keeping a safe distance, and when Nora had tugged at her hand, she had fallen onto her lap without complaint. Nora had worked half-heartedly with 4B in her lap, and she had described what she was doing. But 4B had been too occupied kissing Nora's neck to really hear what Nora had been saying. Remembering, 4B wasn't sure Nora had accomplished any of the checking she had intended to do, because it wasn't long before 4B had swung her leg over to straddle her, pulling Nora's hand to the heat she pressed into her.

4B sighed at the memory and sat down in the chair. She caressed the soft leather arms and imagined Nora sitting there. On the polished wood desk in front of her was an impressive array of monitors, all of them dark. Just a line of blinking dots, indicating they were actually on, just waiting for the command to come to life. A line of computer towers Nora had told her were servers hummed on a low shelf behind the chair. A time zone chart was printed out on a piece of paper and taped to one of the terminals, converting Juneau's time to Massachusetts time. 4B let her finger slide over the columns and a twinge of longing pierced her. She wished she could just pick up her phone and call her. But she'd tried that already. The calls had gone directly to voicemail. She was sure she would have felt something if anything bad had happened to Nora, but the nothingness she felt was almost worse.

❊❊❊❊❊

The snow dumped and let up, off and on, for the next couple of days, as 4B wandered aimlessly through Nora's house, waiting and hoping. During that time, 4B made frequent trips over to Aunt Mace's house, especially when the waiting became too painful to do alone. The party at Aunt Mace's house never completely ended as the community mourned the loss of a beloved friend and 4B wasn't sure when the wake became a lookout party for Nora and Tack, but eventually the question came up more and more often, and 4B heard people making plans to launch search parties up near the last drop site as soon as the snow stopped. Radio calls to the last site had confirmed that Tack and Nora had taken off for the airpark shortly before the snow had hit. That news had threatened to steal 4B's hope, and she struggled to maintain positive about Nora's return. When it became too hard to hope, she called her mother, who always seemed to help, urging her never to give up.

People came and went at Aunt Mace's, and 4B asked everyone if they had heard from Nora or Tack. But no one had. At first, everyone told her not to worry. Tack knew what he was doing. He'd probably set down to wait out the storm. They'd both be taxiing down the tarmac when the snow let up a little. But after a couple of days, even the most confident of those who said that Tack and Nora were fine started to wring their hands. The day Nora overheard Santa Claus telling Elphie that they could have hiked out by now, the rock of fear sitting in 4B's stomach was joined by an avalanche of others, and 4B began to fear she'd never see Nora again. Still, Nora's friends tried to ease 4B's concern by continuing to tell her that Tack knew what he was doing, and getting grounded while doing drops happened all the time. But they had no answer when she asked about the lack of radio contact, and after a while, words were replaced by compassionate eyes, an offer of strong liquor, and pats on the shoulder.

To ease the waiting, 4B sat down to play cards with Elphie and Ship a few times and found that, although she could do without the constant bickering, the more time she spent with them, the more she liked the two women. Ship had slowed down a little on her drinking, at least during the day, but Elphie still had to pour her into bed each night. And 4B's beginner's luck—which she found was bonafide once she regained her memory—continued, which irked Elphie more than it did Ship. So, 4B had to keep an eye out for Elphie's sleight of hand—the cheating Elphie preferred to call "evening the playing field", and which Ship called "'fucking criminal". 4B soon found herself in the mediator role that she had watched Aunt Mace play. It was sometimes tiresome, but it never grew boring. 4B was grateful for the distraction. Heeding Nora's advice, she didn't play for money. No matter how often they asked. And they asked often.

Eventually, even the distraction of the card games wasn't enough.

The snow didn't dump, but after a few lulls, it kept coming at a steady pace, and 4B didn't try to go down to The Strut, but others who came by the house did, and each time, there was still no word from Nora. By the end of the third full day, 4B was numb with worry and feeling very alone. She was also going stir crazy. The quiet in Nora's little house was almost deafening, but she didn't always want to be at Aunt Mace's, where the noise and constant speculation about Nora and Tack were even more difficult to bear. She barely knew most of the people she saw over there, but they took her in like one of their own. She wondered if it had something to do with the bonding power of grief and fear.

The waiting and the quiet became too much for her. She was alone at Nora's and needed something to do. Her mother was back in Washington and she had to wait until later that evening to call. Finally, she picked up a pen and looked for a notebook. Journaling had been an outlet before. She sat down at the desk to find a pad of paper. A yellow-paged legal pad was in the first drawer she tried. She dropped it on the desk and flipped through pages of hastily penned snippets of code, sketches of webpage layouts, and crude little drawings of cats. It looked like Nora often turned to pen and paper when her agile fingers weren't flying over a keyboard.

4B lingered over some of the doodles, longing to see the woman who had probably sat right where she was sitting on long quiet afternoons. On a page somewhere in the middle of the pad, 4B saw a little heart and the initials N.K. + E.T. scrawled in it. But the E.T. had been crossed out, and 4B had been written next to it, along with a sideways smiley face—the doodled emoticon showed how much more time Nora spent on the computer than with a pen and paper.

4B flipped the page and came across two folded pieces of paper nestled between the pages of the notepad. One had been torn from the notebook and was half-filled with writing, dated the morning of Nora's last trip. It was addressed to her. Her heart stood still in her chest. She opened the other folded page and saw the sketch she had drawn of Nora printed out on it. She stared at the beloved face, alive with wonder and discovery. The longing that filled her was painful and a tear slipped down her cheek. She impatiently wiped it away and told herself she would not start crying. If she started now, she would never stop. She placed the drawing on the desk and began to read the letter addressed to her.

Dear 4B

Yes. 4B is who you are to me. Not Grace or Elizabeth. Just 4B.

Actually, you're way more than that to me, but it's what I have right now. You once told me you liked that your entire memory started with me. I liked that, too. At first it was selfish. I wanted to be everything to you. I still do. But, then I realized all of my important memories are of you, and it just seems right to want to start my life where 'we' began. I just hope I get a chance at that, a chance that consists of more than picking what name I want to call you.

But you have your memory back, and you've been spoken for by the life you had before. How can 'we' stand up to your entire life and the people who already claim you?

I think the fear of that is what allowed me to even entertain the things I brought up on the phone yesterday morning. You must think I watch too many soap operas or something, crafting such an elaborate story from such flimsy data. In development speak, they call it not following a logical path. In doctor speak, it's called making a poor diagnostic impression. Either way, I didn't consult the source, and I allowed my imagination and fear to run away from me. Now, I know I was just looking for something to help me separate from you, because the prospect of losing you is too painful to compute.

I do that. Push things away when they hurt too much. Stop thinking about them when it gets too hard. I ran away from my dad, I ran away from my career, and then I ran away from my failed marriage and life in Denver. It's what I do. I don't want to do it with you.

You said you weren't keeping any of the things we spoke of away from me on purpose. Just like I'll never know what series of events allowed 33 of us to be tossed out almost unscathed from the airplane, I'll probably never know what series of events led up to where we are today. But I have no other choice but to believe you. And I do.

I hope I get a chance to talk to you about all of this. But for now I want to give you the space you need to work it all through as you put your life back on track. I have nothing else to offer you, except what I already have, but I can give you freedom to do what you need to do. I'll always be here for you.

So, I'm writing this letter, which I will probably just tear up when Tack and I get back from our trip today. I just wanted to download my thoughts so, hopefully, I can speak clearly with you if—no, when—I get another chance.

I wish you were here. I have so much to say to you, so much to tell you.

Above all else, I'm not sure I can handle losing you and Aunt Mace at the same time.

I'll wait however long it takes.

There was no signature or sign off. It just ended.

4B reread the letter, and her heart ached. 4B had been so focused on whether Nora felt betrayed that she hadn't thought that Nora was only trying to be strong for her. Again. Nora was always the rock. She wanted to be Nora's rock this time. Her yearning was so intense it bent her double. She begged the Universe to give her another chance.

❀❀❀❀❀

That evening, 4B looked down the slope of Aunt Mace's backyard toward the creek from her perch on the wooden stoop of Aunt Mace's back porch. It was already dark, and fairly cold, although the snowfall had stopped late that afternoon after having dropped about three feet over the last three days. The sky was clear, finally, and the quarter moon illuminated the shadow landscape before her in silver. She sat in a square of yellow light pouring from the kitchen window behind her.

A cup of coffee was cradled in her hands and she huddled over it watching the landscape through the tendrils of heat snaking from its caramel colored surface. She'd been drinking too much coffee, but it was the only comfort she knew. However, at the moment, besides warming her hands, it wasn't doing much for her except exacerbating the anxiety trying to shatter her. Even so, she was numb with unanswered hope and exhausted from worry. She heard someone come out through the back door.

"Hey, squirt. Ain't your backside freezing down there?" asked Ship.

4B took another sip of her coffee and crooked her head to see the figure standing just behind her. Ship carried a coffee mug, too. 4B hadn't seen her drink anything other than coffee all afternoon and she wondered if Ship's bender had come to an end. The cold didn't seem to bother Ship very much even though she was clad in only jeans and a flannel shirt worn over a thermal pullover. 4B noticed no one complained about the snow or cold in Alaska. They just accepted it, like everything else. Ship's boots were still unlaced, and 4B knew she'd slipped them on just to come out there, to check on her. She realized Ship and Elphie were watching out for her now, and the realization gave her comfort.

"It went numb about fifteen minutes ago, so I'm fine. There's room if you want to sit with me," offered 4B, indicating the wooden step beside her.

"I think I'll just lean on the rail. At my age you get piles sitting in the cold like that. You mind if I smoke?" Ship brushed snow from the wood railing and placed her coffee mug on the cleared spot. She dug into one of the breast pockets of her shirt until she pulled out a red and white package of cigarettes.

"They're your lungs," said 4B. "Just stay downwind."

She heard the hiss of a match and the long draw of a breath before the faint smell of smoke wisped her way. Most of the smoke was floating away from her, so she didn't complain.

4B glanced again at Ship, who stared at the lit end of the cigarette she held.

"I gave these things up twenty-three years ago."

"Oh?" asked 4B, knowing the story would follow.

"Yeah. Macie wouldn't stop hounding me. Kicked it cold turkey, just so she'd stop nagging me. This here is my fifth pack since Saturday."

"That isn't good for you. I'm telling you as a doctor and a friend."

"Probably not," replied Ship taking another long drag and blowing the smoke away from 4B. "You want to hear something stupid?"

Besides picking up smoking again after almost a quarter of a century? 4B wanted to ask, but she didn't. It was just concern she felt. She didn't need to be shitty, even though she felt more snappish and edgy as each day without Nora dragged by.

"Sure," she said instead.

"I keep thinking Macie's ghost will appear and kick my ass for picking it up again."

"Yeah?"

"Yeah." Nora heard Ship suck a lungful of smoke in, hold it in, and then blow it out. "But she hasn't. And I'm kinda pissed off about that." There was a long pause. Without turning to look at her, 4B imagined Ship leaning against the rail, eyes half squinted as her mind turned. "I really thought she would have come back to give me a sign or something, you know? But I don't feel her. I haven't seen her ghost, I haven't heard her voice. Not even a sign she's hovering around me, looking out. Not a single sign. And that's what pisses me off."

4B was intrigued about the otherwise practical woman's belief in ghosts, but she knew exactly what that felt like. She'd been waiting for Nora to show up or send her some sort of sign, but she'd been stuck there with nothing for three days. As if reading her mind, Ship said:

"Hey, I know it's tough, but she's gonna be back. Nora will be here soon."

"I hope so."

"She will. I have no doubt. Macie might not be haunting me right now, but I know she wouldn't let nothing happen to her little sister's kid. She's watching over Nora. I'm positive about that."

"It's reassuring," said 4B, but she didn't really feel it. She'd never believed in ghosts and she didn't have the expectation of an interactive afterlife.

They sat there for a few more minutes in quiet. Ship smoked her cigarette and 4B drank her coffee.

"Hey, thanks for taking care of the cat for me," said Ship.

"Java?"

"Yeah, when Macie got too sick to check on her when Nora and Tack was out of town, that was my job. I shoulda been doing it these last few days, but I know I been too drunk to function for most of it. So thanks."

"The cat needs to eat," she said. It made her feel more connected to Nora, too, but she didn't say it.

"So, what happens when she gets here? You gonna stay a while or are you gonna go back to wherever it is you're from?"

"Massachusetts," supplied 4B.

"Yeah. I knew it was one of those M states. You going back there?"

"I don't know."

"I can't see Nora leaving Juneau, but weirder things have happened," said Ship.

When 4B had jumped on the plane, she'd been focused on making sure Nora was okay. She hadn't really thought about what came next.

"I wouldn't ask Nora to leave here."

It struck her then: she didn't want to leave either. She loved it here. Not just because Nora lived here, though it did play a large role. The physical location called to her, grounded her, made her feel like she belonged. Before, when she'd been staying there with Nora, before she remembered where she was from, it was Nora who dominated her thoughts, gave her a sense of being where she should be. But with Nora not there, and her memory securely back, she still felt like she was where she needed to be. She felt more like she was exactly where she needed to be than she'd ever felt in her life. She chose it. Something opened up inside of her at the realization. She was home.

"So, there's a chance you'll stay?" Ship asked.

4B considered her answer, but before she had a chance to reply, Ship continued.

"You're a doctor, right? We need doctors here. Pay's really good, too. To attract doctors. They pay school loans off, too. Things like that. If you're thinking about it, it's good to know." Ship lit another cigarette from the butt of the last. And 4B thought about the epiphany she'd just had as she watched Ship pinch off the cherry on the old one, rub the filter on the bottom of her boot, and stick the filter in her jeans pocket. She wondered how many times Ship had burnt a hole in her pocket doing that. "Besides, I'm gonna need a new doctor. Mine's gonna kill me when she finds out I picked these up again."

"If I was your doctor, I'd kill you, too."

Ship looked down at the tip of the cigarette she had just lit and blew out a long stream of smoke. Then she looked at the pack she still held in her other hand.

"Fuck," she groaned, pinching off the cherry from the new cigarette, sliding it back into the pack, and then crumbling up the remainder of the pack in one of her enormous hands. "Maybe Macie's haunting me through you."

❀❀❀❀❀❀

The morning of the fourth day broke bright and clear, and Nora still wasn't back. Almost three feet of snow covered the ground.

And 4B gave up.

Nora wasn't coming back, and it was like a switch had toggled in 4B's head. Hope had left.

When 4B went outside to escape the sense of aimless drift that came

317

with giving up, the world was the kind of frozen beauty that crystallized the lungs and sent knives of bright light into her eyes. She stood on the top step of Nora's front porch and tried to feel something in the stunning scenery, but it wouldn't come. It had failed to come four days earlier, and her present was an empty container of time she had no interest in filling. Her memories were a brilliant kaleidoscope of color at which she couldn't bear to look anymore. Her future was colorless and blank.

A tree, stark and brittle, stood in the middle of the yard. 4B stepped off the porch and went to stand below it, the fresh powder she walked through feeling lighter than the snow she was used to back on the East Coast. She had no idea what kind of tree it was. She couldn't remember what it looked like a few weeks ago when the leaves were still on it, except a hundred glass bulbs had hung from the low branches. Now the branches were mostly bare and someone had taken the bulbs down, probably in preparation for winter. She figured she should start learning the local vegetation if she was going to stay. But even that thought couldn't get her back to hope.

She pressed her hand against the cold bark and knew it was a good tree. It was a tall tree, with an interesting trunk, and lots of branches. A short, frayed rope hung from one of the lower branches, the seat part of the swing long gone. The bark had swelled around the rope, consuming it. Tall stacks of powdery snow lined the skinny branches and rested on the few straggler leaves, giving the tree an eerie reverse shadow look against the high blue sky. A breath of wind, barely perceptible, moved through them, and a spray of snow fell gently to the ground.

The sunlight, shining bright and clear, cast itself against the tiny falling snowflakes, and the effect was that of a million diamonds floating in the air. 4B looked up, and the sight of the branches, and the diamonds, and the infinite clear blue sky made her dizzy. She fell backward into the newly fallen snow and it puffed up around her, partially burying her in the white fluff as it settled back down. She felt the snow hit her cheeks and melt immediately against her warm skin.

Tiny drops of water on her face, like mercury, seemed to find each other and join, making tiny paths that slid into her hair and down along her throat. It tickled her skin. Trails of beautiful poison. Cold was her cocoon, nestled in the snow in her brand new parka. She closed her eyes, felt the emptiness of her life, and decided, if she fell asleep right then, and froze right there, it would be okay. She didn't have it in her to take her own life, but if her life took her, she figured it would be a fitting end. She'd cheated death once before, when she didn't have a life worth living. Now she welcomed death when the life worth living stood just out of her reach.

But it wasn't. She thought about staying in Juneau. She could get a job at the local hospital. She could learn the local wildlife and vegetation. She could help Aunt Mace's friends carry on the legacy of a wickedly funny old bean's work. She could be whoever she wanted to be, and do whatever she wanted to do. There were a lot of things worse than wandering down to The Strut a couple of times a week to sway next to the jukebox with a cold beer in her hand. Maybe she'd even get Crystal to teach her gymnastics. Someone needed to take care of Java. She receded into her thoughts and sensed the beginning of something new.

"Hold still."

Her eyes were closed. She felt a shape hovering somewhere above her. Warmth filled her world and she opened her eyes. The light was almost too much, but in the middle of the brightness she saw two blue eyes, the shade of brilliant cerulean. It hurt to look, but she kept her eyes open.

The woman above her seemed so close, but she was too far away. 4B's head cleared, the woman kneeled closer and a chorus of happiness filled her heart.

"It's you."

"Hold still. You look so pretty there in the snow. I want to remember this, coming home and finding you buried in snow."

4B reached up and pulled Nora down to her and the world was right side up again.

"Where have you been?"

"The snow came faster than we thought it would. We had to land at an abandoned claim site when it hit and couldn't leave until we shoveled enough runway. The site was next to a river between two ridges and no one was picking up our radio calls as we sat it out."

Just like Crystal and the others had said.

"I've been waiting for you."

"I'm here now. The thought of you brought me back." Those were the best words she'd ever heard—until the next ones brushed her ear. "I love you, too."

The end.

Also by Kimberly Cooper Griffin

Life in High Def

CPSIA information can be obtained
at www.ICGtesting.com
Printed in the USA
FSOW04n1518110617
34979FS

9 780997 219036